Books in  **:**

More books coming! For a current list, please visit
www.dianehenders.com
Or sign up for my New Book Notification list at
www.dianehenders.com/books

Humour by Diane Henders

SPY NOW,

PAY LATER

Book 8 of the NEVER SAY SPY series

Diane Henders

SPY NOW, PAY LATER
ISBN 978-1-927460-18-4

Copyright © 2014 Diane Henders

PEBKAC Publishing Inc.
P.O. Box 67, Station Main
Qualicum Beach, BC   V9K 1S7
www.pebkacpublishing.com

First printed in paperback July 2014 by PEBKAC Publishing Inc.
v.11

Since You Asked...

People frequently ask if my protagonist, Aydan Kelly, is really me.

Yeah, you got me. These novels are an autobiography of my secret life as a government agent, working with highly-classified computer technology... Oh, wait, what's that? You want the *truth*? Um, you do realize fiction writers get paid to lie, don't you?

...well, shit, that's not nearly as much fun. It's also a long story.

I swore I'd never write fiction. "Too personal," I said. "People read novels and automatically assume the author is talking about him/herself."

Well, apparently I lied about the fiction-writing part. One day a story sprang into my head and wouldn't leave. The only way to get it out was to write it down. So I did.

But when I wrote that first book, I never intended to show it to anyone, so I created a character that looked like me just to thumb my nose at the stereotype. I've always had a defective sense of humour, and this time it turned around and bit me in the ass.

Because after I'd written the third novel, I realized I actually wanted other people to read my books. And when I went back to change my main character to *not* look like me, my beta readers wouldn't let me. They rose up against me and said, "No! Aydan is a tall woman with long red hair and brown eyes. End of discussion!"

Jeez, no wonder readers get the idea that authors write about themselves. So no, I'm not Aydan Kelly. I just look like her.

Oh, and the town of Silverside and all secret technologies are products of my imagination. If I'm abducted by grim-faced men wearing dark glasses, or if I die in an unexplained fiery car crash, you'll know I accidentally came a little too close to the truth.

I hope you enjoy the book!

For Phill

Thank you for being my technical advisor and the most tolerant husband ever. Much love!

To my beta readers/editors, especially Carol H., Judy B., and Phill B., with gratitude: Many thanks for all your time and effort in catching my spelling and grammar errors, telling me when I screwed up the plot or the characters' motivations, and generally keeping me honest.

To Rick and Sandy H. at Hand Crafted Images: Your talent makes my covers extra-special, and your sense of humour makes photo sessions fun even for a camera-hater like me. Thank you!

To Steve A. and the staff at The Shooting Edge: Thank you for lending us your excellent facilities for our cover photo sessions. You guys rock!

To everyone else, respectfully:
Canadian English is an unholy hybrid of British and American English, so I apologize if spellings in this book look odd to you. But if you find typos, please send an email to errors@dianehenders.com. Mistakes drive me nuts, and I'm sorry if any slipped through. Please let me know what the error is, and on which page (or at which position in e-versions). I'll make sure it gets fixed as soon as possible. Thanks!

CHAPTER 1

Choking on frantic sobs, I yanked the lever of the last remaining fire extinguisher. Only a few droplets dribbled out, sizzling uselessly in the flames that ravaged Kane's motionless body.

It was too late. He was already dead.

I had killed him...

"*John!*" I bolted up in bed, my scream ripping the dark silence.

Panting, I wrapped my arms around myself. "Oh, Jesus. God..." I sucked in a shuddering breath and drew my knees up to rest my sweaty forehead on them. "Shit, stop it! He's fine, I'm fine, everything's okay, nothing bad is happening..."

Another deep breath. "Okay. It's okay..."

I flopped back on the pillow, pawing my tangled hair away from my face with a shaking hand.

"Okay. Breathe."

I stopped babbling to follow my own advice. Eyes closed. Belly breaths. Nice and slow. In, two... three... four. Out, two... three... four. Ocean waves rolling in...

At last my heart consented to resume a more-or-less normal rhythm, and the end of my exhalation turned into a groan when I opened my eyes to the glowing numbers of my bedside clock.

Six A.M. Just over an hour since I'd last woken

screaming.

"Fine," I croaked. "Screw this. I'm done." I hauled myself out of bed, hissing quiet but sincere obscenities when the two-day-old bruises on my knee and elbow reminded me of their presence.

I was trudging toward the bathroom when the ring of the phone slammed adrenaline into my veins. I spun, tripped over sleep-clumsy feet, and sprawled across the bed to snatch up the receiver.

"Ow! Shit! What?" My raw-throated rasp drew an instant of silence at the other end of the line.

"Is this Aydan Kelly?"

"Yes! Who-"

"Surveillance cameras just picked up Paul Hibbert heading for your front door. Looks like he's carrying a bouquet of flowers."

"*Shit!*" I dropped the phone and snatched my gun from under the pillow before lurching to my feet to grab for the jeans and sweatshirt I always kept beside my bed.

"What the hell does that asshole want?" I demanded in the direction of the receiver as I jerked the clothes on.

The faint crackle of the analyst's response was drowned out by the sound of my doorbell, and I yanked the spare blanket off my bed and threw it around myself. Hurrying for the door, I draped a fold of blanket over my gun hand.

The doorbell rang again, and I hesitated. What the hell was Hibbert up to? I couldn't imagine him bringing me anything but poison ivy in an exploding vase, unless I had somehow misinterpreted 'I'll get you, bitch'.

Maybe he'd meant to say 'I'll get you *flowers*, bitch'. I snickered despite my pounding heart.

Loud knocking made me twitch my gun into ready

position.

"Flowers from Mr. Parr!" Another barrage of knocks rattled my door. "Open up, bitch! I know you're in there!"

Yep, Mr. Sweetness-And-Light as usual. But he wasn't kicking the door in. So far, so good.

"Fuck off!" I yelled.

"Open the fucking door! Parr will chew my ass off if I don't deliver these flowers right into your hands!"

"Stick them up your ass! He can enjoy them while he's chewing!"

The door shivered under what sounded like a vigorous kick. "Open the fucking door or I'll dent every square inch of it!"

Well, wasn't that interesting? He was threatening my door, but not me. Parr must have thrown some serious fear into him.

A series of loud thuds convinced me to make a decision, pronto.

"All right, I'm coming! Take a pill already!" I tucked my blanket-wrapped gun close to my body and unlocked the door left-handed, stepping back rapidly. He probably wouldn't attack me, but...

The door swung open and Hibbert shoved a magnificent bouquet in my direction. "Here. Choke on them."

He let go of the flowers so fast I had to make a two-handed grab to save them. Fortunately he was already wheeling to stalk away, so he couldn't have heard the muffled clunk of my blanket-wrapped gun against the heavy vase.

Christ, that vase looked like crystal. What the hell?

I swung the door almost shut against the frigid air and watched through the crack while Hibbert stomped down my lane into the darkness, his shoulders hunched around his ears. A few minutes later the slam of a car door shattered the country silence like a gunshot and headlights blazed to life on the opposite side of my gate. I closed the door on the angry revving of his engine as his taillights receded down the snowy road.

Shivering, I propped the vase awkwardly in the crook of my elbow while I re-locked my door, then trailed over to place the ostentatious bouquet on my kitchen table and extract the card from its blown-glass holder.

The creamy envelope was lined with rich metallic foil, and the heavy matte paper of the card would have screamed 'big money' if it hadn't been far too well-bred to communicate in anything but a discreet murmur:

'Dear Arlene – I hope you are recovering. Please don't hesitate to contact me if you need anything. Sincerely, Nick Parr'

Shit, Parr had written it personally. I had thought he was in Vegas or Ibiza or Monte Carlo, but maybe he had come back to do damage control.

I sank into a chair and drew my icy bare feet up under me, my tired mind groaning into reluctant action. Why would Parr send me flowers at six o'clock on Christmas morning? And why the *hell* would he send them with Hibbert when he knew about our mutual loathing?

The flowers and note supported Parr's carefully-cultivated façade as the respectable and philanthropic CEO of Fuzzy Bunny's international toy empire, so that made sense. Just a good PR gesture, buttering up a distraught passenger after a fire on their corporate jet. But he wouldn't send flowers at an ungodly hour on a holiday. That had to be Hibbert's little gesture of goodwill.

So maybe Parr was testing Hibbert's loyalty by assigning

him a demeaning delivery-boy errand. And since Hibbert had to know that crossing Parr was a good way to end up dead, waking me with insults at six A.M. would be his passive-aggressive way to goad me without too much risk to himself.

Dangerous game. But no more dangerous than the one I was playing. If Parr found out I wasn't really Arlene Widdenback the cheesy porn star and fraud artist, I'd end up unpleasantly dead, too.

I shook off that thought with a shudder and rose to stumble back to the bedroom. The phone still lay on my bed, and I hurried over to pick it up.

"Hi, are you still there?" I asked.

"Of course." The surveillance analyst sounded peeved. "Is everything secure there?"

Poor bastard. He must be low man on the totem pole if he had drawn surveillance duty on Christmas morning.

"Fine. Thanks for being there."

"You're welcome." He sounded slightly mollified, and I hung up and hauled myself to the bathroom.

The mirror reflected a baggy-eyed hag who looked closer to sixty-seven than my actual forty-seven, and I sighed and dragged a brush through my tangled hair before throwing my shoulders back, sucking in my gut, and pasting on a fake smile.

Better. Now I only looked ten years older than my real age.

My reflection twisted its face into a rude grimace, and I retreated to the heavenly embrace of a hot shower.

Forehead pressed against the cool tile, eyes squeezed shut while the steaming water cascaded down my back, I summoned the previous evening's happy memories, hoping to calm the weak trembling of too much adrenaline and not enough sleep.

Just relax. Think good thoughts...

...Spider's and Linda's faces glowing with happiness, their eyes sparkling as brightly as the brand-new diamond on her finger. The sound of Christmas carols and the lively chatter of their family and friends. Eggnog blessing my tongue with its creamy caress. Jack and Germain stealing a kiss under the mistletoe, her golden curls gleaming like angel wings against his black hair. And Kane, tall and strong and miraculously *alive*, his smile and murmured 'Merry Christmas' still warming my heart...

I let out a long breath, the knots slowly easing from my shoulders. "Merry Christmas, John," I whispered. "I hope you're having a better Christmas than this."

A smile softened my lips. I knew he would. He was headed for Calgary this morning for some precious family time with his dad and Arnie.

When I emerged from the shower at last, I was alert enough to consider the flowers with renewed suspicion. Even after a reprimand from Parr, I wouldn't put it past Hibbert to sabotage the bouquet. Hell, I'd be shocked if he *hadn't* sabotaged the bouquet. And pissed on my doorstep, to boot.

I considered calling the surveillance analyst and asking about the state of my doorstep, but I decided I didn't really want to know. Instead, I threw on some clothes and took out my bug detector, feeling slightly foolish at my own paranoia.

My heart clutched when the indicator light blinked red.

Long intervals between flashes. The listening device was in my house, but probably not in this room.

I had just cleared the house last night.

So that's what the flowers were for. Parr had bugged the bouquet. Or Hibbert had.

As I moved toward the kitchen, the cadence of the flashes accelerated. Heart pattering, I halted in the hallway to think.

What if there was a surveillance camera in the bouquet, too? My cover would be completely blown if I walked around the corner with classified technology in my hand.

A sudden thought made my mouth go dry. God, had I kept my gun concealed the whole time I was in the kitchen?

I must have. I had still been wearing the blanket when I'd gone back to the bedroom to pick up the phone.

I tucked the bug detector into the pocket of my jeans with an unsteady hand and drew a deep breath before strolling into the kitchen.

My face felt frozen in an 'I'm-on-camera' stare, and I tried to relax it with a fake yawn as I approached the table. I coaxed my stiff lips into a smile and murmured, "Let's see, where should I put you beauties?" as I picked up the vase, turning it in my hands as if admiring it.

Sure enough, the gilt sticker on the bottom of the vase looked too thick. But not thick enough to hide a camera, and anyway, Fuzzy Bunny probably didn't have a burning desire for a close-up of my tabletop.

Just a bug, then.

Unless there was a camera hidden in the flowers.

"Maybe I should trim your stems," I added for the benefit of my audience, and proceeded to dismantle the entire arrangement, diligently trimming stems and scrutinizing every bloom, leaf, and stalk.

When I finished reassembling the bouquet, it was a sad caricature of the once-beautiful arrangement, but I was certain it didn't contain a camera. I sent a mental apology to the high-priced floral designer who would undoubtedly blanch at my desecration, and replaced the vase in the middle of the table. Then I threw on my jacket and boots and hurried out to my heated garage.

A check of my bug detector revealed a reassuring green light, and I extracted a secured phone from my car's glove compartment and pressed the speed dial button.

The phone rang and rang, and I braced myself for Dermott's wrath. At last, the connection clicked open.

"What?" he snarled.

"It's Kelly," I said crisply. "Parr just sent Hibbert over with a bugged flower arrangement for me."

"At six o'fucking-clock on Christmas fucking morning?" Dermott sounded like he'd been gargling battery acid and wouldn't hesitate to spit some my way, so I refrained from pointing out that it was actually almost six-thirty.

"Just sharing the joy," I said instead. "What do you want me to do?"

"Nothing. Or disinformation; whichever you want. We can discuss it in the briefing with Stemp. Merry fucking Christmas." The line went dead in my ear, and I sighed and retraced my steps to the house.

Only two more days of Dermott's crankiness. I couldn't believe I was actually looking forward to having Charles Stemp back in his rightful position as director. Stemp might be a ruthless bastard, but at least he was instantly alert at any hour of the day or night, and his customary emotionless façade precluded any displays of temper.

Inside, I shed my jacket and boots and shivered over to ransack the cupboards. A bowl of cereal soothed my growling stomach, but the early-morning blackness outside the windows encroached like a malevolent presence.

"Fuck it," I muttered, and crept to the bedroom to burrow back into bed. I was floating on the hazy edge of slumber when the phone jolted me awake again, and I stared in disbelief at the clock.

Seven-thirty.

"Jesus, *seriously?*" I fumbled the receiver to my ear, clamping my eyes shut. "Hello?"

"Hi, Aydan, it's Germain. I hope I'm not calling too early..." He trailed off uncomfortably.

I prodded my Little Miss Sunshine persona into reluctant wakefulness. "Hi, Carl! No, it's fine, I've been up since six. Merry Christmas!"

"Oh, good." Relief warmed his voice. "Merry Christmas to you, too. I knew you were a morning person and I was afraid I'd miss you if I waited any longer. I really hate to ask you this, but I was wondering if I could borrow your truck today. My car won't start, and I have to be in Calgary by eleven. I called Kane hoping to catch a ride, but he's already halfway there."

I ground the heel of my hand into my forehead. "Well, normally I'd say sure, but when I was on my way home last week the steering started pulling. If it's a ball joint or tie rod end, it's not safe to drive. I was going to get it up on the hoist and look at it, but I haven't had time yet."

"It's all right, I'll risk it. I have to be there." His uncharacteristic intensity made my eyes pop open.

"I'll come and give you a boost. Maybe that'll do it. "

"No, I already got the hotel manager to boost it. It didn't help. The starter's probably gone."

I squeezed my eyes shut again, thinking out loud. "Shit. If it's your starter it'll take days before the garage can get a new one in. Don't worry, I'll come and get you and drive you down-"

"No, that's too much trouble," he protested. "I'll take my chances with the truck. I hate to bother you at all, but..." I sensed his embarrassed shrug at the other end of the line.

"Carl, you saved me from a fiery plane crash less than forty-eight hours ago. This is the least I can do, and it's no trouble at all. I was going down to meet friends for brunch anyway, so I'll just go a little earlier and drop you wherever you need to go. Then you can rent a car while you're there."

"Oh." His breath of relief floated over the line. "Thank you. That would be great."

"Okay, good. I'll be waiting in front of the hotel by..." I did a rapid mental calculation. "...eight-thirty."

"Thanks!"

We said our goodbyes and I hung up slowly. Germain was the most laid-back agent I knew. Dodging bullets or landing a burning 737, his easy calm never faltered.

So what could possibly make him sound this anxious?

CHAPTER 2

I dragged my complaining self out of bed for the second time to dress and sleepwalk to the kitchen. When another phone call interrupted my tea and toast, I glared at the clock and mumbled a peanut-butter-muffled epithet.

Gulping my mouthful, I eyed the unfamiliar number on the call display and let it go to voice mail. A few moments later, a crisp voice emanated from the answering machine. "Hello, Ms. Widdenback, this is Earl Anderson. I'm the investigator from the Transportation Safety Board-"

Shit, did these guys normally work every day of the year, or was he on Fuzzy Bunny's payroll? Either way, with an active bug in the room, I couldn't ignore the call.

I snatched up the receiver. "H'lo?" I cleared a patch of peanut butter from the roof of my mouth and tried again. "Hi, sorry, this is Arlene. You caught me in the middle of breakfast."

"Hello, Ms. Widdenback, I was hoping you'd have time to clarify a few points in the report you provided at the hospital yesterday. I'm sorry to bother you so early on Christmas morning, but you said you were a morning person."

Damn, I had to stop telling people that.

"No, it's fine, I was up..." My mouth kept talking while I mentally reviewed the cover story Kane and I had agreed on. "...I have to leave in ten minutes, but if I can answer a few quick questions, I'll be happy to."

That was pure bullshit. I wasn't happy about it at all. But he didn't need to know that, and neither did Fuzzy Bunny.

"Oh, good, I won't take too much of your time. Would you please walk me through what happened again?"

"I... can't really remember it very well," I prevaricated. "It was such a... I was in shock, you know?"

"Perfectly understandable. Just do your best." He sounded patient and reassuring, and I wondered how many times he'd had to coax reports out of terrified people.

Uncomfortably aware of the invisible audience behind the bug, I swallowed. "Okay... Um... I was just sitting there reading-"

"I'm sorry, sitting where?" he interrupted.

"Oh. In the sitting room. The second cabin from the front. I smelled smoke, and when I looked up, Thomas..." My voice wavered and I stopped to steady it before continuing. "...the cabin steward... was doing something at the counter. I couldn't really see, but something must have been hot because the next thing I knew a bottle fell over and then there was fire everywhere..."

I squeezed my eyes shut, reliving the moment when my plan had gone so horribly wrong.

"What bottle? Where was the bottle that fell over?" He still sounded patient, but there was a keen note in his voice that hadn't been there before. Damn, maybe I hadn't mentioned the bottle earlier.

I pulled myself back from the memory and dropped into

a chair, clutching the phone like an anchor. "It was a bottle of brandy. Sitting on the counter. There was a lot of turbulence. It must have fallen over..."

Dammit, if Thomas had still been alive, he never would have let that happen. He had been so smart and professional. My throat tightened at the memory of his handsome young face and sparkling smile slackening into death.

"...I think one of the passengers put it on the counter. There was a problem with the guy in the back." My voice came out husky, and I cleared my throat.

That part was true. The next part, not so much.

"The guy was drunk," I went on. "He'd been drinking brandy, and Thomas was cooking something for him just to keep him happy while we landed. Thomas tried to get him to go back to his seat, but he argued and then he shoved Thomas."

"Do you know the man's name? Can you describe him?"

"Um... he was sitting in the rear cabin so I didn't pay much attention to him." At least not until his hands went for my throat. "Maybe, um, five-foot-ten, kind of heavyset? Brown hair..." I trailed off.

"So there was a physical altercation and the bottle fell over. Then what happened?" The investigator sounded as though he had all day.

I shot an anxious glance at my watch. If I didn't leave in few minutes, I'd be late. Then Germain would be late for whatever critical thing had him so edgy. Dammit.

"It broke." I squeezed my eyes shut and reeled off my lies and half-truths. "The brandy caught fire and went everywhere. Thomas used a fire extinguisher on it and the fire was almost out, but the other guy was yelling and freaking out and the drink cart fell over and broke a bunch more bottles and then the alcohol from it caught fire and then the wood panelling caught fire. Thomas pushed me to the back and put the breathing mask on me and told me to stay in the bedroom and keep the door shut. He was grabbing more fire extinguishers when I closed the door."

"And what about the other passengers?"

Shit, I was pretty sure he hadn't asked me that before.

"Um... I don't know. I didn't really notice, with that big hood on my head and Thomas yelling and pushing me into the bedroom. I was so scared..."

The story about Thomas was a bald-faced lie, but I didn't have to fake the tremor in my voice. 'Scared' didn't even come close to the terror I'd felt. Was still feeling. I swallowed hard and eased my sweaty grip on the phone.

"Just take a moment if you need to," Anderson said gently.

I drew a deep breath. "Thanks. I'm sorry, but I have to go very soon. Was there anything else?"

"Did you see another female passenger?"

Yana Orlov, the bitch. May she roast in hell for killing Thomas.

I kept my tone grave and concerned. "Yes, I think she was in the front cabin. But I didn't see her after the fire started."

"And how did you come to be holding the cabin steward's shoe?"

Shit! I had forgotten about that, and Kane and I hadn't discussed it when we were coordinating our cover stories at yesterday's debriefing.

"Um... I just..." My brain hurled out the most plausible reason I could manufacture on short notice. "I was so scared. In the bedroom by myself. I opened the door hoping they'd gotten the fire out, and he was... he was... lying there..."

The nightmare struck again full force. The hungry jaws of the fire, the horrible constriction of the breathing mask's seal around my throat...

"I... I grabbed his legs and tried to pull him..."

I wrapped my free arm around my shaking body. Thomas had been long dead by then. He hadn't suffered, hadn't felt the hungry flames consuming his flesh.

"Just breathe for a minute. Nice and slow." Anderson's voice pulled me back to the warm safety of my kitchen.

I drew a shuddering breath. "His shoe came off in my hands. He was... his upper body was on fire. I tried to put it out, but... I couldn't... I guess I just hung onto the shoe..." My voice cracked and I gulped, fighting the memory, smelling the smoke.

...Clinging to the shoe thinking it was Kane's. Believing I had killed him with a fire I'd started through my own stupidity...

"I really have to go," I croaked.

"Of course. Thank you for your help, and I'm sorry to make you relive this again."

When he hung up, I threw my cold toast in the garbage and yanked on my boots and jacket, thankful I'd have Germain's company for the drive. I really didn't need another two hours inside my own head.

"I'm sorry I'm late," I apologized as Germain slid into the passenger seat. "The crash investigator phoned and I couldn't get rid of him."

"It's okay, if I'm a few minutes late it won't matter."

I put the car in gear and shot him a worried glance, but he sounded sincere and I couldn't detect any strain in his posture. Still, there was that tiny edge of tension in his voice.

"It sounds important, though," I prodded cautiously.

He smiled, the attractive laugh lines crinkling around his brown eyes. "It is to me. This is one of the three times a year I get to see my kids."

"Your k...?" I gaped at him for a second before directing my attention back to the road. "I, um, I didn't know you were a dad."

"I'm not a dad," he replied quietly. "I'm a biological father. I only see Ryan and Tanya on Christmas and birthdays. They call me Uncle Carl."

"*Why?*" I blurted. "That's..." I managed to contain myself. "Sorry. None of my business."

He blew out a long breath. "It's okay. I know it's a little weird. But that's what the judge ruled."

"He said you couldn't tell your kids you were their dad?"

"She." He rubbed a hand over his face. "No, she didn't say that. She just assigned the visiting rights. But this is best for Ryan and Tanya. They weren't old enough to remember me when Melanie and I split up, and we agreed it was better if I didn't confuse them by claiming to be their dad when I only saw them three times a year."

"I don't care if it's only three times a year. Kids need to know they have a dad!"

"They do have a dad. Melanie remarried right away." He hesitated. "I guess they were probably seeing each other before we divorced. I was away a lot." He scrubbed a hand through his short black curls, not looking at me. "Anyway. Derek's an accountant. Nice guy. And Ryan and Tanya have a dad who comes home every night."

"But..." I knew I should drop it, but I just couldn't. "They need to know. It's not fair to them or to you."

"Melanie will tell them when they're a little older. They're only five and three. Right now, they have a stable family life and they love their dad. That's the best thing I can do for them."

I clamped my teeth on my tongue and shut the hell up.

After a moment, Germain went on as if to himself. "I should've listened to Kane. He told me I should get a desk job when Ryan was born. But no, I had to go and be a big hero for my country."

The bitterness in his voice made my heart twist for him. "I'm sorry," I murmured.

Germain shrugged. "My fault. I should have been there for my family. I was undercover when Melanie filed for divorce and I didn't even get the papers until weeks later. Then when the custody hearings came up, I was undercover again and couldn't attend. The judge decided I was a schmuck, and it was all over."

He stared through the windshield. "She was right. I was a dumb schmuck."

"Carl, that's not true. You're doing a tough, dangerous job and you've sacrificed so much. You *are* a hero."

"Yeah, that keeps me warm at night." He shook himself and turned to me, his usual smile restored. "Sorry, I didn't mean to dump on you. And I really appreciate the ride. I can hardly wait. Melanie says the kids have been going absolutely crazy about Santa Claus. It's going to be a great visit."

"Merry fucking Christmas," I muttered to the steering wheel.

"Sorry, what was that?"

I shoved a smile onto my face and spoke a little louder. "I said it'll be a very fun Christmas."

Driving away from the sprawling house in its upscale Calgary neighbourhood, I scowled at the sparse traffic. A lump had risen in my throat while I watched the little black-haired, brown-eyed boy in Batman jammies and the tiny girl in a pink spangled dress race out to dance around Germain, tugging him toward the house amid jubilant cries of 'Uncle Carl, Uncle Carl!'

His ex-wife and her husband smiled from the doorway, arms around each other, and as much as I wanted to hate his ex I couldn't find any villains in the scene. They were all trying to do what was best for the kids.

Dammit, that just sucked.

The gloomy sky mirrored my mood and I pulled into the nearest park, hoping a bit of fresh air and exercise would cheer me up. When I stepped out of the car, a raw breeze cut through my parka directly to my bones. I blew out an irritable breath and frowned at my watch.

Still an hour to kill before I was due at Nichele's place.

I squared my shoulders and started walking.

Tapping on the door of the posh downtown condo an hour later, I braced myself for Nichele's usual squeal and bear hug. Instead, my jaw dropped when the door swung open to reveal a distinguished-looking man in a suit and tie, his thick grizzled hair cropped close in a precise cut that flattered its waves.

His faded blue eyes crinkled with his mischievous smile. "Hi, Aydan."

"Wha...?" I gaped at him, my mouth stretching into a widening grin. "Who the hell are you and what did you do with Dave?"

He laughed, and I stepped forward to hug him. "Jeez, Dave, you look fantastic! You've lost a ton of weight! And are you the chairman of the board these days?"

He returned the hug and patted me on the back before drawing me into the apartment. "Hel... heck, no, still the same old dumb trucker." He waved a hand at his sartorial splendour. "This's for Nichele. Part of her Christmas present."

"Aydan!"

There was the squeal I'd been expecting.

Nichele rocketed down the hall to throw her arms around me. "Girl, how the hell are you? It's so great to see you!"

"It's great to see you, too!" I extricated myself from her embrace to examine the elegant gown that flattered her curvy figure. "Shit, you guys didn't tell me this was a black-tie brunch!"

Nichele giggled. "Like you would've dressed up. Not. But I didn't know." She gave Dave an adoring glance. "This is totally a surprise. And he still won't tell me where we're going, he just said to wear my best dress. And look at him!" She stepped over to cuddle up to Dave, stroking his lapels. "Armani. Mmmmm. There's nothing sexier than a man in Armani."

Dave's ears turned crimson but he grinned, sliding his arms around her. "You're always going on about it, so I figured I better get some."

I laughed. "Hey, while you two are getting some, I'll just go grab lunch somewhere else."

"Smartass!" Nichele released Dave and grinned at me. "Come on, I'll get you a beer."

"Just one." I followed her into the kitchen and accepted the icy bottle. "I have to drive in a couple of hours."

"No, you can stay as long as you-" Nichele broke off, eyeing us suspiciously. "Wait, did you cook this up with Dave?"

"Nope, I'm as much in the dark as you," I assured her. "All I know is Dave called me last week to let me know you guys have to leave at three-thirty."

"But..." Her smile faded. "You're not coming with us? But this is our Christmas *thing*. You and me, hanging out on Christmas Day. It's a *tradition*."

I shot a glance at Dave's worried face.

"And here we are, hanging out on Christmas Day." I toasted her with the beer bottle. "But I'm bagged and I want to get back to Silverside tonight, so I was planning to leave while there was still a bit of daylight."

"Oh. Okay." Nichele's smile came back and she gave me a quick squeeze. "You do look tired. In fact, you look like hell, girl. For God's sake get some sleep when you get home. You always work too hard."

"I look like hell because I'm starving. When do we eat?"

She laughed, and the conversation turned to our usual banter.

"Ah, that was great!" I eased back in the chair and massaged my belly. "But I can't believe the two of you sat here all dolled up eating scrambled eggs and bacon and hash-brown casserole."

Nichele grinned. "You know that's all I can cook. And Dave can barely boil water."

Dave shrugged. "Never needed to do anything else." He winked at Nichele. "Know the best fast-food joints all through Canada and the States though."

She shook a reproving finger at him before shooting me a conspiratorial grin. "But he eats healthy when he's on the road now. He's a changed man."

"Right," Dave agreed, deadpan.

"And speaking of men..." Nichele turned an avid gaze on me. "Please tell me you've been getting busy with Hot John."

"Um." I tried to will the heat away from my cheeks.

"Gotta go." Dave scrambled to his feet, his ears aflame. "Gotta check on... uh... something." He backed away.

"Wait, Dave, don't go," I implored. "We're not having this conversation."

"Oh, yes, we are, girl," Nichele assured me with a leer. "I know what that blush means! You did do him, didn't you?"

"Dave!" I begged, but he had already fled.

CHAPTER 3

I turned my best poker face toward Nichele and lied my ass off. "Of course I'm not sleeping with John. We're co-workers. Strictly professional."

She eyed me quizzically. "So you're still booty-calling Mister Ugly?"

"Don't call him that! It's not his fault his waste-of-skin father broke half the bones in his face when he was five."

"Kidding." She patted my hand, looking contrite. "He's a nice guy. It's just that he's so ug-" She broke off and tried again. "Does he prefer to be called Arnie or Hellhound?"

"I don't think he cares. His army buddies call him Hellhound. I usually call him Arnie." My words came out sounding stiffer than I'd intended.

Nichele's eyes widened. "Oh-em-gee, Aydan, you actually love him!"

"Yes." I raised my chin.

She blinked and stared, and I had to swallow my amusement at her discomfiture. Her mouth opened and closed a couple of times before she stammered, "Are, you, um... are you guys, um... going to...?"

I relented and let my smile escape. "No. We're really good friends and we sleep together sometimes. That's all either of us wants."

"Oh, thank God!" She flushed. "I mean... sorry. Um..."

"Forget it, you goof." I reached over to hug her. "If you actually pretended you liked him, I'd figure the real Nichele had been abducted by aliens or something."

She blew out a sigh, relaxing into a relieved smile. "Girl, don't scare me like that! Anyway, I do like him, I just don't want to think about waking up next to him." She shuddered. "Eeuw. Now, tell me how good Hot John was!"

"Amaz-" I bit off the word.

Her eyes widened.

Shit. Busted.

"Oooh, Aydan, *seriously?* You're doing both of them? Oh-em-gee, you bootylicious babe! Tell me, tell me!" Her jaw dropped. "Wait, they're best friends. Are you doing them at the same time? *Ménage à trois?*"

My vision unfocused for an instant before I recovered from the mental image. "Not at the same time! Jeez, Nichele!"

"You thought about it!" She poked a finger into my ribs, chortling. "You did, you thought about it! Ha-ha! The strait-laced bookkeeper has a secret wild side!"

"I'm not strait-laced!"

She leaned over to pluck contemptuously at my baggy sweatshirt. "Girl, I know nuns who show more skin than you do."

"Yeah, so?" I tweaked the sweatshirt back into place, secretly giving thanks I'd worn my ankle holster instead of my waist holster.

"So; strait-laced!"

"Strait-laced is an attitude, not a fashion statement," I said primly.

"Yeah, girl, you just keep telling yourself that," Nichele teased. "Now, dish!"

"There's nothing to dish. It never would have happened unless-"

Shit. I couldn't say 'unless we were about to die in a fiery plane crash'.

"Um... it was a one-time thing," I lied. "Anyway, we talked it over afterward and it won't happen again," I added, and seized the offensive. "What about you and Dave?"

"You *talked?* Girl, are you nuts? That man's hot enough to melt panties from across the room!" Nichele squinted at me suspiciously. "What aren't you telling me?"

I brazened it out. "I'm not telling you anything about my sex life, that's for sure. But it looks like you and Dave are getting along pretty well."

She smiled, roses blooming in her cheeks. "Yeah." She dropped her gaze, watching with apparent fascination while her perfectly manicured fingertip traced hearts on the shiny glass tabletop.

My heart warmed at the glow in her smile, and I glanced down the hall to make sure Dave was still out of earshot. "So how's it going with... well, you know, living together? What has it been, two months? You've never lasted this long, even with... um, what's-his-name..." The name eluded me. "Whatever. The love of your life that you kicked out after seventeen days."

Nichele waved a dismissing hand. "He was boring."

"After seventeen days?" She shrugged, and I left the topic for dead. "So... you and Dave...?"

"Oh, we're completely incompatible. He likes country music, for God's sake." She gave a theatrical shudder before continuing, "I'm a stockbroker. He's a long-haul trucker.

We have absolutely nothing in common." Her lips curved into a smug smile.

"And..." I prompted, grinning.

She gave a happy little bounce in her chair. "And it's perfect! When he's on the road I go clubbing with my friends. By the time he gets home, I'm ready for some cocooning time. We like all the same food and he's happy if I tell him what to wear, and he's finally gotten over being weirded out because I make more money than he does-"

"Hey, um..." Dave's voice drifted from the hallway. "You done your girl-talk?"

I turned to beckon him in. "It's okay, Dave, it's safe. Come on back."

He shot me a relieved grin before turning to Nichele. "You better get ready, honey. We leave in half an hour."

She bounced up and kissed him thoroughly before vanishing down the hall, leaving him smiling as though somebody had just handed him the moon and stars.

As the bedroom door closed behind her, he turned to me, sobering. "Gotta ask you something."

His seriousness sent a quiver of trepidation to my stomach. I kept my tone casual. "What's up?"

Dave shot a cautious glance down the hall before speaking quietly. "That you in the plane fire a couple days ago?"

I froze.

He raised a calming hand and spoke before I could decide whether to lie. "It's okay, you don't need to tell me. Was watching the news and saw long red hair when they wheeled the stretcher into the ambulance. Thought it looked like you, but I didn't say anything to Nichele. Been worried sick."

"I'm sorry, Dave, you should have texted me or something."

He shrugged and grimaced. "Didn't dare. What if Nichele caught me? She doesn't know about your spy stuff, does she?"

"No." I struggled with the knowledge that I should deny the whole thing, but this was Dave. I owed him my life.

I sighed. "And I'd like to keep it that way."

He nodded. "I figured." Anxiety creased his forehead. "They said five dead; crew and two passengers. Good guys or bad guys?"

My hands clenched into involuntary fists and I swallowed hard. "Two bad, a woman and a guy. The flight crew was innocent as far as I know."

"Shi... crap." He pulled me into a quick hug and patted my back before pulling away to frown earnestly. "Listen, Aydan... If you ever need help, you know you can call me, right? Any time. No matter what."

I swallowed the tightness in my throat. "Thanks, Dave, but you've already gone above and beyond. Now you need to settle down and enjoy life. You've got more to lose now."

He glanced down the hall, his face softening. "Yeah." He returned his gaze to me. "But you're the one that gave it to me. Any time, Aydan. Remember that."

I squeezed his hand. "Thanks, Dave. I will."

We smiled at each other, and before the short silence could get awkward I let go of his hand under the pretext of gesturing at the window. "Wow, look at that snow."

Dave shot an assessing look at the flakes whipping by outside the glass and his brow furrowed. "Yeah. They didn't forecast that, but it sure blew up fast. It'll be bad on the highway. You should stay with us tonight."

"Hardly." I gestured at his suit. "Wearing Armani in front of Nichele is like waving fresh meat in front of a tiger. You won't want any listening ears when she gets you home tonight."

He flushed and a grin tugged the corners of his mouth, but he persisted. "Don't want you out on the highway by yourself."

"I'll be fine. I've got winter tires, and I have my survival kit and winter gear and sleeping bag in case I get stopped."

"Yeah, but the ground drift'll be bad. Can't get above it in that little car."

I shook my head at him and headed for the door. "It's a full-size sedan, and it's all-wheel drive. It just seems small to you because you're so used to your highway tractor." I paused, frowning. "Um, Dave, you know Nichele can't climb up into the cab wearing that tight dress and high heels, right?"

He laughed. "Nope, I know. Hired a limo. Gonna let somebody else do the driving so I can have a few drinks."

"You're a professional driver and you actually trust somebody else to drive you around?"

Dave winked. "Hel... heck, I was in your back seat while you drag-raced a train. Nothing scares me anymore."

We were grinning at each other when Nichele emerged from the hallway. She shot us a suspicious glance. "What are you up to?"

"Nothing." I stooped to lace up my boots. "I was just leaving."

"Stay here." Dave's smile was gone, his bushy brows drawing together. "Believe me, it's gonna be bad out there."

"Dave, you drive in weather like this all the time." I pulled on my parka.

His scowl deepened. "Not the point. You're not me."

I leaned over to give him a quick hug. "And I'm sure Nichele is profoundly grateful for that. Thanks, Dave, but I'll be fine. You guys have fun tonight."

"Be careful." Nichele pulled me into a bear hug. "Call me as soon as you get home."

"I will. Talk to you later." I made my escape, avoiding Dave's troubled gaze.

I was second-guessing my decision before I even finished cleaning off my car. Wind-driven snow stung my face while I wielded the brush, and a layer of white had already accumulated on the windshield when I slid behind the wheel only a few minutes later.

I turned on the wipers and stared out at the whirling flakes. A gust of wind shook the car.

Shit, Dave was right. The highway would be bad and getting worse. And I only had an hour of daylight left, just enough to put me in the most desolate part of the trip by dark.

I clenched my teeth and plugged my phone into the hands-free outlet. I wouldn't spoil Dave and Nichele's special evening. If the roads were really that bad, I'd go to a hotel instead of driving beyond the populated areas. And anyway, I had my survival gear if I got stopped.

Muttering reassurances to myself, I started driving.

Half an hour later, I drew a deep breath and eased my shoulders down from around my ears for the umpteenth time. The main expressway out of Calgary was a confusing expanse of crisscrossing tire tracks fading into several inches of snow. Disoriented drivers wavered uncertainly across the invisible lanes, and cloudbound twilight darkened the sky already.

I feathered the brakes as some shit-for-brains SUV driver sped past only to slide into a butt-puckering skid a few hundred yards ahead. Fortunately, Shit-For-Brains managed to regain control without causing an accident, and I released my pent-up breath in a hiss between my teeth.

This was stupid. I should just pull off and find a hotel here in the city.

My phone rang before I reached the next exit and I eased the car to a stop on what I sincerely hoped was the shoulder, peeling a white-knuckled hand off the steering wheel to engage the four-way flashers.

"Hello?" My voice came out high and tight.

"Aydan? Are you still at Nichele's place?" Kane's warm baritone held a note of concern.

I swallowed. "No, I'm just heading home," I said with as much confidence as I could muster.

"That's what I was afraid of. Where are you?"

"Northbound on Deerfoot at Country Hills."

"Turn around and come back to my place. Don't leave the city."

I hesitated. Despite my fervent desire to follow the second part of his advice, I wasn't quite ready to face him after our sizzling induction to the Mile-High Club. The body-baring had been fabulous. The subsequent soul-baring, not so much.

I made my voice easy and relaxed. "Thanks, John, but I'd really like to get home tonight-"

"That's why I'm calling. You can't. There's a twenty-car pileup north of Airdrie and the highway's closed."

"Shit."

My mouth uttered the expletive automatically, but a tendril of relief crept into my heart. The decision was out of my hands. I could hole up in a warm, safe hotel...

Kane's voice interrupted my thoughts. "Come down to my place. Dinner's almost ready and we have far too much food as usual."

"Thanks, but you're in the opposite direction to where I want to be, and anyway, I don't want to intrude on your family time-"

"Aydan, I told you last night, you're more than welcome. Dad would love to see you again. The turkey's in the oven and we have all the trimmings." His voice dropped to a seductive rumble. "I'm making garlic cream cheese mashed potatoes."

My mouth watered.

"Gravy," he coaxed. "Stuffing. Roasted root vegetables. Fresh cranberry-orange sauce. Pecan pie with whipped cream for dessert..."

I failed to suppress a small moan.

I could hear the smile in his voice as he continued, "...a bottle of Sauvignon Blanc chilling-"

"Stop!" I protested. "Thanks, but I really-"

"Tell her I'm comin' to get her," a gravelly voice spoke in the background. "Where is she?"

"Hellhound will-" Kane began to relay the message.

"I heard, but tell him it's okay. I don't want to leave my car by the side of the road."

"But you're turning around now, aren't you?" Kane pitched his voice into an ominous growl. "If you're not here in forty-five minutes, I'll get Webb to trace your cell phone and we'll hunt you down and drag you back here kicking and screaming."

I laughed, the icy tension easing from my belly. "All right, all right. Jeez, creepy stalkers or what?"

Kane laughed, too, but when he spoke again, his tone was serious. "Drive carefully. Call if you need help."

CHAPTER 4

My car wallowed into a snowy berth in Kane's condo parking lot at last. I pried my aching fingers off the steering wheel one by one, half-expecting to leave deep dents behind. Letting the blessed safety ease into my quivering muscles, I sat for a long moment staring out at the snow slashing almost horizontally in front of the windshield.

A gust of wind made the car shudder before settling deeper into the snowbank as if in relief of its own, and the taut corners of my mouth creaked into a smile at the notion. I patted its dashboard and crooned, "You're such a good car!"

It made no reply, and I let out a breath that felt as though it came from my toes and punched Nichele's speed-dial on my cell phone.

She answered on the first ring. "Aydan, where are you? Are you okay?"

"What are you doing answering your phone?" I teased. "Pay attention to Dave."

"Girl, where are you? Just tell me you're safe."

"I'm safe. I'm staying in Calgary tonight after all."

"Oh, thank God! I was so worried about you but I didn't want to spoil Dave's plans."

"She okay?" Dave's gruff voice spoke in the background.

"She need me to come and get her?"

"Tell Dave thanks, but I'm fine and he'd better pay attention to his date."

Nichele giggled. "I'll tell him. Thanks, Aydan. Now we can relax and enjoy ourselves."

"Enjoy," I agreed. "Get back to your date. I'm going to go and collect a turkey supper."

Cold was already penetrating the car when I hung up and stowed my phone in my waist pouch. Feeling as though I'd aged twenty years, I dragged myself out into the savage gale and tottered to the front entrance to ring the buzzer for Kane's apartment.

When the security door released, I crept up the stairs clinging to the handrail, the soft light and warm silence wrapping around me like a blanket.

By the time I gained the third floor, Hellhound stood in Kane's doorway. His battered face creased into a smile as I approached, and a moment later his arms closed around me, their strength tempered to gentleness as always.

"Jesus, darlin', ya look like ya got nothin' left but eyeballs an' asshole," he rasped, and bestowed a kiss on my lips. "An' lips," he amended. "Lucky for me."

I let out a shaky giggle and cuddled into his warmth, tucking my head under his bearded chin and giving him a careful hug in case his injuries still hurt as much as I suspected they did. "I *feel* like nothing but eyeballs and asshole," I mumbled against his chest. "And actually, the eyeballs are questionable."

"Well, come on in an' get a drink. Ya look like ya need one." He drew me into the apartment with an arm around my shoulders.

Shedding my boots and jacket in the entry, I inhaled the

mouth-watering scent of roasting turkey. When I straightened, Kane and his father stood regarding me with almost-identical smiles.

My gaze locked onto Kane despite my attempt to control it.

God, no man should be allowed to look that good. His wide shoulders and bulging biceps filled his snug black T-shirt to perfection. A dishtowel was tucked into his jeans as a makeshift apron, emphasizing his hard midriff and triggering a smoking-hot memory of what was behind that towel. Strong, square features, short dark hair with a sprinkling of silver at the temples, warm grey eyes bracketed by sexy laugh lines... yum. The bruised and sutured cut above his left eyebrow only added to his deliciously dangerous vibe.

And I had nearly killed him.

A cold wave of guilt swept the warmth from my belly and I gave him what I hoped was a casual smile before turning to greet his father.

Beside his towering son, Doug looked smaller than the last time I'd seen him, but his square shoulders and straight military bearing left no doubt as to the origin of Kane's stature. The maze of wrinkles on Doug's face folded into his widening smile as he stepped forward, extending his arms.

"It's so nice to see you again, Aydan," he said. "Especially since it's under much happier circumstances this time. Merry Christmas!"

I stepped into his hug, guilt twisting my guts. If not for sheer dumb luck, we'd be meeting at another funeral. And I doubted he'd want to hug the woman who had killed both his biological son and his unofficially-adopted one.

"It's nice to see you, too, Doug," I mumbled, and

summoned up a smile. "Merry Christmas."

When Doug stepped back, Kane and I hesitated before giving each other a short, awkward hug. The brief contact brought back steamy memories and my cheeks were hot when I pulled away to offer him a fake smile and too-hearty 'Merry Christmas'.

We both shot warning glances at Doug and Hellhound.

"Don't tell-"

"You didn't see that-"

Kane and I spoke at the same time, and Hellhound laughed. "Shit, guilty consciences or what?"

I silently cursed my burning cheeks as Doug's fatherly gaze darted between Kane and me. Doug's smile widened, mischief sparkling in his eyes. "Is there something I should know about you two?"

"No."

Our simultaneous denial came too quickly. If I hadn't been stewing in my own mortification, I would have been amused at the way Kane's customary aplomb had deserted him.

Kane faced his father. "We're not trying to hide anything from you. But after that faked rape and sexual harassment charge a few months ago, we can't afford any hint of impropriety, and that includes any physical contact that might be misconstrued." He waved an encompassing hand. "We can relax here, but it has to stay inside this condo."

Doug and Hellhound nodded seriously, but the twinkle still danced in Doug's eyes.

I seized on the first diversion that occurred to me. "Wow, this is better than the last time I was here." I indicated the warm, bright room with the cheery fire crackling in the fireplace. "You even have a Christmas tree!

When did you find time for that?"

"You can't have Christmas without a tree." Doug shot a conspiratorial glance at Hellhound. "Arnie and I set it up while you two were at the debriefing last night."

Hellhound slung an arm over my shoulders. "Well, come on an' sit down before ya fall down, darlin'. I'll bring ya a beer."

I sighed. "I'd better not. I still have to drive to a hotel tonight."

"Fuck that." His arm tightened around me. "I'll drive ya. You're done for the night."

I sank into the soft leather sofa and stretched trembling hands toward the warmth of the fireplace. "Thank you. In that case, I would love a beer until death did us part."

Sedated by beer, Sauvignon Blanc, and far too much delicious food, I was struggling to keep my eyes open when Kane rose from the table with a smile. "Aydan, why don't you relax and we'll clean up?" He gestured to the sofa, its dark leather gleaming softly in the mellow firelight. "Get comfortable, and I'll bring you another drink."

I stifled a yawn and rose, too. "No, that would be a really bad idea. I'd be snoring in seconds."

"Bad night last night?"

"Um. The usual." I avoided three sets of sympathetic eyes by bustling around collecting plates and silverware.

The men trailed me into the kitchen bearing the last of the dishes, and Kane set his load down to turn an expression of mock severity on me. "You're not doing any work tonight. We'll handle this. Dad, take her to the living room and sit on her."

Doug laughed and linked his arm through mine. "Yessir, Captain Kane. I'll guard the prisoner."

I laughed, too, and let him lead me back to the living room. Sinking into the softness of the couch, I leaned my head back with a sigh of contentment.

"So, have you been enjoying your visit?" I asked.

Doug smiled. "More than you can imagine, thanks to you."

"Good... Um..." I eyed him in confusion. "Why thanks to me?"

His smile widened. "You don't need to pretend. John and Arnie told me how you saved both of their lives. I can't thank you enough."

"*I*... saved...?"

Shame rose to strangle me and I stared down at my hands knotted together in my lap.

"Doug..." A glance at his seamed face and patient eyes wrenched my heart with the memory of my own dad, dead nearly ten years. It would be so nice to relax into Doug's fatherly fondness. So easy to pretend.

But I didn't deserve his gratitude.

I swallowed hard. This was only the second time we'd met. His anger and rejection couldn't hurt me.

"Doug, I nearly killed them both." My voice seared my throat like dry ice. "I started a fire that damn near burned John to death. And Arnie wouldn't have been beaten within an inch of his life if I hadn't been involved. It's my fault they're both injured, and it's my fault they nearly died." My throat closed.

"I'm sorry," I whispered.

His silence stripped the skin from my body, leaving nothing but raw nerves and my stupidly aching heart.

"I'm sorry. I'll go." I stumbled to my feet, not looking at him.

"Aydan, for heaven's sake!" His hands closed around my shoulders, the firmness of his grip undiminished by age. "Sit down. You and I need to have a talk." He pressed me gently down on the sofa and sat beside me.

"Now." He took my hand. "Look at me."

When I reluctantly looked up, I met eyes of grey steel. "Aydan, my sons don't lie to me." His gaze bored into me. "John said that without you, the plane probably would have crashed and killed you both. Is that true?"

"That's not the point-"

"Answer my question. Is that true?"

I swallowed, silently cursing the prickling behind my eyes. "Yes, but-"

"Shush. Arnie said you broke into his apartment and found him barely conscious and called the ambulance, which probably saved his life. Is that true?"

"Well, yes, but-"

"Aydan." The steel softened, his eyes warming with a bittersweet smile. "You and my sons do dangerous work. Someday they might not come home, and I've prepared for that as best I can. You've given me more days with them than I would have had otherwise, and I will always be grateful for that."

My vision blurred with unshed tears. "B-but..." My voice came out in a child's quaver. "What if I'd k-killed them? It almost happened. I can't-"

"What *almost* happened doesn't matter." His grip tightened on my hand. "If not for you, I would have been spending this Christmas alone." He smiled, his gaze steady. "Live in today, Aydan. You can't change yesterday with regret and you can't change tomorrow with worry." He rose and squeezed my shoulder. "I'll get you another beer."

I had regained my composure by the time he returned bearing a frosty bottle, and he smiled as he handed it over and resumed his seat in the chair across from me. "Now, tell me how that '53 Chevy restoration is going."

I seized the subject gratefully, and we were deep in car talk when Kane and Hellhound returned from the kitchen. Kane took a seat at the opposite end of the sofa and Hellhound sank into the other chair, reaching down to the leather motorcycle saddlebag that sat on the floor beside it. He withdrew a beautiful jewel-coloured afghan and began to ply a crochet hook, the yarn twisting into complex stitches under his deft musician's fingers.

I couldn't suppress my smile at the big badass biker with his 'Live to Ride' T-shirt and a lap full of crocheting. He glanced up, his bruised face softening into an answering smile.

"Where's your guitar?" I asked. "Don't tell me you left her at home by herself on Christmas."

"Hell, no. She's over behind the Christmas tree." He gestured with his crochet hook. "But I started this blanket last week when the doc said I hadta take it easy after that concussion, an' I wanted to get it done. What d'ya think?" He held the almost-complete afghan up for inspection.

"I love it. You have such a great eye for colour and your designs are always so sophisticated."

His smile widened. "Thanks, darlin'. Yeah, I don't do that lacy shit. I make blankets, not fuckin' doilies. An' I'm glad ya like it, 'cause you're gettin' it for Christmas."

"Oh, thank you!" My rush of warm pleasure subsided into chagrin. "But... I'm sorry, I didn't get you anything."

Another uncomfortable thought occurred to me and I avoided glancing at Kane. Shit, what was the gift-giving protocol after having red-hot adrenaline-fuelled sex but rejecting a relationship?

Hellhound's reply pulled my attention back to the conversation at hand. "Jesus, darlin', ya know I got a shitpile of 'em at home an' you're doin' me a favour takin' it off my hands." He sent a not-too-convincing scowl my way. "We ain't doin' the gift thing. It's too much like commitment, so stop scarin' me with that shit. I'm too full a' turkey dinner to run away tonight."

I let out a breath of relief. "Have I told you lately how much I love your commitment phobia?"

"Nah, but now's a good time."

We exchanged a grin.

The knots in my belly slowly eased under the soothing effects of beer and an evening of laughter while the men reminisced, regaling me with tales of outrageous childhood exploits. At last I hauled myself out of the seductive comfort of the couch to stand blinking at the four empty beer bottles on the coffee table beside me.

So much for my usual limit of two. Not to mention the wine with supper. And the beer before that.

"I guess I'd better get going if I'm going to find a hotel tonight," I enunciated carefully. The carpet felt distant under my feet as I concentrated on walking a straight line over to the window to peek out between the blinds into the whirling whiteness. "Shit, that's ugly," I mumbled.

"You don't need to go to a hotel," Kane said. "You can sleep in my bed."

I turned, my brain splashing through the alcohol to rummage for a polite way to decline in front of our audience. "Um..."

A flush climbed his neck. "...and I'll sleep on the couch," he finished.

"Oh, no, don't do that." Dammit, that sounded like an invitation. I tried again. "I mean, I don't want to kick you out of bed."

I hid a wince. My Freudian slip was definitely showing tonight.

Come on brain, get it together.

"I'll go to a hotel," I said firmly. "Arnie, will you take me?"

"Sure, darlin'," he began, but Doug overrode him.

"Nobody should drive in this unless it's absolutely necessary, and it's not. John's got his bed, I'm in the spare bedroom, and Arnie's been using the hide-a-bed in the office. It's a double, so..."

Doug trailed off as if suddenly sensing our discomfort. He eyed Hellhound and me in the short silence, obviously wondering if we'd stopped sleeping together since we'd stayed at his place in the summer.

Awkward.

My booze-soaked brain blundered through rationalizations. Why shouldn't I sleep with Hellhound? After our conversation on the plane, Kane knew I wouldn't offer him a commitment regardless of any jet-fuelled orgasms. And he knew Hellhound and I had been lovers long before anything ever happened with him.

But it still seemed like a slap in the face to bed down with Hellhound right under his nose.

"I gotta sleep diagonal in the double 'cause it's too short

for me," Hellhound said casually. "So Aydan can take it an' I'll sleep on the couch."

"Uh, okay, thanks," I muttered. "I'll go and get my stuff from the car." I hurried to the door and bent to lace my boots, hiding my burning face.

CHAPTER 5

Flames tore at Kane's flesh. His eyes met mine, filled with agony and desperate appeal. I jerked the lever of the fire extinguisher frantically. Only a few drops trickled out. Kane was burning...

Hellhound lunged out of the smoke-filled darkness and yanked the cylinder from my hands. The flames leaped to consume him, withering skin and muscle to expose stark white ribs, his heart still beating inside them.

My gun kicked as I shot Hellhound once; twice; his naked heart spurting crimson blood into the flames. Screams ripped my throat.

The two corpses burned, their beloved features slagging into charred oblivion while I screamed and screamed...

"Aydan, wake up! Wake up, darlin'!"

My eyes jerked open, my last scream tearing the air. Disoriented in the bright light of an unfamiliar room, I struggled against the big tattooed man who pinned me against his chest...

"Aydan, wake up! Just a dream." Hellhound's rasp chased away the last of the nightmare and I collapsed in his arms, burying my face in his shoulder.

"Oh, Jesus. Jesus. Shit." I gasped a couple of ragged

breaths. "Shit. Sorry."

A moment later I woke up enough to register the scene I'd glimpsed when my eyes opened.

I mashed my face into Hellhound's shoulder and vented a groan of sheer humiliation before dragging myself upright to face my audience.

Pajama-clad Doug peered around the doorjamb, his brow furrowed in concern. Kane filled the doorway beside him, gun at the ready, wearing nothing but extremely well-fitting black briefs. His combat stance relaxed as I looked up, hard muscles rippling into smooth curves like running water.

God. Damn. Even waking from the jaws of a nightmare, that body was enough to send a flush of heat from my head to my toes.

Or maybe that was embarrassment.

Thank God I'd borrowed one of Kane's T-shirts for nightwear. The only indignity that could top screaming everybody awake would be screaming everybody awake to see me naked.

"Hey, darlin'." Hellhound smoothed my hair with a gentle hand. "Ya awake now? Ya okay?"

"Yeah." I sank my face into my hands. "God, you guys, I'm so sorry. Go back to bed. I'll sit up for a bit."

"No need to apologize," Doug said. "We've all been there. Good night."

"Good night," I mumbled through my fingers.

After a moment, I looked up. Doug had left, but Kane still lingered in the doorway. His uncomfortable gaze flitted between Hellhound and me. "Can I bring you anything?" he asked. "A glass of water?"

I sighed. Yep, that heat was definitely embarrassment.

"No, thanks. I'm fine. I'm really sorry. I hope you can get back to sleep."

"It's all right." He hesitated. "I hope you can, too. Good night." He turned and left, and a moment later I heard the quiet closing of his bedroom door.

I turned to Hellhound. "You should go back to bed, too. I'm sorry I woke you. I'll just sit up for a while so you can get some sleep."

"Hell, darlin', no big deal. I wasn't asleep. It's only a little after midnight."

"Oh, God, really?" I groaned and leaned my forehead against his shoulder. "I should have gone to a hotel."

"Why, so ya could wake up a buncha strangers an' have 'em call the cops thinkin' somebody was gettin' axe-murdered?"

I winced, and he dropped a whiskery kiss on my temple. "It's better that you're here. Like Dad says, we all been there, so don't feel bad. Why don't ya lie down an' see if ya can get back to sleep? I'll stay with ya for a while."

I shuddered. "I'm not quite ready to try again."

"Well, shove over, then, darlin'."

I squirmed over and he swung his legs onto the bed, reclining to prop himself against the sofa back. He raised a welcoming arm and I cuddled under it, soaking up his warmth. Sliding a hand across the solid planes of his chest, I paused over his heart.

The story of his life was inked in his skin, and the tattoo under my hand was his first. He'd gotten it as a teenager decades ago, an ugly crudely-drawn heart oozing blood, pierced by swords and bound in chains. His later body art swirled in complex patterns that flowed into finely executed vignettes, but the ugly heart had always lain alone in a barren circle on his chest.

I didn't know if it commemorated his mother, beaten to death by his alcoholic father before his five-year-old eyes; or maybe his pregnant high-school girlfriend who had been brutally gang-raped and murdered. Overwhelmed by the magnitude of pain expressed in that tattoo, I had never asked.

But now...

I traced the lines of a new tattoo. Graceful hands occupied the previously empty space on his chest, tenderly cradling the suffering heart while angel wings unfurled to shelter it from above.

"You got some new ink," I murmured.

"Yeah." He took my hand and kissed the palm before returning my hand to his chest, pressing it against the tattoo.

Tears stung my eyes.

"I ain't gonna forget what ya did for me," he whispered against my hair.

I blinked back the moisture and summoned up a teasing grin. "Well, you know what they say. A good friend will visit you in jail, but a really good friend will help you hide the body."

He snorted, laughter fading into seriousness. "That ain't supposed to be literal." He hesitated. "Everythin' okay with...?"

I slid my arms around him, avoiding the worst of his bruises. "Everything's fine. Stemp believes I did it. He gave me a little lecture about too many dead bodies and assigned me to an anger-management class, and that's it. The body's long gone and nobody has any reason to access the redacted records."

Hellhound blew out a long breath and rested his

forehead against mine. "I'm the one that should be takin' the anger management class. I should be takin' the responsibility for-"

"Arnie, no!" I gave him a little shake. "You have more self-control than anybody I know. If you'd feel better taking a class, that's fine, but don't ever feel guilty about killing that rat-bastard. It was self-defence, pure and simple. He killed your mother. He beat the shit out of you as a kid. He assaulted you a dozen times as an adult. He flat-out told you this time he was going to beat you to death-"

"Yeah, but I shoulda called the cops an' told them that, 'stead a' lettin' ya pretend ya killed him."

"Arnie." I sat up to face him, grasping his powerful shoulders to make sure he was listening. "It's done. Trying to change it now would just get us both in trouble. You're finally free of your father, and you don't have any reason to feel guilty. Don't let him hold any power over you now that he's dead."

He regarded me for a moment before letting out a short breath as if in resolution. "You're right, darlin'. I'm gonna let it go. Thanks."

I settled back into his embrace and we lay in silence, my cheek pillowed on his chest while he stroked my hair. The strong steady beat of his heart lulled me into drowsiness, and my eyelids were drooping when he spoke again.

"Somethin' change between you an' John?"

I yawned. "No. Ye... Well, kind of, I guess..."

"Thought ya looked kinda uncomfortable when Dad said we should sleep together." He hesitated. "I figured maybe two people gettin' ready to die in a plane crash might have some talkin' to do. Maybe work a few things out."

"Yeah. We talked. Among other things." I pressed my

face into his chest. "He gets it now, Arnie. He knows I won't give him a commitment."

His hand went still on my hair. "Ya explained? Or did ya just say it can't happen?"

"I explained. He gets it." I drew a deep breath. "And you know? I think he's okay with it. I think... we're okay."

"Well, I guess that's good, darlin'." His hand resumed its stroking. When he spoke again, I could hear the smile in his voice. "'Among other things', huh? So ya banged him an' then told him it ain't ever gonna happen again. What did I tell ya about sendin' mixed messages, darlin'?"

I smacked his chest lightly, smiling in spite of myself. "It wasn't like that."

His chuckle rumbled under my ear. "Uh-huh."

I sighed. "Okay, it was... but it was complicated. I wouldn't have done it otherwise, but I thought he had just lost the love of his life."

Incredulity tinged Hellhound's rasp. "Ya pity-fucked him? Jesus, darlin', guys like me get pity fucks. Guys like him get supermodels crawlin' all over them an' beggin' for it. I'm surprised he's even talkin' to ya."

"Like I said, it was complicated." I sat up and kissed him. "And you will never be a pity fuck."

"No kiddin'. Even when I begged, ya wouldn't give me any." He pulled a long face.

"You didn't beg; you suggested. And anyway, I'd only known you for a few days then. I made up for lost time later." I gave him an appreciative up-and-down appraisal and ran a hand up his denim-clad thigh. "I like the jeans-only look, but I'm surprised you're not commando as usual."

He shrugged, grinning. "I'm sleepin' on the couch. Didn't think Dad an' John'd wanna see me salutin' the flag in the mornin'.'" He pulled me closer, sprinkling kisses up my neck. Whiskery shivers tingled my skin.

"But since ya brought it up, darlin'..." His hand drifted down my shoulder and rounded the curve of my hip, and the tingles spread. "...Maybe ya wanna check out my flagpole," he rumbled in my ear.

"Mmm. You think?"

"Uh-huh." He nibbled my earlobe, sending a delicious shiver down my spine. He pulled away a fraction and sent a smiling glance downward. "Well, look at that. The girls are salutin', too." He stroked a fingertip over one of my nipples, shamelessly pressing toward him under the soft T-shirt.

I sucked in a breath, heat pooling between my legs. Hellhound nuzzled the neck of the T-shirt aside to find that magic spot near my collarbone, his tongue and teeth and whiskers playing a symphony of pleasure on my skin. A small moan leaked out between my lips.

His hand coasted down to the hem of my T-shirt but I captured it as it crept underneath.

"I can't," I whispered. "This bed squeaks. If you get started with those fabulous hands of yours, I can't hold still. I'll wake everybody all over again."

He chuckled. "Ya say that like it's a bad thing." His fingertips traced a feather-light path under the T-shirt, making my hips press involuntarily toward him.

The bed emitted a squeak and I froze.

"We don't hafta use the bed, darlin'," he murmured.

I sighed. "I can't." I pulled away, generating another tell-tale squeak. "Not with John right in the next room. If he heard, it'd be like rubbing it in. I'm sorry."

"It's okay, darlin', don't apologize." Hellhound withdrew his hand and brushed a kiss onto my forehead. "It's fun just teasin' ya."

"And I expect you to deliver as soon as we're alone." I grinned at him. "Just teasing, huh?" I cast a significant glance down to the bulge in his jeans. "I call bullshit. If I hadn't shut you down, I'd be coming my brains out by now."

He chuckled. "Nah. I prob'ly woulda got up to close the bedroom door first. That'd slow ya down by a few seconds."

"You *probably* would have? You're such a gentleman."

"Hell, yeah." He dropped a kiss on my lips.

CHAPTER 6

I woke slowly, clinging to the warm lassitude that enveloped me. Despite my best efforts to remain asleep, a niggling sensation of guilt prickled just below my level of consciousness.

My sleep-sodden brain paged through the possibilities. Was I missing work? No, it was a holiday, I was sure of it.

Something I was supposed to do? No, I didn't need to make any phone calls. Nobody I had to meet...

The comforting familiarity of Hellhound's quiet snores lulled me back toward sleep, his hand warm and heavy on my bare stomach.

Shit!

My eyes popped open.

The bedroom door still wasn't closed and light streamed down the hallway from the direction of the living area. Soft clinks and the smell of coffee assured me we'd been caught by at least one of the Kanes passing by on the way to the kitchen.

Fortunately our position wasn't as explicit as I'd first thought. My T-shirt had ridden up, but the blankets were pulled high enough to hide my partial nudity. And since I didn't remember having a mind-blowing orgasm, I was pretty sure Hellhound's magic hand hadn't strayed too far from its current position.

Still clad in his jeans, Hellhound lay on top of the blankets, curled protectively around me. My heart warmed.

Guarding my dreams, as always. How many times had he woken during the night to dispel my nightmares and soothe me back to sleep?

I eased out from under the covers, tugging my T-shirt down into place. Hellhound mumbled and stirred, and I bent to brush a kiss onto his lips.

"Go back to sleep," I whispered, and drew the blanket over him.

"Mmhmm." He settled without opening his eyes, and a moment later his snores resumed.

I gathered my things and retreated to the bathroom. Inside, I threw on some clothes and splashed water on my face before glowering at myself in the mirror.

So this was awkward. So what? We were all adults. And it wasn't like Hellhound and I had been screwing each other's brains out in the middle of the living room. Kane could just deal with seeing us sleeping in the same bed.

Get out there and get it over with.

I glared at the embarrassed-looking woman in the mirror. "Get going," I hissed at my cowardly reflection.

After a deep sigh, it obeyed.

When I peeped around the corner into the kitchen, my heart rose in cautious hope. No sign of Kane. His father looked up from his coffee with a smile.

"Good morning," I murmured.

"Good morning. What are you doing up so early? I hope I didn't wake you."

"Um, no..."

I hovered in the doorway. What the hell should I do? I really wasn't in the mood for small talk at five-thirty in the morning, but having successfully avoided awkwardness with Kane, I didn't want to go back to bed and set myself up for it all over again. And it didn't seem fair to wake Hellhound and make him go back to the couch.

Doug raised his cup. "Coffee's on the counter. Just fresh a few minutes ago."

Coffee. Blech.

"Um, thanks. Maybe half a cup." I sidled into the kitchen and poured myself a small portion.

Doug smiled and cocked a thumb toward the kitchen cabinets. "You might want to eat something with that. I make it strong enough to dissolve the spoon."

"Thanks for the warning." I followed the direction of his gesture and discovered some bagels in a breadbox. There was no toaster in sight and I doubted Kane was a peanut butter fan, so I snagged a naked bagel and trailed back to perch on the stool beside Doug at the breakfast bar. Taking a sip of the tarry substance in my cup, I couldn't prevent a shudder.

"So how many spoons are in this batch?" I asked.

He chuckled and took a slug of his own brew. "None this morning. John gets testy when his cutlery disappears."

"Good to know." I nibbled in silence for a while, pacing my sips of the corrosive fluid. "Did you, um... sleep okay? Um... I mean, after...?"

"Just fine." He smiled and patted my hand. "Don't beat yourself up, Aydan. I've done my fair share of screaming after combat, too. All of us have. It's nothing to be ashamed of."

I sighed. "Thanks, but..."

There wasn't really anything more to say. I grimaced and took another bite of bagel.

We sat in silence for a while, Doug sipping his coffee while I worked on my bagel. I was beginning to relax when he spoke.

"I see Arnie has a new tattoo."

"Um... yeah." I grabbed my coffee cup and took a gulp.

He stared at the wall, but his eyes looked far beyond it. "I don't usually notice when he gets a new one. He has so many. But this one..." He spoke as though to himself. "He's had an empty place there all his life." He turned to me, his gaze probing too deeply. "Does it mean what I think it means?"

I clutched my mug like a shield between us. "I, um... I don't know what you think it means."

He appraised me in silence for a moment before his shrewd grey eyes softened. "I think you've given him... comfort. He's never let any woman get as close as you." He gazed into the past again. "My wife Ellen worried over Arnie until the day she died nearly fifteen years ago. I think..." He took a sip of coffee, and when he spoke again, his eyes were bright. "I think she'd be happy today."

"I hope so," I murmured.

Doug returned from his reverie, his gaze sharp again. "John thinks the world of you, too."

"Uh." I took a large bite of bagel and chewed with intense concentration.

He smiled. "I won't pry. I don't care how, or if, things work out between you and either of my sons. I just want you to know that in my books, you're family."

"I... Doug, I don't feel like I deserve that, but..." I swallowed the lump in my throat with a swig of coffee.

"Thanks, I'm honoured." My voice came out husky anyway.

Doug smiled and reached over to pat my hand. "You don't have to finish the coffee, Aydan. I know you're a brave woman. You don't have to prove it."

I laughed, grateful for the change of topic. "Thank God. This stuff is killing me."

He chuckled. "Go ahead and dump it. You won't hurt my feelings." When I returned from the sink with a cup of water, he glanced at my face. "Don't take this wrong, but you still look tired. Why don't you go back to bed for a while?"

The first caffeine jitters vibrated in my hands as I reached for the remains of my bagel. "I don't think I can sleep after drinking that rocket fuel."

"Try. You might be surprised."

That sounded like a fine idea. If nothing else, I could avoid more conversation.

I swallowed the last of the bagel. "I think I will. Thanks."

Escaping to the couch, I snuggled into the nest of bedding Hellhound had abandoned. Hyper-alert to Doug's movements in the kitchen, I lay tensely. Caffeine buzzed in my veins.

I wouldn't sleep. Even without caffeine overload, I could never sleep when someone might be watching me.

A soft voice and a gentle touch on my shoulder lifted me from my troubled dream. "Shhh, Aydan, it's okay. You're safe. It's just a dream."

I dragged my eyes open to focus blearily on Doug leaning over me. He smiled, his maze of wrinkles framing eyes full of compassion. "Shhh. Go back to sleep."

My eyelids dropped like stones.

The comfortable rumble of male voices roused me. I yawned and hauled myself upright to massage my aching neck, thankful Hellhound had spent the night in the hide-a-bed instead of here. The couch wasn't very comfortable even for my 5'10" height. For someone several inches taller and close to a hundred pounds heavier, it would be a chiropractic nightmare.

"Good morning." Kane emerged from the kitchen to eye me quizzically. "You ended up on the couch."

"Um. Yeah..." My groggy brain didn't supply any other useful comment.

Keep it simple.

"Good morning," I mumbled. "Is everybody up but me?"

Kane chuckled. "No, it's only eight. Hellhound will sleep as long as we let him."

A glance at his freshly shaved face and still-damp hair made me feel grubby and rumpled, and I rose self-consciously to begin folding blankets. "Is it okay if I have a shower?"

"Of course. Here, I'll take those." He appropriated the bedding and inclined his chin toward the bathroom. "I left a fresh towel and washcloth by the sink for you."

"Thanks." I beat a hasty retreat.

When I emerged from the bathroom, the sound of Hellhound's guitar drifted to my ears and I followed it into the living room. Kane and his father sprawled in the chairs nursing mugs of coffee while Hellhound sat on the sofa, his quiet music accompanying the conversation.

I curled into the corner of the couch beside him, the last of my tension ebbing away. Another yawn took me by surprise and I cuddled deeper into the cushions, feeling safe and relaxed for the first time in weeks.

Hellhound chuckled. "'Mornin', darlin'. Ya look like Hooker, all curled up smilin' there."

I laughed. "Good morning. Lucky I know you're talking about the cat, or I'd take serious offence. Is Miss Lacey looking after him while you're here?"

"Yeah." His eyes softened as they always did when he mentioned his elderly neighbour. "I'm lucky to have her."

"She's lucky to have you to take her grocery shopping and to her appointments, too."

"Mm." He smiled and returned his attention to the guitar, though his music hadn't faltered while we talked.

A faint vibration caught my ear and I sprang up. "That's my phone." I hurried for the bedroom.

"Jesus, darlin', ya got ears like a fuckin' bat," Hellhound teased.

"Well, I'm just not deaf from playing loud music half my life," I tossed over my shoulder, and left their laughter behind to grab my waist pouch from beside the hide-a-bed.

I punched the button without taking time to look at the call display.

"Ms. Widdenback?" The precisely modulated voice slammed tension back into my body. "This is Archibald Rankin, Nicholas Parr's assistant. I was calling to see when it would be convenient for you to return Mr. Parr's credit card."

"Uh. Sorry, I completely forgot about it."

"That's quite understandable, and I'm sorry you went through such an ordeal. How are you feeling?"

God, it was hard to remember these guys were violent, ruthless criminals. I shook off my sense of unreality. But maybe Rankin wasn't a criminal. Parr kept lots of innocent employees on his payroll, too.

"I'm sorry to bring back unpleasant memories," he added.

"It's okay. Um, I'm in Calgary right now..." I bit off the words '...staying with friends'. Shit, all this damn pleasantness threw me off guard. "Is there a place where I can drop it off?"

"Oh, I don't want to trouble you. Just give me the address where you're staying and I'll be happy to come and get it."

I snapped fully alert.

Yeah, wouldn't they like to know where I was staying? They must be pissed after going to the trouble of bugging my house only to have me depart before they could hear anything useful.

"I'm checking out of my hotel in a few minutes," I lied. "I'll be driving anyway, so just let me know where I can drop it off."

"We're in a rather inconvenient location in the industrial park," he demurred.

Parry, thrust, parry...

"...but since you're here, Mr. Parr would be pleased to take you out for lunch," he finished. "You can give it to him then."

Touché.

Shit.

I stalled, racking my brain for excuses. "Um, I thought he was out of the country on his Christmas gambling holiday."

"No, when such a serious situation arises in his company, Mr. Parr is always on hand to deal with it. Frivolities like vacations come second. He's very dedicated to his business and his employees."

Yeah. And he was undoubtedly also very dedicated to finding out what had happened to the deadly weapon prototype we'd swiped from his burning plane.

"Uh..." I couldn't think of a way around it. "Okay. I'd like to have lunch with Nick."

About as much as I'd like to cuddle a pit viper.

I sighed. "Where and when should I meet him?"

There was a distinct note of satisfaction in Rankin's pleasant tone. "He has a reservation at La Chaumière for eleven-thirty."

Inspiration seized me. "I'm sorry, I got caught here in the storm yesterday, and I wasn't intending to stay the night. All I have is jeans and hiking boots. That's not appropriate for La Chaumière, and I wouldn't want to embarrass Nick."

The faint sound on the other end of the line might have been grinding teeth, but when Rankin spoke again his voice still radiated warm concern. "Please, use the credit card to purchase anything you need. It's the least we can do."

Now I was the one grinding my teeth. "That's so kind of you," I cooed. "But I really-"

"Please. I insist." This time there was a hint of iron in his tone.

I dealt the bed a vicious kick. "Oh, thank you. You're so kind." My sweetness was enough to cause diabetic shock inside a three-mile radius. "I'll look forward to seeing Nick at eleven-thirty."

I pressed the disconnect button. "Fuck, fuck, *fuck!*"

CHAPTER 7

I shoved my phone back into my waist pouch and stomped down the hallway, teeth locked together to prevent more obscenities from spilling out.

When I stepped into the sudden silence of the living room, the three men eyed me with concern.

"That didn't sound good, darlin'," Hellhound said.

My lips peeled back in a snarl. "It's not fu-" I bit off the f-bomb with a glance at Doug. "It's not good."

"Relax, Aydan," he said. "I was a drill sergeant for years, remember?"

I acknowledged his graciousness with a tight-lipped smile. Drawing a deep breath, I let it out slowly, trying for composure. "I guess I'll get going. I have to go *shopping*..." The snarl was creeping back despite my best efforts. "...for *dress clothes*." Yep, definitely a snarl. "For a fancy lunch with-"

I clamped my mouth shut, remembering at the last moment that Doug was a civilian without a security clearance.

He rose with an understanding glance. "Excuse me. I'll just..." He gestured in the direction of the hallway and disappeared into the bathroom. A moment later the sound of running water assured me he would give us the privacy we needed.

"What is it, Aydan?" Kane demanded.

"Fucking Parr. I have to have lunch with him to give back the credit card he lent me in Vegas. And of course we're going to La Chaumière, so I have to go shopping for fucking *dress clothes!*" My voice was rising, and I shut up and sucked air through my nose.

"Who's Parr?" Hellhound asked.

Shit, he hadn't been briefed. Me and my big mouth.

But he was already peripherally involved anyway...

"You didn't hear me say that name," I said. "But he's the owner of that weapon prototype you transported to Sirius Dynamics after we, um... acquired it... on his corporate jet."

"Oh. Shit." He and Kane exchanged a frown. "Ya want backup, darlin'?"

The thought of Hellhound's fearsome face and tattoos in a fancy French restaurant made me smile in spite of myself. "No, I'll be fine. I'm safe with Parr. He's busy playing a pillar of the community and a concerned business owner. He can't afford to let anything happen to me." Cynicism twisted my lips. "Especially while he's trying to find out what happened to his secret weapon."

Kane's brow furrowed. "Maybe. He has to be going crazy over losing that prototype. He might be desperate enough to play hardball."

Icy fear clutched my heart. "I don't think so," I argued, hoping to convince both of us. "We know how smart and careful he is. I don't think he'll do anything rash. And I doubt if he would have bothered to put a bug on me if-"

"What?" Kane barked, whisking a bug detector out of his pocket.

"No, at home," I hastened to reassure him.

Nevertheless, we all peered anxiously at the bug detector until the green light glowed.

What a useless so-called agent I was, blindly assuming his apartment was secure.

Then again, this was Kane, the top agent in the service. If his secret apartment wasn't secure, no place was.

"Parr sent Hibbert with a bugged bouquet of flowers for me yesterday," I explained. "So the asshole delivered them at six o'clock in the morning, along with a few choice insults." I paused. "Actually, that's interesting, now that I think of it."

"How is that interesting?" Kane grated. "And when were you planning to tell us?"

I suddenly realized how much my mistake could have cost. What if Kane had called or visited thinking my house was secure? His cover would be completely blown.

Oh, God. This kind of incompetence was exactly how I'd nearly killed him a couple of days ago. Why couldn't I convince Stemp I was just a clueless civilian bookkeeper, when it was so abundantly obvious to everybody else?

"I'm sorry." I made fists in my hair and tugged. "I reported it right away, and Dermott said to discuss it in our briefing with Stemp tomorrow. I wasn't expecting to see you until then and it just slipped my mind." I squeezed my eyes shut.

Idiot. That mistake could have cost his life. All our lives. Fucking moron.

"I'm sorry," I repeated.

Hellhound's arm closed around my shoulders. "It's okay, darlin', it ain't like we were gonna call ya up an' start yakkin' about classified shit."

I opened my eyes to his sympathetic expression. "I know, but..." A glance at Kane made me cringe inside. He didn't look sympathetic. He looked disappointed.

Shame scalded my throat, as bitter as Doug's coffee.

"I'm sure you would have dealt with it if it became necessary," Kane said, his voice neutral. "So, how is it interesting?"

I swallowed, wishing I could just drop dead on the spot. "Um... The bug itself isn't particularly interesting; just Hibbert's mouthing off. If he was that free with his insults, I'm guessing he didn't know about the bug. So that means Parr doesn't trust him."

"Hm. That is interesting," Kane agreed. "But I wouldn't say the bug guarantees your safety. Now that Parr knows where you'll be, he could arrange to have you snatched outside the restaurant. Then he can let his people work you over while he waits in the restaurant, tries to call you, expresses his regret to the waitstaff that you cancelled without telling him, and has a leisurely lunch surrounded by witnesses. And if I was in his place, I'd report my credit card stolen and then express shock and outrage when I discovered the woman who'd disappeared with it had three prior fraud convictions."

I groaned, drowning out his terrifying and all-too-likely scenario. "I'm going to kill Stemp for saddling me with this shitty cover identity."

"...and when they finally find what's left of your body," Kane continued mercilessly, "There won't be a whiff of suspicion directed at Parr. And nobody will cause a big stir over the death of a small-time criminal like Arlene Widdenback. You need backup."

Hellhound's arm tightened around me. "He's right,

darlin'."

I clenched my fists to hide my shaking hands. "Well, I don't have backup. And you can't do it." Kane began to protest, but I kept talking. "We can't afford to let Parr think we're too chummy. If I was him, I'd divide and conquer. Buy me a fancy lunch and try to find out what I know. I don't think he suspects me, but if he decides you stole the weapon, you're going to be the one captured and tortured. If I can string him along today, we'll both be safer."

Kane gave me a flat stare. "Unless you're dead."

My fear burst out in its usual angry disguise. "Then my problems are over, aren't they?" I silenced his rejoinder with a savage chop at the air. "I'll call Dermott and see what my orders are."

"Dermott is a-" Kane stifled whatever he'd been about to say. "All right," he finished evenly.

I pulled away from Hellhound to extract a secure phone from my waist pouch and punched the speed dial button, scowling.

Ring. Ring. Ring.

Come on, Dermott, you lazy bastard.

Ring. Ring.

At last the connection clicked open. "Dermott."

I didn't waste any time with preliminaries. "I'm invited to lunch with Parr. Instructions?"

"Fine. Go."

"Fine." I was about to hang up when Kane snatched the phone from my hand.

"It's Kane," he snapped into the phone. "What if it's a trap? What about backup?"

He listened to the brief response, and the phone's plastic case emitted a small crackling noise under the clenching of his hand. Then he disconnected, his expression impassive and his movements deliberate. He placed the phone quietly on the coffee table before facing me again, still wearing his neutral cop face.

A shiver tracked down my spine. How could anybody look so dangerous while doing and saying absolutely nothing?

When Kane spoke, his voice was calm. "He says there are no other agents available today and it's your op. Up to you."

I swallowed and attempted placation. "Well, I'd really like to have you for backup, but I don't think it's a good idea for you to be seen anywhere near me or the restaurant. How about if we set some prearranged times for me to check in with you? I could just text you."

"Leaving me with no idea where you were or how to help you if you missed the check-in."

"Well... yeah, but..."

His tone was like a brick wall. "And if you're right and Parr does suspect we're involved together in the disappearance of his weapon, what will happen to you if he catches you texting me repeatedly?"

"Um, well... I could-"

"Ya ain't thinkin' this through," Hellhound interrupted. "You're both right, an' there's an easy answer. I'll tail Aydan into the restaurant. Cap, you're the fallback. If this goes to shit, it ain't gonna matter whether Parr sees ya, but there ain't any point in ya showin' up an' blowin' the whole thing right off the bat."

I turned to face him. "Arnie, you can't. In the first place, I don't want him to be able to identify you, and there's no way he'll miss a guy your size who looks like he just stopped a Mack truck with his face. And in the second place-"

"...you're off active duty," Kane chimed in. "You don't just recover overnight from a concussion. Until you get medical clearance-"

Hellhound snorted. "It's been ten days. I'm fine. An' remember how I'm the one that got sent to the airport to pick up that weapon from ya? Dermott doesn't give a shit about med leave, an' I ain't gonna sit here while Aydan goes out an' gets herself killed. Deal with it."

They glowered at each other, and my shoulders knotted with fear and frustration. "Look, you two, I really appreciate your concern, and I'd take your help if I could figure out a way to make it work, but here's the deal."

I drew myself up into my most authoritative posture and glared at them. "I have to go. I only have an hour and a half to buy clothes and makeup and get my ass downtown. You are not to do anything that might allow Parr to identify you. John, you're backup. Don't show yourself unless it's an emergency. Arnie, I'll text you when I get to the restaurant, when I leave, and when I'm clear of Parr. Then we can meet at your place as long as I'm sure I'm not being followed. If I am, I'll text you an alternate location. My op; my orders."

I spun and headed for the door, ignoring the quaking in my belly along with their chorus of arguments.

As I shrugged into my parka and turned the doorknob, Hellhound laid a hand on my shoulder. "Hang on, darlin', you're forgettin' somethin'."

"What now?" I gritted.

"This." He drew me into a hug and placed a gentle whiskery kiss on my forehead. "Good luck, darlin'. Be safe."

I hugged him back, hoping he couldn't feel my trembling. "Thanks."

When I pulled away, I met Kane's eyes. He didn't offer me a hug or kiss. He looked like he wanted to throttle me.

"Good luck," he said.

I nodded and slipped out the door, wondering if he'd offered me a blessing or a curse.

By the time I cleared the snow off my car and extricated it from the snowbank in Kane's parking lot, I was sticky with exertion and nervousness. Clenching my quivering hands on the steering wheel, I headed for the nearest mall.

A snotty department-store saleswoman deigned to dress frizzy-haired, sweaty me in an outfit she assured me was the latest fashion, casting glances of distaste at my jeans and hiking boots all the while. I resisted the urge to fling Parr's credit card at her head.

The mental image of a credit card lodged like a throwing star between her botoxed brows kept a pleasant smile on my face while I paid, wearing the new items and carrying my own clothes in a shopping bag. After a quick trip to the cosmetics counter for lipstick and something to conceal the dark circles under my eyes, I fled as though pursued by elegantly-coiffed, impeccably-made-up vampires.

No, wait; I *was* being pursued by an elegantly-coiffed, impeccably-made-up vampire. I shook off the persistent woman who kept trying to spritz me with some truly vile perfume, and escaped to my car.

Blowing out a long breath, I rested my forehead against the steering wheel for a moment. Even torture and death would be better than the shopping ordeal.

As I started the car, I sent a mental 'just kidding' skyward. No need to tempt fate.

CHAPTER 8

By the time I pulled into the restaurant parking lot at eleven-twenty, the sweat seemed to have frozen on my body. I pried icy hands off the steering wheel and scanned the parking lot for the goons Kane had predicted.

A gigantic black Hummer idled near the other end of the lot, taking up two parking spaces. A bulky figure occupied the driver's seat, but I couldn't make out any details behind the tinted windows. I eyed the vehicle nervously. It sure looked like a goonmobile. But it was too far away to be an immediate threat.

A black Cadillac pulled in beside me and I froze, heart pounding. More tinted windows. That couldn't be a coincidence.

A suit-clad old man with a face like an emaciated prune climbed out and circled behind his car to approach my door. I slid my hand toward my holster.

He looked more like a stick-man caricature of a disapproving butler than a hired killer. But that wouldn't matter if he put a gun to my head.

Ignoring me, he opened the passenger door of his car and bent to offer his arm to the fragile elderly lady in the seat. She rose slowly, and he stood with courtly patience while she patted her white hair into place and looped her purse over her arm. A few moments later, they tottered across the snowy parking lot toward the restaurant, and I let out the breath I'd been holding.

Jesus, I was such a coward. Scared of little old people.

Another glance around the parking lot assured me the potential goon was still in his Hummer. I eyeballed the distance to the restaurant door. Unless he was Superman, he was too far away to intercept me. I extracted my phone to type 'I'm in'.

Finger hovering over the 'Send' button, I hesitated, then backspaced and retyped 'Hey, I'm at La Chaumière. See you later.' If Parr grabbed my phone and read my messages, at least that wouldn't look quite so suspicious.

I took one last look at the Hummer and decided not to press 'Send' until I was actually inside the restaurant. Just in case.

It took all my willpower not to scuttle to the door with my head swivelling frantically. Schooling myself into easy, confident strides, I crossed the parking lot without incident and let myself inside. As the maître d' looked up with a smile, I pressed the 'Send' button inside my pocket and eased out a shaky breath. So far, so good.

The tinkle of cutlery and murmur of well-bred voices mingled with discreet background music and a delicious aroma. Clinging to the peaceful ambience, I returned the maître d's smile with as much composure as I could summon. "I'm meeting Nicholas Parr."

"Yes, of course, Madame, please follow me."

He led me through the dining room, skirting tables clothed in pristine white. Well-dressed patrons were sprinkled throughout, and a handful of empty tables awaited the influx that would no doubt arrive later. As we passed the old gentleman and his wife, he inventoried me with a single glance before apparently deciding I was good enough to grace the restaurant. His disapproving wrinkles rearranged themselves into a pleasant expression and he offered me a nod before resuming his conversation with his wife.

Parr rose from a table near them with a gracious inclination of his head. "Arlene. It's nice to see you looking so well." Stepping behind me, he helped me off with my coat and handed it to the maître d'.

In the winter-bright daylight from the window beside us, his sharp features and prematurely white hair reminded me even more forcefully of a bald eagle. Incisive blue eyes raked me as the maître d' offered me a chair.

"Thank you," I murmured, and sank into it hoping Parr hadn't seen my trembling legs.

He remained standing until I was seated, then sat with a smile.

After assuring the attentive waiter that I only wanted water to drink, I delved into the large handbag I'd bought to hold my waist pouch and extracted Parr's credit card. "Thank you for the credit card. I'm sorry for the extra charges on it. I told Archibald I didn't want to spend any more of your money, but he insisted."

"It's quite all right." Parr tucked the card into the inside pocket of his suit jacket. "It's the least I could do." He leaned forward solicitously. "How are you feeling?"

"I'm-"

I was interrupted by a hearty voice with a distinct Texas twang from the vicinity of the entrance. "So this's La Choo-meer! My buddy told me, 'Son, if you're ever in Calgary, ya gotta eat at La Choo-meer', an' dang if he don't know his restaurants, so here I am. Reservation for Al Hamlin."

The old gentleman at the other table stiffened and sent a reproving glance in that direction before returning to his conversation.

Parr didn't bat an eye. "I'm sorry, what did you say?" he inquired politely.

"Oh. I'm okay. A few bruises here and there, but..." I suddenly realized I should be playing this for all it was worth. I dropped my voice to a murmur and widened my eyes, going for pathetic. "...but when I think about poor Yana..." I let my lips quiver and took a sip of ice water. "I'm so lucky to be alive," I whispered. "You can't imagine the nightmares..."

My act was interrupted again by the voice of the boisterous Texan, who was apparently being seated only a few tables behind me. "Al Hamlin, son. Here's my card. You tell the owner if he's ever lookin' for a way to pop this little restaurant right into the limelight, he should give me a call. I got the top advertisin' sales record in our company for the last three years straight."

The old gentleman's prune face folded into sour disapproval and he exhaled audibly through his nose.

I dragged my attention back to Parr. "I'm sorry, what did you say?"

"I said I'm sorry to hear you're having difficulties. If you'd like help dealing with the trauma, Fuzzy Bunny keeps a qualified psychologist on staff. I can arrange some sessions with her for you, free of charge, of course."

God, not another shrink. Dr. Rawling was more than enough.

"Thank you, but I think I'll be all right."

"If you change your mind..."

The waiter glanced in our direction, and Parr leaned back in his chair. "I'm sorry, how rude of me. Please." He gestured at the menu I hadn't even opened yet. "I hope you'll find something you enjoy. The food is excellent here."

I opened the menu but my overstressed brain refused to process the offerings. Closing it again with a sigh, I appealed to Parr. "Would you choose something for me? You have such good taste, and I..." I eased out a sigh, hoping I wasn't overdoing my act. "I'm having a hard time concentrating after..." I made a helpless gesture and took another sip of water.

Parr gave me a sharp look.

Damn, I had overdone it. He wasn't likely to forget my ball-crushing performance at his office Christmas party. The shrinking-violet act wasn't going to cut it.

He didn't call me on it, though. When the waiter returned, he placed our order in fluent French before returning his attention to me. "Let's talk about more pleasant things. Did you enjoy your day in Vegas?"

He probably didn't want the truth. I didn't give it to him.

"It was great, thanks. The Venetian was amazing. And the wedding was..." I hesitated. "...lovely," I finished, and swallowed before quavering, "Poor Yana. And poor John."

Satisfaction flickered in Parr's face for an instant before warm concern masked it. Yep, definitely pumping me for information.

"How is he holding up?" Parr asked. "I haven't been able to contact him to offer my condolences."

"I don't know. I haven't seen him since the morning at the hospital," I lied. "He looked terrible. He said he had a concussion, but... I'm sure it's shock and grief, too. I can't imagine how hard this is for him, to lose her right after they got married."

Parr assumed an undertaker's expression of grave comfort, sympathy practically oozing from his pores. "At least they were married." He sighed. "So very sad. I hope you'll be able to comfort him."

"Um. Me?"

"Of course. You're friends, aren't you?"

"Uh, kind of..."

"Ex-lovers, I believe you said." He gave me a narrow-eyed look.

"Well, yes... but like I told you, he obviously wasn't that interested in me. It would be pretty tacky to come onto him now."

Parr looked as though he was considering the irony of a middle-aged porn star objecting to tackiness, but fortunately he chose not to go there.

"Of course," he said instead. He rubbed his chin thoughtfully. "Though... if you're interested in a small business opportunity..." He hesitated for a perfectly-timed interval before leaning back in his chair again with a smile. "I'm sorry, I shouldn't discuss business before our entrée even arrives."

Oh, he was good. Dangling a shiny lure in front of a petty criminal.

I pretended to bite.

Leaning forward and pitching my voice a little lower, I murmured, "It's all right, Nick, I know you're a busy man. Please, go ahead."

He smiled and leaned forward again. "Well, Yana had just taken over as director of operations here in Calgary-"

"Well, I'll be danged! If it ain't Charlie Daniels!" The loudmouth was in full cry again. Beside us, the prune-faced old man stiffened.

A moment later, a mountain of expensive suit pushed by to slap the old man's bony back. "Charlie Daniels, as I live an' breathe! How the hell are ya?"

Pruneface froze, his nostrils flaring and whitening while he stared with obvious revulsion at the man looming over him.

I stared, too.

He looked close to four hundred pounds. The fancy western-cut suit jacket barely contained a gigantic swell of white-shirted belly tucked into voluminous slacks, all of it supported by elaborately tooled western boots. A florid tie encircled a massive neck bound by a crisp white collar, and ostentatious diamond rings flashed on two of his fingers. He reached to pummel the old man good-naturedly again, revealing a gold watch the size of a fried egg on his wrist. I glimpsed a tattoo above it before the starched white cuff resettled.

It got worse.

A black moustache and beard adorned a far-too-familiar face. Hellhound's bruised features grinned out from under the most atrocious comb-over I'd ever seen.

I quickly averted my gaze. Parr was staring up at Hellhound with the same horrified expression I felt on my own face, and he hurriedly looked away, too. The little old lady let out a mew of shock.

Parr began to say something to me, but the words died on his lips as Hellhound seized the woman's hand and planted a big smacking kiss on it. Frozen, Parr and I sat facing each other, eyes trained sideways to watch the drama unfold.

"Now, ma'am, you're lookin' lovely today," Hellhound

declaimed in his Texan accent. He swept her a gallant bow, the lank black strands of the horrible comb-over flopping into his eyes. He flung them back with a flamboyant gesture and turned again to the speechless old man. "Charlie, ya ol' dog, how's tricks?"

"Who...?" The old man shook his head as if recovering from a punch before drawing himself up to his stiffest disapproving-butler posture. "I have no idea who you are. Please leave us." The ice in his voice would have frozen anyone but a salesman.

Hellhound bellowed out a guffaw. "You're such a card, Charlie! It's me, Al Hamlin! Maybe ya don't recognize me 'cause my face's a little beat up. A guy took a poke at me a coupla days ago, for no reason at all 'cept I told his wife she was real purty. Some folks sure are excitable."

"I do not know you. I do not wish to know you. Go away." If poor old Pruneface got any stiffer, he was going to shatter into a million pieces.

Hellhound took a step back, frowning. "Ya really ain't Charlie Daniels? Ya ain't pullin' my leg?"

"Most certainly not."

Hellhound shouted with sudden laughter and slapped the poor man on the back again. "Well, shut my mouth! Ma'am; sir; I surely do beg your pardon. You're the spittin' image of my buddy Charlie. I'm sorry to disturb ya. Let me buy your lunch."

"That won't be necessary. Excuse us." The old man gestured to the maître d' who had been hovering anxiously. "May we have a different table, please?"

"Of course, Monsieur, this way please."

"Well, dang it, who'd a' thought?" Hellhound exclaimed to the restaurant at large before turning to waddle back to his table, shaking his head and chuckling.

Parr and I sat in shell-shocked silence until Parr recovered enough to take a largish sip of his scotch on the rocks. "I'm sorry for that. Not at all the usual clientele. Would you like to change tables?"

"I... uh..." I gulped some ice water. "No, it's okay."

Goddammit, I was going to tear Hellhound a brand new asshole. And Kane, too, for letting him do this.

"Where were we?" Parr asked.

My brain was still paralyzed. I stared blankly at Parr. "I haven't a clue."

The waiter chose that moment to arrive with our food, and I seized the distraction with gratitude. The beautifully-plated salmon fillet garnished with golden caviar should have made my mouth water, but it might as well have been cardboard. I ate mechanically for a few minutes, completely oblivious to the flavours.

"How is your meal?" Parr inquired.

"Uh, really good. Thanks." I swallowed another mouthful without tasting it.

"So, we were discussing business," Parr prompted.

"Right." I gathered my scattered wits. "You were telling me about Yana."

"Yes. As I was saying, she was our director of operations, but also a personal friend."

"Oh, I'm sorry," I said automatically.

"Thank you. Her death was a terrible shock." His undertaker's expression returned. "I wish I had a keepsake to honour her memory."

Yeah, like maybe a deadly secret weapon?

"I'm sure that would be a great comfort," I agreed.

"It's doubly hard, because we had such a lovely

conversation before she died," he continued. "She was so happy when she called me from Vegas after the wedding. I can still hear her voice. She had such a lovely accent..." He trailed off and I nodded sympathetically. What a load of shit.

Parr gazed into space, his face a tragic mask. "She said, 'Nick, I got for you the most perfect present to say big thank you for the trip'." He sighed. "I wish I knew what it was. But it probably burned."

"Maybe it was in her luggage," I offered with my best fake concern. "Mine was okay. The fire didn't get to the cargo area."

"No, she told me she was carrying it onboard, that she didn't want it to break. So it must have been fragile."

I pulled a frown. "Oh."

Wait for it...

"Did you notice her carrying anything when she got on?" Right on cue.

"I wasn't really paying attention. You don't have any idea how big it might have been, do you?"

Parr had stopped eating and his expression of fake sadness had faded to expose the hard calculation in his eyes. As if realizing his slip, he took another drink and sighed, shaking his head. "I really don't know. She knew of my fondness for fine spirits, so it might have been a bottle of something exotic. Did you notice any unusual bottles in the cabin?"

Bingo. He was definitely fishing for the bottle-shaped weapon.

I put on a worried face. "I hope it wasn't one of the bottles that broke in the serving cart. Most of them smashed. But maybe the crash investigator would let you check them to see if there was anything unusual in the cart. Maybe you could salvage some pieces of the bottle, just for a keepsake."

"No, I already inventoried the remaining contents of the cabin. There was nothing unusual."

I leaned back in my chair. "I'm sorry to hear that. You've lost so much."

"Insurance will cover the material damages." Parr brushed a hand across his eyes. "The loss of a friend... no money can compensate."

I nodded sympathetic understanding and applied myself to the remains of my salmon. Come on, Parr, get to the point.

As if heeding my mental command, he swallowed the last bite of his meal and leaned forward. "Which brings me to ask a favour of you. I'm devastated by the loss of a dear friend, so I can only imagine what her husband is experiencing. I can't bring myself to ask him about her personal effects at a time like this, but..."

He hesitated.

I played along. "Would you like me to ask him if she had something for you? I know how hard this is for you, so if I can help..."

"Would you?" He flashed me a pleading look. "I think it would be so much easier for him to bear... coming from a close friend like you. It would mean a lot to me."

Enough, already. Time to let Arlene's gold-digging personality out to play.

I sat back in my chair and gave him a flat stare. "How much?"

CHAPTER 9

Parr's jaw dropped as if I'd slapped him. "I beg your pardon?"

I eyed him over the remains of our expensive meal and shrugged. "We're businesspeople. What's it worth to you for me to ask John about your present from Yana?"

His eyes narrowed. "You seem to forget you're already on an extremely generous retainer from my company."

I let my lip curl. "And you seem to forget I already did you a favour attending that wedding in Vegas. And I haven't seen any money yet. And I damn near got killed on your shitty airplane. Your fifty grand is used up, and you're lucky I'm not suing you for damages into the bargain. If you want any more *favours*, you better cough up the fifty K and then some."

His civilized façade dropped, unmasking the soulless stare of a raptor about to shred its prey to bleeding ribbons. I hid my shiver and used every ounce of my self-control to hold his gaze.

Bad, bad idea to piss this man off.

A moment later he blinked and his eyes came to life again above a smile as thin as a surgical incision. "Fine. I'll issue you a certified cheque in the amount of fifty thousand dollars. In exchange, you will sign a release stating that you waive all rights to any further damages in respect to the airplane incident and any further... issues... that may arise as a result of it."

"Fine." I managed not to dissolve into a quivering puddle. "So how much will you pay me to look for Yana's gift?"

"That depends on whether you deliver anything or not."

"Suppose I do?"

"That depends on what it is."

More damn jockeying. My nerves were stretched to breaking point. Hellhound had been silent for too long behind me. The back of my neck crawled with the expectation of another Texas-style outburst.

I forced a bored sigh and tucked my hands under the table to dry my sweaty palms on the napkin. "What do you want it to be?"

He studied me in silence, that predatory blue gaze flicking over me. God, please don't let him see the pulse pounding in my throat.

"Intact," he said at last. "I want it to be intact. Bring me an inventory of everything she had, excluding clothing. Don't let him throw anything away."

"That's going to be difficult. And it might take me a while."

"Ten thousand dollars if you deliver in three days. A thousand less for every extra day it takes."

I injected a whine into my voice. "That's not fair. I don't even know where he is. And for all I know he's thrown her things away already."

"Then you'd better hurry."

The waiter approached to whisk our plates away. As

soon as the waiter departed, Parr rose. "Enjoy your dessert. The meal is paid for."

He turned and strode away.

As my crème brulée arrived, the hearty voice boomed behind me again. "Well, that was mighty fine eatin', an' I thank ya. Here's an extra hundred for ya. Don't spend it all in one place now, y'hear?" Another bellowed guffaw made everyone in the dining room flinch. In the ensuing silence, I tracked Hellhound's progress toward the door by the sound of shuffling chairs and jovial exclamations of "Excuse me, ma'am! Pardon me, sir! Y'all have a good day, now!"

At last the disturbance ceased and a collective breath of relief rose from the patrons. The murmur of conversation slowly resumed.

I picked up my dessert spoon with quivering fingers and tried to relax. Just breathe...

"Madame?"

The waiter's voice made me start violently, the spoon flying out of my hand to clatter loudly against the plate.

"J-" I bit off my reflexive blasphemy and clutched my chest instead.

"Madame, I am so sorry to startle you." He offered me a deferential half-bow. "Would you like tea or coffee?"

"Tea. Please," I stammered.

He bowed again and withdrew, and after letting out a long unsteady breath, I made another attempt with the spoon.

By the time I scraped out the last vestiges of crème brulée, I had recovered enough to taste it. I finished my tea, pondering.

I was probably pretty safe now. Surely Parr wouldn't assign me to retrieve Yana's personal effects if he intended to murder me before I had a chance to comply.

Though there was a pretty good chance he'd murder me afterward.

Worry about that later.

Replaying our conversation in my head, I sighed. I didn't think I had said anything that would lead Parr to believe Kane or I might know more than I had admitted. But I couldn't be sure. I had been so rattled, I couldn't remember exactly what I'd said.

Dammit, if I'd known Hellhound was going to show up despite my orders, I could have taken advantage of his phenomenal memory. If he'd been within earshot, he would have been able to repeat the entire conversation verbatim.

But I was pretty sure I hadn't said anything incriminating.

Pretty sure Parr wouldn't have goons waiting in the parking lot to snatch me and torture me.

I sighed and pushed to my feet. Might as well get it over with.

When I emerged warily into the cold afternoon sun, the sight of the black Hummer parked near my car made my heart accelerate. The bulky figure still sat behind the wheel.

Dammit, why, *why* couldn't I develop some common sense to compensate for my complete lack of spy skills? I hadn't even researched what kind of vehicle Parr drove. Was the Hummer registered to him? Or...

A moment later I brained up enough to check the license plate. Rental. Likely not Parr's vehicle, then.

Realizing I was conspicuously hovering, I drew a deep breath and strode toward my car, my fingers itching for my gun.

As I drew nearer, the figure began to gesticulate and I

sucked in a breath of relief when an obnoxious drawl emanated from the inch of open window on the driver's side.

"...an' tell that young pup to get out there an' start diggin'. Ya gotta work your way up in this business an' never take no for an answer..." Hellhound continued his cellphone monologue without looking at me, waving a hand now and then as if for emphasis.

I slid into my car and pressed the button to send my superfluous text message: 'Leaving now'. Hellhound made no sign of recognition and I drove away, leaving him to harangue the parking lot and his imaginary caller.

It couldn't be that easy.

Eyes peeled for any vehicle that stayed in my vicinity, I took a circuitous route away from the restaurant, stopping at a corner store, a coffee shop, and a pharmacy long enough to purchase a small item in each while watching traffic through the glass. When I spied no sign of pursuit after half an hour, I sank into the driver's seat and sent my final text: 'See you at home'. Then I headed for Hellhound's condo, the ebbing stress leaving my muscles as limp as dishrags.

I drove on autopilot, my brain spinning while my body guided the car. A few blocks from Hellhound's place, a sudden thought jabbed a lance of fear into my heart.

Parr had handled my coat. What if he'd tagged me with some kind of locator device?

Ignoring the honking of the outraged drivers behind me, I jerked the wheel over and cut across two lanes of traffic to dodge into the nearest parking lot. Trembling, I aimed the car into a slot and jammed on the brakes before yanking my bug detector out of my waist pouch.

I nearly fainted at the sight of the reassuring green light.

Thank God.

I leaned back in the seat and breathed. The bug detector would indicate any kind of transmitter in the area, no matter what type of signal was being broadcast. I was still safe.

More to the point, Hellhound and Kane would be safe.

I dragged a trembling hand back to the steering wheel and resumed my trip.

Tucked into one of the visitor parking slots at Hellhound's condo building, I turned off the ignition and sagged in the seat, debating whether to rip a wide, bleeding strip off him for disobeying my orders, or kiss him for being there to watch my back.

Too strung out to decide, I hauled myself out of the car and made for the front door.

There was a note of trepidation in his gravelly 'yeah' when he answered the buzzer.

"It's Aydan," I said, and the security door released.

The stairs seemed extra steep. About half-way up, it occurred to me that I could have taken the elevator, and I was mumbling obscenities when I rounded the corner on the third floor.

Hellhound hovered in his doorway with Hooker tucked into the crook of his elbow. As I approached, he turned slightly as though to shield himself behind the big cat.

"Hey, darlin'," he offered cautiously.

The dreadful comb-over was gone, his head clean-shaven as usual. There was a small smudge of black on his neck, but his beard and moustache were back to their normal salt-and-pepper. The hard bulk of his chest and his flat, muscular midsection were a welcome sight after the corpulent image still seared on my retinas.

"Hi," I said noncommittally. "Is John here yet?"

"Yeah." Hellhound ducked his chin, not quite meeting

my eyes. "Come on in."

When the door closed behind me, Hellhound opened his hand to reveal a bug detector's glowing green light. Then he stooped to release the cat before straightening into parade rest, his chin high. "Okay, darlin'. Let me have it."

"Not just you." I shot a stern glance at Kane sprawled on the sofa. "John's as guilty as you are. More so. He's the ranking officer."

"Officially I'm retired," Hellhound mumbled.

"Bullshit!" I snapped, and levelled a glare at Kane.

Kane shrugged, studying the ceiling. "What was I going to do? You know how pig-headed he is. Short of handcuffing him to the balcony railing, I couldn't stop him."

"And you didn't try! What the hell were you thinking?" I rounded on Hellhound. "And you! I told you not to let Parr see you! And you waltz right in there, right in his fucking face!"

Suddenly I was furious. I slammed my fist down on the half-wall beside me. Cushioned by Hellhound's jacket, it made only a muffled thud, which maddened me even more. "Now he's seen you! How the hell can I protect you if you won't fucking follow my orders?"

Hellhound's parade rest stiffened, his gaze locked on the wall behind me, and I recalled that an ass-chewing for disobeying orders was pretty much the story of his entire military career.

"Well now, darlin'," he said diffidently, "Ya didn't actually say 'don't let Parr see ya'. What ya actually said was 'You are not to do anythin' that might allow Parr to identify ya'. An' I followed that order to the letter."

"You... wha... Bullshit! How the hell do you figure that? You were damn near in his face! You couldn't have been more conspicuous if you'd sat in his fucking lap!"

"Yeah." His moustache didn't quite hide the smile tugging at his lips. "But I guarantee there ain't a single person in that entire restaurant that could pick me outta a lineup. The surest way to keep people from lookin' at your face is to make sure they don't wanna make eye contact. An' they sure as hell wouldn't make eye contact with a fuckin' jerk like Al Hamlin. They saw a big fat fucker with a beard an' a bad comb-over, but that's it. Not a single one of 'em looked me in the face."

"You..." Words failed me, and after a moment I shut my open mouth.

He was right.

They had all looked anywhere but at his face. Nobody was willing to risk being the next recipient of his unwelcome attention. Even I had looked away from the train wreck of ostentatious bad taste.

"You..." I tried again. Behind him, I caught sight of the horrible black toupee, dangling like a grotesque spider from his guitar stand. "You... you..." A bubble of hysterical laughter rose in my chest.

A moment later a snicker erupted despite my effort to hold onto my scowl.

When Hellhound grinned and waggled his eyebrows at me, I lost it completely. Howling with laughter, I collapsed against the door and slithered to the floor. "You... fucking... *slay* me! Goddammit..." I sprawled among the boots on his floor mat, still laughing. "That was the most... The most... Ohmigod..."

Hellhound abandoned his parade rest to sink to the floor beside me, chuckling. Kane's laughter joined in from the direction of the living room, hidden behind the half-wall.

"You..." I thumped my fist on Hellhound's knee. "That was... The most horrible..." I gasped for breath, tears rolling down my cheeks.

"Aw, hell, no, darlin', it wasn't anywhere near," he said modestly. "I was gonna start fartin' an' talkin' about eatin' too many burritos last night, but I figured that might be over the top. Didn't wanna get kicked out before I got my food."

The mental image doubled me over. "Please... please... don't tell me... you can fart... on command!"

"Nah. But I can fake it like a champ."

The accompanying sound-effect convulsed me. I clutched my aching sides and surrendered to the storm of laughter until at last it died down to feeble giggles and whimpers.

"Oh, help," I moaned. "God, help me. I'm in pain."

Still chuckling, Hellhound pulled me close and dropped a kiss on my forehead. "All better now?"

"No. I'm scarred for life." I flopped against his shoulder, wiping away tears. "Don't ever, *ever* do that again."

"Can't make any promises, darlin'." He planted a gentle fingertip under my chin and raised it to regard me seriously. "Forgive me?"

"Of course." I hugged him, forgetting about his bruised ribs until he winced. My arms flew open. "I'm sorry! Are you okay?"

"Fine, darlin'."

I touched his face, tracing my thumb across the undamaged part of his cheek. "Thanks for being there," I whispered.

His arms tightened around me. "I'm always gonna be there." Before I could react he added, "An' don't go freakin' out, 'cause that ain't a commitment. That's just a fact a' life."

We smiled at each other and I disentangled myself to struggle to my feet. Tottering over to the sofa, I fell onto it and poked a finger into the belly-shaped mound of padding lying beside me. "This is gross."

Hellhound sank into his favourite chair, grinning. "Yeah, but it works. Face it, darlin', put a suit on a guy like me an' everybody stares. When I'm Al Hamlin, nobody wants to look at me. Works like a damn when I gotta mingle with some suits for my PI business."

"Okay, I can't argue that." I raised an eyebrow at him. "But seriously: 'Charlie Daniels'?"

He reached for his guitar. His fingers danced over the strings and the intro to 'The Devil Went Down To Georgia' filled the room.

Hellhound shrugged. "First name that came to mind."

CHAPTER 10

Kane leaned forward, elbows on knees. "So how did it go?" He shot a sidelong glance at Hellhound's still-grinning face. "Other than Hellhound's performance."

"Fine, I think." I massaged the ache at the back of my neck. "Parr offered me ten thousand dollars to get a full inventory of Yana's luggage to him in three days. He laid out a bunch of bullshit about how they were close friends and he thought she might be bringing him a special bottle of booze as a gift."

Kane's lips twisted in a cynical smile. "Special bottle. Right."

"Yeah. He wants me to get close to you and find out if Yana mentioned bringing anything to him."

Kane leaned back with a long breath, tucking his arms behind his head. "Good. So you're not in immediate danger."

"Doesn't look that way. He'll probably wait to see if I deliver. And he's got the bug at my place, so he'll be keeping tabs on me. He's probably got eyes on your place in Silverside, too."

"Likely. That's fine; there's nothing for him to see there. And the Calgary condo isn't registered under my name, so it should be secure." He rose. "Speaking of which, we'd better go. We're taking Dad to the airport in a few hours."

"Tell him goodbye for me. It was nice to see him again."

"I will. I know he enjoyed seeing you, too. See you tomorrow at the briefing." Kane donned his boots and jacket and hesitated, hand on doorknob. "Unless you want me to follow you home. The highway report said the roads are still bad."

"Thanks, but that's okay. I'll be fine."

"All right. Drive carefully."

"You, too."

When the door closed behind him, Hellhound and I both rose. I stepped into Hellhound's waiting embrace and reached up to kiss him.

He rumbled satisfaction and kissed me back slowly, his lips savouring mine for long moments before he lightly traced the inside of my lip with the tip of his tongue. A shiver electrified my spine, sending a burst of anticipation sizzling southward. He gradually deepened the kiss, and my body heated with the memory of exactly what else that amazing tongue did so well.

And those amazing hands. A purr escaped me as they coasted down to fondle my ass, pulling me against him. Hellhound broke the kiss to smile down at me, and I linked my arms around his neck.

"So..." I swayed in sensuous S-curves, sliding my breasts across his chest and my hips against the hard ridge in his jeans. "What are you doing for the next couple of hours?"

He groaned. "Ridin' back to Kane's place with a helluva hard-on, an' sittin' there with blue balls for the rest a' the afternoon."

"What?"

"I gotta go. Kane'll be waitin' downstairs. He drove me to the car rental place 'cause we didn't wanna take a chance on somebody matchin' my license plate to my real name. Didn't ya catch the part where he said '*we* better go'?"

Disappointment drenched me like cold water. "Well, shit."

He sighed. "Yeah. But hold the thought, darlin'. I'll see ya soon."

"The sooner the better." I gave him a quick kiss and turned for the door before I could start whining.

Nearly three hours later I was whining in earnest when I got out to unlock my gate in the cold twilight. The highway had been sheer ice, and my entire body throbbed with the pain of my tension headache. Creeping into the sanctuary of my house, I swallowed a couple of painkillers and fell into bed fully clothed.

The vibration of my cell phone roused me from a restless sleep. I groaned and rolled over, yanking the blanket over my head.

After a few seconds, it vibrated again.

"Leave a message, asshole," I growled into my pillow.

A moment later tremendous thuds from the front of the house galvanized every muscle in my body. Flailing free of the blankets, I snatched my gun from the holster I still wore.

Comprehension penetrated my haze of adrenaline as the thuds continued.

Pounding on my front door.

Shit, *again*?

Gun in hand and my back to the wall, I slipped around the corner into the hallway. The shouting from my front porch was audible by the time I reached the kitchen.

"Open up, bitch!" The door shivered under another

barrage of kicks. "Get the fuck out here, you suck-ass cunt!"

The c-word. Guaranteed to piss me off even at the best of times. But after a shitty day and a shattered sleep...

The world went red except for a small aperture of clarity around my gun sights as I drew a bead on the door.

About chest height. I'd give him two rounds to be sure, plus one just for shits and giggles.

Or... My sights drifted lower. Could I blow his nuts off with my first shot? I could try...

Fortunately Hibbert chose that moment to bang on the door again, dragging me back to reality.

Parr's bug would pick up the sound of the shots. Bad idea to let him know I was armed. Not to mention having to clean the blood off my porch and get rid of another damn body.

Hibbert was still bellowing insults and obscenities punctuated by kicks to my door, and I let out a shaky breath and returned my gun to its concealed holster.

"What do you want?" I shouted when he paused for breath.

"Open up, bitch! I've got something for you!"

"Fuck off! I'm calling the police!"

A moment of silence. "Better not if you want your cheque for fifty grand!"

Now it was my turn to hesitate. Arlene Widdenback loved money above all else.

"Leave it in the mailbox!" I yelled.

"You sign the release or you get fuck-all!"

"Leave the release in the mailbox!"

"What's the matter, bitch? Too scared to face me after you ratted me out to Parr?"

"I didn't-" I began, but he was still shouting, hitting the

door so hard I began to worry it might give way.

"You better be fucking scared!" Bang. "You might be Parr's pocket pussy now, but he'll dump you fast!" Bang. Bang. "And when he does..." Bang. "...I'm going to pay you a little visit..." Bang-bang. "...and fuck you up the ass so bad you'll have to shit in a bag for the rest of your life!" Bang-bang-bang...

The sound of his kicks faded under the hammering of my heart as the flashback seized me.

His vicious hands forced me down. His thick tongue gagged me...

I sucked in a breath and crushed the memory. That wouldn't happen. I was armed.

Open the door. Face the fear.

"Put the papers on the porch and back away!" I hoped he couldn't hear the weak terror in my voice. "Or in five seconds I call the police! Five! Four! Three..."

Silence reigned outside, and I tottered forward to peer through the fisheye lens.

Hibbert stood at the bottom of my porch steps. I couldn't see my door mat. Had he put an envelope there?

Or something worse?

Drawing my gun again, I held it behind the door frame while I unlocked the door and opened it a crack.

Hibbert was still taunting me but my fear blanked out his words.

Envelope on my door mat.

I grabbed it and slammed the door shut again, twisting the deadbolt home.

Back pressed to the wall, gun trembling in my hand, I forced my shallow panting into slower, deeper breaths.

Hibbert started kicking the door again, but he seemed a

little less enthusiastic. Maybe his foot was getting sore.

I silently wished him the joy of a stress fracture and heaved myself away from the wall to stagger to the table, fumbling the papers out of the envelope.

My brain refused to comprehend even the most basic words on the pages of legalese.

Screw it.

I scrawled a shaky signature on the bottom. It was an alias anyway. Let Sirius's lawyers deal with it.

Hibbert had stopped kicking the door and switched to graphic descriptions of the atrocities he planned to commit on various parts of my body. Gun in one hand, papers in the other, I jammed the heels of my hands against my ears to block him out.

"Back off or else!" My shrill cry wasn't the intimidating roar I'd intended, but it seemed to work. When I cautiously unstopped my ears, I couldn't hear him anymore.

Another peek out the fisheye lens revealed that he had retreated to the bottom of the steps again. I cracked the door open, flung out the envelope, and relocked the door almost in a single movement.

"Leave the cheque in the mailbox," I bellowed.

My trembling legs barely carried me into my office to watch the security camera feed. Sure enough, Hibbert was marching down my lane. He paused to stuff an envelope in the mailbox at my gate before driving away.

I collapsed into my desk chair.

Breathe. Just breathe.

I closed my eyes.

Inhale. I willed my quivering belly to expand. Nice and slow. Draw in the calm.

Exhale. Let out the fear.

In, two... three... four... Out, two... three... four. Just like ocean waves...

At last I regained enough strength to drag myself out of the chair, and eventually back to bed.

I didn't sleep.

The next morning I shuffled into Sirius Dynamics and propped myself in front of the security wicket a few minutes before nine. The guard greeted me with a wide smile.

"Good morning, Aydan! Did you have a good holiday?"

I plastered an answering smile on my face as I signed for my security fob. "Yeah, thanks, Leo. How about you?"

"Great! Ate too much; drank too much." He practically glowed with complacent cheerfulness, and I squelched my surge of bitter envy.

"That's great. See you later." I turned away to slap my fob on the reader with perhaps a little more vigour than necessary.

I was the last to arrive at the meeting room. Sliding into a chair with a mumbled apology, I took stock of the assembled group.

Dermott and Stemp sat near the head of the table, a study in opposites. Dermott's ruddy complexion and frizzy, thinning hair made him look almost clownish next to Stemp's monochrome colouring and subtle aura of reptilian menace. Their clothing reinforced the impression, with Dermott's rumpled casual shirt and slacks in sharp contrast to Stemp's sober business suit.

Kane offered me his usual friendly nod and smile from across the table, and Spider's youthful face lit up. "Hi, Aydan! Merry belated Christmas!" His almost-palpable happiness brought a smile to my lips despite my exhaustion, and I gave him a fond 'hi' in return.

"Good morning, everyone."

I turned toward Stemp's greeting automatically, but a flicker of concern distracted me from his first words as my gaze coasted over Germain and Jack on the other side of the table. They sat side by side, but they were leaning subtly apart and not looking at each other.

Germain was too good an agent to betray any emotion, but Jack's flawless forehead was slightly puckered and as I watched, her blue gaze darted to Germain for an instant before returning to Stemp, her full lips tightening.

Uh-oh.

"...reports," Stemp was saying. Shit, he didn't waste any time. I shelved my concern over my friends and focused on Stemp. "Anything new?" he asked.

I spoke into the short silence. "Yeah, Hibbert dropped by my place in the middle of the night."

"Yes, I noted that in the surveillance records this morning," Stemp said. "The analyst on duty texted you instead of calling, in case they've wiretapped your phone as well as planting the bug. I've assigned a tech to check for a wiretap today. For now, we'll leave their listening devices in place. If the analysts need to alert you, they'll text the words 'thinking of you', followed by one or more smiley emoticons to indicate the number of people approaching your house."

On top of every detail, as usual.

I repressed the sudden urge to tell him I was glad he was back. It probably wouldn't last. He'd find some way to piss me off as usual.

"Thanks," I said instead. "I'll watch for texts from here on in."

Stemp eyed me with his usual lack of emotion. "Hibbert looked agitated. What did he want?"

I kept my tone casual. "Oh, the usual. Threatened to rape me until I had to shit in a bag for the rest of my life. Burning, mutilation, yadda, yadda." I kept talking over Jack's small cry of horror. "He thought I'd complained to Parr about him. He obviously doesn't know the bug is picking up all his lovely insults. Oh, and..." I slid the certified cheque across the table. "He brought me a little present."

Dermott leaned forward to gape at the cheque. "Christ, Kelly, another fifty grand? That's a hundred grand from two different high-rollers in a week. Did you grab Parr by the nuts, too?"

Everyone turned to me with raised eyebrows. Germain passed a hand over his chin as if hiding a smile, and the corner of Kane's mouth quirked up.

I fought the heat rising in my cheeks. "No. This is the retainer Parr promised me. When I met him for lunch yesterday to return his credit card, I told him I'd sue him for the plane crash if he didn't pay up in full..."

Dermott barked laughter, and I went on. "...and then I told him I wanted an extra payment if he wanted me to track down the so-called 'special present' Yana was bringing back from Vegas for him. So that'll be another ten grand if I deliver in three days."

Dermott fell back in his chair with a guffaw. "Jesus Christ, Kelly, you've got more balls than any three guys I know! You torch his plane, kill his operatives, steal his secret weapon, and then put the screws to him to the tune of sixty grand. That's fucking beautiful!"

I shot a glance at Stemp's expressionless façade. Shit, he

was going to keep thinking I was a capable agent until my dumb luck ran out and my incompetence killed somebody.

"I only killed one of his operatives and it was an accident," I mumbled. "I'd have been dead if John hadn't killed Yana before she could nail me with that weapon. And it was probably a really bad idea to piss Parr off."

"Maybe," Stemp conceded. "But it was in character for Arlene Widdenback, and it's useless to second-guess at this point. And three days gives us time to come up with a plan. Well done. Anything else?"

"Nothing I can think of." I slouched back in my chair.

"Travers, Honey, have you got any analysis done on that weapon yet?" Dermott asked, smirking.

Jack flushed.

I winced. After they'd locked horns last week, I had thought Dermott would be smart enough to back off. Jack's parents might have saddled her with blonde gorgeousness and the moniker of 'Honey', but I guessed Dermott was about to get a major dose of vinegar.

"That's 'Dr. Travers' to you," she said coolly. "Unless you're inviting me to call you by your middle name..." She paused for a single devastating instant. "...Shirley."

A choking noise came from Spider's vicinity and a tide of crimson suffused Dermott's face. "No," he muttered. "What about that weapon?"

I did my best to hide my delight. Brent Shirley Dermott. Jack wasn't the only one with sadistic parents.

"As I told you..." Jack paused, letting the razor-edged phrase take another slice out of Dermott before continuing, "...weapons are not my area of expertise. I did a preliminary analysis and then passed it on to Dr. Chow, the head of weapons R&D."

"That weapon is top-secret priority-one classified-" Dermott began to bluster.

"Yes, Dr. Chow was a good choice." Stemp's dispassionate tone silenced him. "Can you give us the preliminary results, Dr. Travers?"

Jack turned to Stemp with obvious relief. "It appears the weapon uses a heretofore unknown technology that focuses ultrasonic waves into a destructive beam. As I'm sure you know, ultrasound is used in many applications from healthcare to industrial testing, but its fundamental characteristics cause the ultrasonic waves to diverge and disperse rapidly. That severely limits its effective range-"

Stemp raised a hand to stem the didactic flow. "So the weapon does what, precisely?"

Jack gave the small sigh of a scientist asked to grossly oversimplify an explanation. "*Precisely*, we don't know yet. In general terms, based on my very superficial analysis and John and Aydan's description of its effects, I would surmise that it..." She hesitated and swallowed, her creamy skin paling. "...it... essentially reduces human tissue to... pulp. At a selected depth."

She swallowed again and her voice trembled when she continued, "...which appears to be a few inches below the skin surface. That would create massive disruption in the brain and/or major organs, causing instantaneous death without making a sound or leaving a mark on the skin. And the weapon appears to be mostly constructed of graphite composites and ceramic. So it can pass undetected through any security scanner in general use today."

CHAPTER 11

Dermott's voice broke the heavy silence in the room. "Holy shit. So it really is a fucking death ray."

"Yes." Jack's pallor made her look ill. "That is my preliminary conclusion. Dr. Chow will, of course, provide a much more comprehensive analysis after he has completed his testing."

"But..." Spider's voice trembled. "We have the only one, right?"

Stemp's clinical tone chilled me. "Maybe. But someone out there has the schematics and has successfully created at least one working prototype. They can create others, if they haven't already. We need to trace the origin of that weapon, quickly."

"Did you obtain any physical evidence from the device?" Kane's strong baritone sounded as confident as ever, but I sensed tension in the set of his broad shoulders. "Fingerprints, fibres? We handled it with gloves, so we shouldn't have disturbed anything."

Jack looked stricken. "I didn't think of that. But..." Her expression firmed. "I didn't touch it with my hands at any time. Dr. Chow-"

Stemp was already barking orders into the phone. When

he hung up, he faced us with his usual composure. "Dr. Chow says it hasn't been compromised. I've assigned a forensic specialist to his team. If there's any physical evidence, we'll find it."

The air pressure lightened around the table.

"Anything else?" Stemp inquired. Silence and negative headshakes answered him, and after a pause he continued, "Very well. Next item."

He pinned me with his reptilian gaze. "Kelly, Kane, Germain, your top priority will be monitoring Parr and tracing this weapon, code reference Afterburner. Tammy Mellor will be joining you today to transition into Kelly's former role in decryption."

Spider stiffened. Dermott shifted uncomfortably.

Oh, shit.

Spider would refuse to act as Tammy's controller again. Would Stemp fire him the way Dermott had? And now that Stemp had Tammy for decryptions, I'd better prove my worth as an agent or he wouldn't just fire me; he'd arrange for me to take a permanent dirt nap.

Shit, shit...

Stemp was still talking. "...Kelly, whenever you aren't actively involved with Project Afterburner, you can continue with your decryptions. Webb, you'll oversee Ms. Mellor's work and when Kelly is here, work with her as usual."

Stemp paused and his flat gaze took in everyone at the table, lingering on Spider. "Ms. Mellor is, and will remain, unaware of her role in the decryptions. As far as she knows, she is simply acting as a super-user in our simulation network. Does anyone have any issues to bring forward?"

Spider and I exchanged a glance. When he spoke, his voice was shaky but determined. "I won't control her mind in the network without her knowledge."

"That won't be necessary," Stemp replied crisply. "We have assigned another analyst, Tyler Brock, to be her controller, and Jill Francis is her handler. You'll meet them both this morning. Brock is, by necessity, aware of the clandestine decryptions. Francis has been briefed on the brainwave-driven virtual reality network and the way in which super-users enhance its operation, but she is not aware that we are hacking and decrypting external data."

Stemp glanced around the table. "Those operations are strictly need-to-know. Unless it's absolutely necessary, Francis is not to be briefed." His gaze snapped back to Spider. "You will be the team lead for the expanded decryption program, coordinating with Brock and Francis and facilitating Kelly's work with your usual technical support. I trust that will be satisfactory."

The last sentence was delivered with exactly the same inflection as the others, but the unspoken 'or else' lingered in the air.

Spider flushed and knotted his skinny fingers together. "I... guess... Okay. Yeah."

"Don't guess." Stemp's voice was deadly dry.

"No, I mean..." Spider's blush deepened. "I meant... thanks. For... keeping me."

Stemp inclined his head gravely. "After your exemplary work in preventing the loss of two valuable agents and the weapon prototype, it would be foolish to do otherwise."

Not fired. Promoted.

Suck on that, Dermott. I prevented myself from looking in his direction, hoping my triumph didn't show.

Stemp glanced at his watch. "We'll take a short break. Brock will join us here in ten minutes for a briefing on the decryptions, after which we'll meet with Mellor and Francis to hand off the decryption project. Then Kane, Germain, and Kelly..." He nodded at each of us in turn. "...we'll meet regarding Afterburner. Thank you, Dr. Travers; you can return to your regular duties now. Dermott, I'll take it from here."

Dermott nodded without making eye contact, and everyone rose to head for the door.

"Just one more thing." Jack's clear voice cut through the shuffling of chairs. She smiled at Stemp. "It's good to have you back, Director."

His expressionless façade softened into an answering smile. "Thank you, Dr. Travers."

Dermott pushed through the group and left. By the time we spilled into the hallway he was nowhere to be seen, and I heaved a sigh of relief.

The men straggled toward the lunchroom, and I headed for the ladies' room. Jack followed, and we reconvened at the sinks after using the facilities.

Grinning, I cast a sidelong glance at her elegant ivory profile as we washed our hands. "*Shirley?* How did you find that out? My God, his parents must have hated him."

Her patrician features twisted into unholy glee. "Know your enemy. I'm not the bimbo he thinks I am."

"If he thinks you're a bimbo, he's even more of an idiot than I thought."

Her smile vanished. "He's a man. And I'm a blonde with big boobs." She slapped the water tap closed and jerked a paper towel out of the dispenser. "I am so sick of men and their *issues!*"

"Um..." I detoured around her to take a towel of my own. "Is everything okay... um, with you and, um..."

"Carl?" She crushed the towel and shoved it into the garbage. "Fine. There is no 'everything'. No anything. It was one kiss on Christmas Eve. Just two lonely people reacting after a stressful situation. Nothing more." She grabbed another towel.

"Uh..."

She was still talking, staring at her hands while they slowly shredded the paper towel. "It was actually quite funny." She let out a bleak laugh. "We parted ways on the sidewalk in front of Spider's house. Both of us fumbling like idiots, explaining how we liked each other but it couldn't turn into anything."

"Uh..."

"But it can't." She stuffed the remains of the towel into the garbage. "I refuse to date a man with a dangerous job like Carl's. If I'm going to let my children get attached to a man, he has to be there to stay. Not like my ex. I won't put them through the pain of another loss."

"Um, you don't usually get a guarantee..."

"...And it doesn't matter anyway." Jack frowned at the garbage can. "He won't date a woman with children."

"Wha...? Why the hell not? He-"

I shut up before I could blab about his kids. None of my business.

"He said he failed his own children, and he won't fail somebody else's, too. Anyway, it's no big deal. It was just a kiss." She stared into middle distance and sighed, pink rising in her cheeks. "But what a kiss! My heavens, Aydan..."

She shook herself and turned to face me with a grimace. "I can't believe I'm gossiping about a man, a co-worker no less, in the women's bathroom. Please forget I said any of that. How was your Christmas?"

I slam-dunked my paper towel and headed for the door. "You don't even want to know."

She sighed and followed. "I don't know how you do it, Aydan. I'm going back to my nice safe lab, and I'm thankful for every minute of it. Let's have lunch later, and you can update me on the new team members."

"Sure." I held the door open for her. "Brock is probably your typical computer geek, but I'm looking forward to meeting Jill Francis. I've never met a female agent before."

Jack paused, frowning. "You *are* a female agent."

"Um." Heat rose in my cheeks.

Jack laughed. "You're amazing. I've never known anybody who maintained their cover as convincingly as you do. If I hadn't read your mission reports, I'd swear you really are just a civilian bookkeeper." She shook her head, still smiling. "See you later."

I repressed the urge to beat myself senseless against the wall and turned back to the meeting room instead, massaging my aching temples.

I was the last to arrive again. Kane, Germain, and Stemp leaned back in their chairs cradling coffee mugs, their expressions and posture identically cop-neutral. Spider was bandying incomprehensible tech-talk with the skinny personage draped against the wall beside him.

Tyler Brock. Yikes. Not exactly your typical computer geek.

From the toes of his retro black-and-white hightop sneakers to the tips of his shaggy hair, everything about Brock screamed 'non-conformist'. Tight red jeans hugged toothpick legs, and a 1950s-style plaid suit jacket slouched over a white shirt and yellow sweater-vest. The ensemble was completed with Elvis Costello glasses and a bulky knit scarf and tuque. I barely registered thin forgettable features and patchy facial hair behind enough lip, cheek, and eyebrow piercings to make my face ache in sympathy.

"...seriously, that's lame as eff," Brock was saying, waving a disparaging hand at Spider's beloved laptop. Spider's face fell, and Brock heaved a theatrical sigh. "Don't go all emo. You know I'm right."

Spider turned to me instead of responding. "Aydan, this is Tyler Brock," he said. "Brock, Aydan Kelly."

Brock raised a double-pierced eyebrow, the ring-bedecked corner of his mouth rising in a half smile. Or a sneer; I wasn't sure which.

"Yo," he said.

"Uh... hi." I sank into a chair, trying to tear my gaze away from the discs that stretched holes the size of loonies in his earlobes.

He poked a finger through one of the holes, his lips twisting. "Like my plugs?"

Okay, that was definitely a sneer. And he had insulted Spider.

I gave him a sneer of my own. "Nothing cooler than having earthworms dangling from your head."

"Earthw...?" His smirk faded into confusion.

"Yeah." I adopted a bright, helpful tone. "That's what your earlobes look like when you take those discs out. The bottom part looks just like a dead earthworm hanging there under the hole."

Germain's sudden cough sounded as though it concealed a laugh.

"Let's begin." Stemp's dry tones overrode any rejoinder Brock might have intended. "Webb?"

Spider straightened and faced Brock. "You've read the reports?"

Brock nodded, his snotty attitude fading. "It'll take me a while to assimilate it all, but I get the basics. Mellor holds a unique authentication key that gets her invisibly into any network and lets her decrypt everything on the fly; I have a unique counterpart key that interfaces with hers to let me drive her through the networks wherever we want to gather data. We record the data; she doesn't know anything about it..." He trailed off, eyeing me.

"That's how it will be with you and Tammy," Spider agreed. "Aydan uses her authentication key standalone, and she goes where she wants."

Brock frowned. "But you can control her if you want. Your key overrides hers. She's just a slave."

Spider stiffened. "No."

"Bull. I studied the schematics. That's how the hardware is designed."

"It is, but Aydan can override it."

Brock's metal-studded eyebrows climbed his forehead. "Seriously? You mean she can control *you*?"

"No." Spider hesitated. "But she can break the control."

Brock scrutinized me, dubious lines scoring his brow. "How?"

"Well, um..." Spider gave Stemp a questioning look and received a nod in return. "By killing the controller," Spider said apologetically.

CHAPTER 12

"What?" Brock stared at Spider. Then he swivelled his unbelieving look toward me. A heavy silence hung in the room.

"This is, like, um... theoretical, right?" he asked after a few moments. "You mean, like, a kill-switch in the software, right?"

"No." Spider shifted, his gaze darting over to me before returning to Brock. "I mean, like, the guy who tried to control her dropped dead."

Brock's eyes went wide as he reared back in his chair. "Holy mother of God!" He turned an accusing glare toward Stemp. "Dermott didn't tell me this was dangerous! He said it was-"

"An analyst's position; that's correct," Stemp said smoothly. "You won't be working with Kelly. Ms. Mellor has never entered the network without being controlled. She isn't aware of your control in the first place and even if she was, she has no ability to break it nor any reason to try."

"That you know of," Brock snapped.

Stemp acknowledged that with a tiny dip of his chin.

Shit, if Brock backed out, Stemp would probably try to force Spider to take his role. As far as I knew, there weren't any other analysts with a high enough security clearance.

"If it makes you feel better, I've been inside Tammy's mind," I offered. "And I'm quite sure she won't fight back."

"You've been inside her mind." Brock sounded as though he couldn't decide whether I was joking.

"Yes, when two super-users meet inside a data tunnel, they instantly assimilate each other's memories," Spider explained. "That's why Aydan won't usually be in the network with Tammy. It's a huge strain for her to keep Tammy from seeing inside her mind. And as Tammy's controller, you'll be able to read everything in Tammy's mind, too, unless you put up a mental shield."

He didn't look at Kane or me, and I suppressed the guilty urge to glance at Kane. Thank God Spider had shielded himself from my mind as soon as he accessed the topmost of my memories. And thank God he was a good enough friend not to blab about the hot sex Kane and I never should have had.

"So you've done this before. With her." Brock jerked his chin in my direction, apparently unwilling to look me in the eye. "And she didn't kill you."

"I was fine," Spider said. "And it was really fun." His face lit up at the memory. "It was so totally cool, it was like... like... I was part of all the data in the world, just riding around in a big rollercoaster of data and I could read everything..." He trailed off, grinning. "I can't explain it. But it was so totally *cool!* You're going to love it."

Brock lifted a superior brow. "'*Totally cool*'? Cool is fin. You're so midtown."

The words made no sense to me, but the insult was clear. Spider's sparkle vanished and spots of colour reddened his cheeks.

I locked my teeth together. Time to have a little heart-to-heart with Brock. With no witnesses.

Brock studied Kane and Germain, who formed an imposing wall of muscle beside Stemp. "So why are you guys involved?"

"We protect Aydan inside the network," Kane began, and Brock stiffened. "From herself," Kane hastened to add. "If she doesn't stay focused when she's inside the virtual reality..." he hesitated, obviously searching for a non-scary way to say I was likely to kill myself and everyone around me. "We just help her stay focused," he finished lamely.

"Aydan doesn't really need me at all," Germain added, deftly diverting the conversation. "I'm normally based in Calgary, but I've been posted here for the last couple of weeks working on an op and doing the annual agent requalifications. I'm just helping out with Aydan's project in my free time."

"Okay..." Brock sat back, eyeing us suspiciously.

I willed my blandest expression. Come on, Brock, you lily-livered little shit.

"I want to practice with Kelly before I meet Mellor," Brock said finally. "I don't want to take a chance that Mellor will realize what I'm doing."

My words came out dead flat. "If you ever try to control me, I'll k-" I bit my tongue. "It wouldn't be safe for you," I finished instead.

Brock blanched and everyone except Stemp shifted suddenly in their chairs.

I didn't look at Stemp. We'd already had this conversation. And even if I didn't kill Brock the instant he took control inside the network, Stemp would execute him afterward, as dispassionately as he'd killed the last man who had read my mind. I wondered if Stemp's wife and little daughter in Bulgaria knew exactly how far he was willing to go to protect the secret of their existence.

Hell, did *I* really know? Maybe getting Tammy on board was just Stemp's first step toward turning me into daisy fertilizer.

Spider's hurried voice interrupted my dark thoughts. "Your key isn't customized to Aydan's, so you couldn't control her even if you wanted to."

"Okay..." Brock perched nervously on the edge of his chair, his gaze darting toward the door as if he was about to make a run for it. "So... how would we do this?"

"You'll just go into our internal brainwave-driven virtual reality network," Spider said cheerfully. "Then you pick Tammy up and go into the external network."

"And *she'll* be in the network at the same time as me?" Brock gave me an apprehensive look, and I tried to feel guilty about enjoying his fear.

Guilt eluded me, and I gave him a hard stare. You hurt Spider. You'd better be scared, you little shit.

"Don't be so lame," Spider scoffed, and I clamped down hard on the grin that tried to seize my lips. Spider was the sweetest, most tolerant person I knew, but he'd obviously reached his limit.

Spider flushed, apparently taken aback by his own effrontery, but he continued with lofty disdain, "I told you, most of the time it'll just be you and Tammy. And your controller chip can't even connect to Aydan's, so get over it."

Brock straightened, colour flaming into his pasty cheeks. "Fine," he snapped. "Let's do it." His show of resolve was somewhat marred when he fumbled and dropped his man-purse twice in quick succession. When he finally straightened clutching it, he shot a glare around the room, but met only straight faces.

I silently congratulated myself on my restraint while we all filed out the door.

Didn't laugh at his discomfiture. Only threatened to kill him once.

Go, me.

Stemp led our little procession down the hall and into the office next to mine. As he motioned me to precede him through the door, a voluptuous brunette rose from the couch to step forward, hand extended. "You must be Aydan. It's nice to meet you. I'm Jill Francis."

"Hi, Jill, it's nice to meet you, too." I accepted her firm handshake, appraising her with interest.

I had half-expected a butch female counterpart to Kane's and Germain's breath-taking physiques, or maybe a willowy, dangerous femme fatale. But Jill was a few inches shorter than me and much curvier, her glossy dark hair framing sparkling hazel eyes and a mouth that looked accustomed to smiles. An elegant scarf draped casually over her soft-looking sweater, and chunky jewellery finished her outfit to perfection.

Great, just what I needed. Another gorgeous, fashionable co-worker.

At least her companion's unstyled greying auburn hair and rumpled clothes showed she spent about as much time on her grooming as I did on mine.

Then again, she was blind.

I repressed a sigh.

The small, round woman surged forward, passing her white cane to Jill and extending her hand, her dark glasses trained in my direction. "Hi, Aydan, I'm Tammy Mellor!

We're going to be working together!"

"Hi, Tammy-"

I had just accepted her handshake when she stepped closer, her small soft hands patting up my arms, across my shoulders and up my neck to skim over my features and stroke down my hair. I held myself still, barely suppressing the urge to recoil from the invasion.

Heedless of my discomfort, her hands skimmed back down to squeeze mine again. "It's so nice to *meet* you, oh, you have beautiful *hair*, I'm so *excited* we're going to be working together to power the sim, this is so much *fun* for me to meet all these new people and it's so *exciting* to start a whole new career but I miss my Terry *so much*, he would have been so *excited* about my new job, we shared *everything*, you know, and it was just a *tragedy* when he died, I miss him so *much* but thank *God* Charles was here for me and he's been so *lovely* and I just can't tell you how *grateful* I am!"

I extricated my hand from Tammy's chummy grasp to edge away, but I couldn't resist a glance at Stemp. Nobody ever called him Charles.

No reaction, as usual.

Tammy reached out again before stopping herself. "Oh, I *forgot*. Dr. Rawling said sometimes people don't like being touched if they don't know me. But *you* don't mind, do you? We're going to be such great *friends* and I *always* do that, it's just *me*, it's just the way I *am*. It's so *complicated* to be around new people, there's so much to *remember*, it was always just me and my Terry before and it's so *funny* to think that some people don't like being touched, but you know, I was just *saying* to Dr. Rawling..."

Stemp slid smoothly into the miniscule gap caused by

her need to breathe. "Ms. Mellor, Charles Stemp here. Your other team members are with me. This is Clyde Webb."

Spider stepped forward to shake her hand. "Hi, Tammy! It's nice to meet you. You can call me Spider."

"Hi!" Her hands fluttered up his arms, and he folded his beanpole six-foot-two obligingly as she stretched up. She giggled. "Oh, *thank* you for coming down where I can reach you. I just *know* I'm going to like you. Why do they call you *Spider*? Do you *like* spiders? When I was a little girl I thought spiders were *icky*, but that was when I could *see* them, but now I can't *see* them anymore and they don't bother me at all-"

"And this is Tyler Brock," Stemp interrupted.

"Hi, Tyler! I've been *so* looking forward to meeting my new knight! My knight in shining armour!" She beamed about two feet to the left of Brock, holding out her hand.

Brock stepped up and took it reluctantly, grimacing as she patted her way to his face.

When she touched his first piercing, she jerked her hand away. "Oh!" Her forehead scrunched up. "I'm sorry, did I *hurt* you? Did you have *surgery* or something?"

He wasted a sullen glare on her, obviously forgetting she couldn't see it. "No. Those are piercings."

"Oh..." Her busy hands returned to categorize the hardware. "You stuck these things in your face on *purpose*? Why would you *do* that? I can't imagine how that must have *hurt*... Ooh, what's that in your *ear*?"

Brock pulled away scowling and took a seat on the opposite side of the room. Her hands floated down forlornly, her dark glasses searching the air in his direction.

Stemp's voice drew her attention back. "Carl Germain and John Kane are also here. They work with Ms. Kelly."

Germain stepped forward first, taking her hand. "Hi, Tammy, I'm Carl."

"Hi, Carl!"

He stood patiently while she patted up his arms. When she reached his bulging biceps, she let out a little cry of appreciation. "Ooooh, you're really *muscular*!" Her hands danced up to his face and hair. "I bet you're really *handsome*, Carl!"

The mischief glinting in Germain's eyes belied his solemn tone. "I'm hideous. Children cry when they see me. Women run screaming."

She giggled, her hands drifting down to skim across his powerful shoulders and chest. "Oh, I bet you're *fibbing*, I can *tell* when a man is handsome, my *Terry* was handsome, too, that's what he always *told* me, but he might have been fibbing just a *bit*, and he was much older and not nearly as *strong* as you, but he was my knight in shining armour and-"

"Tammy, let go of Carl. You're invading his space." Jill's reproof was delivered with quiet humour, and Germain gave her a grin and a wink as he withdrew from Tammy's clutches to offer Jill a handshake, too.

She returned his smile and kept the handshake short, but she looked as though she wouldn't have minded subjecting him to a little handish inquisition of her own. Hell, any woman in her right mind would. And Germain and Kane together in the same room? Serious eye candy.

And speaking of Kane...

"Hi, Tammy, I'm John," he rumbled.

"Hi, John, oh, you have such a *sexy* voice!" There went the hands again. "Ooh..." A little indrawn breath when she encountered his biceps.

I could relate. The memory of those smooth hard

muscles under my hands was enough to make me suck in a breath, too.

"You're really *muscular*, too! And I bet you're just as *handsome* as Carl!" She was already stretching to her full height just to reach his shoulders. Those massive, ever-so-tasty shoulders...

"Oooh... oh, my... you're..."

Kane stooped and her hands traced the strong square planes of his face.

"*Wow*. You're so... *big*... and *tall*." Tammy sounded a little breathless. "Oh..."

Stemp interrupted. "Ms. Mellor, you can get acquainted later. Kelly, you'll observe and be ready to enter the network if necessary. Let's get to work."

Unabashed, she turned an expression of shining admiration in his direction. "Oh, yes, Charles, it's so *exciting* to have work to do again, I can hardly *wait*..." Her hand searched the air and Jill offered the crook of her arm, handing back Tammy's white cane.

Tammy reclaimed both, chattering again with apparent relish as Jill led her back to sit on the small sofa. "...you know I was so *lost* when my Terry died, it was such a *tragedy*, I don't think *anybody* can really understand unless they've been through a *tragedy* like that themselves, you know, I *always* say people who have never experienced that kind of *tragedy* just don't know what it's like, when *I*-"

"Tammy," Jill interrupted gently. "It's time to stop talking now."

Tammy beamed in her direction. "Okey-dokey, Jilly-Bean!"

Kane and Germain exchanged a glance, and I could practically read the thought-bubble above their heads:

'Thank God I'm not assigned to her.'

I sank into one of the chairs, fervently hoping I wouldn't have to enter the network. One experience of Tammy's memories was more than enough. I suppressed a shiver of claustrophobia and eased out a long, slow breath.

Spider and Brock held a whispered consultation before Spider rose and crossed the room to stand in front of Tammy.

"Tammy, it's Spider," he said. "If you hold out your hand, I'll give you your network key."

"Oh, *thank* you, Spider." She thrust out a hand to accept the tiny cube. "I'm all ready to work now!" She smiled and leaned back on the sofa. Her body went limp.

CHAPTER 13

We stared at Tammy's motionless body for an instant before comprehension dawned. "She's in the network already!" Spider yelped. "Go, Brock!"

Brock's eyes widened, then he gripped his key and his face settled into the blank stare that indicated he'd entered the network, too.

"Brock should have Tammy under control now," Spider said a moment later, his gaze riveted to his laptop. "He should be moving her any time... Ah, there they go," he finished.

Being on the observing end of a network session was a new experience for me, and it was boring as hell. Kane and Spider must have the patience of saints to have put up with me for the last nine months. When Brock and Tammy blinked and straightened nearly fifteen minutes later I drew a breath of relief.

Tammy cocked her head. "I didn't get *dizzy* this time, so that was nice, but your network is *funny*, I felt all light and kind of *floaty* when I first went in! I'm so lucky, all I ever did was get dizzy but poor Patty used to throw up, *every single time*. It was *awful*, and her knight was so *mean* to her, that was Martin Brewster and he was just so *mean*, *none* of us mages liked him. And I heard one of the other mages went *crazy*, that was Irina, but she died before I could meet her. And don't you think *mage* sounds so much more *romantic* than super-user? That just sounds so *cold* and *boring*, but being a *mage* is so much more-"

Shit! She was about to blab the whole story behind our network keys, and Jill didn't have a security clearance.

I shot a wild-eyed glance at Stemp.

He interrupted Tammy's babble, as unruffled as always. "Ms. Kelly gets a bad headache when she comes out of the network, and sometimes she loses consciousness."

"Oh, I'm *sorry* it hurts you that much," Tammy said. "And oh my God, you actually *pass out*? Is that why *Betty* went into a coma when you were in the network together? I *hope* not, because I was really *hoping* I'd get to go into the network with you and see your memories, my *Terry* said if I ever went into the network with another mage, I'd see her memories and it would be so *nice* to see again even if I wasn't seeing through my *own* eyes."

"Somebody ended up in a coma?" Brock's trembling voice broke in. "You didn't tell me that!"

"It was another super-user." Stemp's neutral expression didn't alter, but I got the distinct impression it was taking some effort for him to hold onto it. "It was a small technical problem, and we determined the cause and fixed it. She recovered with no ill effects."

Not even the flicker of an eyelid. God, he was a good liar.

"A small technical problem?" Brock's voice soared to a pitch that made me wonder if his tight pants had caused some long-term damage. "Since when is a coma considered a *small technical problem*?"

Jeez, lucky he didn't know Betty had actually withdrawn

into trauma-induced catatonia after encountering my memories.

"We can discuss this later," Stemp said firmly. "Thank you for coming, Ms. Mellor," he continued in his usual dispassionate tones. "That's all the testing we require for today, and we'll expect you tomorrow morning at nine o'clock for your first full day of work."

"Oh, *thank you*, Charles!" Tammy rose, her white cane sweeping her path as she hurried over to reach toward him. He offered his hand and she hugged it, beaming. "It was so *exciting* to meet everybody and I can hardly *wait* to work with you, you know I'll do *anything* I can to help, I just owe you so *much* and you've been so *good* to me-"

Jill intervened to extricate Stemp's hand and transfer Tammy's grip to her arm instead. "It's time to go, Tammy. Nice to meet you, everybody." Jill steered Tammy toward the door.

"Oh, yes!" Tammy chirped. "Aydan, I can hardly *wait* for tomorrow, it was so *nice* to meet you all and I can hardly *wait* to get started, this is going to be so much *fun*, if only my Terry was here it would just *perfect*, wouldn't it, Jilly-Bean? I just *wish* you could have met my Terry, I just *know* you would have *loved* him, I miss him so *much*..."

Tammy's chatter receded down the hallway, and I let out a sigh of relief just as Kane released a breath of his own. We caught each other's eyes and looked away hurriedly.

"Brock, report," Stemp said.

Brock blinked, massaging his temples. "Uh, I guess it went okay. I went into a couple of sites that I knew were securely encrypted and I could read the data no problem. And I don't think Mellor knew what was going on."

"That's what it looked like to me while I was watching

from the outside, too," Spider seconded, but he didn't look happy.

Stemp leaned back in his chair. "Kelly, based on your recollection of Ms. Mellor's mind, please brief us on exactly what she knows regarding the decryptions. She may turn out to be a liability due to her..."

My mind supplied the words 'verbal diarrhea', but Stemp continued, "...unrestrained enthusiasm. Francis is an excellent handler, but even she can't control every word out of Ms. Mellor's mouth." His inscrutable façade wavered for a moment in what might have been a shudder. "No one could control that."

"Yeah. Okay, give me a minute." I closed my eyes, drawing a deep breath to begin sifting through the alien memories. Too bad the really disturbing ones stayed freshest.

I suppressed a shudder and forced my mind past them into the innocuous reams of Tammy's accumulated minutiae.

"Okay." I drew a deep breath and opened my eyes again. "Her Knight..." At Brock's look of incomprehension, I paused. "Didn't you read her mind while you were driving her?"

"You seriously think I'd go into *that*?" He shuddered. "No."

Jerk.

I tried to soften my attitude. He wasn't a jerk. He hadn't invaded her mind.

But his reasons weren't exactly altruistic.

I sighed. "Short version, then." I rubbed my aching temples. "The original eight creators of the controller keys called themselves the Knights of Sirius. They called the super-users mages. That's what she was talking about earlier, when she said you were her new knight."

"Oh. Good." His nose piercing jiggled unattractively as he sniffed. "I was afraid she was coming onto me."

I left that alone and carried on. "So 'her Terry', that's Terry Sherman, her knight... controller... he was a lot more than that."

My stomach tried to climb my throat again at the memories, but I gulped it down determinedly. "She's been blind since she was a little girl, and the Knights arranged to take her from her family when she was only eight. She had no family life at all after that. Sherman started out as a handler and father figure and ended up as a lover. Or pseudo-husband, whatever. He was her whole world."

"That's sick."

I breathed carefully. "Yeah. Anyway, the Knights were using the mages to secretly gather data and sell it to the highest bidder. None of the mages knew they were doing anything but powering the brainwave-driven simulations."

I spoke to Stemp. "And she still doesn't know about that part. That's what she meant when she said she felt light and floaty."

Stemp nodded, and I returned my attention to Brock's puzzled frown. "When a mage is being controlled in the network by someone who's reading her mind, it feels... heavy. Like being trapped in tar."

That mental image wasn't helping my claustrophobia. I sucked in a breath.

"...but when the controller shields his mind, it's not as heavy," I finished hurriedly. "Tammy has never been in a network without somebody riding her mind, so she felt 'light and floaty' because she went in on her own before you gained control of her and you kept your own mind shielded."

Brock nodded, and I turned back to Stemp.

"So she isn't aware we're using her to hack and decrypt data," I finished. "And she wasn't aware the Knights were doing that, either. But Sherman didn't try to hide any information about the brainwave-driven network or the other Knight/mage pairs, so there's plenty of classified information for her to blab if she gets going."

"Yes." Stemp sat in silence for a moment, then nodded decisively. "We'll have to bury her."

"What?" Spider and I chorused.

Spider sounded horrified. I sounded... dangerous.

"It's the only answer." Stemp rose. "We'll keep her underground in the secured area."

"For how long?" I grated.

Stemp wasn't stupid. He had to sense my impending explosion.

He eyed me dispassionately. "Indefinitely, of course."

"You can't do that to her. She hasn't done anything wrong. She's not a prisoner-"

Stemp's cool tone cut across my rising voice like a blade. "I can, and I will. National security is my top priority."

Just like that.

No rights, no appeal, just locked away in a dungeon forever. He'd bury Tammy just like he'd tried to bury me. But Tammy was blind, alone in the world, unable to fight back because she didn't even know what was at stake.

My claustrophobic terror rushed back wearing rage as a disguise. I rocketed up from the couch, fists clenched. "Listen, you fucking dickhead-"

"Kelly!"

His admonition didn't even slow me down. I stepped closer, fists and voice rising. "...who the hell do you think you-"

Spider's gasp was loud in the sudden silence when I shut up, staring at the gun Stemp had whipped out to train on me.

Goddamn him. I knew how fast he was, but I'd never thought he'd actually draw on me in front of everybody.

As if suspended in time, I observed our little tableau.

Spider, poised half-way off the couch, his hands outstretched in a warding gesture. Brock's mouth hanging open in an 'O' dotted with piercings, dark against his shock-white skin. Kane's hand on his holster, his jaw taut. Germain's arms extended, whether to restrain Kane or intercede with Stemp I couldn't tell.

Stemp's voice broke the silence, as emotionless as ever. "In my office, Kelly." He angled his chin a fraction toward the doorway, the gun rock-steady in his hand. "If you please."

I let out a breath, eerie calm supplanting my anger. "You won't need that." I nodded at his gun.

"Good." He holstered it without changing expression and swept the others with a glance. "Brock, you're dismissed for the day. Be here tomorrow at zero nine hundred to continue with Ms. Mellor. The rest of you meet back here in twenty minutes for Afterburner. After you, Kelly."

As I moved slowly toward the door, I wondered if he actually trusted me not to attack him or if he was just so deadly in hand-to-hand combat that it didn't matter. Either way, he didn't blink when I passed.

He followed several paces behind me while we marched down the hall toward his office. The skin crawled on my back. Had he drawn his gun again?

At the door to his office, his voice halted me. "Do I need to ask for your weapon?"

I turned. He wasn't holding his gun.

The knot of tension loosened between my shoulder blades. "No. I promise not to pull it on you this time. But you can take it if you want." I held my arms out from my sides. "It's in my waist holster."

"No need. I trust you." His gaze bored into mine. "This time." He gestured through the door. "Please sit."

I tottered over and sank into his guest chair, heart thumping while he closed the door and took a seat across the desk. He regarded me in silence for a moment before extracting a bug detector to contemplate its glowing green light.

The corner of his mouth lifted in what might have been the smallest smile ever issued. "I knew I could count on your legendary temper. Thank you for obliging me."

"Wh..." My lips were barely framing the word when he continued.

"As much as I don't particularly appreciate being called a dickhead yet again, your predictability does create a convenient method for arranging confidential meetings with you. So. I need to know..." His intense amber gaze transfixed me like prey before a predator. "Can you extract memories from Ms. Mellor's mind?"

I blinked. "What?" My brain caught up with the first part of his statement and I straightened indignantly. "You played me."

"Of course." His impersonal tone never altered. "Please answer the question."

I opened my mouth to tell him where to stick it, but clamped it shut again. This was Stemp. I might as well rage at the lush Boston fern in the corner of his office. I'd get more reaction from the plant.

I held my voice level. "I'm not really sure what you're asking."

"I'm asking if you can selectively remove memories from her mind."

I stared at him, the ramifications of the question slowly sinking in. Sick anger hollowed my chest. "You want me to... *mind-rape* her? That's fucking disgusting!"

"No. That's not what I want at all. I want to know if you can remove certain very specific memories that pose a major threat to national security and to all of your team. Just like you did for Betty Hooper when you removed your own memories from her mind and restored her sanity."

"It's not *just like* that!" My fingers bit into the arms of the chair. "With Betty I was retrieving my own memories, memories she never should have had, memories that were destroying her. What you're asking is like... like... secretly cutting out a piece of Tammy's brain! Her fundamental... person! Who she is!"

"That's not what I'm asking. Please calm down and I'll explain."

Stemp eyed me in silence for a moment as if making sure he had my attention.

I pried my fingers loose from the chair. A few months ago I would have jumped down his throat with both feet. Now...

"I'm listening," I growled.

He exhaled and leaned back in his chair. "Since you discovered the existence of the Knights and their mages a few months ago, I have been scrambling to make sure our national security remains uncompromised. The Knights are no longer a threat, thanks to you."

He inclined his head in my direction, and I nodded

grudging acknowledgement.

He went on, "The three mages you freed when you eliminated the Knights were all citizens of the United States. They have been repatriated and assigned to join Betty Hooper on the U.S. project, which is continuing. Since they are all under strict oversight by the U.S. Department of Homeland Security, I don't consider their knowledge a major threat."

"However." Stemp pressed his fingertips briefly to the bridge of his nose as though trying to suppress a headache. "Ms. Mellor is a Canadian citizen. I assigned Francis immediately after we acquired Ms. Mellor, and Francis and several other agents have been supervising her constantly since then. Dr. Rawling has also been evaluating Ms. Mellor under the guise of grief counselling sessions. She has normal intellect, but her social and emotional development were severely stunted by her isolation with Sherman. She is naively trusting and easily manipulated, with no emotional boundaries or impulse control to speak of. That makes her a constant threat as long as she remains free and retains her memories of the scope of the project."

He held up a silencing hand as I leaned forward to protest. "I'm not asking you to *do* anything at this point. I'm simply asking if you think it's *possible* to remove selected memories."

"I don't know."

Stemp eyed me wearily. "Consider it. Please. Because otherwise I'll have to bury Tammy Mellor."

CHAPTER 14

I glared at Stemp. "You're playing me *again*, you bastard! Trying to force me to rip an innocent woman's mind apart by threatening to stick her in prison for the rest of her life if I don't. You *dickhead*!"

He closed his eyes for a moment. "Please don't shoot the messenger." The quiet resignation in his tone drained every vestige of heat from my anger.

I slumped back in my chair. "Shit." I ground the frown wrinkles out of my forehead with the heel of my hand and added, "Sorry."

He sighed and nodded acceptance.

We sat in silence while I wrestled with the problem and all its complications. I knew Stemp was right, but there had to be another way.

I just couldn't think of anything at the moment.

I blew out a long breath. "Suppose I did actually figure out a way to... edit her memories. What would happen to her then? I thought you wanted her to take over my decryptions. If she doesn't have any memory of the network, she can't do that."

Stemp shrugged. "That is the least of my worries. I can concoct a plausible 'job' to bring Ms. Mellor here daily. Once

Brock perfects his control, she need never know there is a network."

"But she's going to wonder why she has no memory of ever doing anything at work besides arriving and leaving."

"Let me worry about that."

Something about the way he said it made suspicion bloom into certainty.

"False memories." I stared at him, my stomach twisting. "You don't just want me to remove the classified memories, you want me to make up new ones to take their place. That's... that's..."

He held up a hand. "I don't want you to do any of this. I don't want it to be necessary in the first place. I want to find another solution. I hope you can help me do that."

My fingers were digging into the chair again. "But you're considering it as an option."

"Yes." Stemp met my eyes squarely. "It is my job and my sworn duty to protect national security. I can't dismiss any option, regardless of how distasteful I may consider it personally. That's why we're having this conversation in strict confidence. I hope it turns out to be unnecessary. Take some time to think about it. She's secure for now under Francis's constant supervision, but we will have to deal with the issue at some point, preferably in the not-too-distant future. I would appreciate your input."

He rose. "We should get back to your office. You can pretend you've received a reprimand and use this incident as a plausible reason for being sent to the anger management class. The series begins tomorrow at sixteen-thirty in the meeting room at the end of the hall."

I suppressed a groan. Ten long weeks under Dr. Rawling's too-perceptive observation.

But it was worth it. As long as Stemp was sending me to the class, it meant he still believed I'd killed Arnie's father. Arnie would be safe.

I stood, squaring my shoulders. "Okay."

If Stemp heard the reluctance in my voice, he didn't react to it. "Also, I've scheduled your requalification tests for tomorrow." His eyes narrowed. "I expect you to pass this time."

"Tomorrow?" I couldn't hide my gulp. "I thought you said you'd give me a few weeks. I've been pushing hard with my workouts and doing the training simulations at the shooting range whenever I have time, but..."

"It has been over two weeks. And Germain may be reassigned shortly, so you'll need to complete your hand-to-hand combat requalification before he leaves."

"What?" My voice caught in my suddenly-dry throat. "I can't do hand-to-hand combat. I already told you that. I'm just a bookkeeper."

Stemp gave me one of his deadly stares. "And if you hadn't breached your cover, you would have been able to avoid the requalification. But since your last mission report clearly states you killed an enemy agent in hand-to-hand combat, you'll need to complete the requalification."

"I didn't!" I clenched my hands together so I wouldn't grab him by the lapels. "I never said that! Read my report!"

"It was detailed in Kane's report. And the autopsy findings were consistent with Kane's account. They also matched the results of Helmand Senior's autopsy report. A broken neck; no other significant injuries."

"No, Kane didn't see what really happened," I argued desperately. "I just hurt the guy's arm. Then he tripped and when he fell he couldn't save himself because his arm collapsed, and that's when his head got stuck between two seats and-"

Stemp froze me with a look. "Do you honestly expect me to believe it was an accident? Despite the fact that you already admitted you killed Helmand using exactly the same technique? Or are you saying you lied and someone else actually killed Helmand for you?"

My heart stopped.

God, if he discovered the truth, Arnie and I would both go to jail.

"No," I squeaked.

"Good. Report for your requalification tests in the gym at zero nine hundred tomorrow." He turned and strode out.

After a paralyzed moment, I stumbled after him.

I didn't absorb much at the Afterburner briefing. I was fairly sure I had nodded at the right moments, but as we filed out the door of the meeting room afterward, my mind buzzed like a frantic fly in a Mason jar.

I was so fucked.

I couldn't avoid the hand-to-hand combat test. Even if I manufactured an excuse that got me out of tomorrow's test, Stemp would just keep rescheduling it.

I didn't have a hope in hell of passing. The only self-defence moves I knew were a wrist lock and an arm-bar hold, and those wouldn't even slow Germain down.

But as soon as it became obvious that I didn't know any martial arts at all, Stemp would start digging to find out who had really killed Arnie's father.

Mouth dry, heart pounding, I trailed down the hallway toward my office.

Had they cremated Helmand's body? Please, God, let it be gone. If it was only buried and they exhumed it for a forensic investigation, they might find carpet fibres from Arnie's SUV.

I drifted to a halt in my office, staring sightlessly at my jacket slung over the back of the sofa.

I *might* still be valuable enough to the decryption program for Stemp to overlook my lie. But Arnie would go to jail for murder.

"Aydan..."

"*Jesus!*" My feet left the floor completely as I corkscrewed around to face Kane. He snapped into a defensive stance at the sight of my raised fists, and I hurriedly straightened from my crouch and unclenched my hands to clutch my chest instead. "Christ, John, don't sneak up on me like that! You scared the shit out of me!"

"I'm sorry." He relaxed his combat posture, frowning. "I thought you'd heard me. Since Stemp dismissed us for the day, Germain and I are going to grab lunch and a couple of beers at Blue Eddy's. Do you want to join us?"

"Oh... sorry." I drew a deep breath. "I was... thinking..." I pulled myself together. "Yeah, I was heading over to do Eddy's books this afternoon anyway, so that sounds like a great idea. I could really use a beer."

It wasn't a great idea.

I tried to concentrate on my companions, but most of the conversation faded into static while I nodded and smiled mindlessly. Even my favourite blues music couldn't penetrate my preoccupation.

I ate and drank without tasting the excellent food, and

when I finally retreated to Eddy's office the ill-advised beer conspired with my sleepless night to swaddle me in an exhausted stupor.

The columns of numbers swam in front of my eyes. God, if I could just lay my head down. Just for a minute...

"...Aydan...?"

I convulsed, my knee smashing into the desk. *"Aagh! Snotlicking-shiteating-sonofa-"*

As I doubled over to clutch my knee, a sheet of paper detached itself from my face and floated to the floor. Apparently I'd been drooling.

I managed to smother my high-pitched stream of obscenities and rocked back and forth instead, keening and cradling my knee.

"I'm sorry!" Eddy crouched beside me, his usually twinkling eyes wide and worried. "I didn't want to wake you, but I know you usually go to your next client's now and I didn't want you to be late. I'm sorry." He made a helpless gesture. "Do you want some ice?"

I pried my teeth apart and straightened, swiping at my cheek in case there was still drool on it. "It's okay." My voice came out strangled, and I cleared my throat and tried again. "Sorry for my language."

"It's okay." A little of his twinkle returned. "I've been known to use some creative language myself every now and then." Concern creased his face again as he eyed my white-knuckled grip on my knee. "Do you need to go to the hospital?"

I finally managed to ease my hand away, surreptitiously checking to make sure my kneecap hadn't actually exploded.

"No, it's okay. It's just that I fell a few days ago, so I had a bruise there already."

I rose, biting back a groan when my knee straightened. "I'm sorry I fell asleep on the job." I eased down to retrieve the paper from under the desk and sank back into the chair. "I'll get back to work now. All my other clients are closed for the holidays this week, so I can make up my time this afternoon."

"Don't worry about it." Eddy patted my shoulder. "If you're that tired, you should go home and rest. There's nothing here that won't keep."

"Thanks, Eddy, but I'd rather stay." I gave him an embarrassed grimace and indicated the paper that had served as my pillow. "I've already had my nap for the day."

"All right, if you're sure." He hesitated in the doorway. "Can I bring you anything? Ice for your knee? A drink to dull the pain?"

I laughed. "I think it was the drink that caused the problem. But thanks, I'm fine."

He withdrew with a smile, and I immersed myself in the safe, predictable world of bookkeeping.

When I emerged from his office a couple of hours later, my pleasant communion with numbers had restored some of my equanimity. I waved at Eddy, receiving a cheery salute from behind the bar in return, and headed out the back door into the long shadows of late afternoon. I had barely gotten into my car when my cell phone vibrated. I sighed at the sight of the text message.

'Call home'.

Shit, what now?

I extracted the second-last secured phone from my glove compartment, making a mental note to requisition some more, and pressed the speed dial.

As usual, Stemp picked up on the first ring. "Stemp."

"It's Aydan."

"The surveillance analyst just called to report Hibbert left a box on your front porch, approximately the size of a shoe box. Are you expecting anything?"

I sighed. "No."

"I'll send the bomb squad as a precaution."

I took my time driving home, but when I pulled into my driveway twenty minutes later the unmarked bomb disposal van was still there. I trudged forward to peek around its fender, and a young tech waved me over to where he stood beside a large square device on my sidewalk. Robotic arms protruded from its sides, and it hummed quietly on high-profile three-wheeled tracks. Track marks in the snow led up my sidewalk to the front steps.

"Just retrieved your package a few minutes ago," the tech said. "I've got it in the containment unit and I'm running the analysis now-" An electronic beep interrupted him, and he eyed a readout on the screen of the tablet he cradled in the crook of one arm. "No explosive," he informed me cheerfully. "No biohazard, either. It should be safe to open if you want."

I cast a jaundiced glance at the containment unit. "I don't want."

"Oh..." He eyed me uncertainly. "Well... we have to open it anyway. Just so I can finish my report."

"Knock yourself out. I'm just going to stand behind the truck while you do that."

His brows drew together. "Okay... but there's no trace of explosives or incendiaries. No wires or trigger devices showed up on the scan."

"Maybe not, but with my luck it'll be a big pile of fresh shit sitting on a fan that starts when the box opens."

His face twitched as though he was trying not to laugh. "Does that, um... happen to you a lot?"

I sighed. "I'm just saying."

A smile tugged at the corner of his mouth. "Okay, we'll open it with the remote arm inside the containment unit. Just in case the shit hits the fan."

"Thanks."

He punched a few keys on his control panel before manipulating its small joystick. "Okay, here we go. Ready for the big reveal?"

He angled the screen toward me so we could both watch while the robotic arm flipped the lid off the box.

My stomach clenched, my lips peeling back involuntarily.

"Nice." The word rasped from my constricted throat.

The Barbie doll's broken arms and legs stuck out at grotesque angles, deep knife slashes crisscrossing its naked limbs and torso. The source of the slashes was immediately obvious. A jackknife had been driven between the doll's legs with such force the plastic torso had split almost up to its torched and half-melted breasts. The doll's remaining blue eye gazed up with macabre serenity from the scorched and slagged remains of its face.

I swallowed rising bile. "Well, at least it's not shit." I stretched my stiff lips into a smile-like grimace.

The tech let out a puff of nervous laughter. "Yeah." He hesitated. "You want to call the cops?"

Keep breathing. Use short words. "No need."

"You okay?" he persisted.

I put every ounce of my acting ability into a smile.

"Yeah. Thanks." Another breath. "Can you take that with you?" I didn't look at the screen again.

"Yeah." He returned to his controls and the robot pivoted on its tracks and hummed over to crawl up the ramp into the back of the van. The tech tucked the control unit under his arm and scrutinized me. "You sure you're okay?"

The tremors were starting. Twisting my guts, dislodging the underpinnings of my control.

I unclenched my teeth and forced another smile. "Yeah. Freezing my butt off, though. Th..." A shudder shook me, my voice quavering into silence for a moment. I jerked it back under control. "Thanks for coming. Sorry it was for nothing. Have a good evening."

"Thanks, you, too," he said automatically. He grimaced. "Um, I mean... You better get inside and get warmed up."

I gave him a tight-jawed nod and hauled myself up the stairs to totter into the house, my muscles vibrating like overstressed cables.

I managed to get the door closed and locked behind me before the deluge of hideous memories crushed me to the floor.

The searing agony of blue flame and the smell of my own flesh burning. The bite of restraints on my wrists and ankles. The terror of utter helplessness and the sick certainty of prolonged rape and barbaric torture...

White-hot panic blotted out my world.

CHAPTER 15

I gradually regained awareness. Curled in a ball on my doormat, I was shaking so hard my teeth rattled together and knots of blazing pain scorched my neck and shoulders. My face was cold and wet, but I didn't remember crying.

I was pretty sure I wasn't crying.

Maybe I was.

I unlocked one arm, then the other from around my body, my muscles creaking their protest. After a moment, I uncurled enough to push myself semi-upright and slump against the door.

Knees clasped to my chest, I stared into the gathering darkness, shivering. Time passed while I huddled there, my mind carefully blank.

At last the nagging sensation at the edge of my consciousness became too irritating to ignore.

The floor was too damn hard. My ass hurt.

And it was freezing, pressed up against the drafty bottom of the door. I really should install some new weatherstripping.

I groaned and dragged myself to my feet.

When I flipped the light switch the sudden brilliance seared my eyes, making me flinch and swear. Blinking away afterimages, I shuffled over to fill the kettle before dropping into one of my kitchen chairs, still hugging my jacket around me.

When the kettle boiled I attended to my tea-making ritual with deliberate concentration.

Chamomile. Soothing.

My legs didn't want to carry me into the living room so I sat at the kitchen table again, losing myself in the clear golden depths of the tea, absorbing its warm summery scent.

When nothing remained but a few flower-flecks clinging to the inside of the mug I stared at them for long minutes, marvelling at their delicate tenacity.

At last, cradling the cooling cup in my hand, I rose slowly.

Crossed to the sink.

And spun to hurl the mug at the wall with all my might.

It exploded into porcelain shrapnel, the sound of its destruction shattering the brittle shell that contained my rage.

"*Fuck this!*" I roared. "*I am fucking DONE!*"

I swept up Parr's crystal vase. My aching muscles sang with fierce effort and sudden release.

The heavy crystal smashed with a thunderous report, punching a gaping wound in the drywall and spraying water and flowers in all directions. I stamped over its remains, my hiking boots fracturing the shards.

I was still screaming, the feral shriek of a cornered wildcat. "*No fucking more! Finished! Done, done, done, fucking DONE!*"

I crushed the listening device under my heel, stomping and grinding until the broken crystal gouged splinters from the hardwood floor.

At last my berserk strength faded and I hunched over, panting. The tiny gilt bug winked up at me from its sparkling bed of pulverized crystal.

Was it dead? Or was it still invading my house and my life?

I growled and plucked it from the floor, puncturing the tip of my finger on a shard. Cursing, I tossed the bug into a baking dish and rummaged for the small butane torch I used for crème brulée.

The click-hiss of its ignition made me flinch with the memory of the same flame burning my skin.

"No fucking more," I grated, and shoved the memory back.

The tiny electronic device glinted mockingly in the ramekin and I snarled, pushing the flame so close it rebounded from the surface of the porcelain. The bug sizzled and bubbled.

A curl of acrid black smoke recalled the choking terror of the burning plane.

My lips peeled back in a hellish grin. "No. Fucking. More."

As if in response, the bug emitted a tiny gout of flame and melted into a black puddle. Teeth bared, I held the torch on it until it stopped bubbling and grey wisps of ash dotted its surface.

At last, I snapped the torch off. The reek of burning electronics filled the kitchen. The smoke detector activated right on cue, its ear-splitting squeal lashing my nerves. I flung the window open and flapped a dishtowel, trying to hunch my shoulders up high enough to plug my ears.

A few minutes later it quit.

Blessed silence.

I stood in the middle of the kitchen, trembling with reaction while the wind moaned, wringing icy fingers over the destruction I had wrought.

After a long time, I drew a deep breath.

"Well then." My voice sounded loud in the silence.

I blew out a sigh and crunched over the broken crystal to close the window. Turning back to the table, I bent to examine the remains of the bug, now permanently fused to what used to be a perfectly good baking dish.

"Shit," I said mildly. I poked a cautious fingertip at the edge of the ramekin. Still hot, but not hot enough to burn me.

The dish shifted and I spotted the scorch mark on the table under it.

"Well, shit."

I eyed it for a moment, then shrugged. Picking up the ramekin, I pegged it at the wall, too. I didn't put much shoulder into the throw, and the dish split disappointingly into a few large pieces instead of smashing into oblivion.

I wandered over. Maybe I should stomp the remaining pieces, too. Do the job right.

The hole in the drywall caught my attention and I poked at it, idly pulling a few loose chunks off the edges.

"Ah, whatever." I turned away and stretched my arms above my head, the freshly-used muscles lengthening pleasantly and emitting a few crackles. Then I rotated my neck, releasing another snap-crackle-pop.

Crunching across the mess again, I retrieved my phone. My hands were rock-steady when I dialled Parr's number.

To my surprise, he actually answered. "Nick Parr."

"It's Arlene Widdenback." My voice was flat. "You can take your ten grand and shove it up your ass. I'm done with you. And tell Hibbert if he shows up here again, I'll kill him."

"Wh...?" He recovered in an instant. "Would you care to explain what this is about?"

"I don't work with assholes no matter how much they pay," I snarled. "You can take Hibbert and his threats and go fuck yourselves." I punched the End button.

A moment later, the phone vibrated in my hand. Private caller.

Gee, who could that be?

I laid the phone down gently and went to get the broom and dustpan.

Belting out 'I Got Stoned And I Missed It' along with my Dr. Hook CD, I stroked my taping knife over the wet drywall compound, finishing the patch for the night. My hands were steady, my anger banked to a heartening glow in my belly.

I picked up my beer bottle from beside its two empty companions and took another healthy swig. Maybe I'd sleep tonight. That'd be a nice change.

Surveying the fresh patch, I tipped the last swallow of beer down my throat. Tomorrow morning I'd put on a final coat, then sand it when I got home from work; maybe sand some of those gouges out of the floor, too...

My phone vibrated again.

Probably Parr.

Fuck him.

I crossed to the sink and rinsed the last of the mud off the drywall knife before drying it on my comfortably baggy work jeans. Dr. Hook launched into 'Get My Rocks Off', and I growled happily along with the lead singer.

This was the life. Beer, tools, and raunchy music. If only

Hellhound was here, I could top it off with some hot sex. The four basic pillars of happiness.

My growl smoothed to a purr at the thought of Hellhound's fine upstanding pillar of happiness. Mmmm, wouldn't that be nice right now? Too bad he was two hours away and I was in no shape to drive.

Maybe I'd plan a road trip to Calgary in the next day or two.

Grinning, I gathered up my tools. I was carrying them across the basement when the vibration of my phone transmitted itself through the floor above me.

Jesus, how long was Parr going to keep trying? Asshole.

I ignored the urge to run up and check the call display immediately, and finished stowing my tools instead. Climbing the stairs a few minutes later, I froze, listening.

What the hell?

Rhythmic tapping came from the vicinity of the front door.

I hurried up the last couple of stairs to listen again.

It wasn't tapping on the door; it was something else. Dull reports like somebody chopping wood in my front yard.

...crack ...crack.

Silence.

My brain automatically counted back. I'd heard about ten, but there might have been more. It could have been going on the whole time I was in the basement.

Ten made me uneasy. Same as the maximum number of rounds allowed in a handgun magazine.

I shook off my paranoia. It couldn't have been gunshots. Not loud or sharp enough. But what the hell was it?

I was heading toward my office to check the surveillance cameras when the sound of my doorbell made me jump.

Torn, I hesitated in the hallway.

Maybe it was Hibbert with his knife and blowtorch. An involuntary shudder shook me.

But probably not. He'd be kicking the shit out of my door and yelling. Unless he was dropping off another horrible 'gift'.

I swore and hurried to the door to peek out the fisheye lens.

Nothing moved, but there was a bulky dark object draped over my porch railing. It sure as hell hadn't been there earlier.

I couldn't make out its details in the distortion of the fisheye. Fuck, what had Hibbert left me this time?

Stomach clenching, I hurried to my office and powered on the surveillance screen.

"*SHIT!*"

I dashed for the door. Panting more from terror than exertion, I skidded to a halt, my clumsy fingers fumbling the deadbolt.

Come on, come on...

Crouching to present a smaller target, I flung the inside door open.

Oh, God, oh, God, please...

I cracked the screen door to duckwalk sideways onto my porch, my gun tucked beside my leg.

I nearly tripped over a large pistol with an illegal silencer lying on my doormat. Barely glancing at it, I scooped it up left-handed, my heart battering my chest while I stared at my latest gift.

The man slumped over my railing was clearly dead. Only the duct tape binding his hands and feet to the spindles had kept his body from falling. Gunshot wounds had ripped open his knees, hips, crotch, and torso, but the mess of tissue that replaced half his head gave away the end of the story. My porch was slick with blood, the snow beyond darkly spattered.

My heart clenched with fierce relief at the sight of blood-drenched slacks and dress shoes. Not Kane's dark denim or Hellhound's well-worn jeans. Thank God.

So who was this poor corpse?

More to the point, who had brought him here, turned him into a corpse, and then left their gun behind?

Heart pounding, my back to the wall, I sidled toward the door.

I didn't make it.

CHAPTER 16

"Looks like you've got a problem."

I started violently as a huge man clad in disposable coveralls stepped out of the shadow by my garage. He smiled, his gloved hands held away from his body in a conciliatory gesture.

I made a split-second decision. Be Arlene Widdenback.

I jerked up the silenced gun to aim with my left hand, hoping the sudden movement would focus his attention on it while I tucked my own weapon back into its concealed holster. The heavy pistol wavered dangerously in my awkward one-handed grip, and he raised his hands to shoulder height.

"Hey, take it easy," he chided. "I'm a friend. I can help you."

"Bullshit." I straightened out of my crouch and waved the gun at him in a classic novice-shooter move. "Don't come any closer or I'll shoot."

We both knew it was a useless threat. The pistol's slide was fully extended and locked, the magazine's carrier clearly visible in the empty chamber. Completely out of ammo. But he didn't need to know I knew that.

He smiled again, a flash of shark-like teeth below dead-flat eyes. "Calm down. You just killed a guy, I can see you're a little upset."

"I didn't kill him! I don't even know him!"

"Sure you do." Shark teeth again. "Real well, as a matter of fact."

An icy fist of terror crushed the blood from my heart. Was that an Armani suit?

Oh, God, not Dave, don't let it be Dave.

"Who...?" My question ghosted out on a tiny whiff of vapour in the cold air, the gun trembling violently in my hand.

"Check it out." Sharkface waved an expansive hand at the body. "Go on, you're gonna love this."

My trembling legs dragged me the few steps to stand beside the body. Clenching my teeth, I reached out a shaking hand to turn the ravaged head.

A glimpse of the remaining parts of the face made me stumble back, staring.

"What... the..." I slumped against the railing, still goggling at the corpse. I shook myself and tried again. "Why the hell did you shoot Hibbert? On my front step?"

Sharkface grinned. "I didn't. You did. He came to your house and you blew him away just like you told Mr. Parr you would. And now you're going to do exactly what I tell you."

I jerked my chin up in a show of defiance. "I don't think so. I'm going to call the cops."

"You might not want to do that."

I pretended to freeze at the hard edge in his voice, but my heart hammered so hard I didn't have to fake my stammer. "Wh-why?"

"Think about it." He abandoned his pretense of caution and lowered his hands, smirking when I waved the gun at him again. "You punched his lights out in front of a hundred witnesses at the Christmas party. You told the security people he assaulted you. I have witnesses that heard him threaten you and saw him attack you. And you just told Mr. Parr you were planning to kill him. That's what they call 'motive'."

He jerked his chin at the gun in my hand, his smile broadening. "Your fingerprints are on the gun that killed him. I have a guy who'll swear he sold it to you. And don't even think about calling it self-defense. You tortured him before you shot him. Some pretty nasty work with a knife and a blowtorch. And then you shot him in the cock, pumped eight more rounds into him, and then let him suffer some more before you finally blew his head off."

He waved a hand at the blood-splattered snow. "That shit doesn't go away. Even if you clean it up, they can see the residue with special lights. You've got chunks missing from your railing from the bullets, and I made sure to go through some of his soft spots so there are bullets covered with his blood and tissue buried in your yard. If you want to go to jail for a very long time, sweetheart, you just go ahead and call the cops right now."

Christ, Parr was brilliant. Eliminate Hibbert, who was becoming a liability, and force Arlene Widdenback to cooperate at the same time.

Sharkface apparently took my silence for frozen fear. He shrugged. "Or, you can let me help you. I can make this all go away."

"What's in it for you?" I snapped.

"Me? Nothing." He shrugged. "I don't give a shit if you go down." His eyes sharpened. "If you make yourself enough of a nuisance that you need to be removed..." He nodded in the direction of the corpse. "...that would be fun. I like my work."

The winter air bit through my jeans and sweatshirt, and I couldn't suppress my shivering any longer.

His soulless smile widened. "But this is a simple business transaction. Hibbert was bothering you. We solved your problem. Now you say 'thank you very much, Mr. Parr, what can I do for you in return?'"

Nailed! Finally, direct evidence of Parr's shady side.

"Yeah, so he c-can hold this over my head f-forever. F-fuck that." I tried to sound defiant and scared instead of triumphant. Incipient hypothermia definitely helped.

"Honey, you don't have a choice. Mr. Parr owns everybody. Now, put the gun down and let me vanish that body." Sharkface started forward and I made a show of jerking the trigger and looking terrified when the gun didn't fire.

"Now you're just pissing me off." He strode up the steps and I cowered away from his looming bulk as he grabbed my free hand and clamped it over the slide before yanking the gun out of my hands.

My fingerprints on the action. This guy was a pro.

"Pick up the brasses." He jabbed a gloved finger at the empty cartridges scattered on my porch and turned away to release Hibbert's body.

I stooped hurriedly to hide my wolfish grin.

A pro, but a cocky one. Fatal mistake to underestimate me, asshole. I could shoot you right now while you stand there with your big stupid back turned.

But I wouldn't.

Adrenaline pounded in my veins, a heady mix of fear and excitement that heated my blood and froze my fingers. I didn't have to fake the trembling of my hands while I fumbled to pick up the empty cartridges.

"Give them to me."

I straightened to drop the brasses onto his outstretched palm, leaning away as if in terror.

He grinned and dumped them into his pocket. "Jesus, you're a dumb bitch. Fingerprints on the brasses, too. You're making this too damn easy." He withdrew a folded polyethylene tarp from the backpack he wore and shoved it into my hands. "Spread this on the snow under the railing."

I did as directed, and he hoisted Hibbert's body effortlessly over the rail. It thudded into a boneless heap on the tarp and an involuntary squeak of revulsion escaped me.

Sharkface chuckled, a cold merciless sound. "See, that's why you don't want to make a nuisance of yourself. Straighten him out and roll him up."

I shook my head frantically and hunched over to make gagging noises, and Sharkface laughed. "That's it, honey, give 'em some more evidence." He strolled down the stairs to pat me on the ass. "Go on, puke it up."

I jerked away, wrapping my arms around myself and glaring. He ignored me to crouch beside the body, straightening its arms and legs to roll it neatly into the tarp before hoisting the bundle smoothly to his shoulders.

I backed away, pulse pounding. Shit, he could give Kane a run for his money in size and strength. Hopefully not in martial arts, though.

Sharkface jerked his chin at my gory porch. "Better clean that up, sweet-ass. See you later."

"W-wait, you said you were g-going to make this g-go away," I whined.

"I'm making *this*..." he shrugged, hefting the body on his

shoulders. "...go away. Nighty-night, sweet-ass. See you in your dreams."

He strode down my lane into the darkness and a few minutes later I heard the slam of a vehicle door from the direction of my gate. While the engine receded into silence, I stood staring at the slaughterhouse that used to be my front porch. The aftershocks of adrenaline rocked me into violent trembling.

Shit, if anybody drove into my yard now...

Shit, shit, double-shit!

Teeth chattering, I hurried for my garage. Its warmth seemed to emphasize my chill, and I quivered over to my car to check my bug detector before dialling my last secured phone.

"Stemp." He was right on top of it as usual. Thank God.

"Did you catch all that on the cameras?" I demanded.

"Yes. Who was the victim? We couldn't get a positive ID."

"Hibbert." I let that sink in, imagining Stemp's thoughtful expression.

"Interesting," he said after a moment.

"Yeah. And Sharkface made it clear Parr was behind it. We've got him." Fierce triumph vibrated my voice.

"Yes... an excellent development," Stemp said slowly. "Now you'll be in a much better position to gather information."

My elation trickled away. Shit. Of course it wasn't good enough to get Parr on a single murder and extortion charge.

I wrapped my free arm around myself, still shivering. "Let's hope so. Do you have a cleanup crew available? I need to get this mopped up fast in case I have visitors."

"Parr may have you under surveillance. Better if you do

the cleanup yourself."

After a moment of miserable contemplation, I sighed. "I liked the good old days better, when you used to send out helicopters full of armed men whenever anybody threatened me."

"The good old days were never as good as everyone remembers them." His dry tone might have been humour or censure, I couldn't tell. "I'll expect a full report tomorrow after your requalification tests," he added, and the line went dead in my ear, leaving me to whine my self-pity into the unsympathetic phone.

By the time I tottered back into the house and gathered my bucket and rubber gloves, the blood had frozen. Heartily cursing Parr, Sharkface, Hibbert, Fuzzy Bunny, and everyone related to them, I went to work with the frost scraper from my car, scooping the crystalline red goo into my bucket and ferrying it to the bathroom to flush it.

After removing as much as I could, I trotted back and forth to sluice everything with hot water, scrubbing away the remaining stains and splatters. Then it was time to shovel up the bloodstained snow and flush it, too.

At last I straightened slowly, clutching my aching back.

My cleanup wasn't nearly good enough to hide a murder if the police actually investigated, but it was good enough to pass casual inspection. And it was snowing lightly. That would cover any remaining splotches and dribbles.

Note to self: Never shoot anybody unless there's a cleanup crew handy. No wonder Kane and Germain preferred hand-to-hand.

That thought made me groan aloud. In about nine

hours, Germain was going to kick the shit out of me.

Utterly spent, I plodded back into the house and did a nosedive into bed.

Exhaustion and despair made a surprisingly good soporific. When my alarm blared at seven, I slapped it into silence and lay blinking in the darkness for a few moments. It hadn't exactly been a restful sleep, but at least I hadn't screamed myself awake every hour.

Slightly encouraged, I staggered into the shower before heading to the kitchen for a breakfast I hoped would sustain me through the qualification tests.

At least this time I knew what to expect. I was pretty sure I could do the physical fitness portion. And I was almost certain I'd pass the firearms qualification.

But hand-to-hand...

A chill chased itself down my spine and I straightened, squaring my shoulders. Okay, so I was going to get beaten up today. Badly.

But once I was down, Germain wouldn't keep hitting me. Just a bit of pain and then it would be over. A lot less scary than the beatings I'd taken at the hands of men who truly wanted to hurt me.

The large hairy lump in my throat seemed unconvinced by that reasoning. I gulped it down along with a mouthful of toast and peanut butter, and my stomach turned it over distastefully before agreeing to let the toast stay. The hairy lump returned posthaste.

I sank my head into my hands and groaned. If it was only a beating at the hands of a friend, it wouldn't be so bad. But the physical pain would be nothing compared to the knowledge that I had doomed Arnie to prison.

My remaining minutes ticked away in deepening despair, and at last I trudged out to my car, defeated.

CHAPTER 17

Standing in front of the heavy steel door of the secured area, I scraped up every mote of courage I owned.

Okay. I could do this.

Not a big deal. Nice fresh air down there. Not trapped.

I'd done it dozens of times. I'd be fine.

"Good morning, Aydan!"

A little yelp escaped me and I spun to face Jill's fading smile.

"I'm sorry, I didn't mean to startle you." She eyed me with concern. "Are you okay?"

"F-fine." I drew a deep breath and massaged my heart back into place. "It's okay, I was just... lost in thought. Good morning."

She hefted the gym bag she carried. "Looks like we're here for the same thing."

"Uh...?" My sluggish brain made the connection and I loosened my white-knuckled grip on my own bag. "Oh. Yeah. You're doing a requalification, too?"

"Uh-huh." She shot me one of her sparkling smiles. "Let's go do it!"

"Um... you go ahead. I'll be down in a minute." A flicker in her expression prompted me to add, "I'm claustrophobic.

The time-delay chamber really freaks me out, so I'd rather be alone in it."

"Oh. That must suck." Her smile came back. "Well, see you down there, then." She leaned in for the retinal scan and a moment later the chamber swallowed her.

Like being buried alive.

Stop it.

I shoved my face into scanner range and stepped into the chamber before I could run screaming.

Taking a couple of rapid steps forward, I activated the next retinal scan and then stood in front of the locked door with my eyes closed, both hands clenched on my gym bag. Only thirty seconds. I could do this.

The warm, stagnant air still bore a trace of Jill's light cologne. It pressed against my face, slowly smothering me.

My eyes flew open, but the sight of the too-low ceiling made me gasp a panicky breath. I clamped my eyes shut again.

Stop it.

Nice easy yoga breaths. There was lots of air. Only a few seconds left...

I felt for the door handle without opening my eyes.

The muffled click of the lock release made me wrench the door open, catapulting myself into the narrow concrete stairwell.

Stairway to hell.

I abandoned dignity and half-ran, half-fell down the stairs to yank open the door at the bottom. Bounding through it, I sidestepped hard and clapped my back against the wall, squeezing my eyes shut.

Lots of cool fresh air moving across my face. Not trapped. Don't think about the tons of concrete and steel overhead.

Shut up.

Don't think, just breathe.

Breathe...

The previous night's anger roused like a dormant dragon waking in my belly.

Fuck this goddamn shit. There were more than enough people out there trying to scare me. Not going to do it to myself anymore.

Snapping my eyes open, I jerked upright and strode down the hall, spine straight and arms swinging despite the pounding of my heart.

Deep in my belly, I felt my dragon smile.

My dragon blanched a bit when I entered the gym, but I ignored its cowardice and waved an artificially cheerful greeting to Germain and Jill as I headed for the changing room. A few minutes and a stern mental lecture later, I emerged to find them still in animated conversation.

At the sound of the door, Germain glanced over as though he'd forgotten I was there. His smile lines crinkled. "Okay, let's get this show on the road."

As he crossed the gym and bent to pick up his clipboard and paperwork, I caught Jill surveying his rear view with unconcealed appreciation. And what a view it was. Germain's broad shoulders and rippling muscles were deliciously displayed by his snug T-shirt and gym shorts, his dark good looks undiminished even by the harsh gym lights. Jill shot me a mischievous wink, and I grinned back.

"Okay, who's up first?" Germain asked.

"You go ahead, Aydan," Jill said. "I was so busy yakking I haven't changed yet." She vanished into the change room.

I drew a deep breath and stepped up to the starting line

of the obstacle course, shaking out my arms and legs.

"You'll nail it this time, Aydan," Germain encouraged. "Do you want me to call your lap times again?"

"Yeah. Thanks." I sucked in a breath and started to run.

Steady pace.   Up and down the stairs.   Over the obstacles. Controlled fall.

Germain shouted encouragement from the sidelines.

Steady run...

Four laps in, Jill's voice joined Germain's. "Go, Aydan, you're kicking it! Way to go!"

Five laps.   Sweat dampened my T-shirt but I was on pace.

Sixth and final lap. Still on pace. My muscles strained, my breathing accelerating into deep panting.

"Go, Aydan! Go, go! Thirty seconds left! Kill that push-pull!"

I staggered up to the apparatus. Seventy pounds. Six times.

Five. Four. Three...

"Go! Go!"

I threw myself into the pads, sweat slicking the grips. Two.

One...

"You did it!"

I barely heard Germain's triumphant cry as I flopped to the floor, my heart pistoning while I gasped for air.

"Are you okay?" Jill's worried face hovered above me.

I hauled myself into a crouch, propping my elbows on my knees. "...Yeah..." I panted a couple more breaths before shooting a glance at Germain. "How long... before the... carry?"

"Two minutes. Just breathe, Aydan. You're doing fine."

I nodded and concentrated on slowing my breathing. Two minutes. Lots of time to recover. I'd been practicing for this.

I was still breathing hard when Germain spoke again. "Okay, go do it, Aydan."

I wobbled over to the eighty-pound sack.

Only eighty pounds. And I only had to carry it fifty feet. I'd been lugging hundred-pound concrete patio blocks. I could do this.

I squatted and hoisted the sack into my arms. Fuck, since when was this eighty pounds? It felt like a couple hundred.

Shut up and walk.

Muscles straining, I put one foot in front of the other.

Jill's and Germain's shouts of encouragement faded into the thunder of my pulse. The sack slipped and I clenched it tighter. Squeezing the air out of my lungs...

I panted shallow breaths, my vision hazing red, a coppery tang drying my mouth.

Still walking.

One foot in front of the other...

Across the finish line.

The sack fell from my arms and I collapsed on top of it, sucking air.

"Nice work, Aydan!" Germain jogged over to beam down at me. "You nailed it! You just became the oldest female agent to pass the physical fitness qualification! Congratulations!"

I let out a heartfelt groan between gasps. "That'll look... fucking great... on my tombstone."

He laughed and offered me a hand up.

After a moment, I convinced my limp-noodle arm to

raise and accept it.

My victory march back to the bleachers probably looked more like a drunk staggering home after an all-night bender, but I made it. Slumping onto one of the benches, I leaned back to observe the next victim.

Jill's lush curves were accented by modest shorts and a tank top, her shining bob pulled into a clip at the back of her head. Her eyes sparkled as though she was looking forward to the challenge, and she grinned at Germain as she toed the start line.

At his nod, she swung into an easy run, tackling the stairs and obstacles while I shouted as much encouragement as my still-winded condition allowed. Germain joined in occasionally, but in between cheers he watched Jill's voluptuous figure as if mesmerized.

And she was well worth watching. Those soft curves hid a dynamo.

Almost before I realized it, she was powering through the last of the push-pull sequence. I offered a few feeble cheers, but she clearly didn't need them.

At her last pull, Germain clicked the stopwatch, his face alight. "Right on, Jill!" He offered her a jubilant high-five. "That was a joy to watch! Two minutes to the weight carry."

She grinned and wiped the sweat from her forehead, panting.

I had never seen Germain ogle any woman, not even Jack-the-Gorgeous, but I could have sworn he was surreptitiously enjoying Jill's heaving chest.

I sat up a little straighter, amusement tickling me while I watched them exchange a few bantering words. Apparently he had a weak spot for curvy brunettes.

"Two minutes is up."

Jill nodded and squatted beside the sack. Then she hoisted it onto her shoulders and rose to walk slowly but steadily to the finish line.

I joined Germain's applause. Shit, she'd made that look easy. Maybe I could get her to teach me how to do that fireman's-carry thing.

Then again, she was just in better shape than I was. I sighed and tried to comfort myself with the knowledge that she was probably about a decade younger, too. Pushing the big five-oh wasn't exactly the kind of activity that improved my fitness level.

Germain's voice broke into my reflections. "Do you want to do the firearms qualification now, or go straight to the hand-to-hand?"

"I've already done my firearms," Jill said. "So if it's okay with you, Aydan, I'd like to do my hand-to-hand and then I can get cleaned up and go join Tammy and Brock's session upstairs."

I tried not to grimace. Other than the flush in her cheeks and the sweat stains on her tank top, she looked completely recovered.

"Sure," I said. "Go ahead."

At least then I'd have an idea what I'd be up against.

Germain led the way to a large square of mats laid out on the floor, and the two of them faced each other in the centre. Some prearranged signal must have been exchanged, because they suddenly launched at each other.

Jaw sagging, I watched while they fought. Sometimes standing to circle each other warily, other times rolling and grappling on the mats, neither seemed to be gaining the upper hand.

It didn't have the ferocity of a real fight, though. Both

combatants were smiling except for the times when a whoosh of breath indicated a successful strike. At last, Germain pinned Jill to the mat and she tapped out with a groan.

He rolled to his feet and offered her a hand up. She accepted it and they stood panting and grinning at each other, looking for all the world like a couple who'd just rolled out of bed after a particularly satisfying bout of sex.

Jill shook her hair out of its clip and ruffled it as if to dry the sweat, still grinning at Germain. "Well, thanks. Guess I'll get going."

"Thank *you*. Always good to have a worthy opponent." Germain ran a hand through his crisp black curls and offered her a half-bow and a heart-melting smile.

When she turned away, his gaze followed her all the way to the change room before returning to me.

"You're up, Aydan," he said cheerfully.

Heart pounding, I dragged myself to my feet. My mind circled while I plodded over to the mats. Maybe I could miraculously pull something off?

Not a fucking chance.

Come on, think of something! Arnie's life was at stake.

Maybe if I faked an injury?

"Are you ready?" Germain shot me a puzzled frown as I stood across from him on the mats, my arms dangling uselessly.

Of course he expected me to engage him the way Jill had.

And I didn't have a clue how to do that.

"Aydan?" His keen gaze searched my face, his voice softening. "Are you having a problem?"

The words burst out before I could stop them. "I can't do this."

He abandoned his stance to step closer. "I know how

hard it is to fight again after you've killed somebody, but this is safe," he murmured. "I know you can do this. Let's just start with some easy sparring." He stepped back into his stance. "Just relax. It'll be fine."

Goddamn it, I didn't deserve his sympathy. Tears prickled my eyes and I blinked hard.

"I can't, Carl." My voice came out rough and angry. "I can't fight you because I don't know how. I didn't kill that guy with martial arts, it was just a freak accident. I'm just a bookkeeper."

"Aydan..." He dropped his arms and eyed me helplessly. "What do you want me to do here?"

"Just beat me up and get it over with." My voice cracked and I jerked my chin up, cursing my weakness.

His face twisted. "While you just stand there and take it? I don't think so."

Weariness overcame me and I sank to the mat. "Then fail me and call it a day."

I buried my face in my hands. Fail me the way I'd failed Arnie.

Only I deserved it. He didn't.

The mat creaked as Germain crouched beside me. His hand warmed my shoulder. "I'm not going to fail you. Hand-to-hand isn't even a core requirement. If your cover is that deep, you need to talk to Stemp about it. He can be a bit of a jerk sometimes, but he'd never jeopardize an agent's cover."

Slow hope straightened my spine. Germain was right. I might still be able to pull this out of the fire.

All I had to do was stop trying to tell the truth.

I drew a deep breath and faced Germain. "Thanks, Carl, I didn't think of that." I squeezed his hand and rose. "You might have just saved a couple of lives."

He gave me a half-smile. "I thought it might be something like that." His brow furrowed. "So are you going to take your firearms qualification?"

I straightened, my belly warming with renewed optimism. "Hell, yeah."

CHAPTER 18

"That's a relief." I grinned at Germain's thumbs-up as I emerged from the firing range. "I've been worrying that Stemp would change his mind about letting me keep my gun after I failed the first time." I hung the protective earmuffs on a peg and pulled out my earplugs.

"How many times did you have to suck his cock to get that deal?" The rough voice made me spin to face my unknown adversary, my heart kicking my chest while my hand flew instinctively to my holster.

Germain's restraining hand landed on my shoulder. "Is that how you passed your last qualification, Holt?"

The hard-looking blond man flushed, his hands clenching into knots at his sides. "Look who's talking, you fucking brown-noser. You've got your tongue so far up Stemp's ass it's pathetic." His fists jerked as if he was fighting to control them as he took a threatening step forward, his voice rising. "You think you're such a fucking golden boy with your fucking squeaky-clean record and all your fucking black belts! Do you go up to Stemp's office after hours for a nice long suck on his cock? Or maybe you like getting it up the ass!"

His face twisted to sneer at Germain's hand, still

gripping my shoulder. "What, are you sharing pussy with Stemp?" He snapped his steel-blue gaze back to me while I stood flabbergasted by the ugliness pouring out of his lips. "That's it, baby, fuck your way to the top," he spat. "Come and see me later and I'll give you a little boost." He hoisted a hand into his crotch and thrust his hips at me, his lips snarling in a parody of a grin. "Believe me, it'll be better than anything you're getting from *him*."

Germain's grip tightened and he spoke before I could. "That's enough." Through the red haze of anger, I dimly felt the insistent pressure of his hand steering me toward the door. "Come on, Aydan, I'll walk you up to Stemp's office and you can file a sexual harassment complaint."

Holt's face twisted, flecks of spit spraying from his lips as he bellowed, "Yeah, that's it! Take your fucking whore and go crying to Stemp, you fucking pansy-ass..."

The torrent of hate was cut off by the closing door as Germain half-dragged me into the corridor. "Walk away," he urged, his grip propelling me down the hallway. "Just walk away."

"What... who... what the hell was that?" I sputtered. "Who the hell pissed in his cornflakes?"

"I did." Apparently deciding I wasn't going to do anything rash, Germain relaxed his hold but he didn't slow his stride. I hurried to keep up as he spoke again. "I shouldn't have reacted to him, and I'm sorry you got caught in that. Holt isn't... wasn't a bad agent, but an op went south on him last summer and he had some pretty bad trauma. He tried to come back too soon and I had to fail him on his hand-to-hand. That's when we discovered he'd also developed severe anger-management issues."

"I'll say." Reaction set in, and I leaned trembling against

the wall beside the time-delay chamber. "Holy shit. That was downright scary."

"He's actually doing better. He's only attacking with words now. He lost it completely during the combat qualification and I had to lay a pretty serious beating on him just in self-defence. That's why he's got such a hate on for me. Stemp put him on a desk job and confiscated his weapon, so he can only shoot under supervision in the range until Dr. Rawling okays him for duty."

"They actually let him handle a weapon?"

Germain grimaced. "He's usually not that bad."

We stepped into the chamber and I drew a deep shaky breath, mentally counting down the time delay. I twitched when Germain spoke again. "He'll probably apologize to both of us later. He really is trying hard, but it likely set him off when you said you'd gotten to keep your gun even though you'd failed the qualification. And then I sent him over the edge with my smart-ass comment."

"I guess I can understand why it would piss him off that Stemp hadn't confiscated my gun. I wouldn't have said anything if I'd known he was there, but I was wearing my earplugs and I had my back to the door." The lock released and I sprang into the lobby, sucking in a frantic breath of freedom.

Germain eyed me with concern. "You'd better sit down for a minute. You're shaking like a leaf."

"I'm okay." I drew a deep breath and let it out slowly. "It's just that damn coffin-chamber. It always freaks me out."

"All right, if you're sure." He gestured toward the stairs. "Let's go and talk to Stemp and you can file that complaint."

I plodded forward on shaking legs. "If you say he's really

trying and he's getting better, I won't file a formal complaint. But I think Stemp needs to know. And Dr. Rawling."

He relaxed into a smile. "You're a good person, Aydan."

When I tapped on his office door, Stemp looked up from his computer. "Come. Sit. How did the qualifications go?" His eyes sharpened as Germain swung the door shut behind us before taking his seat.

"Passed with flying colours," Germain said easily, pushing the evaluation sheets across the desk.

Stemp glanced over them before his gaze flicked up to pin me to the chair. "This is physical fitness and firearms. Was there a problem with the hand-to-hand?"

"Um... not really." I squirmed under his scrutiny. "Actually, before we get to that, I just wanted to mention that we had a bit of a run-in with, um..." I turned to Germain. "...Holt? What's his first name?"

"Greg Holt." Germain squared his shoulders. "It was mostly my fault. I provoked him."

Stemp's reptilian gaze flattened. "What happened?"

"We just had words," I said quickly. "But he seemed really angry. More so than what was warranted under the circumstances. I thought you should know."

"Do you want to file a complaint?"

"No."

Stemp eyed me for a moment longer. "Very well. Noted. What about the hand-to-hand?"

I drew a deep breath. "I can't do it."

"Can't? Or won't?" Stemp shot a narrow look at Germain. "Did you do any evaluation at all?"

Germain gave him an impassive cop face. "No."

"Why not?"

"Because I can't evaluate combat skills if someone just

stands there and lets me hit them."

Any other human being would have betrayed some of the irritation Stemp had to be feeling.

He didn't even blink. "Thank you, Germain. Dismissed."

Germain rose and left, closing the door quietly behind him.

Stemp contemplated me in silence for a long moment before speaking. "Explanation."

My heart lurched into my throat to vibrate there.

I held his gaze until I was certain my voice would come out level. "A couple of weeks ago I asked you to redact the records when I killed Helmand Senior. Now I'm asking you to redact the part of Kane's report that conflicts with mine in regards to the killing of that enemy agent. And I'm asking you to cancel my hand-to-hand combat requalification. There can't be a record of me having any martial arts skills whatsoever. It's essential to my cover."

Stemp leaned back, crossing his arms over his chest. "If you persist in displaying your martial arts skills for all to see, it's pointless for me to redact records."

I wrung the arm of the chair as a substitute for wringing his neck, and kept my voice even. "I didn't display any martial arts. Kane was mistaken."

"Kelly." This time I could actually hear a hint of frustration in his tone. "Kane is our top agent, and a master in several disciplines of martial arts. If he says he saw you use martial arts, I'm strongly inclined to believe him. Particularly when the autopsy corroborates his report."

"For *fucksakes-*" I clenched my teeth and backpedaled, trying for reasonable tones. "Okay, but it wasn't in public. There were no witnesses. I've worked with Kane for a long time and I trust him. Now I'm trusting you to protect my cover."

His silence expanded to occupy the entire room, closing around my throat while I stared at him. The thought of Arnie behind bars made my stomach twist. Stemp had to do this.

He *had* to.

Emotion rose, choking my voice. "Please. If you don't let this drop, it could cost a man's life."

Stemp moved at last. Pinched the bridge of his nose, squeezing his eyes shut. "You're asking me to simply take you on faith." When he opened his eyes again, I saw a weary man worn down by the betrayals of the world. "I can't take *anyone* on faith. You know that."

I bowed my head, staring at my white-knuckled hands while they throttled each other in my lap.

"If you could just give me a name in your secret chain of command," Stemp said softly. "You've trusted me with the knowledge of its existence. Trust me enough to explain why you can't have this on your record as an agent."

"I can't." My voice vibrated with hollow despair.

His silence made me clench my fists, anger welling up like glowing magma. I jerked my chin up to glare at him. "Why the fuck does it even matter whether I've got the stupid hand-to-hand qualification? Germain says it's not a core requirement. I've passed your basic qualification tests. And I already told you you'd be putting people in danger if you promoted me to being an agent. Why can't you just let this go?"

"Because I need to know the full capabilities of all my agents," he said quietly. "Lives depend on it."

"If you put me in a situation where somebody's life depends on me knowing martial arts, *they will die!* Count on it!" I balled my fists in my hair to keep from slamming them on his desk.

He stared into my eyes. "Is the life of that one man so important that you would sacrifice others to save him?"

My anger deserted me, leaving nothing but an empty shell. I slumped in the chair. "I don't have a choice." My voice came out utterly hopeless.

After a long pause, he said, "I've been in your shoes. Deep cover can be... extraordinarily difficult."

When I dragged my gaze up to his, there was sympathy in Stemp's expression.

He let out a short breath. "All right. I'll alter your personnel records to indicate you're not qualified in hand-to-hand combat, and all future assignments will be based on that. And I'll redact that portion of Kane's report and cancel your requalification. No lives will be lost through unrealistic expectations." He gave me a wintry smile. "Next time, don't get caught snapping necks."

A flood of relief floated my head dizzily to the ceiling. "Th-thank you," I whispered. I sucked in a breath, trying not to faint. "Thank you."

He nodded, expressionless as always. "Dismissed."

After waiting a moment to make sure my legs would hold me, I rose and tottered out.

When I emerged from Stemp's office, Holt stood in the corridor. His hands flexed at his sides and he shifted from foot to foot, his gaze locked on me. I avoided eye contact and kept walking.

As I passed, he snapped, "Wait."

It didn't sound like anger.

I turned, letting the motion place my back to the wall while I regarded him warily. Down the corridor, Germain strolled out of my office and halted, watching us.

Holt spared him an uncomfortable glance before returning his attention to me. "I'm sorry," he blurted.

Germain lingered, eyeing Holt with his neutral cop face firmly in place.

Holt's gaze flickered in his direction, his lantern jaw tightening. His next words strained out between his teeth. "I owe you both an apology. I lost control. I'm sorry." His steely gaze sought mine, and I read his sincerity despite the bunching of his shoulders. "I reviewed the parts of your mission reports that are accessible through my..." The muscles in his jaw rippled. "...current security clearance. You've got nothing to prove to an asshole like me and I deserve that harassment complaint. I'm going to tell Stemp that now."

Cautious sympathy tugged at my heart. As he turned away with his face set in hard lines, I touched his sleeve.

"I only told him you were angry. I didn't file a complaint."

He froze. "Why not?"

"Carl told me you'd had a tough time. I know what that's like."

Holt turned slowly to face me, tension easing from his posture. His gaze searched my face while his jaw worked as if struggling for words. "Thanks," he muttered at last. "But that's no excuse."

"No." I gave him a rueful lift of my eyebrows. "But I've had to make some apologies of my own. All we can do is keep trying."

His jaw eased, his shoulders lowering. "Thanks." This time he sounded as though he meant it. "Can we start over? I'm Greg Holt. Part-time asshole."

I grinned despite myself and shook his outstretched hand. "Aydan Kelly. Part-time fraud artist and porn star, thanks to my Arlene Widdenback cover."

An answering grin softened his craggy features. "Yeah, I got that from your mission reports. It's got to be shitty living with that cover, but it's nice to meet you." He turned to Germain, his smile vanishing into a cop face as unreadable as Germain's own. "Thanks. I'll do better."

Germain's keen brown eyes measured him for a moment before he nodded. "I know you will. You're welcome."

Holt nodded and headed for Stemp's door, squaring his shoulders.

I continued down the hall and Germain leaned close to murmur, "Don't trust him, Aydan. I think he's basically a good guy, but he's unstable right now. And he's almost as advanced in hand-to-hand combat as Kane and me."

I sighed. "Great. Thanks for the heads-up." I glanced at my watch. "Ten whole minutes before our briefing. I'm going to go and get a breath of fresh air."

Germain nodded. "Coffee time for me." He headed for the lunchroom.

Wandering down the sidewalk a few minutes later I drew a deep breath of cold, clean air. My legs still quivered, and I willed strength into them.

I'd passed my tests. Arnie was safe. Parr had played into our hands.

So why wasn't I dancing down the street in sheer euphoria?

Stemp's sympathetic expression rose in my memory and my guts squirmed. Dammit, why was I feeling guilty? He'd screwed me over so many times...

Because he'd had to. Doing his duty for our country.

And now I felt like a total shit for lying to him.

I hissed through my teeth. I hadn't lied. Arnie's life *was* at stake. And this was the right thing to do. At least now any agent who worked with me would be safer because they wouldn't expect me to be Jane Bond, super-ninja.

My waist pouch vibrated and I grabbed my phone, thankful for the distraction.

Private caller.

Tension gathering in my shoulders, I thumbed the Talk button. "Hello?"

"Hey, sweet-ass. Meet me at the drive-in tonight at eight."

It wasn't difficult to sound stiff. "Who is this?"

"You know who it is."

"What do you want?"

"You don't listen very well, do you? I want you to meet me at the drive-in at eight tonight."

I clenched my teeth. "It's winter. The drive-in is closed."

"Aren't you the bright one. Later, sweet-ass." Sharkface hung up.

I swore and spun to stomp back to the office.

CHAPTER 19

Dropping onto the couch in my office, I returned a terse 'hi' to Kane's pleasant greeting. Spider mumbled a dispirited hello as well, and I dragged myself out of my mood.

"Everything okay, Spider?" I eyed him worriedly.

"Yeah."

The gloomy monotone was so unlike him that Kane and I exchanged a glance of concern.

"What's..." I began, only to be interrupted by Stemp's arrival.

Spider pressed his lips together and gave me a tiny headshake, and I let it drop. A few moments later Germain arrived, coffee in hand, and Stemp called our meeting to order.

"Kelly, give us your progress report on Afterburner."

Kane straightened in his chair, his eyes igniting. "There's progress?"

"Um..." I drew a deep breath, schooling my expression into what I hoped was a detached cop face.

Do not let remembered fear get to you. Summon the anger.

I addressed the far wall of my office. "Hibbert left another box on my doorstep late yesterday afternoon. It was..."

My throat went dry.

Calm down. He's dead. It's over.

"...just another personal threat," I said steadily. "So I called Parr and forced his hand. I told him I didn't want his money and I was finished with him and with Hibbert's threats. And I eliminated the bug."

Stemp's emotionless façade was disturbed by the fractional lift of his eyebrow.

"I did it in a plausible way," I assured him before he could ask. "It would have sounded accidental to them."

He nodded and the eyebrow resumed its status quo.

A sudden thought struck me. "Was there a wiretap on my phone line?" I asked.

"No."

"Good. Can you get the analysts to go back to calling me instead of texting?"

I didn't bother to add that I'd failed to get their warning until far too late last night. And since I'd just finished lying to Stemp about being an agent, it seemed like a bad time to display my incompetence.

Stemp nodded. "I'll inform them."

I turned my attention back to the others. "So Parr responded by murdering Hibbert."

"*What?*" Spider's yelp sounded as though something in his chair had bitten him. Kane and Germain jerked forward, their faces intent.

"Sharkface..." I hesitated. "Do we know who that guy was? Is?"

"Kevin Barnett. Suspected enforcer for Fuzzy Bunny," Stemp supplied. "Confirmed, after last night."

"Kevin?"   I   hesitated,   momentarily   distracted.

"Seriously?"

"Yes. Is there a problem?"

"No. He... just... I mean, *Kevin*? He looks like he should be... I don't know, Rocco or Slade or something."

Everyone except Spider eyed me as if questioning my sanity.

I pulled myself together. "Um. Anyway. I guess Parr's bug had picked up Hibbert's threats. So Sharkface... um, Barnett... tortured Hibbert using the same methods Hibbert had promised to use on me..."

Don't think about it. *Don't...*

"...and then brought him to my place," I continued with barely a waver in my voice. "...where he tied him to my porch railing and emptied a magazine into him just for fun before finishing him off with a shot to the head."

"On your *front porch*?" Spider sounded strangled. "That's horrible!"

"It was a hell of a mess," I agreed. "And he left the murder weapon on my doormat to be sure I'd pick it up and get fingerprints on it, and also forced me to pick up the brasses to get prints on those, too. If I really was Arlene Widdenback, I'd be totally hooped."

"Smart," Kane murmured.

"Yeah. Sharkface is a pro, but he's a little overconfident." My grin showed a few more teeth than usual. "He thinks I'm a harmless bimbo."

A tiny smile tugged at the corner of Stemp's mouth. "An impression you ably enhanced. I did enjoy the charade with the empty pistol."

Unexpected pride warmed me. "Thanks." I gave him a grin before returning my attention to the others. "So my good buddy Sharkface offered to solve my little problem by removing the body, but he kept the murder weapon as leverage. And he wants to meet me tonight. I expect he'll have some demands."

"You didn't mention that last night." Stemp eyed me questioningly.

"No, he just called a few minutes ago. I'm meeting him at the drive-in at eight."

"How many times have I warned you about sneaking out at night to meet your boyfriends?" Germain teased, mischief glinting in his eyes.

I hung my head in mock penitence. "Sorry, Dad."

"Do you want backup?" Kane asked.

"Ummm..." I frowned into middle distance. "I'm... not sure."

No one spoke while I pondered.

"On one hand, I'm not too worried because he underestimates me and he doesn't know I'm armed," I thought out loud. "...but he's a fucking big bastard, so if he gets physical I'll have to pull my gun. And he'd report that to Parr if I let him live. But it'd blow my cover if he turned up dead."

"So maybe... yeah," I finished. "I don't want anybody within visual range, but if you can be in the general vicinity, that would be good. I'll leave my phone line open. If you hear anything going wrong over the phone or if you lose the connection, you could show up 'coincidentally'. I'd rather have him think I have to depend on you to rescue me."

Kane eased back in his chair, relaxing. "That's a good idea. If I have to make an appearance, you can pretend you were meeting me to talk about Yana's luggage."

"That'll work." I gave him a smile.

"Very well." Stemp rose. "We'll leave it there for now.

We can strategize more effectively once you meet with Barnett tonight and find out what Fuzzy Bunny's next demand will be." He fixed Spider with a reptilian eye. "Have you determined a way that Ms. Mellor and Kelly can work simultaneously in the network without exchanging memories?"

"Yeah, I think so," Spider mumbled.

"Good. Brief Kane and Kelly, and then you can all go back to your regular decryptions this afternoon. Germain, please join me in my office for a briefing on your next assignment."

Germain stood and the two men strode out.

As soon as they cleared the doorway, I leaned closer to speak softly to Spider. "What's up? Is something wrong?"

"No..." He sighed. "Well... yeah, kind of. I just..." His long fingers worried at his shirt cuff. "It's this thing with Tammy." He twisted the cuff button back and forth, not looking at me. "I'm not controlling her directly, but... I might as well be. I'm the team lead. That makes it my responsibility." He hesitated. "I mean, you know, morally."

"Um." I shot a look at Kane, hoping he'd contribute something useful.

He dropped his gaze to frown at his toes. Damn.

"I don't know what to say, Spider," I said. "I understand what you mean, but it's..."

Shit, do not blurt out 'better than what Stemp wants me to do'.

"...um, she wouldn't object if she knew about it," I said instead. "Remember, I've been in her mind. She's happy to help, and it wouldn't bother her a bit even if she knew she was being controlled."

"Really?" A faint flush of hope stained Spider's cheeks as

he looked up.

"Yeah, really."

"Oh." The word came out on a gust of breath as he leaned back in his chair. "Oh, good." He sat still for a moment as if thinking it over, then straightened, his usual buoyant smile returning. "Thanks, Aydan, that really helps. Do you want to go over my idea for the network now?"

I glanced at my watch. "Can we do it after lunch? I'm starving."

"No problem." He bounced to his feet. "I'm going to go and call Linda. She was worried when I was so down in the dumps this morning."

I eased out a secret breath of relief. "I'm glad you're feeling better. Say hi to Linda."

"I will." He hurried out, smiling.

After he disappeared, I sank back with a sigh.

"You handled that well." Kane's deep baritone warmed me.

I met his smile with a rueful one of my own. "If only all moral dilemmas were so easily resolved."

"True." He chuckled, then sobered, assessing me. "Was that more than a rhetorical comment?"

"N..." I thought about it for a moment. "Actually, yeah, I guess it was." I glanced at my watch. "Do you have time to walk over to the Melted Spoon for a sandwich? I'm stiffening up after all that exercise this morning, and I could use some fresh air."

"Sounds good." He rose. "Let's go."

Strolling down the sidewalk beside Kane a few minutes later, I rolled my neck and shoulders and drew a deep breath of bright cold air. I wasn't quite sure how to broach my question.

"Loosening up?" Kane asked.

"Yeah, a little. I think I'll be stiff tomorrow, though."

He walked on in silence for a moment before shooting me a sidelong glance. "So how did it go?"

I shook myself out of my abstraction. "Um, what?"

"Your qualification tests. How did they go?"

"Oh. Fine. I passed both."

His brow furrowed. "I thought you were taking three."

"No, just fitness and firearms."

"But Germain said he was doing your hand-to-hand this morning."

"Um." My steps slowed and I glanced around us. No pedestrians were within earshot, but I leaned a little closer anyway. "I'm not doing the hand-to-hand. And it's on my record that I don't have any martial arts skills."

He stopped to frown down at me. "Aydan, I saw you-"

"No, you didn't." I held up a silencing hand when he tried to speak. "Really, you didn't. It was just a freak accident. Think back to what you saw. Every detail."

His gaze flicked into middle distance, his brows still drawn together while he reviewed the scene. "Yana stepped into the cabin and raised the weapon. I didn't realize what it was until Thomas dropped dead. She swung it around to aim at you and I jumped her at the same time you hit the floor. Her accomplice ran in from the rear cabin and she yelled at him to get you. You were rolling to your feet. You ducked under his arm and got behind him and broke his neck."

I hissed a breath of frustration between my teeth. "No, I didn't. You were dealing with Yana, so you only saw me moving and then when you looked up again he was dead. I got him in an arm-bar hold and tore something in his arm. Then he tripped and couldn't save himself with his bad arm.

His head got caught between two seats and he broke his own neck when his body fell."

Kane stared at me in silence for a moment. "I suppose that's what you told Stemp," he said at length.

"Yes. And I asked him to redact the description of the fight from your report."

Muscles rippled in his jaw. "Aydan, why do you persist in diminishing yourself like this? I know what a competent agent you are. So does Stemp, and Germain, and anybody else who's ever worked with you. Why-"

"Stop."

To my surprise, he did. He stood looking down at me in silence, his hurt and frustration showing in the hard lines around his mouth.

My heart clenched. "John..."

What the hell could I say? The truth only made things worse between us.

Resignation bowed my shoulders. Truth was a luxury only civilians could afford. And no matter how I tried to deny or avoid it, I wasn't a civilian anymore.

For the first time since I met John Kane, I looked up into his troubled grey eyes and did the kindest thing I could think of.

I lied.

CHAPTER 20

"Look, John." I glanced around the deserted sidewalk, then sighed. "I'm going to tell you something. If you bring it up again, I'll deny I ever said it."

"Wait." He dipped into his coat and extracted a bug detector. We both eyed its steady green light for a moment before he pocketed it again. "Let's walk."

I pushed my reluctant feet into motion. It didn't help.

"What do you want to tell me?" he murmured.

"I don't want to tell you anything..."

Right there. That was the last moment of honesty between us. Maybe I should build a little memorial cairn by the sidewalk.

I forced the words out. "...but you're right. I've been deep undercover for years, in a mission so secret that it's even above Stemp's pay grade. I'm supposed to be just a bookkeeper. Finding the network key and getting sucked into working with you has been a disaster for my cover. I can't walk away from my work with you, but every time somebody reports a skill I shouldn't have, it jeopardizes my other mission. That's why I can't use any martial arts, that's why I make stupid mistakes in my missions, and that's why I can't even think about having any kind of committed relationship. I just can't drop this cover. I'm sorry you've gotten involved, and I'm sorry I keep hurting you, and-"

"Shh. It's all right." When I looked over at him, the hard lines had eased from his face. "Thank you," he said quietly. "Thank you for finally trusting me with the truth."

My groan erupted despite my best efforts.

"Don't worry, Aydan," he said gently. "You know I'll protect this with my life."

I rubbed my hands over my face, wishing I could scrub away my guilt. "That's what I'm afraid of."

"Don't be."

"John." I clutched his sleeve, drawing him to a halt. "This doesn't make things better. Nothing is going to change."

He gazed down at me with a bittersweet smile. "I understand that nothing's going to change. But..." His eyes softened. "Now that I know why, it's already better."

Unable to face him, I turned away and he fell into step beside me again.

After a couple of minutes of silent walking, I turned to him again. "Can I ask you something?"

"Of course."

"Do you ever..." I stopped.

Tried again. "Last night. When I found the body. It was... pretty ugly. Blood everywhere. And I..."

I stopped again. Maybe I didn't really want to know.

"You what?" Kane prompted after a moment.

"I..." The words rushed out before I could stop them. "How fucked up is it that I looked at Hibbert and thought, 'Oh thank God it's nobody I care about', and my next thought was 'Jeez, this is going to be a real pain in the ass to clean up'? I mean, another human being was tortured and killed practically in front of me, and I... I just..."

Kane's hand found mine, giving it a brief squeeze. "You turned off your emotions and did what had to be done."

My throat closed and my voice came out very small. "I hate this."

"Me, too."

I stared up at him and his lips twisted in a bleak smile. "What, you think I'm some gung-ho action hero who loves danger and violence?"

"Well, I... I mean, you're the top agent in the service. You've been doing this for a long time."

He blew out a breath. "I gain satisfaction from knowing I'm protecting innocent people. The results are important to me. But the process? And the emotional toll? No."

We reached the Melted Spoon and he held the door for me. We stood in silence in the queue and didn't speak again until we were seated at one of the corner tables, our backs to the wall with a commanding view of the tiny bistro.

I swallowed a bite of my chicken and brie panini. "So... what would you do if you weren't doing... what you do?"

"I don't know." Kane sipped his coffee and his gaze flicked over the scattered patrons as if automatically evaluating threat levels. "I've been thinking about that more and more lately." He grimaced. "I'm not getting any younger. Big five-oh next year. I promised myself that the day I feel like I'm losing my edge, I'll quit. Everybody makes mistakes and I've had to live with the consequences of mine, but at least I know anyone would have made the same decisions given the knowledge I had at the time."

He stared into middle distance for a few moments, old ghosts haunting his eyes. He gave his head a tiny shake and returned his attention to me. "But I refuse to endanger anyone just because my ego doesn't want to admit I'm past my prime."

"Is it that easy? Can you just walk up to Stemp and say 'I quit'?"

"It won't be easy." He took a bite of his sandwich and chewed, his eyes focused somewhere beyond the opposite wall. After a moment, he swallowed and returned his gaze to me. "There are always loose ends. They'll always need me for just one more thing. There's always the knowledge that something from my past could come back and bite me. But sooner or later everybody has to make that break. Stemp did it when he was a lot younger than I am now. I don't think I'd want to transition into management the way he did, but..." He shook his head. "I just don't know."

"You could always open a restaurant. You're such an amazing chef. Or how's your book coming along? Maybe you'll become a famous children's author."

He chuckled. "Maybe. How about you? What's your end game?" He took another bite of his sandwich, clearly returning the ball to my court.

"I..." My panini suddenly lost its flavour and I laid it on the plate to sink my head into my hands. "If I survive it'll be a fucking miracle," I mumbled.

"Plan on it," Kane growled.

Startled, I looked up to meet eyes like grey lasers.

"Plan on it," he repeated fiercely. "You need that vision. You need something that's so important to you that you'll keep fighting even when you know you can't win."

"I do that anyway. It's called being too stupid to know when to quit," I quipped, trying to lighten the mood.

"I'm not joking." The intensity of his gaze made me shiver. "Aydan, we've worked together for nine months.

You've proved over and over that you're willing to die for your team, and I can't tell you how much I admire your courage. But being brave enough to die isn't what really matters. You need to be brave enough to live, too."

My throat closed. Unable to speak or even swallow, I dropped my gaze.

Get it together. Gulp down that lump in your throat and make a joke.

I watched my hands wrapping the remains of my panini in a napkin.

Say something, dammit.

Say anything.

I sprang up and hurried out, my sandwich squishing in my grip.

"Aydan-"

The closing door cut off Kane's words, and I broke into a jog. The icy air felt good on my hot face and I blinked away the wetness in my eyes. Goddammit, I was so sick of being afraid.

Fuck this shit. Maybe I should just march into Stemp's office and tell him I quit.

But even if I quit, I wouldn't be safe. Not until I was free of Fuzzy Bunny.

Trapped.

"Aydan, wait!"

I picked up the pace, my breath coming in sobs that weren't from exertion. Goddammit, they all want something from you. It's never enough. No matter how much you give, they demand more and more and more until there's nothing left...

The sound of running footsteps made me accelerate again. Gaining on me. Dammit, dammit, just leave me the hell alone!

"Aydan, stop. I'm sorry." Kane caught up to run beside me. "Please stop and talk to me."

I slammed on the brakes so suddenly he overshot, pounding forward a couple more strides before whirling to hurry back.

I hunched over to avoid his eyes, bracing my elbows on my knees and panting.

"I'm sorry, Aydan. I didn't mean to-"

"Forget it."

"No. I was out of line. I had no right to preach to you and I'm sorry-"

"It's fine." I smeared my sleeve over my face and straightened to face him. "You weren't preaching, and you don't need to apologize." I straightened my spine and started down the sidewalk toward the office, dumping the mangled panini into a convenient garbage bin.

"Come back to the Melted Spoon and I'll buy you another sandwich," Kane coaxed.

"I can't eat right now." I kept going.

"You only ate a couple of bites. You need to eat. Aydan, please." He caught up again to lay a restraining hand on my arm. "If you won't accept my apology, at least accept a sandwich. I promise not to bother you while you eat it."

I stopped and blew out a sigh. "No, it's fine. I told you, you don't need to apologize. You haven't done anything wrong. I'm not mad at you. I just... need some time alone, okay? I'll see you back at the office at one."

He hesitated, the storm-grey of his eyes betraying his distress. "All right," he said at last.

I walked away without looking back, trying to hide my trembling.

CHAPTER 21

By the time I tottered back into Sirius Dynamics at ten to one, I felt as though I'd been chewed up, digested, and shit out on gravel.

Dragging myself to the security wicket, I signed in, my shaking hands barely managing the pen. Leo laid his half-eaten submarine sandwich on the desk behind the bullet-proof glass before activating the turntable that delivered my fob. It arrived with a waft of bacon scent that made my stomach unleash a ferocious growl, and I cursed the idiocy that had made me walk the only route in town where there were no food stores.

Well, tough. I'd just have to wait until coffee break.

I turned for the stairs, still berating myself. Why the hell had I let Kane get to me? He wasn't trying to manipulate me; he was just being a friend. Watching out for me.

The truth niggled at the back of my mind. Now that he'd made me think about it, I realized I honestly didn't expect to survive. Every damn day I expected to be captured, tortured, and killed. Every one of my plans was subconsciously prefixed with 'if I'm still alive'.

What the hell kind of life was that?

A shitty one, that's what.

Time to change that.

I growled and hauled myself up the stairs. Trailing into my office, I was peeling off my jacket when a delicious aroma made my head snap around like a bird dog on point.

There was a paper bowl on my desk. I hurried over.

Soup. The Melted Spoon's signature cream of celery and blue cheese. My favourite.

With a chicken-and-brie panini beside it.

And a paper napkin folded into a rose.

For a moment I just stood there wearing a big sappy smile. Then I dropped into the chair and started inhaling food.

By the time Spider arrived a few minutes later, there was nothing left but crumbs and a grin. My smile widened at the sight of Spider's cheerful face.

"You look a lot happier," I greeted him.

He flopped onto my sofa, smiling. "I feel so much better! I was just... I felt so guilty, but I didn't know what to do. If I quit they'd never hire me back, and there are no other jobs for me in Silverside unless I want to sling burgers. And with Linda working at the hospital here, and our wedding coming up..." He shook his head. "Thanks, Aydan. You're the best friend ever."

Embarrassed, I mumbled, "I'm glad I could help," and changed the subject. "So you've set a date?"

"Yes." His cheeks glowed, his hazel eyes bright. "Well, kind of. Middle of August for sure, but we haven't decided which weekend yet."

"That's great..." I trailed off as Kane appeared in the doorway.

He hesitated and I waved him in, feeling suddenly shy. As he took a seat, I forced myself to meet his eyes despite the heat in my cheeks.

"Thank you for lunch," I said. "I was starving. And it was delicious."

He smiled. "You're welcome."

I was sinking into the warm grey of his eyes when Spider's voice rescued me. "Here, Aydan, let's trade places and then we can get started. I think I've figured out a way for you to avoid Tammy in the network."

Several hours later I handed over my network key to Spider and he accepted it and strode out, whistling. I rose and stretched the kinks out of my stiffened muscles.

Kane wandered over to lounge against the doorframe, and I tried not to let my attention drift away from his face and across those broad shoulders. Over that hard-muscled chest and down those beautifully-defined abs to...

I jerked my gaze up again when he spoke. "Do you have time for a beer?"

"Um." I squinted at my watch and let out a sigh. Five minutes to spare. "I'd like to, but I can't. I have to go to... um, a class. And then I need to get organized to meet Sharkf... Barnett tonight."

"Oh, what class are you taking?" Kane's interested expression turned uncertain at the sight of my grimace.

"It's, um..." I averted my eyes under the guise of massaging my headache. "An anger-management class. Stemp's making me go."

"Oh."

There was an awkward pause while I waited for him to assure me I didn't need the class and Stemp was an idiot.

"Well, that's good," he said. "You'll get a lot out of it."

"Thanks," I muttered, determinedly holding onto my temper.

He chuckled. "I didn't mean that as an insult. It's a good class. I found it quite helpful when I took it a few years ago."

"Oh." I met his eyes with relief. "Does Stemp make everybody take it?"

His sexy laugh lines crinkled. "No, just hotheads like you and me." He sobered. "I'll see you tonight. I'll be in place by seven-thirty. Call me with one of the burner phones when you're on your way to the drive-in. Good luck."

He left, and I sighed and gulped a couple of painkillers before trailing reluctantly down the hall.

When I poked my head in the meeting room door, my heart sank. Shit, of course Greg Holt would be there.

A couple of other men sat at the table, too, and Dr. Rawling looked up from his seat at the end of the table. "Hi, Aydan. Welcome. Please come in."

I sidled in to perch in the chair closest to the door, defiantly facing the scrutiny of my classmates.

"Aydan, I believe you've met Greg, and this is Ashley, and Calvin. This is Aydan," Dr. Rawling introduced us.

Holt offered me a welcoming grin with an understanding lift of his eyebrows, and the other two nodded silently, unsmiling. I nodded back at them and faced Dr. Rawling, bracing myself for an excruciating couple of hours.

He smiled. "All right, today we're going to talk about cognitive restructuring."

It was as bad as I'd expected. Holt and the others were obviously doing their best and I tried to play along, but discussing my feelings in a group of strangers was about as likely as flapping my arms and flying to the moon. And God knew I was willing to try that, or any other means of escape.

The painkillers never had a chance. By the end of the class my neck and shoulders were twisted into fiery knots, and I dug my fingertips impotently into the base of my skull as I shuffled out of the room.

"You okay?"

Holt's voice made me start, and I squinted through my pain. "Yeah. Just a headache."

I made for the lunchroom, hoping a cup of tea and a snack would help. Pacing beside me, Holt leaned closer and dropped his voice.

"So Stemp stuck you with this class, too. Who'd you kill?"

My instant of frozen immobility made Holt draw back, his craggy features twisting into a surprised grin. "You did kill somebody."

I regained my composure and summoned up a scowl without too much difficulty. "It probably had more to do with the fact that I called Stemp a dickhead."

Holt barked out a laugh. "Yeah, that'd do it. The guy's got a major stick up his ass."

A reluctant urge to defend Stemp took me by surprise. "Well, I kind of jammed my gun in his throat, too."

"Shit." Thunderclouds began to gather on Holt's face. "And he's still letting you carry?"

Dreading another explosion, I leaned forward to whisper. "Greg, can I trust you with something?"

The gambit worked. His scowl faded into interest. "What?"

I hesitated, my mind spinning through possibilities. Something plausible. Not classified, not a lie, but juicy enough to make him feel entrusted with something important...

"You can trust me." Now he looked intrigued. "Remember, I'm a spook. I know how to keep a secret."

Shit, what could I tell him? The longer I hesitated, the better my 'secret' had to be.

No inspiration came to mind. My headache thumped behind my eyeballs.

I sighed and went with the truth. "I'm involved in something so big they can't afford to take away my gun. But I shot a guy's face off a couple of months ago, and if they decide I'm too much of a risk they won't just confiscate my gun and assign me to a desk, they'll probably kill me. Or worse, put me in jail. I have to get through this anger management course."

Apparently that was a big enough 'secret'. Holt's lantern jaw sagged. "Holy shit." His scowl came back. "Those fucking management bastards. They put us out there with our asses on the line and then they won't back us up when we have to get our hands dirty. But that might change soon. Keep your fingers crossed."

I was about to ask what he meant when he spoke again. "You shot a guy's face off?"

"Seven rounds. Point-blank."

He winced. "That'll leave a mark. So they figured you were serious about doing Stemp."

I grimaced. "I was."

Holt followed me into the lunchroom and leaned against the counter, eyeing me with interest while I filled the kettle and rummaged for a cereal bar. "You probably shouldn't say that out loud," he offered after a moment.

"Too late. I threatened him in front of General Briggs."

"Jesus."

"There were extenuating circumstances."

"Fuck, I hope so. You're lucky they didn't double-tap you right on the spot."

"Yeah." I turned to him, cradling my mug and wishing I'd just braved his fury and told him to bugger off. "So don't tell anybody, okay? I just have to get through this."

"No problem." He offered me a fist bump. "Team. We'll get through it."

CHAPTER 22

At a quarter to eight, I slid into my car and dialled Kane's cell phone. He answered on the first ring.

"Hi." I hesitated. "How's it going?"

"Fine. I'm at the bowling alley."

"Oh, that's good." I couldn't hear the clatter of the pin-setting machines, so he must be parked outside. Only a few blocks away from the drive-in, thank heaven.

I carefully tucked the burner phone into my jacket pocket. "Can you still hear me?"

"Yes." Kane's voice crackled out of the tinny speaker.

"Okay... Well, I guess maybe I'll see you later?"

"Count on it."

I withdrew the phone and deactivated its speaker before easing it back into my pocket. Now, as long as I didn't bump my pocket and accidentally hang up, everything should be fine.

Putting the car in gear, I drew a deep breath and let it out slowly. Nothing to worry about. Parr still needed me, so I shouldn't be in any danger from Sharkface. And Kane was only minutes away.

I'd be fine.

Really.

Nothing to worry about.

Apparently my stomach was unconvinced. It knotted around the cereal bar that had served as my supper, gurgling so loudly I was afraid Kane would hear it over the phone.

A few minutes later I pulled up in front of the drive-in, its serving windows boarded up, its colourful picnic tables floating like bright islands in the monochrome snowscape under the streetlights.

No other vehicles.

I glanced at my illuminated dashboard clock. I was right on time.

So where the hell was Sharkface?

Then I spotted the fresh tire tracks in the snow beside the kiosk, disappearing into the trees of the small campground behind it.

Shit. He must be waiting in the year-round picnic area behind the drive-in.

Following the tracks, I drove into the trees. A cheerful orange glow beckoned from one of the picnic sites, but he surely would have avoided the rowdy teens who hurriedly concealed their beer cans as I rolled by.

Sure enough, a single set of tire marks continued past the party site. I followed the tracks deeper into the campground, my headlights barely piercing the blackness. Spruce trees extended dark menacing arms over both sides of the trail.

I eased my sweaty grip on the steering wheel and gulped at the dryness in my throat.

Nothing could go wrong. Parr needed me.

How long would it take Kane to find me out here in the woods if something went wrong?

Suck it up. I had a gun. I could shoot Sharkface if I had

to.

I rounded a bend in the narrow road and braked to a halt.

Shit.

"Barrier across the road," I murmured for Kane's benefit.

I eyed the log that lay across the trail. The tire tracks continued beyond it, disappearing into the darkness. Footprints and drag marks showed the log had been deliberately placed there.

"Asshole," I muttered, not exactly certain whether I meant Sharkface, Parr, or myself for being dumb enough to go out in the middle of nowhere alone.

Then again, that was my job now.

I suppressed a groan and rested my throbbing forehead against the cold steering wheel for a moment before turning off the headlights to plunge myself into inky blackness. Waiting for my eyes to adjust, I stared wide-eyed into the night. My heart banged like a kettledrum in the profound silence.

Should I follow the tire tracks on foot? Or just wait for Sharkface to show up? He had obviously planned to stop me here.

What if this was just a ploy to get me out in the middle of nowhere so he could shoot me? He could have a night-vision scope trained on me right now.

I resisted the urge to curl into a ball under the dashboard.

If he'd wanted to shoot me, he could have done it last night. Parr still needed me.

The crunch of approaching footsteps in the snow made my pulse hammer in my throat. Homing in on the sound, I made out a dark shape approaching from the black-on-black landscape.

A moment later a flashlight blinded me.

"Ugh!" I flung up an arm in protest and shouted, "Turn it off!"

The beam bobbled as the flashlight tapped sharply on my side window.

I powered the window down an inch and snapped, "Turn off the fucking light!"

A grunt that might have been amusement came from behind the glare, and the light flicked over the interior of my car while I blinked away glowing spots.

"Open the trunk."

"Why?"

"Because I said so."

Heart pounding, I reached for the door handle instead.

"Keep your hands on the wheel and stay in the car or I'll shoot you right where you sit. Now open the fucking trunk."

I returned my clammy hand to the steering wheel. "I can't open the trunk with both hands on the wheel."

"Don't. Piss. Me. Off." His growl raised icy gooseflesh on the back of my neck. "Open the trunk, then put your hands back on the wheel. Do anything else and I'll blow you away."

Swallowing hard, I inched my hand over to press the trunk release before resuming my deathgrip on the wheel.

"Sit still." The footsteps crunched around to the back of the car, the light still trained on me.

What was he doing back there? Putting a locator device in my trunk? Or a bomb?

The light disappeared behind the trunk lid for only a second. Then the trunk slammed and the footsteps came back.

"Good, sweet-ass, you came by yourself. You're smarter than you look." He laughed. "Or dumber. Out here in the middle of nowhere all by your lonesome."

"What the hell do you want?" I demanded, not bothering to hide the fearful quaver in my voice.

"Aw, don't worry, sweet-ass, you're safe with me. Even if you came out here stark naked and gave me a nice little lap-dance, I wouldn't lay a finger on you." I could hear the grin in his voice. "You can try it if you want."

"Fuck off."

His voice went as cold as the black winter air. "When you stop being valuable to Mr. Parr, I'll make you regret saying that to me."

My sweaty hands slipped on the steering wheel and I tightened my grip. "Enough with the threats. Tell me what you want."

"Two things. A white ceramic bottle from Yana's luggage. And a picture of George Harrison."

I couldn't help it. Nervousness popped the words out before I could stop them. "The Beatle?"

My window exploded and a huge hand clamped around my throat, slamming me back against the seat. Fireworks ignited behind my eyes as the blood flow to my brain dwindled.

He shoved his face so close his breath fanned my cheek. "George Harrison. From Sirius Dynamics. And the bottle. You have two days. Or you and I are going to have a little party. You won't enjoy it. Clear?"

I managed a fractional up-and-down movement of my chin and his grip loosened enough to ease the roaring in my ears.

"Now get your ass over to Kane's place tonight and get

that bottle. Or else."

He let go and I collapsed forward, sucking big shuddery breaths. The icy air pouring in my broken window carried the receding sound of his footsteps.

Leaning my forehead against the steering wheel, I concentrated on breathing.

Slow, even breaths. In, two... three... four. Out, two... three... four...

After several minutes, the faint sound of an engine drifted back on the still air. I tracked its progress around the remainder of the camping loop before it faded into the dark silence.

I sat trembling for a few moments longer before peeling a hand off the steering wheel to open the door and force my quivering knees into standing position. Leaning over, I shook broken glass out of my hair and off my jacket, then staggered several yards away from the car before pressing the trunk release button.

The trunk clicked open obligingly and I flinched, half-expecting an explosion.

None came.

After a few moments I crept close enough to look inside. My usual winter survival gear looked undisturbed. And I hadn't heard him messing with anything. A glance at my bug detector indicated all clear. He must have just been checking to make sure I hadn't hidden anybody in my trunk.

I sighed and used the snow brush to flick the broken glass out of the driver's seat before sinking into it again. Hopefully I'd waited long enough to be sure Sharkface wasn't coming back.

I pulled out a secure phone and punched the speed dial.

"Stemp." His voice crackled over the line after the first

ring, and I swallowed a small sob of gratitude at the reassuring sound.

I held my voice steady with an effort. "I have two days to deliver a white ceramic bottle from Yana's luggage and a picture of George Harrison. From Sirius," I added. "Not the Beatle. And Sharkf... Barnett wants me to search Kane's house for the weapon tonight."

In the momentary pause, I imagined Stemp calculating all the possibilities. "Very well," he said. "We've confirmed Kane's house is under surveillance, so coordinate with him to get into his house tonight and make it appear you're following their orders."

"Okay," I said, but he had already hung up.

Easing out a sigh, I pulled the burner phone from my pocket. "John, are you still there?"

"Yes. Are you all right? What was that crash I heard earlier?"

"Just Shit-for-Brains breaking my car window. Did you hear the conversation with Stemp?"

"Yes. I'll go home now. Call me there using your personal cell phone and we can arrange something plausible. Assume they have the phone line tapped."

"Okay. I'll give you ten minutes."

"Good. Talk to you soon."

I hung up.

Ten minutes to wait. I could do that.

I leaned my head against the headrest. Distant laughter and whoops indicated the teenagers' party was warming up, but the only other sound was the whisper of the breeze through frozen spruce trees.

Willing my clenched muscles to relax, I stared out at the darkness. Now that I knew Sharkface was gone, the silent blackness seemed peaceful, and I closed my eyes and breathed the cold spruce-scented air.

Ten minutes later, I turned the ignition key again, shivering. Communion with nature was all fine and dandy, but it'd be better if it was above zero.

I cranked up the heat and pulled out my phone to dial Kane.

It rang a few times on the other end, and I was beginning to wonder if I'd called too early when he answered with a cautious 'hello'.

"Hi, um... it's Arlene..." I let the sentence trail off. When he didn't reply immediately, I added, "I was just calling to see how you were doing... after, um..."

He sighed, and when he spoke again my heart clenched with automatic sympathy even though I knew he was faking the weary sadness that infused his voice. "I'm... all right, I guess... How are you?"

"I'm okay... Um... I wondered... Do you feel like some company tonight? Would you like to have a drink over at the hotel bar?"

"Not really..." He hesitated as if changing his mind. "Well, all right... Yes. If you're free."

"I'm free. And I'd like to see you."

"Oh. All right. Good... When?"

Christ, we sounded like a couple of teenagers arranging a first date.

"I'm heading over there now, so whenever you get there."

"All right, I'll see you in a little while."

CHAPTER 23

Shivering, I pulled into a parking spot at the Silverside Hotel. Damn Sharkface. I was going to freeze my ass off driving on the highway with a missing window. Maybe I could borrow some tape and a garbage bag from Kane for a temporary repair.

I hurried across the parking lot and into the hotel lobby. As soon as I stepped through the door the din of the sports bar assaulted my ears, and I squared my shoulders to prepare myself.

Sidling into the dingy cavern, I squinted through the gloom at the usual mix of rowdy oil-rig workers and mummified old-timers whose only movement was the mechanical raising and lowering of beer bottles. A moment later I spotted a broad-shouldered figure backlit by the giant-screen TV, and I wove between the tables to slide into the chair beside Kane, our backs to the wall.

His lips quirked. "Nice place. Do you come here often?"

"Smart-ass." I leaned closer to put my lips to his ear. "I didn't want to go to Eddy's tonight. I'm planning a grand seduction scene to justify going home with you, and I didn't want to have to do the walk of shame in front of Eddy tomorrow."

He drew back, laying an aggrieved hand over his heart. "What, you're ashamed to be seen with me?"

I grinned. "Oh, shut up. Where's the waitress? If I don't eat something pretty soon I'm going to pass out. And that'll totally spoil my plans."

"You have plans. I like the sound of this."

Even competing with the blaring of the hockey game, that sexy rumble sent a hot shiver to places I'd been trying to ignore.

I ignored them harder. "Only if I don't starve to death first... There she is." I beckoned to the waitress and she slouched over.

"Whaddaya want?"

"A glass of water and an order of poutine."

Her lip curled. "We only have bottled water. It's two-fifty. And it's a ten-buck minimum order."

I held onto my patience. "I thought the poutine was eight bucks. That makes ten-fifty with the water."

"Minimum *drink* order."

"I'm driving..." I began.

"It's all right," Kane interrupted. "We'll get some beer. You can have a couple of sips and I'll drink the rest." He turned to the waitress. "We'll have two bottles of Corona."

She eyed him up and down, blatantly ogling his arms and shoulders before batting her eyes. "Sorry, hottie-cakes, we only got Canadian, Coors Light, and Kokanee in the bottle. Canadian on tap."

"Two Kokanees please." Kane returned her scrutiny, feigning appreciation of the tattooed spiders crawling over her bountiful cleavage as she bent in front of him, ostensibly to put a coaster on the table.

At least I was pretty sure he was feigning. But what the

hell did I know? Maybe he had a thing for inked arachnids. Or more likely, bountiful cleavage.

I successfully resisted the urge to glance down at my own chest, which wasn't looking bountiful at all under my baggy sweatshirt. Maybe I should've gone home and put on a V-neck T-shirt. With that tiger print push-up bra.

Kane shot me a teasing grin. "Jealous?"

"Yes." I pushed my lips into a pout. "Don't forget who's seducing you here."

"I won't." His fingertips traced the line of my jaw and he pressed his lips to my ear. I forgot how to breathe as he murmured, "Just playing the part. If I was the kind of guy who'd go out on a date a few days after my new wife died, I'm probably not the epitome of class."

Those bad-boy words in that velvet voice generated all sorts of naughty thoughts. And even naughtier sensations.

I sucked in a breath as he drew back, smiling.

Be cool. For chrissake, at least wait until the drinks arrive before you fling yourself at him.

"I'm sure you were just angling for good service," I said. "Your noble sacrifice is duly noted."

He gave me a slow smile. "I'll look forward to my reward."

Christ, I'd been trying to forget how devastating he was when he turned on the charm. It wasn't fair, dammit. His business persona was hard enough to resist.

Sudden realization brought a smile to my face.

I didn't have to resist. This was all in the line of duty.

Game *on*.

I glided the tip of my tongue over my lips. "I have a suitable reward in mind."

Kane's mouth opened, and the waitress chose that

moment to slap the bottles down on the table, adding a stink-eyed glare as a bonus before flouncing away.

Kane groped for one of the bottles, his eyes never leaving my lips while he took a long swallow. Then he placed the bottle back on the table and leaned closer.

"Do that again, and we won't be here long enough for you to get your food."

The huskiness in his voice ignited sparks of bright lust that completely obscured my better judgement.

"What makes you think you're in control here?" I purred. I traced his lower lip with my fingertip before letting it drift down his chin.

Over his throat.

Slowing while I trailed it down his chest.

Bumping over the hard contours of his abs, watching his eyes dilate.

Lower still to make slow circles around the button of his jeans.

He stiffened, and I dropped my voice to a sultry tease. "I'm going to make you wait while I take my time finishing my food. And you're going to sit there thinking about it the whole time." I picked up a beer bottle, holding his gaze.

Licked lazily around the rim.

When I flicked the tip of my tongue into the opening of the bottle before closing my lips around it to take a drink, he groaned.

"Aw, what's the matter?" I leaned over to nibble up his jaw to his ear.

Oh... my...

Leather overlaid with the scent of gun oil and a hint of citrus. The erotic sandpaper of his five o'clock shadow stimulating my lips. That mind-melting salty/spicy flavour that was pure Kane...

Thankful my moment of slack-jawed lust had been concealed by darkness, I murmured against his earlobe, "It's all for our cover story. I'm just making sure everyone's convinced you'd take me back to your place."

"Any man in his right mind would," he muttered. "And if you don't stop doing that, we'll be facing public indecency charges when I take you right here on this table."

That breathtaking thought made my head spin, but I pulled back and ran teasing fingertips up from his knee, ending with a light smack on the inside of his thigh. "Behave yourself."

His hand shot out, his fist clenching in the hair at my nape. He dragged me closer, forcing my head back. "You forget," he growled. "You told Parr I'm not a very nice guy."

His lips claimed mine, hard and possessive, his grip on my hair dominating me. I tensed, my hands bracing against his chest.

Kane broke the kiss to pull me close as if ravishing my neck. "Are you all right?" he whispered next to my ear. "I didn't mean to trigger anything."

Relax. This was Kane. Kane's glorious chest hot under my palms, his lips drifting lightly down my neck...

I turned to meet his kiss again, summoning a grin. "Don't worry, you're going to make that up to me."

"Oh, I plan to," he rumbled against my lips.

He deepened the kiss and I sank into the haze of lust. Our tongues tangled, my body igniting at the thought of a long hot night, unmarred by impending death for a change.

A thump on the table pulled us apart.

"Y'know we got rooms," the waitress sneered. "Maybe you oughta get one."

"Yeah, thanks," I mumbled in the general direction of her receding back, my attention riveted by the plate of french fries, gravy, and melting cheese curds she had dropped in front of me. The rich scent of hot fat made my stomach twist with hunger, my mouth watering.

Kane laughed. "I'm suffering a severely bruised ego here. If you looked at me like you're looking at that poutine, we'd be halfway to my house by now."

"Sorry, I missed supper..." I began.

"Don't apologize. I'm joking. Eat." He leaned back in his chair and raised his beer bottle to his lips, holding my gaze with hot eyes. "Trust me, you're going to need the strength."

Hunger of another kind almost made me ditch the poutine and drag him out the door, but I contented myself with giving him a slow smile and turning my attention to my food instead.

No rush.

Tonight I could take time to savour the ache of anticipation. Let my need build...

Under the table, his strong fingers kneaded my knee. I forgot to swallow while he worked upward, the heat of his hand burning through my jeans.

"I thought you were hungry." He gave me a devilish grin while his hand continued its northward migration.

With circling fingertips.

Ohmigod.

I drew in a shaky breath. "I... uh..."

His hand slid down to cup my knee again. "Hurry up and eat. I'm hungry, too."

I didn't need to ask what kind of hunger he meant. It was burning in his eyes, practically consuming me where I sat.

I shovelled in a few mouthfuls without tasting them. "Okay, I'm done."

"No, you're not." The wicked glint was back. "Not until you eat at least half that plateful." He raised his beer bottle to his lips. "And I want to finish my beer."

"I'll give you something better than beer."

"And I'll take it." He leaned close to growl in my ear. "And give it to you. Over and over. Until you forget everything but my name."

A wave of desire floated my eyelids half-closed, my breath easing out in a tiny moan.

Kane chuckled, the low sexy sound vibrating my eardrum. "Which is why you need to eat now." He sat back, smirking, and took another drink.

"You..." My voice came out in a breathy whisper. "...are a very bad man."

He grinned.

At last the bill was paid and we made for the door, stealing kisses every few steps. Outside, Kane's arm tightened around me. "We'll take my vehicle."

My mind still reeling from his last kiss, I began to demur but he silenced me with his lips.

When we came up for air he rasped, "My vehicle. Now." The raw edge of need in his voice sent a fresh burst of heat to places that were already verging on combustion.

I hurried to his SUV and jumped in.

The short drive to his house seemed to take forever. Reaching across to the driver's side, I dragged my fingernails up his thigh to scrape lightly over his straining zipper.

He hissed a breath, his knuckles whitening on the steering wheel. "Aydan, stop. I want to make it home at least."

I made small circles, feeling him swelling beneath my fingertips. "You'd better drive faster then."

"I'm... a cop. Laws... still apply." The words grated from between his teeth. He gripped my wrist, immobilizing my hand.

"You don't want me to touch you?" I asked, my innocence slightly spoiled by the hunger vibrating in my voice. "Maybe I should touch myself then."

I slid my free hand up my thigh, parting my legs.

Kane swerved over to the curb and slammed on the brakes, startling a yelp out of me.

"If you don't stop..." His voice growled low and breathless. "...you're going to cause an accident."

I gestured at the empty street ahead of us. "It's a small town. I think we're safe."

"I didn't mean a vehicular accident."

I leaned over to kiss him, easing my hand closer to my goal. "Would that be so bad?"

He groaned as my fingertips brushed his bulging denim again. "No, it would be mind-blowing. But we're thirty seconds away from my house. Please let me get there with my dignity intact."

"Oh, all right." I grinned. "Since you asked so nicely."

"Begged." He steered the SUV back on course. "I'm not too proud to admit it." He shot me a look hot enough to melt every snowflake inside a ten-mile radius. "But it'll be your turn to beg soon enough."

I shivered, my breath catching in anticipation.

When we parked in his garage a few minutes later, he

punched his seatbelt release and the garage door closer before lunging over to pin me to the seat in a ravenous kiss.

My hands slid inside his jacket, roaming over those hot, hard muscles. His tongue parted my lips and I moaned into his mouth, knotting my fists in his T-shirt and arching to press my breasts against him.

He fumbled for my seat belt button and grunted satisfaction when it released. Dragging me closer, he slid a hand down my back to knead my ass, the rough caress jolting more heat into my already-melting body.

When he pulled back, I whimpered and clutched at him, far beyond the ability to form words.

"Stick to the mission," he rasped. "Surveillance... Get in the house."

"'Kay." My voice was as hoarse as his.

Somehow I managed to slide out of the SUV. Locked in each other's arms, we performed a stumbling dance across his yard to the back door. He pinned me to the door frame beside it, kissing me breathless before unlocking his door.

A couple of steps inside, he deactivated his alarm system and swung the door shut behind us, glancing at the blinking light on his answering machine. "Sorry," he muttered. "Have to check this..."

He pressed the play button and pulled me into his arms, devouring my lips.

"Mr. Kane, this is Sunny Drycleaners."

He froze in mid-kiss.

"We're calling to remind you to pick up the two shirts you left with us. This is your final reminder. If you don't pick them up within forty-eight hours, we will donate them to charity. Thank you for your cooperation."

His body turned to iron in my arms.

I stared up at him. "What? What's wrong?"

His hands closed hard on my shoulders. "Goddammit! Aydan, you have to leave. Now!"

CHAPTER 24

"*What?*" I goggled up at Kane, caught between frustrated lust and sudden fear. "What the hell-"

"I'm sorry." He pressed his keys into my hand. "Take the Expedition. Get your car and go home."

"I can't, we're under surveillance here and I'm supposed to be searching your house-"

"Dammit, no damn blood left in my brain." He scrubbed both hands over his face and gave his head a shake, visibly switching to tactical mode. "Fuzzy Bunny has remote cameras trained on the front and back doors of my house." He hurried me toward the basement stairs while he spoke. "Go out the side basement window and over the fence into the neighbour's yard. You can get to the back door of my garage from the alley. Take the Expedition. Leave it in the hotel parking lot. I'll get it from there."

I planted my feet at the bottom of the stairs and refused to move. "If you need the Expedition, I can walk."

"No, take it; it's cold out-"

I cut him off with a gesture. "You need it, don't you?" When he hesitated for an instant, I nodded. "Yeah, I thought so." I handed him the keys. "What's happening? How can I help?"

Kane blew out a short breath. "I don't know what's happening yet. And you can help by leaving." He jabbed a finger at the high window on the east side of the basement. "It opens on about four feet of space between my house and the fence. Their dog's name is Max; black lab; friendly; not much of a barker. Stay away at least an hour. I'll leave the window unlatched so you can sneak in again and go out the door for the cameras." He unlatched the security bars and pushed the window open.

"Wait..."

Kane seized me by the shoulders and looked into my eyes. "I'm sorry for this. I will make it up to you, I promise. Go. Hurry. Be safe."

He pressed a kiss to my lips before letting go to make a stirrup of his hands under the window.

"Be safe, too," I whispered, and stepped into his hands.

Several seconds of ungraceful heaving and squirming landed me in the dark recess between Kane's house and the fence. Heart pounding, I hauled myself to my feet and took stock.

The damn fence was a good six feet high, its smooth boards taunting me. I pressed an eye to the tiny gap between them, but it was too dark to see anything on the other side.

Surely the dog would have been attracted by my struggles if he was outside. And I couldn't see any lights on in the house. Small mercies.

I clamped trembling hands on the top of the fence. Jesus, another workout. Just what I needed.

Scrabbling and straining, I hooked one foot over the top and hauled myself up, stretching my mouth wide in a silent scream when I whacked my goddamn knee again.

Perched atop the fence with the boards digging into my

thighs, my breath puffed out on the cold air in steamy gasps while I shot a glance around the yard before lowering myself as quietly as possible.

No barking greeted me, but judging by the smell the neighbours weren't too fussy about picking up after the dog. And he'd been out recently enough that his latest contributions hadn't frozen yet.

Great, just fucking great.

I scuttled along the edge of the yard, staying low against the fence. At the back gate I eased the latch open, wincing at its rusty squeak. Still no barking, thank God. I whisked through the gate and latched it behind me before collapsing against it to pant and tremble for a few moments.

Then I blew out a long breath and dragged myself away from the fence to skulk down the dark alley, accompanied by the lingering stench of dog shit.

A few houses down, it occurred to me that anonymity would probably be a good idea. Muttering a curse, I yanked my hood up to hide my face and hair. Then I spent several seconds grinding my boots into a snowbank trying to clean them.

At last I set a brisk pace toward the hotel. The cold bit through my jeans, and the thought of the warm ski pants in my emergency kit mocked me. Smooth move, leaving the kit behind in the car. That'll teach me to give in to lust.

And speaking of lessons learned, didn't something bad happen every damn time I even came close to getting lucky with Kane? Getting unlucky was more like it. Fights, explosions, plane crashes, court-martials... or was that courts-martial?

Whatever. But fate was probably trying to tell me something.

I pushed that thought away and rubbed my hands over my icy thighs, picking up the pace despite the fatigue dragging at my muscles.

What would Kane be doing now?

He had probably left already, going into God-knew-what danger to respond to that coded message.

I briefly considered calling Stemp, but discarded the idea. Kane would report his new mission, and mine hadn't changed. Make Sharkface think I'd searched Kane's house.

After that, who knew? I hoped Kane and Stemp had a plan to appease Sharkface when I didn't hand over the weapon, because I sure as hell didn't. And my two days were ticking away.

By the time I strode into the hotel parking lot twenty minutes later, my legs were blocks of ice and sweat trickled down the back of my neck inside my hood. Growling, I slid into my car and fired it up, cranking on the heater.

It was hard not to feel conspicuous driving around the tiny town at ten-thirty on a Wednesday evening. Even after driving every street twice I still had time to kill, but I didn't dare stop where I might be noticed. Keeping my fingers crossed that the hard-working populace were all in bed early on a week night, I orbited the town a couple more times, my shoulders slowly climbing up around my ears.

The frigid breeze from the broken window did nothing to improve my mood. By the time I parked a couple of blocks away from Kane's house around eleven P.M., my sweatshirt clung cold and clammy to my back and my legs had gone numb. I quivered out of the car and pressed the lock button before realizing how pointless that was with the driver's window open to the world.

Head down, fists jammed deep in my pockets, I trudged

for the back alley, too exhausted to even swear. Stumbling down the snow-rutted lane in the darkness, I pulled up sharply at the sound of a low 'whuff' from the yard beside Kane's.

"Oh, for chrissake, *seriously*?" I muttered.

As if in reply the neighbour's gate rattled against its latch, accompanied by more whuffing and some vigorous sniffing from inside the yard. And there was a light on in the house.

I groaned, generating another soft whuff on the other side of the gate. "Shhh, Max," I muttered. "Who's a good boy?"

That didn't help. Max started scratching, his nails rattling against the fence boards like hailstones while he whined and whimpered.

Shit, shit, shit!

I hovered, pulse pounding. Should I run? Come back later? Max whined again and redoubled his efforts against the gate.

"Max, shut up," I hissed. "Shut the hell up!" Sudden inspiration struck. "Sit, boy. Sit!"

The scratching stopped abruptly.

I drew a shaky breath and eased closer to the gate. "Good boy, Max. Good dog. Sit."

Did I dare?

Going into the yard seemed like an extra-special flavour of stupidity, but Kane had said the dog was friendly. I'd probably be okay. And if I made some noise going back over the fence, the neighbours would chalk it up to Max instead of freaking out and calling the police.

"Hey, Max. Hey, boy. Sit, that's a good boy." I reached for the latch with trembling hands.

This probably ranked right up there as one of the stupidest things I'd ever done.

I held my breath and lifted the latch, wincing at a squeak that sounded loud enough to alert everyone on the block.

"Sit, Max." I inched a cautious hand in the direction of the black shape panting eagerly inside the gate. When a cold wet nose nudged my hand and a warm tongue slurped in its wake, I sidled a little closer, blocking the opening with my body. "Good boy, Max. Sit."

I was almost inside the yard when a sudden thump nearly rocketed my heart out of my chest. The series of rhythmic thumps that followed made me gasp a hysterical little giggle.

"He's such a good boy. Maxie's such a good boy. Sit..." I quavered, and Max's tail thumped even harder against the fence.

I edged the gate shut behind me, wincing again at the squeal of the latch. Tearing my attention away from the dog and the gate for the first time, my heart froze when I glanced up at the window.

Sock feet propped on his coffee table, a man sat facing me, bathed in the flickering glow of his television. If he transferred his attention away from the screen for even a moment, my black parka would show up against his white fence like a dog turd in the snow.

"Keep sitting, Max. Good boy." My whisper was so high-pitched the dog was probably the only one capable of hearing it.

Paralyzed, I stood vacillating between making a mad dash for the side of the house or easing my way over slowly so I wouldn't attract attention.

Max whuffed and rose to lean against my legs, his tail

whipping the air.

Okay, a black dog against a white fence. Camouflage.

I hunched down to creep along the fence line, trying to make myself approximately dog-sized. Surely the owners were so used to seeing Max moving around out here that they wouldn't be alarmed.

Nothing to see out here, folks. Just keep watching TV...

Apparently delighted with our new game, Max bounded beside me, letting out little whuffs and whimpers and pushing his wet nose over to lick my face.

"Jesus, dog, fuck off," I crooned in loving, encouraging tones. "I don't want to- Bleah!" Slinking steadily toward the side of the house, I wiped the dog slobber off. "...get frenched by some big dumb pooch that probably just finished licking his own dick."

The dripping tongue went into overdrive, nailing me square in the mouth.

"Gross!" I spat and scrubbed my sleeve across my lips before cooing some more. "Good boy, Max, you big dumb shit-pumping spit factory-" The tongue slathered me again. "Blech!"

Past the side of Kane's house at last. Out of camera range. Now all I had to do was get over the fence without getting caught by the neighbours.

"Sit, Max," I hissed. "There's a good boy. Sit."

Max obediently thumped his hindquarters into the snow, his lashing tail sending frozen turd bombs hurtling in all directions.

"Great, fabulous. Good boy. Why does this corner of the yard have to be your favourite place to take a dump?" I grabbed the top of the fence. "Sit, Max, good boy."

It took everything I had to clamber to the top of the fence

again. The reek of dog shit closed my throat and I had to suppress my gag reflex when I looked down at the dark smears on the white boards below me.

Oh, God, please tell me I don't have dog shit all over me.

"Good dog, Max," I choked, and toppled over into Kane's yard.

Max immediately began to whine and scratch at the fence.

"Sit, Max," I hissed. "Sit, dammit!"

The stench surrounded me and I scuffed my boots frantically against the snow. Max's whimpers got louder and he emitted a sharp little 'let's play' bark.

Dammit, if his owners came out now and found my footprints in the snow they'd call the police for sure.

But I just couldn't bring myself to track dog shit onto Kane's nice basement carpet.

Cursing under my breath, I whipped my boots off and stepped onto what I sincerely hoped was a clean patch of snow. The frigid moisture bit through my cotton socks instantly, and I dropped to my knees to fumble Kane's window open.

The fence rattled under a barrage of scratching.

I gave one last despairing hiss of "Sit, Max!" and dropped to my belly to squirm feet-first through the window, boots clutched in one hand, the other hand flailing for purchase on the window frame. My jacket and sweatshirt bunched up under my arms as I slid. Snow bit my bare stomach and I bucked at the icy shock, throwing my descent completely out of control.

My wildly waving feet slammed against a flat, hard surface that hadn't been under the window when I left.

My wet socks slipped on it. Oh-God-this-is-going-to-hurt...

A moment later my upper body jounced over the windowsill, my fingers raking uselessly past the frame.

Falling-oh-*shit!*

I tumbled off the hard thing and crashed to the floor.

For a moment I sprawled unable to move or breathe, my arms immobilized above my head by the bonds of my scrunched-up parka, my stinky boots still clutched aloft in a rigor-mortis grip.

Then pain and oxygen deprivation hit simultaneously and I sucked in an agonizing breath.

My exhalation was a piteous whine that put Max's efforts to shame, and I lay immobile for a few more torturous breaths while the apocalyptic agony faded slowly to garden-variety pain.

"Oh-God-oh-god*damn!*"

Groaning and whimpering as quietly as possible, I eased onto my side, still holding my boots clear of the carpet. After a few more moments of intense contemplation of life and the universe, I managed another quarter roll, then gradually straightened into kneeling position.

Everything seemed to be working. Not willingly or comfortably, but working nonetheless. Emerging from my painful preoccupation, I gathered my wits enough to take stock.

A tiny nightlight provided the only illumination. The house was completely silent. Kane must still be gone.

I dragged myself to my feet to stagger over and close the window, leaving it unlatched so he could return later. The hard object under it proved to be a sturdy wooden dresser. He must have used it to get out the window himself, or maybe he'd left it to provide me with a landing zone.

That would've been nice, if I'd known about it.

The smell of my boots was even worse in the warm enclosed space. Holding them at arm's length, I stared around the dim basement.

Maybe a washtub? There should be a laundry room.

The first door I tried gave onto an exercise room, the chrome bars of the equipment gleaming softly through the darkness. When I opened the next door, a hint of Kane's citrusy scent tickled my nostrils while I surveyed the small tidy space with its washer and dryer. No sink or washtub. Damn.

Heaving a painful sigh, I trudged for the stairs, enveloped by the vile canine miasma. God, that was one sick dog. What the hell were they feeding him?

I limped upstairs, mentally cataloguing my injuries as the all-over pain began to resolve into distinct areas. My poor kneecap felt as though it had been replaced by a pulsating grapefruit, and a jab when I bent my elbow made me catch my breath. A largish ache in the vicinity of my hip indicated one of my landing points, but it didn't hurt enough to be serious.

I'd live. Unfortunately.

Shuffling through the darkened hallway, I headed for the kitchen. Should be garbage bags there.

It seemed like sacrilege to bring my disgusting boots into the pristine steel-and-granite kitchen where Kane produced such delicious meals. My arm was beginning to ache from holding the boots as far away from my nose as possible, and I ransacked the cabinets one-handed, finally discovering plastic garbage bags under the sink.

With a breath of relief I double-bagged my foul footwear and carried the bag to the back door.

The reek persisted and I hovered uncertainly. Was it just the lingering fumes from the boots? Or did I have something unspeakable stuck to some other part of me?

The urge to strip and shower immediately was almost overpowering, but I decided against it. Better to get the hell out before anything else went wrong.

Bag in hand, I slipped out the back door and scurried down the frigid sidewalk, my wet socks alternately freezing to the concrete and pulling loose with muffled Velcro-like noises. In the back alley, I reluctantly unwrapped my smelly boots and stuffed my half-frozen feet into them before trudging back to my car.

When it came into view, I dragged to a halt, my shoulders slumping.

I had forgotten about my broken window.

No tape, no extra garbage bag, no hope of repair.

Well, fine. Fuck me.

A one-hundred-kilometre-per-hour windchill at sub-zero temperatures provided the perfect finishing touch for my shitty evening. Even though I ran the heater full blast, my ear and the side of my face ached with cold after fifteen minutes on the road. I drew a breath of relief when I slowed to turn the corner into my lane.

Home at last, thank God. Now for a hot shower with lots of soap. Some painkillers, a warm bed...

I had just parked in front of my gate when headlights turned onto my road from the highway a couple of miles away.

Damn, hardly anybody drove this road in the winter. And I was really not in the mood for a neighbourly chat.

I struggled out of the driver's seat and hurried to unlock my gate, fumbling at the combination lock with cold, stiff fingers. Squinting in the glare of my headlights, I finally flipped the lock tumblers to the correct combination and swung the gate open.

Too late.

A dark SUV pulled to a stop behind my car, its headlights blinding me. A large all-too-familiar silhouette approached from behind the glare.

Fear slammed my pulse into overdrive.

CHAPTER 25

Too late to make a grab for my ankle holster.

My heart scaled the inside of my chest to batter my throat as Sharkface approached, the muzzle of his gun looking like a giant gateway to hell. Christ, what was that thing, a .50 cal? He could blow away half my torso with a single shot.

"Give it to me." His voice broke into my frantic thoughts.

I had to swallow twice before a dry croak emerged from my throat. "Wh-what?"

"*Give it to me*, bitch!" He must have seen the blank incomprehension on my face. He elaborated. "The fucking bottle. That you took from Kane's."

"Wh... I d-didn't..."

I managed to throw up a defensive arm an instant before his pistol would have shattered my cheekbone. The blow slammed me to the snow, exploding my bruises into fresh agony.

He loomed above me while I lay gasping, his inhuman grin thrown into deep-shadowed contrast by the blaze of our combined headlights. "You left Kane's place carrying a bag. Where is it?"

Involuntary tears of pain and fear chilled my cheeks. "B-boots, it was j-just my b-boots in the b-bag, I d-didn't f-find anything!"

The high-pitched quaver of my own voice infuriated me. Goddamn snivelling chickenshit, about to die grovelling in a snowbank from your own fucking stupidity...

"Try again, bitch." He levelled his gun at my head. "Last chance."

"D-driver's seat of m-my c-car," I gabbled. "B-bags in the f-footwell. I s-stepped in d-dog shit and p-put my b-boots in the b-bag in the h-house b-but I had to p-put the b-boots back on-"

He swooped down, his massive hand driving toward my face. I jerked my arms up to protect my head, but his fist clenched on my hair, hauling me to my feet. His gun muzzle jammed into the back of my skull as he shoved me in front of him. "Move."

I stumbled forward, pain and terror fuzzing my mind while he herded me to my car door before yanking me to a halt.

The driver's door was still open, the dome light revealing the two white garbage bags I'd worn over my boots while driving. The aroma of overripe shit hung in the air.

Sharkface barked out a laugh. "Okay, sweet-ass. But let's just make sure. Open the back door and the trunk."

Still restrained by his painful grip on my hair, I leaned slowly in to press the lock button and trunk release. Sharkface kept his gun at my head while I opened the back door for his inspection.

Then he pushed me around to the rear of the car to survey the almost-empty trunk. "Dump that shit out."

The only 'shit' was my emergency kit and toolbox, so I

reached slowly for them, my hands trembling in the illumination of his headlights. When my ski pants and sleeping bag and tools were scattered across the snow, he grunted and stepped back, mercifully releasing his grip on my hair at last.

My wobbling knees almost gave out. I propped my hands on the back fender of the car, gulping shaky breaths.

"Strip."

I froze at his command, my heart and breath dying in my chest.

"Now. *Strip*."

As if controlled by an invisible puppet-master, I turned slowly to face him, my surge of adrenaline sweeping me beyond panic into cold detachment.

His massive form was backlit, his features lost in the glare of headlights, but I could make out the shining length of his gun barrel. Still levelled at me.

So that was it. I'd die broken and naked in a snowbank, alone in the icy darkness.

I drew a breath at last, my heart kicking my ribs. I wasn't dead yet...

I reached for my parka zipper with numb fingers.

Unzipped it and let it fall.

My breath plumed in the cold darkness. My trembling hands closed on the hem of my sweatshirt. Tugged it up and over my head.

The arctic air bit my naked skin.

Waist pouch next.

Sharkface said nothing as I dropped it beside me. Gooseflesh pebbled my body, tremors rocking me.

Easy now...

I unbuttoned my jeans.

Slid the zipper down.

Pushed the denim over my hips and eased it down my legs.

Closer and closer to my ankle holster...

Sharkface laughed, a sound as dark and cold as the frigid night air. "So you weren't hiding anything. You're not as dumb as I thought. Get me that bottle. Two days. Or else."

Snow crunched as he strode to his vehicle and got in. A moment later he reversed onto the road and drove away.

My knees gave out completely. Sobbing and shaking, I struggled into my sweatshirt, barely feeling the snow that sifted onto my icy skin.

Parka. Hood up. Conserve body heat.

Violent tremors wracked my body and I lurched to my feet, hauling my jeans up. My shaking fingers couldn't manage the button or zipper, and I stumbled around to the driver's seat holding my pants up with one hand.

Falling into the car, I slammed it into drive and stomped on the gas, leaving tools and emergency gear strewn behind in the darkness.

It took two tries for my shaking finger to hit the button for my garage door opener. At last the door rolled up, the warm light of safety spilling out over the snow.

The car was halfway into the garage before my tear-blurred eyes focused and my brain registered what I was seeing.

I coasted in and shifted into park, mechanically turning off the ignition and punching the button to close the garage door. Then I sat quaking in the seat with both arms locked around my body, my mind fading to merciful blankness while I absorbed the chaotic scene.

Of course he had searched my place while I was at

Kane's.

Of course.

I blinked and drew a long shuddering breath.

I was still behind the wheel of my car, sitting in darkness.

The garage door opener's timed light had gone out, so at least ten minutes had passed. Probably more, judging by the screaming muscles in my arms and shoulders.

I eased my arms down from their taut hug around my body, wincing.

Thank God my garage was heated. It would have been the height of stupidity to freeze to death huddling brainlessly within a few yards of a warm house.

Assuming the house was still warm. Maybe he'd broken the windows and the whole place was frozen by now.

I didn't really want to know.

I eased out a breath, trying to relax my rigid diaphragm. Belly breathe. Slow like ocean waves.

Quivers still shook me, the constant fine vibration of overstressed muscles.

I should call this in to Stemp.

But I needed to check the house before I could give my report.

I couldn't face that yet. Not alone.

I needed Kane.

My shaking hands fumbled my phone free, but I hesitated. If Fuzzy Bunny was monitoring my calls...

But wouldn't it be natural for me to call him? Wouldn't they expect that?

Too strung out to care, I pressed the speed dial button

and listened to the ringing on the other end. After four rings, his usual terse voice message played. "Kane. Leave a message."

I disconnected and let my hand fall to the seat beside me, staring through the windshield into the darkness.

Arnie would come if I called him. A single word, and he'd leave his bed and drive two hours in the middle of the night on icy highways just to offer gruff comfort and gentle kisses. The thought of his steadfast bulk brought tears to my eyes.

I wouldn't ask that of him.

And anyway, it would be pathetic to just sit here for two hours waiting to be rescued.

So suck it up.

I shook myself and blew out a breath. So I'd gotten a little chilly standing half-naked in the snow, so what? Nothing bad had happened. True to his promise, Sharkface hadn't laid a finger on me.

And there weren't any breakables left in my house after they'd trashed it a couple of months ago, so the cleanup should be easier this time.

And I was safe as long as Parr still needed me. Sharkface wouldn't harm me.

"Get going," I said aloud, and pressed the garage door opener.

Driving back to my gate brought a rush of reflexive terror.

I drew a deep breath and let it out slowly. Just a reaction. No need to let it control me.

Hauling myself out of the car, I limped over to retrieve my tools and gear. In the glare of the headlights, my shadow swooped and undulated, the dark movement a horrible reminder of Sharkface.

Cut it out.

Clutching my sleeping bag to my chest, I straightened and tipped my head back to study the distant serenity of the stars sparkling across the black velvet sky. The country silence wrapped around me and I concentrated on relaxing the tension in my muscles, absorbing the tranquillity.

I wouldn't let him take this from me. This was mine.

This peace. This place. This life.

Mine.

Spine straight, shoulders square, I strode back to reload my trunk and lock the gate behind me.

CHAPTER 26

I hesitated shivering on my front porch, trying to prepare myself for the disaster that likely awaited me inside.

Maybe it wouldn't be too bad.

Sharkface's search of the garage hadn't been wanton destruction. He had ransacked any spot that might have concealed something the size of the bottle-shaped weapon, but left my tools still neatly arranged inside the flat drawers of my floor-standing tool chest, just as I'd left them.

I blew out a breath between my chattering teeth. Stop stalling.

Pushing my key into the lock, I swung the door open and stepped inside. My security system chimed as the door opened, but it didn't emit its warning tone. He must have disarmed it with a valid code. How the hell did he get that? I wasn't in the habit of mumbling my master code aloud while I punched it in, so they couldn't have gotten it via the bug.

I braced myself and flipped on the lights.

"Oh, fuck you, Sharkface!" The words spilled from my mouth before it occurred to me that I might be bugged again.

I whipped out my bug detector, and sure enough its light flashed red. I groaned and took off my boots before hurrying over to gather up the frozen food scattered across my floor.

After replacing it in the chest freezer, I padded over to survey the rest of the damage.

It wasn't as bad as I had feared. He hadn't smashed my plates or glassware. The contents of most of the cabinets had been swept out onto the floor, but he had spared any place that could be checked at a glance. Unfortunately, that didn't include the shelves of my fridge, and I picked my way around puddles of milk and pickle juice decorated with silvery shards of broken glass.

In the living room, the contents of the open shelves were undisturbed but the furniture had been upended. The larger cushions had been slashed, their stuffing spilling out of the wounds.

The rest of the house bore witness to the same thorough but ruthless technique. By the time I reached the basement I was numb. After a cursory glance at the disarray I dragged myself up the stairs again, holding back whimpers while my bruised knee flexed and straightened.

Back to the door. Back into my parka and stinky boots. Back out to the garage, my dragging feet bulldozing twin trenches in the fluffy snow.

When I stepped back into the garage, the mess struck me with even more force than the damage in the house. My house had been violated before, but my garage... my garage was my sanctuary. A place untouched by my spy life; full of the soothing smells of warm rubber and motor oil and memories of the cold crisp tang of beer and happy summer afternoons sprawled on the cool concrete with a wrench in my hand.

I gulped down impending tears.

Took a long breath.

Okay, get it together.

When I pulled out my bug detector, it shone steady green. I extracted a secured phone from the glove compartment of my car and crossed to the next bay to slide into my half-stripped '53 Chevy, dangling my boots outside. Stroking a loving hand over its chrome-and-enamel dashboard, I inhaled its faintly musty old-car scent and rested my head against the big chrome-buttoned steering wheel.

Thank God it was undamaged. If Sharkface had vandalized it, my heart would have shattered completely.

I drew a deep breath and hit the speed dial button.

The phone rang on the other end.

Rang again.

And again.

Fear twisted my stomach. Something was wrong.

Ring-

"Dermott! What?"

"Wha..." My voice came out in a dry whisper and I cleared my throat. "Where's Stemp?"

"Hell if I know. Personal emergency is all he said. You calling to kiss him goodnight, or what?"

I was too worried to be irritated. "No, I'm reporting that I pretended to search Kane's house as planned tonight. They saw me leaving on the surveillance cameras and Sharkf... Kevin Barnett followed me home and..." My voice wanted to wobble, but I wouldn't let it. "...searched me to make sure I didn't have the weapon. He also searched my house and garage while I was at Kane's."

"Yeah, the analysts saw him going in to your place."

Okay, *now* I was irritated.

"Why the hell didn't you call and tell me?"

"Analysts texted you; you didn't reply. Get your shit

together, Kelly!" He disconnected.

Fuming, I pulled out my cell phone. Sure enough, there was a text from a couple of hours ago: 'Call home'.

"*Fuck!*" I stowed my own phone in my waist pouch and lunged to my feet to fling the burner phone at the concrete floor with all my might. It exploded in a satisfying spray of plastic shrapnel, and I aimed a savage kick at the largest part, forgetting my aching hip and knee.

"Fuck, fuck, *fuck!*" I flung my arms wide, head back, and shrieked *"FUUUUCK!"* at the top of my lungs before trampling the remaining pieces of the phone in a berserk tantrum, shrieking obscenities and pouring all my pain and fear and frustration into the annihilation of the inoffensive device.

At last I dragged to an exhausted halt. My throat was raw, my entire body aching.

But the hot anger in my belly had loosened the icy grip of fear. Nicholas Parr and Sharkface had no idea what a world of hurt they'd just brought on themselves.

They were going *down*.

But first I needed a shower.

I trudged back to the house, growling under my breath.

My shower had to wait while I unearthed my bucket and scrub brush from the shambles in the basement and tackled my boots. After several scrubs and rinses while I shivered and cursed on the front porch, I deemed them clean enough to return to the house.

Then I retraced every step I'd taken in those boots, scrubbing my stairs, porch, doormat, garage floor, and the floor mats from my car.

At last I retreated to the house and extracted a towel from the heap in front of my ransacked linen closet before creeping into the shower to scrub myself with copious amounts of soap. When I was positive every trace of dog shit had been eradicated, I dressed in fresh clothes and swallowed a couple of painkillers before tackling the most pressing parts of the indoor cleanup.

By the time I finished cleaning the kitchen floor I was ready to take on Fuzzy Bunny with nothing but fists and attitude.

Shooting was too good for those assholes. They deserved to be stripped naked and rolled through the broken glass and pickle juice they'd left on my floor. Then rolled through Max's rotting shit. And then shot and pissed on.

The hot current of rage carried me through the triage of the kitchen and into my bedroom to heave the box spring and mattress back onto the bed frame. As I was stirring through the jumble in search of my pillows, fatigue suddenly caught up to me, dragging me down like a leaden overcoat.

I staggered to the front door to set my apparently-useless security system before sleepwalking through the tangles of clothing on my bedroom floor to fall into bed.

Murder was my last conscious thought.

Morning was more than enough to take the edge off my badass attitude. Groaning, I hauled myself out of bed. Maybe I should try to be grateful for my crappy sleep. All that screaming and thrashing had kept me from stiffening up too much.

Or maybe I was in better shape than I thought after pushing to prepare for the physical qualification.

That optimistic idea was enough to sustain me through the arduous journey from my bed to the shower. I shoved my face into the hot spray and stood there, eyes closed and brain in neutral until I remembered I'd practically scrubbed my skin off only a few hours before.

Eyes still half-closed, I stumbled out again and dried off before taking stock of the new bruises blooming on my skin. My knee had been a murky yellow-brown before, but now black and purple had been added to the mix. I turned it from side to side, admiring the artistic blending of hues. At least the ice pack I'd applied last night had taken care of the swelling. It hurt like a bitch, but it worked.

My elbow and hip were only slightly discoloured and I dismissed them after a brief examination. All systems go.

By the time I'd finished my milk-less breakfast and trudged through the cold morning darkness to the garage only to realize I still had to fix my car window, I was fully awake and pissed off enough to start swearing again. I slogged through the knee-deep snow to my shed wondering what destruction I'd find there, but everything was undisturbed.

I thumped my forehead with the roll of clear plastic vapour barrier I'd retrieved from my stockpile of construction supplies. Duh. No tracks in the snow. He hadn't bothered to check the shed because he could see nobody had been there recently. Sharkface was smarter than I was.

That revelation didn't improve my humour. I stomped back to the garage, fully expecting the snow to melt from the heat of my invective.

After several minutes of cutting, taping, and cursing, I finished securing my makeshift window and headed for town, the sharp rattling of cold plastic sounding like the hail of bullets Sharkface so richly deserved.

When I parked at Sirius Dynamics, I caught sight of Dermott and Holt crossing the street toward the building, grinning and bantering. As I got out of my car, Holt socked Dermott on the shoulder and they both guffawed as they climbed the steps and vanished into the building.

When I arrived a few moments later, Dermott was just turning away from the security wicket, fob in hand. He grunted when he saw me. "Kelly. Briefing for Afterburner at nine."

I nodded and he slapped his fob on the reader and vanished through the doors.

Holt finished signing for his fob and stepped away from the wicket looking happier than I'd ever seen him. "'Morning, Aydan," he greeted me with a smile.

I did my best to summon up a smile in return. "'Morning." I took my turn at the wicket. "'Morning, Leo."

"Good morning!" Leo offered his usual grin and spun my fob through the turntable.

Holt was still lingering when I turned away, and he fell into step with me as I headed for my office.

"Good news." His grin widened. "Stemp's gone somewhere and Dermott's back in charge. Dermott's not afraid to let us do what we have to do. And he's starting the paperwork to get me reinstated. Man, I wish we had him for a permanent director."

"Um."

The thought of Holt being reinstated scared the shit out of me. And I wasn't sure Dermott was a good choice for director, either.

Holt leaned closer to mutter confidentially, apparently oblivious to my lack of joy. "It could happen. Stemp's up for review in a few months, and if Dermott can pull off a couple of good ops, the mucky-mucks might consider giving him Stemp's position."

"Oh... uh... well, I guess that would be good for you, right?"

"Too right." Holt bopped me lightly on the shoulder. "Good for all of us."

He turned and strode into an office on the main floor while I made for the stairs, wondering if Stemp knew Dermott was gunning for his position. And whether Dermott would push Holt's reinstatement through before Stemp got back, whenever that might be. And what Stemp's 'family emergency' really was.

A chill snaked down my back. As far as I knew Stemp didn't have any family except Katya and his little daughter Anna in Bulgaria. And it would have to be a real emergency for him to leave so suddenly.

My mind filled with a vivid memory of his ashen face when he'd thought Anna had been harmed the previous summer, and I floated a heartfelt three-word prayer skyward.

Please, not that.

CHAPTER 27

I trailed into my office frowning, and tossed my jacket over the back of the chair before wandering to the window to peek out through the blinds at the lightening sky.

Could I trust Dermott?

Stemp never failed to irritate me, but I trusted him. Well, trusted his competence, anyway. Dermott's bluster was annoying, but did it conceal capability or inadequacy? I was going to need all the help I could get to nail Sharkface and Fuzzy Bunny.

"Good morning, Aydan!"

I yelped and spun to see Spider leaning into my doorway.

His smile dissolved into concern. "I'm sorry, I didn't mean to scare you."

"It's okay." I tottered over to flop onto my sofa. "I was just..." I hesitated. Not the time or place to discuss Dermott. "...um, preoccupied," I finished. "Come on in."

"I can't." He twitched his shoulders. "I'm working with Tammy and Jill and Brock this morning."

I raised a restraining hand. "Hey, Spider, before you go... do you have a minute?"

"For you? Of course." He glanced up and down the corridor before coming into the room to fold his lanky body into the chair opposite me. "What's up?"

"That's what I wanted to ask you. Is Brock... um, are you okay with... um... You guys don't get along, do you?"

He grimaced. "Was it that obvious?"

"Well... yeah." I eyed his youthful features fondly. "You don't have much of a poker face."

"I know. My face doesn't seem to learn from experience." He blew out a breath and crossed his arms, scrunching deeper into the chair. "It's no big deal. Brock and I were in the same classes through CSIS training. He's an okay guy, but..." He hesitated and I could tell he was trying to come up with something nice to say.

"He's a bit of a prick," I said.

Spider blushed, but laughed. "Ooh, burn!" He sobered. "He's really smart. A lot smarter than me and really good at what he does. He just..."

"Spider, you're the smartest guy I know." I leaned over to pat his bony knee. "Don't let him intimidate you. He's trying to make himself look good by making everybody else look bad, and that's just stupid and childish. You're a better manager and a better person, and that's why Stemp made you the team lead."

Spider flushed, his expression brightening. "Thanks, Aydan. That makes me feel better." He hesitated. "Was that all you wanted to ask me?" At my nod, he rose smiling. "I'd better go. See you later."

After he left I slouched on the sofa a few moments longer, picking at an errant cuticle and fighting my rising uneasiness. Why hadn't Dermott included Spider in the Afterburner briefing? We needed his technical wizardry.

I climbed to my feet, wincing when my knee straightened, and limped over to check my email. Sure enough, there was the meeting request for nine o'clock. Kane and I were the only ones invited. What was Dermott thinking? Why hadn't he invited Germain or Spider?

A glance at my watch assured me I'd find out soon enough, and I trailed down the hall toward the meeting room.

It was empty, and I sank into a chair with my back to the wall. Nerves twitching, I fidgeted with my pen and watched the clock. Its hands crept toward nine at the pace of a crippled snail.

Then past nine.

Shit, had I gotten the location wrong?

I was on the verge of scurrying back to my office to recheck the meeting request when Dermott strode in. He scowled. "Where's Kane?"

A knot of worry tightened around my heart. "I don't know. I haven't seen him. Didn't he check in?"

"I don't know." Dermott crossed to the phone and dialled. "It's Dermott. Did Kane check in yet? ...Damn!" He slapped the receiver back into its cradle. "He's late."

I swallowed rising fear. "No, I meant, did he check in after his op last night? Maybe something happened-"

"What op?"

The sight of Dermott's deepening scowl drained the blood from my face. "What do you mean, 'what op'?" I quavered.

"This isn't the Three fucking Stooges, Kelly! *What* op? Kane didn't call in anything new to me last night and Stemp didn't leave anything in his notes."

"Oh, shit." My words strained out between cold, stiff lips. "He got a coded message last night and took off like a bat out of hell. He must have forgotten to call it in."

Even as the words left my mouth I knew they were wrong. Kane would never forget something that important.

And now he was missing.

"You don't just fucking *forget* to call in an op-" Dermott's ire was interrupted by the phone. He snatched up the receiver. "What!" His knuckles whitened on the receiver and I could have sworn wisps of steam rose from his forehead. "No, it's Dermott. Stemp's buggered off. What the hell's your problem?"

The crackle at the other end of the line had an instant effect. Dermott's ruddy face blanched, the change so startling I thought he might faint.

"No... No, I didn't. And if Stemp did, he didn't leave me any note about it." He groped for a chair and dropped into it, staring wide-eyed at the wall. "Oh, *shit*."

The receiver crackled vociferously as Dermott's hand sagged. After a moment he gave his head a shake and raised the receiver again to break into the tirade on the other end.

"Yeah, I know. Yeah. Yeah, I fucking *get* it, okay? You're not telling me anything I don't already know. I'll get back to you... I don't know, later! Once I figure this out!"

He slammed the receiver back into its cradle before raising it to dial again, his hands shaking. "Yeah, it's Dermott. Get me the access records for the secured weapons lab between five o'clock last night and nine this morning... Yesterday! I need them fucking *yesterday*! *Move it!*"

I clenched my icy fingers together as Dermott turned to face me at last.

"What's wrong?" My words fluttered weakly into the silence.

"The weapon's gone from the secured lab."

My jaw dropped. "But... almost nobody has access...

could they have just misplaced it?

Dermott sprang to his feet. "It's a fucking top-secret weapon in a fucking classified lab, for fucksakes! They're not going to fucking *misplace* it!"

Even if I hadn't already realized that a split second after the words left my mouth, Dermott's spate of f-bombs would have convinced me not to pursue that line of questioning. We were staring at each other in silence when the phone rang.

Dermott snatched up the receiver. "Dermott!" He listened for a moment before shouting, "Who the hell is George Harrison? ...Well, *find out!*"

The receiver went down again, only long enough for him to disconnect and dial again. "Send Webb to the second-floor meeting room. Now!"

Silence descended except for loud, regular pops as Dermott systematically cracked one knuckle after the other. My mind hurtled in frantic circles.

The secret weapon, gone. And the mysterious George Harrison somehow involved. Stemp gone. Kane gone. What the hell was happening?

Spider hurried in looking anxious, his ever-present laptop tucked under his arm.

Dermott practically pounced on him. "Who the hell is George Harrison?"

"Um..." Spider eyed him uncertainly. "...the Beatle? He's dead."

"Not the fucking Beatle! The George Harrison that waltzed into the secured weapons lab at eleven o'clock last night and waltzed out again with the fucking weapon prototype!"

"The George Harrison that works here at Sirius. The one

Nicholas Parr was trying to contact," I added.

"*What?* Oh, *crap!*" The colour drained from Spider's face as he sank into the nearest chair, whipping open his laptop. For a few minutes the only sound was the frenetic clicking of keys, his hazel eyes blazing with fierce concentration.

At last he looked up, gnawing his lip. "There's no George Harrison in the personnel records. Not even the black ops."

"But he was on the Sirius Dynamics phone list Stemp gave me to take to Fuzzy Bunny last week," I protested. "Could he have quit in the last few days?"

"No, I searched a years' worth of records."

"Bullshit!" Dermott burst out. "I just talked to the head of security. Last night at eleven-oh-six P.M., the lab door was opened using a fob that showed a valid top-level security clearance for George Harrison. So don't give me any bullshit about how there's no George Harrison in the system!"

"Hang on..." Spider ducked behind his screen, his fingers flying over the keyboard again. "Okay," he said a few minutes later. "I accessed the point-in-time rollback for the security database, and George Harrison was listed with a top-level security clearance at eleven o'clock last night. At eleven fifty-seven, he was removed. But he never existed anywhere in any of the personnel databases."

"What the f-"

Spider kept talking over Dermott's incipient outburst. "So I pulled the surveillance camera records. Here's our guy going into the lab." He swivelled his laptop so we could see the screen.

We all peered at the rotund man with a paper file folder clutched in his hand, obscuring his features. Pink scalp peeked through the top of his slightly too-long thinning hair, and his rumpled casual pants and open-necked shirt could have belonged to any of the dozens of researchers who occupied labs in the secured area.

"Get his face," Dermott snapped.

"Um... that's a bit of a problem," Spider mumbled. "He knew where the surveillance cameras were, and he blocked every one of them with that file folder. This is the best shot we've got."

"Shit!" Dermott bent closer, as though staring harder at the screen could somehow help. "Can you enhance it? All I can see is a piece of his beard."

"He slipped up and moved the folder just for a second," Spider said, zooming and manipulating the view. "We've got a bit of cheekbone and temple, too, see? And that ear will help. I'm enhancing the image and running facial recognition now, cross-referencing against all known personnel. We won't get a positive ID, but at least we can narrow down some basic characteristics. And using the door frame in this shot for reference, I figure our guy is about five-nine to six feet tall, so I'm filtering for approximate height. It'll just be a minute."

Dermott paced while Spider stared at the screen, his knee bouncing with nervous energy. I slouched in my chair, racking my brain for every time I'd heard George Harrison mentioned.

First, at Parr's Christmas party. Parr had noticed his name on the phone list Stemp had provided and asked me if I knew his 'friend' George. Other than that, I was pretty sure nobody had mentioned Harrison again until Sharkface demanded his photo.

But if Harrison was a friend of Parr's, why would Parr need a photo?

Unless Parr had been lying to me. Well, gee, there was a shocker.

"Okay..." Spider's voice interrupted my thoughts, and I looked up to see his troubled face. "It's a pretty long list." He turned the laptop toward us again.

I frowned at the faces and names filling the screen. "Well, it's a start. I guess there's no point in filtering by security clearance, since it was obviously faked..." I trailed off, pondering. "Hey, Spider, just for the hell of it, can you filter out everybody who's checked in for work today? I mean, if our guy was smart, he'd grab the weapon and then show up today pretending to be as worried as everybody else, but if he took it and ran..."

Spider was already typing. He pressed a key and froze for a moment before flopping back in his chair, blank-faced.

"What?" I demanded.

Dermott and I both swooped in to peer over Spider's shoulder, and I felt my jaw sagging as we stared at the single face remaining on the screen. We exchanged a glance.

"No, that doesn't make sense," I protested. "He's totally the wrong build and he's not bearded and balding like our guy. And anyway, he wouldn't steal the weapon. And even if he did plan to steal it for some reason, he's far too smart to just grab it and run."

The muscles bulged in Dermott's jaw. "Maybe, maybe not. It's easy to stick padding under clothes, and a fake beard and hair is a no-brainer. We can't take a chance." He spun to snatch up the phone. "Security! Total lockdown on all access for Charles Stemp! If he shows up, detain him!"

CHAPTER 28

I stood rooted to the carpet while Dermott concluded his phone call. Spider gave me a worried look, his hands hovering uncertainly above his keyboard.

Dermott slapped the receiver down and wheeled to glare at us. "What the fuck are you waiting for? Get your asses in gear! Find him!"

"Um... maybe we should try calling him first," I ventured. "You know, see if he answers, maybe find out if he was even around last night at eleven."

Dermott's ruddy complexion deepened its hue. "Webb, check his personnel file. Get me numbers for every family member he has. I'll try his cell number and home phone while you do that. And trace his cell phone location."

Spider went back to clicking keys while Dermott dialled and I stood there uselessly.

A few moments later, Dermott swore. "His cell is offline and there's no answer at his home."

"The GPS location for his cell phone matches his house, so he must have left it behind. Try this number." Spider rattled off the digits. "It's his parents in British Columbia. No siblings or other family listed. His father's name is..." he hesitated. "Um, Karma Wolf Song. And his mother is

Moonbeam Meadow Sky."

Dermott snorted laughter as he finished dialling. I bit my lip and managed not to make a retaliatory crack about 'Brent Shirley Dermott'.

Maybe Dermott read my expression, or more likely he refocused on the matter at hand. His mirth vanished while he drummed his fingers on the desk.

After a lengthy wait, he spoke. "Karma Wolf Song or Moonbeam Meadow Sky, please."

A brief pause. Dermott's fist clenched on the receiver and a muscle jumped in his jaw. "This is the police," he snapped. "Get one of them on the line now."

A tide of red suffused his face at the response, and I suppressed a twitch when he exploded, "I don't care if they're having tea and crumpets with God himself! You've got ten seconds to get one of them on the line, or I'll charge you with obstructing an investigation!"

That apparently had the desired effect, and he subsided into baleful muttering. "Goddamn hippy-dippy bullshit. Communing with the earth spirit, my fucking ass... Yes! Mr. Wolf Song?"

The muscle twitched in his jaw again. "Fine. Karma. Your son, Charles Randall Stemp. Have you seen him recently?"

His lips twitched and he clamped a hand over his mouth. When he spoke again, his voice came out sounding half-strangled. "All right, have you seen 'Cosmic River Stone' recently? ...I see. Are there any other family members he might visit?"

He shot us a scowl and a headshake as he spoke again. "No, not that we're aware of; we just need to contact him regarding an important investigation. If you hear from him please call me as soon as possible at this number." Dermott dictated his name and phone number before hanging up to glower at us. "Kelly, get your ass over to..." He made sardonic air quotes. "...*Cosmic River Stone's* place and search it. Tear it apart. Get me a clue where he might have gone. Webb, hack the public networks, gas station and bank CCTVs, airlines, car rentals, busses, fucking dog sled rental places if you have to. Find him!"

"Um, what about..." I began before silencing myself. If Stemp hadn't listed Katya and Anna as next of kin even in his confidential personnel file, there was probably a good reason. "Where's Germain?" I asked instead. "Can I have him for backup?"

"Reassigned." Dermott spat the word as if it tasted foul. "Stemp made sure every agent was assigned to an op except you and Kane before he made his move. Fucking smart bastard. And now Kane's AWOL. You're on your own, Kelly. Better watch your back."

"But... what about Jill?"

I subsided under Dermott's glare. "She's babysitting Mellor full-time. Fucking security breach waiting to happen. Mellor, not Francis," he clarified. "Suck it up, Kelly..." He trailed off, his face clearing. "Wait. I can give you Holt."

Alarm bells jangled in my brain. "Uh, no, that's okay." Dermott's face darkened and I hurriedly changed the subject. "Um, don't you think we should check some of the other guys that came up in Spider's search? I mean, can we justify a full-scale manhunt for Stemp based on circumstantial-"

"He's gone. The weapon's gone. He had the opportunity and he fits the physical profile. And he lied about a family emergency," Dermott snapped.

"But he might have said 'family' if it was a close friend," I argued. "And if he was with somebody in a hospital, he'd have to turn off his pho-"

"Shut the fuck up and get going!" A vein pulsed in Dermott's forehead. "I'm reinstating Holt, effective now. Meet him at Stores in five minutes where he'll be picking up his weapon. Five seconds after that, I want your ass, and his ass, *hauling* ass over to search Stemp's place. If you find him, bring him in. If he resists, use deadly force if necessary. Got it?"

The vein bulged dangerously and I nodded, my gaze riveted to it with the jittery fascination I usually reserved for watching someone inflate a balloon.

"Good! Now. Get. Your. Ass. Out-of-here!"

I withdrew, my mind whirling.

This couldn't be happening. Stemp couldn't have stolen the weapon. He might be a dickhead sometimes, but I'd stake my life that he wasn't a traitor.

I trailed to a halt in my office.

Shit, I *was* staking my life.

What if he'd been leaking information to Fuzzy Bunny all along? He knew everything about me. I was as good as dead.

Oh, God. No, I was worse than dead. If they captured me, death was a mercy I wouldn't be granted.

Sticky hot/cold sweat prickled my body, my knees wobbling. Oh, God, he couldn't be a traitor.

"Aydan." The whisper from close behind me galvanized every muscle. I spun, my fists flying up.

Spider yelped and jumped back, stumbling over his own feet and thumping into the wall.

"Shit, I'm sorry, Spider! Are you okay?"

"Yeah." He straightened and gave me a weak smile,

rubbing his shoulder. "I've got to remember not to sneak up on you." He glanced toward the hall before stepping closer to whisper again. "You didn't mention Katya."

"No." I studied his worried face. "I just... Maybe that was stupid, but... if he didn't put her in his personnel file, I feel like maybe she's in danger if anybody finds out about her." I scrubbed my hands over my face. "Shit, Spider, I just don't know!"

"Me neither." His brow furrowed. "All we know is that they're lovers. What if she's actually an arms dealer and he's giving her the weapon?"

"I..." I trailed off.

I couldn't breach Stemp's trust. Spider and Kane were the only other people who knew about Katya, but nobody else knew about little Anna. If she was harmed because I blabbed, I'd never forgive myself.

"I know some things I can't tell you," I said finally. "I don't even want to think about the consequences if I'm wrong, but if I say anything it could be just as bad. Maybe worse." I looked up into his unhappy face. "If you think it's the right thing to do, tell Dermott about Katya. I can't make that decision for you."

"No..." he said slowly. "I... Stemp isn't always the nicest guy, but I just can't believe he's a traitor. If you think so, too, I won't say anything."

A slow knot formed in my belly and I gave him a sick smile. "I don't know if that makes me feel better or worse."

"Me neither." He grimaced and handed me a scrap of paper with an address scribbled on it. "Here's Stemp's home address. Maybe you'll find something."

"Thanks." I hesitated, but there wasn't anything more to say. I turned my palms up in a gesture of defeat and trudged down the hall toward Stores.

When I arrived, Holt was just buckling a holster on, grinning from ear to ear. He let out a long breath as his fingertips drifted over the grip of the Glock. "Ah, that feels so much better. I've felt naked for the last six months." His steel-blue eyes blazed with frightening intensity above his grin as he tossed me a lightweight bulletproof vest that matched the one he already wore. "Let's go catch ourselves a traitor."

I put the vest on, wondering how bulletproof it really was. With any luck I wouldn't find out.

Holt turned away impatiently, and I donned my parka over the vest and followed. "Um, we don't actually know he's a traitor," I offered as we strode down the hall.

Holt shrugged. "I didn't necessarily mean Stemp's the traitor. But he's a hell of a good place to start looking. Here." He handed me a pair of disposable gloves and an earpiece with a small transmitter. I threaded the earpiece over my ear and dropped the transmitter into my pocket.

"Test. How's that?" Holt inquired, his voice sounding simultaneously through the earpiece and beside me.

"Fine. You?"

He nodded and picked up the pace.

"Don't we need a warrant or something to search his house?" I asked as we hurried across the lobby.

Holt handed in his security fob at the wicket and waited for me to do the same before answering as we headed for the door. "Dermott will get one, if he hasn't got it already. Don't worry, he'll back us up. Not like Stemp." He nearly snarled the name.

Shit, if Stemp was home I'd better find him before Holt did.

"We'll take my car." Holt's voice interrupted my thoughts. He jerked his chin in the direction of the parking lot, and I didn't argue. No need to piss him off unnecessarily.

We got in and Holt headed for the town's small residential area. "I'll take the front door; you cover the back," he said. "We'll clear the place, then search."

His automatic assumption of leadership might have irritated me if I'd been a real agent, but under the circumstances it suited me just fine. I nodded and said nothing, hoping he couldn't see my hands quivering.

'Cover the back'. Yeah, right. What would I do if Stemp ran out? I couldn't stop him. He'd pull some martial arts move on me and drop me in seconds.

But screw Dermott; I wouldn't shoot to kill. Unless Stemp was actually trying to kill me. But if he was, he'd almost certainly succeed.

My heart drummed my ribs.

Holt slowed and jabbed a finger at a small brown bungalow down the street. "That's it. I'll drop you in the back alley." He turned into the alley and stopped a few houses away. "Give me about a minute to get in position around front. Let's do it!"

I didn't trust my voice so I just nodded and hauled myself out of the car, wincing.

As I turned to close the door, Holt shot me a look. "You okay?"

"Smashed my knee last night," I mumbled.

He grimaced sympathy before jerking his chin toward the house. "Let me know when you're outside the gate. Hold until I say go."

My fears did their best to convince me to run far, far

away while I watched his car recede and turn the corner.

This was stupid. Stemp was an ex-agent and the director of clandestine operations, not to mention a computer expert in his own right. Surely he had some kind of external surveillance system on his house. He'd know we were there long before we ever got in.

And anyway, he wouldn't hide here. In the first place, he wasn't a traitor, so he didn't have any reason to hide. And in the second place, even if he was a traitor, he was far too smart to steal a top-secret weapon and then hide inside his own house.

I hoped.

I hesitated at his back gate, swallowing hard.

If he was here...

I clenched my teeth. If he was, and if I had to shoot, I'd aim for his hip. Disabling but probably not lethal.

I drew a deep breath and murmured, "I'm in place."

"Roger that." A few moments later Holt spoke again. "Get to the back door."

Clenching my teeth, I scuttled up the sidewalk to jitter on the back step. "I'm there."

Should I stand to the left or the right? Against the house?

Oh. Duh.

If Stemp ran out while I was standing here, he wouldn't even need martial arts; he'd knock me out cold when he hit me with the door. I pressed my back against the house, using its support to still my trembling.

"In three... two..." Holt's voice in my ear made me twitch.

"ONE!" Holt's shout was half drowned out by a tremendous thump and a grunt that sounded like pain.

A second later he gritted, "Are you in yet?"

What, I was supposed to get *in*?

"Um, no."

His irritation hissed over the comm link. "So much for the element of surprise. He's probably not here anyway, but stay sharp." His voice trailed off. A few moments later, he spoke again. "Pick-proof locks. It's fucking Fort Knox. I'm drilling out the lock now. Can you get that one?"

"No."

No need to point out that I didn't even have a clue how to try.

I drew a breath and let it out slowly.

Stay calm.

Stemp wasn't here, I was sure of it. We were just going to clear an empty house.

Should I draw my gun?

I shot a nervous glance around the yard. What if the neighbours were watching? I was supposed to be a bookkeeper.

I left my Glock in its holster.

Okay, breathe. I could do this. I knew how to clear a building. I'd seen Kane do it often enough. He always looked so cool and collected, though. My heart skittered like a frantic rodent inside my chest.

Focus. Just get in. Clear the house. Search.

Shit! That's why Holt had given me the latex gloves.

I fumbled them out of my pocket and onto my shaking hands, praying Stemp wouldn't burst out the door and catch me with both hands occupied.

Even in the cold air, sweat slicked the inside of my gloves in seconds.

Calm. Stay calm.

A couple of minutes later Holt spoke again. "Got it. Cross your fingers he's not standing there with a fucking cannon waiting for me. Going in now..."

A grunt.

"...*now*..."

A barrage of thumps accompanied by a roar of rage from Holt sent adrenaline sizzling through my body.

"*Fuck!* Fucking paranoid asshole..." Holt sounded mad enough to take on an army of Stemps singlehanded.

"What's happening?" My words snapped out, sounding ridiculously competent considering that my quivering knees were about to drop me to the back step.

"Some kind of barrier on the door." I was pretty sure I could hear Holt's teeth grinding. "Going in the window now."

The crash of shattering glass underscored his words.

A moment later he spoke again, tension vibrating his voice like a plucked string. "Don't shoot! Sir, please put the gun down."

CHAPTER 29

A surge of adrenaline froze my feet to the porch, my heart stalling in my chest.

Oh-shit-oh-shit-oh-shit...

Holt's voice went on. "Sir, I'm a police officer. Please put the shotgun down." He gave the word 'shotgun' a bit of extra emphasis. Emphasis that sounded a lot like 'Kelly, get out here and cover my ass'.

My breathing restarted in shallow panting. Holt wouldn't need to identify himself if it was Stemp. So who was it?

Go and cover Holt, idiot.

As I crept around the side of the house, Holt's steady voice spoke in my ear again. "Sir, I'd like to show you some identification. Is it all right if I put my hand in my pocket to get it for you?"

I hesitated. This didn't sound like a confrontation with a criminal. Would I make things worse if I suddenly popped around the corner of the house?

Slinking closer, I drew my gun. As I crouched at the corner of the house, a cracked voice drifted to my ears.

"No fast moves, sonny, or I'll give you a taste of double-ought buck."

"I'm just going to reach into my pocket, nice and slow," Holt soothed. "See? Here's my ID."

"Cops don't break windows." The cracked voice was firm. "You can just cool your heels until the real cops get here."

"I'm a plain-clothes officer," Holt argued. "We're searching for a missing person and it's urgent that we get into this house."

"Save your breath. It ain't so urgent that it can't wait for the real cops. They oughta be here any minute."

I drew a deep breath and tucked my gun back into my holster. If Holt's captor had called the police, Holt probably wasn't in immediate danger. Better to stay out of it and call Dermott so he could sort it out with the incoming RCMP.

"Stall him," I muttered into my microphone.

Holt kept talking without acknowledging me and I tuned out his continuing negotiations while I retraced my steps to the back yard and pulled out my phone.

Dermott was going to have a shit-fit.

I sighed and dialled.

For once, he answered on the first ring. "Dermott!"

"It's Kelly. We have a situation. It sounds like one of the neighbours caught Holt trying to break in and he's holding him at gunpoint until the RCMP get here."

"Shit! Do something!"

My strained nerves snapped. "I am doing something! I'm covering the back of Stemp's house, and I'm calling you to give a heads-up to the RCMP so they don't freak out and shoot anybody when they get here. Holt told the guy he's a plain-clothes police officer."

"Hang on."

Interminable minutes passed. I stared at Stemp's back

door until my eyes burned, the phone trembling in my left hand, my right hovering over my holster.

At last Dermott came back on the line. "Talked to the unit. They're inbound just a few minutes away. They'll back you up."

I blew out a breath and hung up before relaying the information to Holt over the comm link. As I spoke the distant wail of a siren caught my ear.

Holt spoke to his captor again. "Here they come. You should probably put the shotgun down now so they don't think you're dangerous."

Apparently that didn't fly. Holt continued his soothing monologue while the siren's volume swelled and finally stopped out front. A few minutes later, Holt's side of the conversation indicated the RCMP officers had defused the situation and the shotgun-wielding man had cooperated.

Holt spoke over the link again. "Kelly, a uniformed officer is coming around the north side to cover the back. Meet me around front and we'll go in together."

I drew a deep, shaky breath and let it out slowly.

Calm. Stay calm.

When the young officer stepped warily into the back yard, I summoned up a smile and made for the front with the most confident stride I could muster.

As I rounded the corner, a skinny elderly man in a plaid shirt and denim overalls glanced over and his bushy eyebrows shot up. His rickety form seemed barely sturdy enough to support itself, let alone the double-barrelled shotgun tucked into the crook of one toothpick arm. His bedroom-slipper-clad feet must have been freezing in the snow, but his weathered hands were steady on the gun.

He smiled, revealing ill-fitting dentures. "A lady cop?

Well, how-do, ma'am? Lordy, I didn't know we had so many undercover cops in town. Here I thought you were that new bookkeeper."

"I am a bookkeeper," I said hurriedly. "I'm not a cop. That's why I was staying out of the way until they opened the door."

The remaining RCMP officer shot a puzzled look at Holt, who gave him a tiny headshake in return.

"I'm a friend of S..." I stumbled over the name. "...Charles. He didn't show up for work this morning, and I'm worried about him. We're checking to make sure he hasn't had an accident, but we don't have a key to his house."

The old man's eyebrows drew together, his wrinkles furrowing into concern. "Wish I'd known that. I'm Bud Weems. I live across the street." He nodded toward the blue house with red trim glowing against the snow. "I keep an eye on Charlie's house for him, and I thought Sonny here was some hoodlum breaking in."

"It's all right, Mr. Weems, please go back to your home now," Holt broke in impatiently. "Let us do our job."

Bud raised an indulgent eyebrow. "Sure, Sonny. But as I was saying..." He turned back to address me. "I watch Charlie's house for him and water his plants when he's away. I've got a key. And I've got the doohickey that takes the bars off the inside of the doors." He shot a disapproving frown at Holt. "All you had to do was ask. You didn't have to smash his window."

Muscles rippled in Holt's jaw. "Thank you, Mr. Weems," he gritted. "May we please have the key and the... device now?"

"Sure, Sonny. Just sit tight and I'll get 'em."

I stepped forward as he turned back to his house. "I'll

come with you," I offered. "You should stay inside where it's warm."

"That's right kind of you, ma'am. It is a little nippy out today, isn't it?"

"A little nippy for a cotton shirt and bedroom slippers," I agreed.

Bud let out a cracked chuckle. "Nothing compared to the army. A few minutes of cold just makes me more thankful for what I got."

I made an encouraging noise as he picked his way cautiously through the snow, the shotgun secure in his two-handed grip.

He went on, "Yep, got my twenty years with the PPCLI." His faded eyes twinkled at my questioning look. "Princess Patricia's Canadian Light Infantry. Retired master corporal. The pension ain't much, but it's nice to have a little something coming in. Bought a farm when I got out of the army, and farmed for another twenty-five years. Then I sold the farm and retired to town."

We reached his front step and he nodded fondly at the brightly-painted house. "I still keep up the regimental colours, though. 'These colours don't run', that's what we always used to say. Are you comfortable around guns, ma'am? Would you be okay holding my shotgun for a moment?"

"I'm sorry, I should have introduced myself," I apologized. "I'm Aydan Kelly. And yes, I like guns. I used to shoot with my dad."

He smiled and handed me the shotgun before gripping the handrail with both hands to haul himself slowly up the three stairs. "It's nice to meet you, Miss Kelly." He sounded breathless, and I eyed him with concern as I joined him on the top step.

"Don't worry about me." He wheezed a laugh as he retrieved his shotgun. "The old lungs ain't what they used to be, but the ticker's good as ever. Hope you don't smoke, Miss Kelly. I quit twenty years ago, but I'm paying for the forty years before that." He opened the door and motioned me in as he continued, "You just wait right here and I'll get the key. I keep it in a safe place..."

His voice receded as he turned down a hallway and I waited as instructed, taking in the small living room with its clean but shabby furniture. The scent of bacon and coffee lingered in the air.

Several minutes later I was sweating profusely and beginning to wonder if he was all right, but before I could call out he reappeared carrying a key and what looked like the fob for a car's electric door locks.

"Here you go, Miss Kelly. You just press this button and the bars will open right up. When you're done, close it up again and bring it back." He frowned. "I sure hope nothing happened to Charlie. He didn't signal me that he was going anywhere."

I snapped to attention. "He signals you? How? Does he always tell you when he's leaving?"

"Yep, any time he'll be gone for more than a couple of days. His hibiscus trees and cyclamens need watering every three days or so. If he knows in advance he mentions it while we're playing cribbage, but if he has to leave real sudden, he lowers the blind half-way in his front room so I know he's gone."

Aha.

"I'd better take this over so we can get into his house now," I said. "But I'd like to talk to you a bit more if we don't..." I trailed off. "I really hope we don't find him."

Lines of worry pinched Bud's face. "I sure hope not, too, Miss Kelly. Let me know as soon as you can, will you please?"

When I retraced my steps to Stemp's house, Holt shot me a sour look. "What the hell were you doing all this time? Having a nice little cup of tea?"

"Gathering intel," I snapped, and pressed the button on the fob.

A muffled thump from the other side of the door indicated the barrier was removed and Holt straightened, his pique vanishing. We exchanged a nod with the RCMP officer, and Holt pushed the door open and slipped inside.

I followed on his heels, sidestepping to put my back to the wall. After a couple of blinks my eyes adjusted from the snow-bright daylight, and Holt jerked his chin at the hallway. I drew my gun and followed his lead to methodically clear the house, my heart pounding so hard I could barely hold my weapon steady.

Every time we opened a door or rounded a corner, I steeled myself for sudden movement and an ear-shattering gunshot. By the time we reached the basement, my shaking legs could barely carry me.

When we finished checking the last corner, Holt and I exchanged a nod and I abandoned bravado to collapse against the wall and slither to the floor, gulping air.

Holt blew out a breath and holstered his weapon before sinking down to hunker opposite me. "Fuck," he muttered. He scrubbed trembling hands over his face and hissed out another long breath.

Sympathy softened my heart. "It's tough to come back," I said quietly.

"Yeah." He met my gaze, the vulnerability in his eyes belying the hard lines of his face. "A hell of a lot tougher than I expected."

I gave him an understanding grimace.

We sat in silence for a few more moments before Holt sucked in a breath and stood, squaring his shoulders. "Okay. Let's do this."

He offered me a hand up and I accepted it to rise, too. "Where do you want to start?"

"I'll do the basement and garage if you want to do the main floor," he offered.

I nodded and headed for the stairs.

On the upper landing, I hesitated. What the hell was I even looking for? I was pretty sure I wouldn't find a to-do list that included '*steal classified weapon*'. Maybe there would be some evidence on his home computer, but that would need Spider's expertise.

I sighed and headed for the bathroom. If I was going somewhere, I'd take a toothbrush.

There was a single toothbrush in a clean glass next to a precisely-rolled tube of toothpaste. The medicine cabinet revealed a sparse assortment of over-the-counter painkillers and some first-aid supplies, and I checked the boxes and bottles, finding exactly what their labels advertised.

The cabinets were equally unenlightening until I pulled out the bottom drawer and sprang back with an involuntary yelp. Thankful that Holt hadn't seen my embarrassing reaction, I let out a breath and bent to examine the 'mice' I thought I'd glimpsed. An assortment of fake beards, moustaches, and eyebrows were neatly laid out in the bottom of the drawer along with a bottle labelled 'spirit gum' and some theatrical cosmetics. Apparently George Harrison wasn't Stemp's only disguise.

I found nothing hidden elsewhere, not even inside the toilet tank, and I sighed and turned my unwilling feet toward Stemp's bedroom. The invasion of his privacy seemed doubly intrusive after the devastation of my own home. And we were supposed to be the good guys.

An hour later, the only new things I'd discovered about Stemp were that he wore silk boxer shorts and liked houseplants. I really hadn't wanted to know the former, and the latter was useless. He had no family photos and few possessions. No scratch pads or jotted notes; not even a grocery list. No liquor. And no weapons of any kind. The only personal item in the whole house was a small dreamcatcher on the wall over the head of his bed.

I rubbed the incipient headache between my eyebrows. God, what if he'd gone somewhere last night and just had car trouble? If he came back and found us tearing his house apart.

And what if Kane needed help? What if he'd been captured? My heart clutched at the thought. What if he was suffering barbaric torture even now, hoping for rescue that wasn't coming because I was pissing away time hunting for a man who was almost certainly innocent.

Holt's voice made me start. "I'm done the basement and garage. He's sure got a shitpile of plants. I'll start on them."

I turned in time to see him uproot a beautiful little bonsai evergreen.

"Don't!" The word snapped out before I even thought.

Holt frowned, the small tree dangling forlornly from his hand, its exposed roots weeping dirt.

"Why the hell not?" He tossed it on the floor and turned to his next victim. "Plant pots are a great place to hide stuff.

Nobody ever thinks to look there." He upended a large pot containing a flowering shrub, breaking its branches and scattering dirt everywhere. One of the bright blooms fell, its red petals like a splash of blood against the dark carpet.

"*Stop!*" I lunged forward to grab his wrist. "Don't you dare wreck his plants!"

Holt gaped at me for an instant before his brows drew down. "Back off, Kelly! You forget we're looking for a deadly weapon?" His scowl deepened. "Or what, are you trying to protect him? Are you screwing him after all?"

"Jeez, you're a pig! No, I'm not screwing him! But we don't even know he's guilty. The poor bastard gets called away for a family emergency and comes home to find everything he cares about smashed and destroyed, do you know what that's like, Holt? It sucks! It fucking *sucks!*"

My voice cracked and I flung his wrist away to turn my back, hiding the stupid tears that suddenly swamped my eyes.

CHAPTER 30

"What the hell, Kelly?" Holt demanded. "If you can't do the job, why the hell are you here?"

"I never asked for the fucking job," I hissed, and dashed the tears away. I held my voice hard and level. "I'll hold the plants while you pull the pots off, *gently*. If there's nothing hidden in them, we'll put the plants back in. Green side up. Clear?"

After a moment of sullen silence he mumbled, "Fine."

We worked without speaking for a time, and I avoided his gaze. At last he said, "Aydan? I was out of line. Sorry."

"It's okay," I muttered, and turned for the next plant.

Another long silence while we methodically evicted and repotted several more plants.

"It wasn't just the crack about Stemp that pissed you off, was it?" he asked at last.

I bit my tongue against the urge to tell him to stick it, and rose from my crouch to head for the kitchen. "Just a few more plants in here."

He followed me, apparently undeterred. "Talk to me, Aydan. Team Anger Management, remember? I felt like you were angry about something more than-"

"Don't go all sensitive on me," I snapped. "I liked you

better when you were an asshole."

He barked out a laugh. "I hate that fucking touchy-feely bullshit, too."

"Good." I picked up a pot and held it out to him. "Here."

He eased the pot off the roots and inspected the root ball before tucking the pot back into place. "But I wasn't kidding about the team stuff." His eyes met mine, the steel softening. "You want to talk about it?"

I turned away before his sympathy could weaken me. "No big deal. My place got trashed last night, for the second time in two months. I know what it's like, that's all."

"Oh. That sucks." He hesitated. "Do you want some help with it?"

"Thanks, but it's okay." I turned to face him again. "Well, I don't know where else we can search. I didn't find anything. How about you?"

Holt scowled. "Fuck-all. No airline tickets, no baggage claim stubs, no personal address book, no lockbox, nothing. And did you find a computer?"

I shook my head. "No. Which is weird, because I know he's a computer expert. His toothbrush is here and there's empty luggage in the closet, and Bud Weems says Stemp would have told him if he was planning to be gone for more than a day or two."

Holt's scowl deepened. "This was a waste of time."

"Yeah." I sighed. "I guess I'll go have a chat with Bud. See if he noticed anything." I picked up a couple of plants to carry to the living room.

"What the hell are you doing?" Holt inquired mildly.

"They'll freeze if they're too close to that broken window."

He shook his head. "Shit, Kelly, you're soft." Before I

could retort, the corner of his mouth lifted in a wry smile. "There's a piece of plywood in the garage that looked big enough, and Mr. Anal-Retentive has his tools all hung up on pegboard. I'll go get the stuff to cover the window."

When Holt returned bearing a hammer, nails, and plywood, I asked, "Do you have a secured phone on you? I used mine up calling Dermott about the RCMP, and my extras are in my car."

His face went blank. "Shit. No." A flush climbed his neck and his jaw tightened. "I forgot to get them from Stores. What the hell kind of spook am I?"

I shrugged. "You only had ten seconds to go from off-duty to active service."

"That's no excuse. It was a stupid mistake." The words grated out between his teeth. "A dangerous mistake."

"It's not that big a deal. Cut yourself some slack." I eyed his darkening scowl, hiding my anxiety behind a comforting tone. "You'd do the same for another agent if they were in your place."

His fist clenched on the hammer handle, his knuckles whitening. "No. I wouldn't." His words came out in a menacing growl. "I'd chew a fucking strip off their incompetent hide. Like I told you, I'm an asshole."

"Well, don't be," I snapped, and hurried outside just in case he decided to swing that hammer.

When he didn't come roaring out behind me, I pulled my personal cell phone out with trembling fingers and dialled the main office line at Sirius Dynamics.

Dermott came on the line with gratifying speed after I'd navigated the receptionist.

"What's new?" he asked.

"Nothing, but we're going to talk to the neighbours."

A moment of silence greeted that announcement. When he spoke again, I couldn't identify the undercurrent in his tone. "We've got news here."

Was that worry straining his voice? Excitement? Grief?

My heart rate ratcheted up and I mentally cursed the unsecured line that prevented me from demanding details.

"It is urgent?" The undercurrent in my voice was easy to identify. Fear, plain and simple.

"No. Finish up there and then come in."

What the hell did that mean? It could mean anything from 'Stemp just walked in and explained everything' to 'We just found Kane's and Stemp's bodies'.

I swallowed a hard knot of dread. "Okay. We'll be back as soon as we can."

As I disconnected, Holt emerged from the house, the hammer dangling loosely from his hand. Apparently the storm had passed. His brows drew together in concern. "What's happening?"

"I don't know." My voice came out in a dry croak, and I cleared my throat before continuing, "They've got some new information at the office but Dermott says it's not urgent. He said to finish up questioning the neighbours before we come in."

"Is that good or bad?"

I grimaced. "I wish I knew."

"Shit." Holt squared his shoulders and drew in a breath. "Okay, give me a hand with this plywood and then we'll canvass. You've got a rapport with Weems, so take your time with him. I'll see what I can get from the rest of the neighbours."

A few minutes later I rang the doorbell of the blue and red house. The door popped open almost immediately.

"Come in." Bud's anxious gaze searched my face. "Please, come in and sit down. Excuse me, I've got the kettle on, I just have to turn off the heat." He hurried for the kitchen, and I seized the opportunity to slip off my parka and the bulletproof vest that would have been tricky for a bookkeeper to explain. Folding the vest inside my parka, I laid both on the scarred deacon's bench beside the door and shed my boots.

Not a moment too soon. Bud rounded the corner from the kitchen. "Did you..." His thready voice wavered into silence.

"No, we didn't find him," I said.

"Thank the good Lord." His shoulders sagged with relief before he shook himself. "I'm sorry, where are my manners? Please sit down. Can I get you a cup of tea, Miss Kelly?" He beckoned me to the sofa.

I sank onto it and kept sinking as the aged springs succumbed to my weight. "Thank you, that would be great. And please call me Aydan."

"Only if you'll call me Bud." The twinkle was back in his eye.

I summoned up my best smile. "Sure, Bud. Thanks."

After considerable fussing with antique-looking bone china cups and a battered silver teapot, Bud finally settled in the overstuffed recliner across from me with a wheezing breath and leaned forward, clutching his tea. "Was everything in order over there?"

I hesitated, and his cup clattered in its saucer.

"Yes," I said hurriedly. "I mean, it was in order when we got there..." I trailed off, guilt making it hard to meet his piercing gaze. "It's a bit of a mess now... after the police searched it," I mumbled, throwing Holt to the wolves with barely a qualm.

"That young hoodlum made a mess, you mean," Bud snapped. "I didn't like the looks of him from the start."

"I think he's just trying to do his job as efficiently as possible. His priority is finding Ste... Charles." When I looked up to meet Bud's gaze, guilt squeezed even harder. "If you want to leave the key with me, I'll go back later and clean up," I offered, fighting off despair at the thought of having to tidy Stemp's place as well as my own. "I made sure the plants were all back in their pots and I carried them away from the broken window, so I hope they'll be okay."

"Oh, now, don't worry about that," Bud interrupted. "I don't have much to do these days. I'll just go over and straighten up."

I tried to hide my breath of relief. "Thanks. Charles is lucky to have you for a neighbour."

I struggled out of the couch to lay the key and locking device on the table beside him, and he raised the teapot inquiringly.

"Thanks, just a half-cup," I agreed.

When he had finished pouring I resumed my seat and sipped before asking, "So have you known Charles long?"

"'Bout seven years, ever since he moved in across the street." Bud grinned. "I remember it like it was yesterday. This proper-looking young buck in a suit and tie, gimping around giving orders to these two dirty old hippies moving stuff into the house. I was sure hoping it was him and not them moving in." He laughed. "Found out later they were his folks, and they're nice as can be. Odd ducks, mind you, but fine people. Charlie'd been in a car accident, so he couldn't lift anything or do much for a while. I offered to help out after his folks went home, and that's how we met."

He waved a self-deprecating hand at his emaciated body. "I was in better shape then. Now Charlie's the one that helps me."

"So you spend quite a bit of time together," I prompted.

"Heck, not that much. We play cribbage a couple nights a week; wave hello across the street; that's about it."

"But he'd tell you if he was going somewhere."

Bud's wrinkles creased into a frown and he passed a hand over his age-spotted bald head. "Not unless he was going away for a few days." His frown deepened. "Aren't you jumping the gun a bit getting the police involved this early? A young buck like him might just be..."

He hesitated. "Sorry, ma'am... uh, Aydan... I don't mean to be crude, but maybe he's just, er, keeping company with a young lady."

I shook my head. "I doubt it. He..." I rapidly considered and discarded several choices of words. "...had an important meeting this morning," I continued. "It wouldn't be like him to miss it without calling in."

A gloomy silence descended, broken only by the ticking of the clock on the bookshelf.

I sipped my cooling tea, every tick-tock winding my nerves tighter with the knowledge that Kane's minutes might be slipping away. Assuming he wasn't dead already.

The sound of the doorbell made me start. Bud levered himself out of the recliner and shuffled toward the door.

"Oh, it's you." Bud's disapproval was evident in the three words. He poked his head into the living room to address me. "Sonny-boy's here."

I set aside my teacup and struggled out of the man-eating sofa again. When I rounded the corner, Holt was wearing his neutral cop face.

"I'm finished with the neighbours," he said. "Are you ready to go?"

I nodded and turned to Bud. "Thank you for the tea. May I call you if I have more questions?"

"Sure, of course. I'll do anything I can to help. I'm in the phone book. I'm the only Weems left in Silverside now." He hesitated. "You'll let me know? If you... find out anything?"

"Of course. Oh, and here's my card." I handed him one of my bookkeeping cards before putting on my boots and tucking my rolled-up parka under my arm. "Please call me any time of the day or night if you hear from him or see any activity around his house."

Bud nodded and we left him standing in his doorway, eyeing Stemp's house with a troubled expression.

By the time we got to Holt's car halfway down the block, my teeth were chattering. I buckled into the passenger's seat and wrapped my arms around myself, shivering.

Holt shot me a look as he put the car into gear. "Why the hell don't you put on your jacket?"

"I've got the bulletproof vest rolled up in it. I didn't want to blow my cover as a bookkeeper."

Holt grimaced understanding and cranked up the heater fan. "So did you get anything from the old fart?"

"No... I don't think so." I nearly added, '...and watch your mouth, Sonny-boy', but I bit my tongue in time. Don't poke the bear.

"How about you?" I asked instead.

"Nothing. Standard serial-killer stuff." When I gaped at him, he elaborated, "You know. Quiet, keeps to himself, never causes any trouble..."

"Right." I sighed and hunched deeper in the seat. "God, I hope it's not bad news at Sirius. Can you drive any faster?"

CHAPTER 31

When I signed for my fob at the Sirius security desk, it wasn't the cold that made my hands tremble. The stairs to Dermott's second-floor office seemed interminable, but when I reached the top I wished they'd been longer. My reluctant feet dragged on the carpet and I avoided Holt's gaze while he paced down the hall beside me.

Until I actually entered Dermott's office, I could pretend everything was fine. Kane would be there. Stemp would be there. Everybody would be laughing over the misunderstanding...

No laughter greeted me when I tapped on the open door.

Dermott looked up from his computer, scowling. "Anything?"

"No." Holt sounded frustrated. I just shook my head, my throat too dry to speak.

Dermott picked up the phone and punched an extension. After a moment, he spoke. "They're back." He hung up the phone and stood, jerking his chin in the direction we'd come. "Meeting room. Webb will be there in a few minutes."

We trailed down the hallway and took our seats in the meeting room in silence. Dermott had just opened his mouth to speak when Spider hurried in, clutching his laptop like a shield. He dropped into a chair as if his knees had collapsed and eyed us worriedly. "Did you find anything?"

Holt shook his head.

I couldn't bear to wait any longer. I turned to Dermott. "What's the new development?"

Dermott looked as though he was chewing something unpleasant. "When I escalated this up the chain of command to get the search warrant, they gave me some more information." He surged to his feet as if unable to sit still and strode over to close the meeting room door.

"What is it?" I tried to keep the impatience out of my voice, but only half succeeded. My pulse hammered in my throat as Dermott scowled.

"Seems they knew about Stemp's alias of George Harrison. And they gave him approval to take the weapon."

"What?" Spider's mouth dropped open. "They *knew*?"

"Yeah." Dermott's mouth twisted. "Fucking nice of them to tell us."

"So we shouldn't have been searching his house at all." I fell silent at the sight of Dermott's scowl.

"Oh, hell yeah, we should." He returned to drop into his chair again. "Apparently Kane did call in last night." He made a 'go-figure' gesture before continuing, "He said he had an informant who had reactivated after years of silence. Kane thought he could get some back-door information about the origin of the weapon, but he'd need to show the weapon to somebody. He didn't say who."

I leaned forward in my chair, my interlaced fingers going cold when the blood squeezed out of them.

"So Stemp reactivated an old cover identity from his last op seven years ago," Dermott continued, his words grating through clenched teeth. "George Harrison. And he got clearance from the chain of command to take the weapon to a meeting place at eleven-thirty last night. He was supposed to return it immediately after their meeting. Instead, he remotely accessed the security database, erased George Harrison, and buggered off with the weapon."

"But... but..." I bit off my pointless objections and stared at Dermott. "So what now?"

Dermott shrugged as if a great weight lay on his shoulders. "Now we find Stemp. And Kane. Find out if they colluded to steal the weapon; find out who their contact was for the meeting or if they had a contact at all; get that fucking weapon back; and drag their fucking traitorous asses to jail. Kelly, you know Kane best, so you're in charge of this investigation. Webb, let Brock take over the decryption program temporarily while you support Kelly. Holt, you're full-time with Kelly. I've gotten clearance for all of you to access personnel and mission files for Stemp and Kane. I..." He rose and made a frustrated gesture. "I'll be finding out what else Stemp didn't tell us about all the other ops."

My nervousness swelled into dismay. "But... um, where should I start?" The dismay trickled into outright dread. "And what should I tell Sharkf... Barnett?"

Dermott shrugged, already halfway out the door. "Your op, Kelly. Let me know what you decide."

I sat paralyzed by the mocking echo of my earlier words to Kane and Hellhound. My op; my orders.

Shit, shit, shit.

"So what's the plan?" Holt demanded.

"I... um... hang on a sec." I sank my chin to my chest and churned my fingers in my hair.

Should I just hand the whole thing over to Holt? He was an experienced agent. He'd know what to do, or at least where to start.

But he hated Stemp. And his self-control was precarious at best. And dammit, even if I wasn't sure about Stemp, I was positive about Kane. There was no way he was a traitor. If Holt railroaded them, or worse, shot them in a fit of rage...

No, dammit, I had to keep Holt under control.

And there had to be an explanation for all this.

I emerged from the cover of my hair to meet Spider's anxious eyes. "Spider, can you bring up the records for Stemp's last op before he retired from active service? Or wait; any op where he used the alias of George Harrison?"

Spider nodded and dove into his laptop. I watched his rapid typing for a moment before adding, "And are there audio records of Kane's and Stemp's calls on the secured phones last night?"

"Yes," Spider mumbled, still typing with his gaze riveted to the screen. "Hang on..."

"Oh, and if we could find any of Kane's old ops where he had an informer... and track his personal cell phone..."

"Okay, hang on..."

I shut up and let Spider work, my mind racing as fast as his flying fingers. If we could identify Kane's informant, we might be able to backtrack to figure out who they had been meeting about the weapon. If something had gone wrong at the meeting and they'd been captured...

But no, that didn't make sense. Stemp had accessed the security database after the meeting. He wouldn't have been able to do that if he was a captive.

Unless they had forced him.

My mind shuddered away from the level of coercion that would be necessary to crack Stemp's icy control. I couldn't imagine him breaking, even under torture.

Shit.

I fell back in my chair, staring wide-eyed at the wall.

The timeframe was too tight. They couldn't have captured him and tortured him into submission in a mere twenty minutes. They had to have some other leverage.

Like the little daughter who meant so much to him.

"What?" Holt's voice cut into the cold horror that gripped me. "You look like you just saw a ghost."

"I..." My voice came out in a dry croak. "I hope I didn't."

"What the hell's that supposed to mean?"

I was saved from answering when Spider spoke. "Okay, I've pulled the mission reports. I'm sending copies to your network accounts now. Kane's personal cell phone matches the GPS coordinates for his house, so it looks like he left it at home. And here's the audio from Kane's call last night."

He pressed a key and Kane's strong baritone spoke from the laptop. "It's Kane. Dawn White has resurfaced. She has connections with a weapons expert who should be able to identify the maker of the weapon. She's set up a meeting so I can show it to him. What do you think?"

Stemp's cool tones responded. "How much do you trust her?"

"Not at all. But the information from the weapons expert... I'd say ninety percent."

Silence hummed on the line for a few moments before Stemp spoke again. "I'll escalate it up the chain of command. Call back in twenty minutes."

"I won't be able to. The meeting is in forty minutes if you can deliver the weapon."

Stemp didn't hesitate. "Where?"

"Drumheller. I don't know exactly where yet. If I tell them the weapon is being delivered, I'll be able to provide directions."

"Wait for my call." A dial tone hummed out of the laptop as Stemp hung up.

Spider eyed Holt and me anxiously. "What do you think?"

I slouched in my chair, frowning. "No surprises there. Stemp obviously managed to get permission to take the weapon to Kane, and then he took it and left."

And neither of them came back.

Nearly twelve hours in enemy hands.

I pushed away the cold fear tightening my throat. Just figure this out.

"Stemp was wearing a disguise." I thought out loud, tugging a lock of hair. "Why do you suppose he concealed his face on the security cameras? If the chain of command knew he was taking the weapon, why would he go to all the trouble of putting on his disguise and hiding his face? Why wouldn't he just go and get the weapon and... oh, never mind." I grimaced. "It was late at night. He would have been at home, not at the office. Okay, so he put on his disguise at home. So he must have been wearing it when he signed for his security fob, right?"

"Right." Spider started clicking keys again. A moment later, his shoulders slumped. "Nope. Here he is, signing in at eleven o'clock." He swivelled the laptop around so we could see Stemp in the security footage, wearing immaculately pressed casual pants and a polo shirt while he signed for his fob and entered the secured area.

It seemed odd to see him out of his usual uniform of quiet suit and tie, but then again, it would be a little silly for him to get dressed up in a suit and tie at eleven o'clock at night.

"Wait, back it up, Spider." I peered at the screen. "Those aren't the clothes he was wearing when he went into the secured lab. They must be in that bag he's carrying."

Holt grunted. "Makes sense. He'd need a bag to carry the weapon out anyway. He'd have his disguise in there, too."

I sat up straight. "And his laptop. So he goes down to the secured area, changes into his disguise, logs into the security database and adds George Harrison, uses that ID to access the lab and take the weapon, then takes off the disguise, puts everything into the bag, and leaves. What was he wearing when he signed out?"

Spider clicked a few more keys, watching his screen. At last he spoke. "You're right. I can track him going into the men's room in the secured area and coming out disguised. At least I'm pretty sure it's him, but he's still hiding his face from the cameras. Then he goes to the lab, then back into the men's room, and then comes out looking the same as when he arrived." Spider turned the laptop again to display Stemp signing out.

"So why would he bother?" I frowned at Holt and Spider. "Why go to all the trouble of disguising himself to get into the lab? The chain of command knew he was taking the weapon. He had to know we'd be able to track him on the security cameras, and it doesn't take a rocket scientist to figure out he's the only one going in and out of the men's room at eleven o'clock at night."

Their blank expressions didn't help. I hissed out a breath between my teeth. "Okay, do you have Stemp's call to Dermott?"

"Yes." Spider clicked a few more keys and a moment later Stemp's dispassionate voice spoke from the laptop.

"It's Stemp. A personal emergency has arisen and I need to leave immediately. Please take over."

Dermott's grunt could have been satisfaction or annoyance. A moment later the call ended.

I slouched in my chair. "Well, that was short and sweet."

"And useless," Holt grumbled.

Sudden realization made me sit up again. "Maybe not completely useless. I thought Dermott said he'd reported a 'family' emergency. He didn't. He said 'personal' emergency."

"Same shit, different pile," Holt drawled. "Still doesn't tell us anything."

"Well, no..." I subsided. "But at least he didn't lie about a family emergency."

Holt sneered. "Oh, well, that makes it all better. He only stole a deadly top-secret weapon. Guess we better cut him some slack. After all, he's not a *liar*."

"Shut up," I mumbled.

He added a scowl to his sneer. "So, oh mighty leader, what's the plan?"

Irritation straightened my spine and I locked eyes with him. "The plan is, we go over Stemp's and Kane's mission reports with a fine-toothed comb. Spider, do you have any way of accessing Kane's cellphone records to see where he called Stemp from last night? I assume he must have called with a meeting location-"

"Or they set this up in advance and just fucked off with the weapon," Holt interrupted.

I raised my voice and kept talking over him. "...and it might help if we know where that was."

"I should be able to," Spider said.

"Good. Anything you can get would be great." I stood,

doing my best decisive-leader imitation. "Let's split up and start reading mission reports. Meet back here at two o'clock. I'm looking for any commonalities between the reports, any names or descriptions mentioned, everything we know about Dawn White and Stemp's George Harrison alias; anything at all that raises a flag."

"That's only a couple of hours," Holt protested.

"And that's two hours too long, so get on it," I snapped, and strode out.

Too rattled to risk human interaction, I took refuge in a cubicle in the women's washroom. Lowering myself onto the toilet seat, I wrapped both arms around my trembling body and closed my eyes, memories of torture and captivity turning my guts to water. A couple of ragged breaths escaped me and I clamped down on control before they could turn into sobs.

Missing for twelve hours already. Twelve hours of unspeakable suffering...

I swallowed a whimper and jerked my spine straight. I couldn't help anybody if I was an emotional mess.

And anyway, maybe they hadn't been captured. Kane was the best agent in the service, and Stemp had been a top agent, too. Together they'd be damn hard to overcome. And Stemp had sounded fine when he spoke to Dermott after the meeting.

But then, he never betrayed any emotion.

I vacated the cubicle and tottered to the sink to wash my hands. Glaring at my strained face in the mirror, I squared my shoulders. Time to suck it up and be the agent everybody thought I was. Too bad if I didn't know what I was doing. I had Holt's experience to draw from, and I'd just have to figure the rest out.

CHAPTER 32

Sinking into my desk chair, I checked my phone messages just in case there was a call from Kane. Think positive thoughts. Maybe he was just staying deep undercover. If he didn't trust his informant, he wouldn't take a chance on reporting to Dermott.

My voicemail was empty, and I shook my head at my own foolish hope. If he was deep undercover he wouldn't call me, either. He'd made it very clear he didn't want me involved when he'd kicked me out of his house last night.

But he might have called someone else. Like his brother-in-arms.

I punched in the number and waited, barely breathing while it rang at the other end. I drew a short hiccupping breath at the sound of Hellhound's cheerful gravelly voice.

"Hey, darlin'. Hope you're callin' to say you're comin' down for a little R an' R."

"Um, no..." My voice came out sounding small and lost.

Tension knifed into his rasp. "What's wrong?"

"I... nothing, I hope... have you heard from John?"

"Not since he left on Boxin' Day. What's wrong?" he repeated.

Conscious of our unsecured connection, I made my tone

light. "I was just expecting to see him today and he didn't show. Let me know if he calls you, okay?"

"Okay..." He hesitated. "Hey, listen, darlin', I was thinkin' of comin' up for the Thursday jam at Blue Eddy's tonight. Ya feel like some company?"

"Um..."

It was my turn to hesitate while I read between the lines. Did I want his help?

Hell, yes. But did I want to risk involving him in something this dangerous?

"It's okay if ya ain't in the mood." Hellhound spoke into the lengthening silence. "I'll be stayin' at the hotel, an' I'll be at Eddy's around eight as usual. Gimme a call if ya wanna see me."

"Of course I want to see you," I assured him. "I'm just a little busy right now."

"That's okay, darlin', I'm gonna be there anyway, so I'll see ya if I see ya. 'Bye now."

He hung up, leaving me to draw a breath of relief mixed with worry. He'd come. He was probably getting ready to leave right now, judging by the undertone of urgency in his voice.

If only I knew whether that was good or bad.

Well, I couldn't change it. I put my worry aside and opened the first mission report.

An hour later I leaned back to massage my aching neck, frowning into infinity while I shuffled the pieces of my mental jigsaw puzzle.

"Aydan?" Spider's voice yanked me back inside the four walls of my office with a start.

"Uh. Sorry, Spider, what?"

"I said, did you get lunch? It's after noon."

For the first time, I spared enough mental capacity to note the weakness in my limbs and my growling stomach. "Uh, no, I guess not."

"That's what I thought." He came in and handed me a small carton of orange juice and a couple of the cereal bars from my stash in the lunchroom. "You'd better eat these."

"Thanks, Spider, you're the best." I tore off the wrapper, taking a too-large bite of cereal bar. "How is your analysis going?" I mumbled around the mouthful.

"Pretty well. It took me a while, but I just finished tracing the records for the secured burner phones. I found an incoming call on Kane's phone last night just before eleven. That must have been when Stemp called to say he could bring the weapon. And then there was an outbound call at eleven-thirty. That would be when Kane called Stemp to give him directions. I pulled the tower and GPS coordinates, and the call came from an automotive shop in the light industrial area south of the highway in Drumheller. Then I pulled satellite imaging data so I have the layout of the place."

The lump of half-chewed cereal went down my throat in a single painful gulp as my mind filled with the thought of Kane tied up helpless in a frigid abandoned building. Or lying injured and alone, slowly succumbing to shock and hypothermia...

"We need to get out there! Good work, Spider, you're friggin' brilliant!" I snatched up the phone and punched Holt's extension. He answered on the first ring, and I blurted, "Spider found out where they met last night. Let's move!"

"Meet you at Stores." The line went dead in my ear.

Sparing an instant of gratitude for Holt despite his

unpredictable temper, I sprang up. "Spider, can you print us off a map and a layout of the area and meet us down at Stores?"

"Okay."

His response faded behind me as I jogged down the hall.

At Stores, I requisitioned a bulletproof vest and a tranquilizer pistol.

After a moment's thought, I doubled the order. Holt had done the same for me in the morning. That must be the proper procedure.

I was fumbling with the trank gun's shoulder holster and feeling thoroughly inept when Holt arrived.

He indicated my armament with a nod. "What are you expecting?" He shrugged into the other holster while he spoke, looking every inch the rock-jawed, steely-eyed action hero.

"I don't know. I figured we'd take everything with us and sort it out when we get there."

I trailed off as Spider hurried up clutching a sheaf of papers. "Here you go," he panted. "A road map; the exterior layout; and I grabbed the building permit drawings for an interior layout."

"Spider, you're amazing! Thank you!" I turned to Holt. "Ready?"

"Let's do it."

When we left the building, I glanced over at Holt. "Will you drive?"

"Sure." He led the way to his car. "But I figured you'd want to. Seeing as you're in charge and everything."

I ignored the dig. "I can if you want, but my car window got broken last night, so it'd be a chilly drive."

"Shit, Kelly." We slid into his car and he gave me a

sidelong glance as he put it into gear. "You're just living the life, aren't you? Busted knee, trashed house, busted car window..."

"You have no idea," I growled. "Throw in some rotten dog shit, get smacked around by some asshole twice your size, and stand naked in the snow for a while, and that about sums up my fun from last night."

"Shit, no wonder you need the anger management class."

I didn't reply, and after a moment he asked, "So what's the plan?"

He seemed to have dropped his challenging attitude, and a little of the tension eased from my shoulders.

"We'd better give it a drive-by and scope it out. It's a weekday afternoon, so hopefully there will be some other traffic and we can blend in. After that we can come up with a plan."

Holt grunted what I hoped was approval.

"Unless you have another idea," I added. "I'm counting on you to speak up if you do."

He glanced over, looking surprised. "No," he said after a moment. "That's what I'd do, too."

"Okay, good."

We lapsed into silence for the rest of the twenty-minute trip. By the time the flat snowy fields gave way to the rough coulees of Drumheller's Badlands, I had imagined and banished dozens of increasingly horrific scenes that might confront us at the automotive shop. My stomach writhed into a queasy coil of nerves, hunger, and fatigue.

Holt spoke for the first time as we turned onto the main highway north of town. "Okay, give me directions from here."

"Just keep heading south until you hit the intersection

with the main highway, then turn west." I was glad my voice didn't betray my fear. I guided him to the industrial area and my guts tightened as he followed my directions. Moments later we cruised past the small automotive shop.

I slumped in my seat. "Shit!"

"Do you mind not doing that?" Holt aimed a pointed glance at my hand, which was alternately rolling and crushing my shoulder belt.

"Sorry." I let go of the wrinkled seatbelt. "Damn. How the hell are we going to search the place? Guys working in both bays, customers waiting in the office..."

Holt shrugged. "Your op."

I was really beginning to hate those words.

"Where do you want me to go?" he added.

"Um." My brain refused to disgorge any useful ideas. "Just head back downtown."

Holt turned east. "Where downtown?"

I clamped down on the urge to yell, 'Shut up and let me think', and contented myself with a terse, "Anywhere. Just drive."

At least Kane and Stemp probably weren't lying injured in there. Some employee would have found them by now if they were. But the bustle of regular work activity had probably destroyed any clues we might have found, too. And how the hell could we get in to search the place?

Kane's informant had set up the meeting after the shop was closed, so that meant either an employee or the owner was likely to have been involved. Bad idea to walk in there claiming to be police officers. If Stemp's and Kane's covers weren't already blown, that would do it.

And pleading car trouble would get Holt's car into one of the bays, but it wouldn't get us access to the office or back areas.

Deep in thought, I blinked when Holt stopped the car outside a sandwich shop several minutes later.

"I missed lunch," he said. "You want anything?"

My stomach let out an embarrassingly loud growl, and I clapped a hand over it and gave him a sheepish smile. "I have one vote for 'yes'."

He grinned, and I hauled myself out of the car to follow him into the tiny restaurant.

I was down to the last few bites of my sandwich when the idea struck me. I jerked up from my dispirited slouch. "Rats!"

Holt frowned. "What's wrong?"

"Nothing. I mean, *rats!*" He eyed me warily, and I hastened to explain. "We can pretend to be rat patrol."

"Say *what?*" His wariness morphed into an 'are-you-crazy' scowl as he edged back in his seat.

"Rat patrol!" When he didn't look enlightened I asked, "You're not from around here, are you?"

"Hell, no. I got transferred to this godforsaken hole from Toronto."

"That explains a lot." I gobbled the last of my sandwich and elaborated. "Alberta is a rat-free province. Well, officially, anyway. Norway rats are pretty much everywhere in Canada but not in Alberta, because they can't get through the unpopulated areas in the west, south, or north. So their only access point is a short piece of the Alberta-Saskatchewan border. And the border is patrolled by-"

Holt burst out laughing. "Rat patrol! You're shitting me!"

"I shit you not. We're not in the official patrol zone here, but all reports of rats are checked out no matter where they are in the province. We just have to say somebody reported seeing a rat and we can get in anywhere we want to go."

"Now I've heard everything." Holt rose, crumpling his empty sandwich wrapper, and I followed suit.

Out on the sidewalk, I surveyed him, frowning.

"What?" he demanded.

I indicated his smart overcoat and neatly creased slacks over expensive-looking leather boots. "You won't pass for rat patrol."

He grimaced. "Like you said, ten seconds notice. Not my usual choice of wardrobe for active service."

"I think we can still make it work." I flashed him a grin. "Wait in the car. I'm going shopping."

A short while later, I slid into Holt's passenger seat and delved into the bag of supplies I'd acquired.

"Here you go, big-city researcher," I said as I passed him a clipboard. "You're visiting from Toronto and job-shadowing me, a biologist who volunteers with the rat patrol." I waved a hand at my scuffed hiking boots and faded jeans. "I already look the part, so all I need is this..." I coiled my hair up and pulled my new tuque over it. "...so I'm not quite so easy to identify."

I finished my look with a pair of heavy-rimmed reading glasses and blinked myopically at Holt. He grinned and put the car in gear.

"We'll have to visit a couple of places on either side of the shop, too," I cautioned. "I hate to waste the time, but I don't want to arouse suspicion. And I want to check the outdoor areas as well. There might be some tracks in the snow or something."

Holt raised an eyebrow. "Rat tracks?"

I grimaced. "Yeah. Human rats."

CHAPTER 33

Nearly two hours later, I slumped in Holt's passenger seat again, defeated. Not a single damn clue in the automotive shop or its surroundings. And the snow had been so trampled, even if Kane had lain down and made snow angels we couldn't have found them.

Maybe we should have stayed longer; looked harder. But that would waste even more time we didn't have.

"Stop doing that!" Holt snapped.

I desisted from mangling the seatbelt yet again. "Sorry."

"Another fucking waste of time," he snarled. "Freezing my fucking ass off poking around in the snow to find fuck-all, and look at this grease on my coat!"

"Yeah." I reached for the seatbelt again, but caught myself in time and locked my fingers together instead. "It was a long shot, but we had to check."

"So now what?"

I made my tone as confident as possible. "Now we go back and finish analyzing those reports."

He grimaced, but didn't argue.

I glanced at my watch. "Three-thirty. I bet Spider's got a complete analysis by now."

Holt brightened. "Is he that good?"

"Better. He's a genius."

"That's good. We're going to need one." Holt gave me a sidelong glance before returning his attention to driving. "We've got a snowball's chance in hell of catching two top agents like Kane and Stemp once they go rogue."

"They haven't gone rogue." I met Holt's skeptical eyebrow with my most confident expression. "I'd stake my life on it."

Holt snorted. "You are staking your life on it."

"Yeah." I slouched deeper in the seat. "But if Kane had planned to steal the weapon, he'd have just killed me on the plane and nobody would have been any the wiser. And even if they were actually conspiring to steal the weapon, they're both far too smart to do something this obvious."

Reaching for the seatbelt again, I caught Holt's glare and converted the movement into a vigorous tug on my hair. "Something went wrong last night, I'm sure of it. Really, really wrong. We need to find them, and fast."

The twenty-minute drive seemed to take forever. Holt drove in silence again, leaving me ample opportunity to work myself into a state of poorly-suppressed panic.

Maybe I should call Spider. See if there was anything new.

But no, he'd call me immediately if anything had changed. So that meant no news.

But no news might be good news, I argued with my jittery self. If Kane and Stemp were undercover, they wouldn't risk calling in. Maybe everything was going according to plan. Maybe it would be better if I didn't try to find them.

Or maybe their time was running out.

I sighed as we pulled into the parking lot at Sirius

Dynamics, and sprang out to make a beeline for the building as soon as the car stopped.

Holt caught up just as I was turning away from the security wicket, and I waited impatiently while he signed in, too.

Wincing at the complaints of my bruised hip and knee, I took the stairs two at a time and hurried for Spider's office with Holt trailing me. When I tapped on his door, Spider twitched, his gaze jerking away from the computer screen.

"Anything?" he asked fearfully.

"Nothing. You?" I took in the rumpled peaks of his hair, a sure sign of his absorption. He churned an oblivious hand through it again, his gaze returning to his screen. "Maybe. Pull up a chair."

Holt sat while I perched, leaning forward as if I could peer through the back of his computer screen. "What did you find?"

"Okay." Spider let out a long breath. "I went back through Stemp's old missions. He only used George Harrison as a cover once, on his very last mission seven years ago. He was trying to trace an arms deal overseas..." He hesitated and his gaze flickered to me before returning to his screen. "...in Bulgaria and Romania."

I held onto the best poker face I could muster. Bulgaria, seven years ago. Katya lived in Bulgaria. And Anna was six or seven years old.

"Something went wrong, and Stemp believed his cover might have been compromised," Spider went on. "We don't know if it actually was or if it's just generally unhealthy to be involved with arms dealers over there, but one night somebody opened fire on his car with an automatic weapon. His passenger was killed and Stemp was injured. We extracted him and brought him back here, and put out the word that George Harrison had died in the attack."

The connection clicked in my brain. "Oh!"

"What?" Holt demanded.

I grimaced. "Nothing useful. It was just something Bud Weems said. Stemp moved into his house about seven years ago, and he'd been in a 'car accident'..." I made air quotes around the word. "...just before that. Go on, Spider."

"So here's another connection," he said. "Guess who took over the mission from Stemp?"

Holt snorted. "Too easy. Kane, right?"

Spider nodded. "So Dawn White, the informant from seven years ago he mentioned last night..."

"...was part of that op, of course," Holt finished. "How did it wrap up? Did they nail the arms dealer?"

"No." Spider frowned. "Thanks to Kane's informant they arrested a few small-time couriers who seemed loosely associated with Fuzzy Bunny, but they couldn't get up the food chain to Parr. The leads went cold and Kane got recalled."

"He said that's what happened the last time he was over there sixteen months ago, too," I said. "That was when Yana Orlov was his suspect."

Holt's lips twisted. "Well, isn't that convenient? Stemp and Kane both investigate arms deals overseas that just never quite get solved. And then Kane calls Stemp and says their informant from seven years ago just showed up, and Stemp decides on the spur of the moment to get involved with an op using his old cover identity even though he's been retired from active service for seven years. And he takes the time to call in a 'personal' emergency."

He shot me a sour look before continuing, "But oddly

enough he doesn't take time to check in with the chain of command and let them know how his meeting went. And then they both just *coincidentally* vanish along with a secret weapon prototype." He scowled. "That's a few too many coincidences for me. What do we know about Dawn White?"

"Um, maybe Stemp couldn't call the chain of command because he was undercover and somebody was listening. Remember, his call to Dermott was pretty general. And, um..." Spider hunched his skinny shoulders, not quite making eye contact. "Dawn White is probably an alias. I've pulled all the official records and there are a couple of dozen Dawn Whites in Canada, but none of them seem likely candidates for our informant. And there's really not much in Kane's reports about her-"

"Fuck!" Holt exploded. "Why not? Why the hell didn't the chain of command make sure the reports were complete? Shit, Stemp and Kane have been colluding for fucking years-"

"I'm sure there's another explanation." I put on my most confident voice to hide the shrivelling sensation in my chest. "There are lots of reasons why he might not mention her in a report. If it would have put her at risk-"

"If that's the case, you redact the identifying information from the general reports," Holt snarled. "But you still report it somewhere."

"I'm still digging," Spider said hurriedly. "It'll probably show up. This is just my preliminary analysis. Oh, and I've got facial recognition software scanning every CCTV feed I can pull from here to Calgary, but no hits yet for Kane or Stemp. I've also got the police watching for either of their vehicles. And I've done a preliminary search on the owner of the automotive shop. Nothing suspicious there either, but I'm also looking into his family members and employees. I dumped everything I've got so far into your network accounts."

I sighed and dragged myself to my feet. "Thanks, Spider, you're doing a great job as always. I'm going to go and read everything you've sent me and get up to speed."

Holt rose, too. "I'll report to Dermott." A hint of smug satisfaction smoothed his face. "Guess he'll be our new director after all." He strode out, leaving Spider and me eyeing each other unhappily.

"This is bad," Spider said in a small voice. "It's like he doesn't want them to be innocent."

I hugged my parka and tried to emulate Stemp's dispassionate tones. "I guess that's what makes a good agent. He needs to be impartial."

"He's not impartial," Spider protested. "He and Dermott are buddies, and they've both got something to gain. If Kane and Stemp get railroaded, Holt gets reinstated and probably promoted, and Dermott gets the director's position."

I sighed. "I wish Germain was here. He'd know what to do."

"It'd be great to have another person on our side, but as long as you're on the case I know it'll work out fine." Spider's confident smile made my gut clench.

"Thanks," I mumbled, and hurried out before I could blurt the truth of my inadequacy.

I had almost reached the safety of my office when Jill stepped out of Tammy's doorway.

She greeted me with her usual sparkle. "Hi, Aydan! Why the long face?"

Casting a wary eye behind her, I muttered, "Where's Tammy?"

"Ladies' room. Why?" Jill frowned.

"Um... I just..." I sighed. Jill would understand. "I'm working on a case and it's getting me down. I really need some help, but nobody's available." I eyed her hopefully. "I don't suppose...?"

Even as I said the words I realized she didn't have the necessary security clearance, so I was relieved when she grimaced and shook her head.

"I'd love to, but I'm full-time and then some with Tammy. And she doesn't know any of us are agents, so I can't break cover."

I scuffed my booted toe morosely at the carpet. "Yeah, I figured. It was worth a try. Speaking of which, I was going to ask you, um... would you maybe teach me some hand-to-hand combat sometime? When you can get away from Tammy, I mean?"

Jill smiled. "I'm not good enough to teach. You should talk to Germain about that."

"Are you kidding?" I gave her an incredulous look. "I saw you fight. You and Germain were evenly matched!"

She laughed, a warm cascade of amusement that made me smile despite my worries. "He could have wiped the floor with me in ten seconds or less."

"But..."

She chuckled again at my confusion. "It was a skill evaluation, not a fight. It's his job as an evaluator to push my limits and find out what I can do, but he wasn't even close to going full-out."

"Oh." I couldn't quite prevent my sigh from escaping. "Damn, I wish he was here. Or that I could at least talk to him. I don't even know where he's assigned or how to get in touch with him, and I know Dermott won't tell me."

Jill leaned closer and dropped her voice, mischief

glinting in her eyes. "I might know that."

Her conspiratorial tone made my lips quirk upward. "Oh, really?"

"Really." She grinned. "You didn't seriously think I'd let that hot hunk of man walk away without leaving me his phone number."

My smile widened. "That would be ridiculously short-sighted."

"Damn right." She beckoned me into the office and extracted a scrap of paper and a pen from her purse. "Here." She scribbled a number and handed it to me. "This is his burner phone. He's not undercover, but he's really busy with his case so it might be pretty late when he calls back." She winked. "Nothing like a late-night phone call."

I grinned, feeling better already. "Thanks, Jill. This really helps."

I had just stepped into the hallway when Tammy approached from direction of the ladies' room, her white cane skimming the carpet and tracking along the baseboard.

I hesitated. I wasn't really in the mood for another deluge of her one-sided conversation, but could I just keep walking? She couldn't see me. It wasn't like she'd know I was being rude.

"Who's there?" Her dark glasses turned unnervingly in my direction.

I gulped. "Hi, Tammy, it's Aydan."

"Oh, *hi*, Aydan! I was *wondering* when we'd meet again. Spider said you're really *busy*, so I'm glad you weren't *sick*, but I was really *hoping* we'd be able to work together again *soon*, and-"

I interrupted as politely as I could. "Actually, I am really busy, so I have to run. I hope you're enjoying your work, though. And I'm sure we'll work together soon." I began to walk away during the last sentence, hoping my receding voice would cue her that I was leaving.

"Oh... well, maybe I'll talk to you later..." She looked so disappointed that my heart smote me.

Fortunately Jill emerged and spoke to her, and I shot her a look of gratitude as I escaped into my office, guilt still nibbling my conscience.

Flopping into my desk chair, I punched Germain's number. Who knew how long I might have to wait for his return call?

The ringing on the other end was cut short by a deep, seductive growl. "Well, hey there, Hotness."

After a flustered moment, I stammered, "Um, it's Aydan."

"Oh!" Germain's sexy tease vanished. "How did you get this num... Never mind. Sorry. What's up?"

"Do you have time to talk for a few minutes?"

"Yes, is something wrong?"

I sighed. "I don't know."

I laid out the entire scenario while he listened, prompting me now and again with questions.

"...and I still need to go and check John's place to see if he's been back, and Spider's still digging," I finished. "I'm sorry to bother you with this, but I just needed to bounce it off somebody who doesn't have an agenda."

"It's okay, Aydan, I don't mind." Germain hesitated. "But honestly, I don't know what else to tell you. I'd do exactly what you're doing if I was in your place."

I slumped in the chair. "Damn. I was hoping I'd missed some really simple solution."

"We're never that lucky."

"Yeah." I heaved a big sigh. "Thanks for listening, anyway. Good luck on your case."

"Thanks. You too. Call me if you think of anything else."

I hung up and scowled at the phone for a few moments before the corners of my mouth tugged into a smile.

'Hotness'. Well, well. Apparently I hadn't been imagining the attraction between Jill and Germain. And they were free to pursue it, since they weren't working together.

My smile slipped away. Not like Kane and me.

Assuming Kane and I were still on the same side of the law. And assuming he was still alive.

I groaned and reached for the phone. "Holt? Yeah, we need to go over and check Kane's place. Bring your lock picks."

CHAPTER 34

Parked in Kane's back alley, I glared at Holt and continued our debate. "No, you're *not* coming in. I only asked you to bring the lock picks as a last resort. If you show up in Fuzzy Bunny's surveillance video, you could blow my cover. I'm going to go and try the back door. If it's still unlocked, it means he hasn't been back. And if he hasn't been back, it means we don't need to search because he didn't know about any of this before he got the call last night."

Holt frowned. "You think it's smart for you to show up on their surveillance?"

"They'll just think I'm searching his place again. I've only got a day left to deliver the weapon, so they'll figure I'm getting panicky." I shrugged to hide how panicky I truly was.

"What if he just left the door unlocked to make it look like he hasn't been back?" Holt argued.

"I'll be able to see the prints in the snow under his basement window. If there are prints on top of mine, I'll know he was back."

Holt scowled. "How do you know he didn't just walk right in the door? If he's working with Fuzzy Bunny, he wouldn't care if he showed up on their surveillance cameras."

"Christ, Holt, he's not working for Fuzzy Bunny! If he was, I'd be dead and we'd never have gotten the weapon in the first place."

Holt eyed me narrowly. "Why would you be dead? What does Fuzzy Bunny care about you?"

Shit, I'd forgotten he didn't have the security clearance to access all my mission reports.

I recovered as fast as I could. "Because he'd have told them I was an agent instead of a cheap fraud artist." I pinned him with a gimlet stare. "Take the car around front. Stay out of sight unless I call for backup."

I was halfway out of the car when Holt spoke again. "Does he have a fucking paranoid security system like Stemp?"

"No. Just a deadbolt."

He put the car in gear without further argument and drove down the alley. A couple of minutes later, his voice spoke in my comm link. "I'm three houses west of his place now."

"Okay. I'm going in."

In the gathering dusk, I let myself in Kane's back gate with a moment's gratitude for not having to navigate the scatological obstacle course next door. At the back door I hesitated, my heart thumping rapidly.

What if it was locked? What if I was wrong about Kane?

Or what if it was open and somebody was waiting to ambush me inside?

I shook myself. It would be open. And I had Holt for backup.

My hand clamped around the doorknob. Turned it and opened the door.

I drew a deep breath and stepped into the dimness.

The unlocked door hadn't diminished my nerves as much as I'd hoped. Pulse racing, I slipped off my boots and drew my gun. My sock feet were silent on the hardwood while I flitted from room to room in approved spy-fashion, clearing every closet and corner. At last I crept down the basement stairs and checked the laundry and weight room before holstering my gun with shaking hands.

"The door was unlocked. The house is clear," I muttered into my comm link. "I'm checking the basement window now."

It was exactly as I'd left it; closed but not latched. I hauled myself atop the dresser to peek outside. In the fading twilight I could barely make out the imprints of my sock feet melted into the snow beside the window and the drag mark from my precipitous entrance. A single set of large footprints near the fence indicated where Kane had apparently exited, but they were facing the fence and my second set of prints overlaid them.

I sighed. Kane was smart enough to walk backward to the window and obscure his footprints as he slid back in, but I doubted if even he could climb over a six-foot fence and drop perfectly back into the same set of footprints in the pitch dark. And anyway, his incoming bootprints probably would have had dog shit in them.

"He hasn't been back," I said. "I'm going to do a quick search."

"You want help?"

"No, I want you watching out there."

Holt grunted assent, and I put him out of my mind while I pondered in the middle of the basement.

Kane had been in such a hurry to get rid of me. Why?

He'd had to leave to meet his informant, sure, but why

did *I* have to leave and then come back? He could have just left me here to make my own way out later.

If he needed me out of the house, that meant either he needed to do something in the house that I couldn't know about, or else somebody was coming to the house.

And if it was the former, he would have just asked me to give him some privacy.

Okay, so that meant somebody was coming to the house. I'd bet it was the mysterious Dawn White. But Kane had said he needed his vehicle. So were they going somewhere together? And how would he know without talking to her? Unless it was in the coded message...

I trailed over to prop my elbows on the dresser, frowning.

That didn't make sense. If Kane went out the window, where did his visitor go? There were only two sets of footprints outside the window; Kane's and mine.

So the visitor must have arrived and left by one of the doors.

And gotten caught on Fuzzy Bunny's surveillance.

Excitement fizzed into my veins. If we had that video, Spider might be able to work his facial recognition magic.

A moment later my excitement went flat faster than a soda in the sun. Yeah, no problem. All I had to do was obtain footage I wasn't supposed to know about, from a criminal organization that was going to kill me in a day or less.

Fabulous.

"You okay?" Holt's voice made me start.

"Yeah, why?"

"You groaned."

"Sorry. I'm fine."

I yanked my mind away from the fear yammering in my backbrain and switched to pacing in small circles. I might as well search for clues while I was here anyway.

So if Kane knew he was going somewhere, what would he have taken with him?

And how would I know whether he had taken anything? I had only been in this house on one other extremely memorable occasion, and I sure as hell hadn't been paying attention to the furnishings. Except the bed.

Don't think about that.

Blowing out a breath, I began in a corner of the basement and worked my way upstairs, using my tiny LED flashlight to snoop. Other than Kane's heavy punching bag and weights in the basement, the house might have belonged to anybody. No hobby equipment or personal items, and no family photos except for the one of his dead brother, a copy of the one he kept at his condo in Calgary.

Even his dresser and closet were devoid of personality. Mostly dark denim and dark T-shirts, though a couple of pairs of soft faded jeans languished at the bottom of a drawer, their wrinkles showing they'd been buried a long time. Black underwear that made my face heat with steamy memories. Some crisp white shirts and a couple of dark suits in the closet along with a dress military uniform. Black fatigues and military gear similar to what I'd found in Hellhound's closet a couple of weeks ago.

Like Stemp's, his bathroom vanity held a single toothbrush, and there was unused luggage in the front closet. If he'd planned to leave, he hadn't packed.

"Nothing," I muttered into my comm link. "Dammit. I'm coming out now."

Trailing up the steps of Sirius Dynamics behind Holt, I glanced at my watch and hissed tension out through my teeth. Six o'clock. An entire day gone.

My mind shied away from what might be happening to Kane while I shuttled uselessly from one dead end to another. God, how long could he hang on?

At the security wicket, Holt eyed me quizzically. "You going to call it a night any time soon?"

"No, I want to get through those mission reports and all the stuff Spider dug up." I bit down on the urge to command him to do the same, and instead said, "You can go home if you want. There's no point in both of us being tired."

He let out a short bark of laughter. "What, you think I'm union or something? This job doesn't come with a time clock. I'm going to hit the reports, too. Maybe we can find something Webb missed."

"Okay, thanks." I trudged for the stairs. "Let me know when you're done."

When I passed Spider's office, I wasn't surprised to see him still hunched over his desk.

"Hey, Spider, how's it going?" I inquired.

He started and straightened, rubbing his eyes. "Not great," he admitted. "I've been going over and over this data and I haven't found anything other than what we talked about earlier." He shot a furtive glance at the open door behind me and lowered his voice. "I found a note in one of the reports that Kane was fostering a relationship with Dawn White in order to gain her confidence, but I didn't want to tell Holt or Dermott that. They're already too gung-ho to make him part of a conspiracy, and anyway, it doesn't help us figure out who she really is or what she looks like."

I surveyed his bloodshot eyes and strained face. "Go home and get some rest, Spider. I might have an idea, but it won't happen tonight."

He shook his head and began to protest, but I overrode him with a raised hand. "Go home. I promise I'll call you if we need you tonight, but right now the best thing you can do is be fresh and ready to go tomorrow, okay?"

He hesitated, scraping his skinny fingers through his tousled hair. "Okay. I'll set up the facial recognition program so it pings me at home if it catches anything. Thanks, Aydan." He rose slowly and rubbed the back of his neck, rocking his head back and forth as if it ached. "Oh, Hellhound called looking for you," he added. "I told him you were out searching for Kane and I didn't know when you'd be back, and he said he'd check in later." He grabbed his jacket. "Good night. Don't forget to get some sleep, too. You look wiped..." He hurriedly corrected himself. "I mean, you look great, you always do, but... you need sleep, too."

Fondness warmed me enough to relax my tense face into a smile. "Thanks, Spider. Good night."

Much later, I blinked heavily at the computer screen as it diverged into two incomprehensible blurs. After another couple of blinks the blurs reluctantly merged into a single document again and I massaged my pounding temples, fighting to stay awake.

Dammit, Kane needed me to be alert. To find some hidden clue in the mission reports I'd already read three times over.

"I'm done." Holt's voice jerked my eyes open and I squinted for a moment until he swam into focus, leaning into the doorway of my office. "I've been through those damn reports backward and forward, and I haven't found anything new. I'm going home to let it stew in my subconscious for a while." His steel-blue gaze evaluated my groggy blinking. "You should, too. You look like shit."

I considered flipping him the bird, but I couldn't summon the energy.

"See you tomorrow," I mumbled instead.

He withdrew, and I stared at my computer screen for a few more minutes before reluctantly admitting he was right. When I dragged myself to my feet, my joints protested bitterly and I whimpered a few feeble curses while I eased the kinks out, feeling the stress vibrating in every muscle.

As I limped down the stairs, the faint sound of music made me stop and scrub my hands over my face. Shit, I must be more tired than I thought. Hearing things.

I resumed my slow descent, but the music got louder until my sluggish brain finally traced its source to the lobby below. When I emerged from the doors it stopped abruptly and Hellhound rose from one of the lobby chairs, guitar in hand.

"Hey, darlin'." He smiled, but his eyes were anxious. "How ya doin'?"

Somehow I managed not to fling myself into his arms and burst into tears. I twisted my quivering lips into a smile-like grimace instead. "I'm okay. It's good to see you, but what are you doing here?"

He hefted the guitar. "Just killin' time."

I squinted at my watch. "Shit, it's nearly ten. I hope you haven't been waiting long."

"Few hours." He waved away my dismay. "No big deal."

"But why didn't you call me? You could have been

jamming over at Eddy's instead of sitting here."

"Wasn't really in the mood for Eddy's tonight after all. An' I figured if ya were still here an' ya hadn't called me, ya prob'ly didn't wanna be interrupted." He stepped closer, lowering his voice. "Any word from Kane?"

"No."

The word trembled out, and he folded me into his arms. "He's okay, darlin', don't worry."

I pulled away, hope surging while I searched his face. "Did you hear from him?"

"No, I didn't mean that. Sorry." His face softened, his voice a gentle rasp. "But this ain't the first time he's dropped off the radar for a while. Just means he's doin' his job."

Disappointment bowed my shoulders, and Hellhound eyed me with concern. "You're shakin'. When did ya eat last?"

"Um..." Food. Suddenly I was ravenous. "I had a sub around two o'clock."

"Shit. Come on, let's get ya somethin' to eat. Go sign out, an' I'll be right there. I just gotta phone Dad an' let him know there's no news yet."

"You told him John was missing?" With an effort I prevented myself from adding, 'What the hell were you thinking?'

Hellhound scowled. "Nah. I wouldn'ta worried him with it, but the cops called him askin' if he'd seen John, an' Dad called me right after he finished talkin' to the cops. I told him I'd let him know soon's I knew anythin'."

"Dermott and Holt. Dammit." At his questioning look, I added, "I'll explain later."

He nodded and tucked his guitar into its case before pulling out his phone. I tottered to the security wicket, barely able to hold myself upright over the emptiness in my middle.

We had just stepped out on the sidewalk a few minutes later when my phone vibrated. My heart leaped into my throat. Hands shaking, I fumbled the phone free.

The call display read 'Private Caller', and I punched the button and snapped, "Hello?"

"Bodyguard won't do you any good, sweet-ass. I can drop him with a single shot from here."

CHAPTER 35

Terror galvanized every muscle and I sprang in front of Hellhound, arms spread wide as I shoved him backward with my body. "Get back in the building!"

His hand closed on my shoulder as if to move me aside. "What the hell, darlin'?"

"*Get in the building now!*" I shrieked.

His big fist clenched on my parka to half-drag me up the steps and back inside Sirius Dynamics. He yanked me to the side and shielded me with his body, tossing his guitar case behind him. I barely saved his beloved instrument with a one-handed grab as he snapped into a combat stance facing the door.

"What's happenin'?" he barked, his gaze riveted on the entrance.

Panting, I laid the guitar case down and raised the phone to my ear again. My hand shook so violently I had to lean against the wall and lock my elbow against my body with my other arm.

Sharkface's laughter sounded clearly over the phone. "Some bodyguard. That was pathetic."

My voice came out in a thin quaver. "He's not a bodyguard. And if you hurt him I will rip your butt-ugly head off and shit down the bleeding hole."

"Easy, sweet-ass, don't get your knickers in a twist. What did you find at Kane's this afternoon?"

"What the fuck's goin' on?" Hellhound demanded.

"If you tell him anything I'll kill him." Sharkface's voice was ice-cold in my ear.

I shot a glance at the security guard behind the bulletproof glass, one hand on his sidearm and the other poised over the alarm button.

I shook my head at the guard and laid a hand on Hellhound's rigid shoulder. "Sorry, it was just one of my stupid friends playing a stupid joke," I quavered.

"Bullsh-"

I clapped a hand over Hellhound's mouth before he could complete the word and waved the phone.

His eyes narrowed in comprehension as he peeled my hand away from his lips. "Well, tell the dumb fuck he scared the shit outta me," he growled. "An' if he does it again I'm gonna find him an' shove his fuckin' phone so far up his ass he'll hafta open his mouth to dial."

"That wasn't funny," I said weakly into the phone. "He's mad, and I don't blame him. Don't do that again."

"Good job, sweet-ass. Now come outside where I can see you. And leave your big dumb boyfriend inside."

I turned to Hellhound. "Sorry, the phone reception's really bad in here. I'll have to take this call outside. You stay here where it's warm. I'll just be a minute."

His eyes blazed and I made a frantic shushing motion before he could explode. Scowling, he flung out his hands, mouthing 'Are you nuts?'

I shook my head and made calming gestures before tottering toward the door again. At the doorway I turned and gave him a silent palm-out 'stay' command.

His face hardened, but he remained standing where I'd left him, his fists bunched by his sides.

Sidling out the door, I peered into the dark parking lot across the street, but I couldn't spot Sharkface's SUV.

Hot anger coursed through my veins at the sound of his amused voice. "Good girl. Now, what did you find at Kane's today?"

"Nothing. If you saw me there then you know that anyway." I didn't try to hide the sullenness in my tone.

"You better hurry up. You have to deliver that bottle tomorrow."

Stall.

"It looks like he left," I said. "I'll need more time to track him down and get the bottle now."

"You don't have more time. And you're lying. We're watching his house. He didn't leave."

"Well, he's gone," I snapped. "There are footprints outside his basement window, so he must have known you were watching and sneaked away."

There was a muffled expletive on the other end. "Well, you better find him fast," Sharkface growled. "Maybe his girlfriend knows where he is."

"If you mean his wife, she died last week. Parr knows that."

"No, his girlfriend. The one that was sucking face with him on his front step while you were in his bed last night." His tone taunted me. "Guess you weren't good enough to keep him interested."

The phone sank from my ear while I gaped into the darkness. Apparently Dawn White was more than just an informant. So that's why he wanted to be rid of me.

After a moment I raised the phone again. "What time was that?"

"I don't know; you tell me. You were there when she rang the doorbell."

Shit!

"He said it was a neighbour dropping off some mail that got delivered to the wrong house," I extemporized hurriedly.

I sounded too unconcerned. Go for indignant.

"No wonder he took so long to come back, the bastard," I snapped. "What did she look like?"

"I don't know; she had her hood up. She rang the doorbell, sucked his lips off, and left. Looked like he sent her away."

"So he could meet her later!" I hoped that sounded more like anger than enlightenment. "Did you get a picture?"

"I'll email you a video. Hurry up and find him, sweet-ass. Clock's ticking." He hung up, and a few moments later his dark SUV pulled out of the parking lot. The bastard had the nerve to wave as he drove away.

My mind raced while I stood watching his taillights recede. So. Another lover from Kane's past. Or possibly present. Apparently he'd been successful at 'fostering' that relationship.

I spared a moment of sympathy for any civilian woman who'd actually tried to have a committed relationship with Kane, and turned to wobble up the stairs again. By the time I reached the top step, hope was warming the chill in my belly. Half my problem was solved. I was getting the video footage. And maybe I didn't have to worry about Kane quite so much if Dawn was that friendly.

When I swung the door open, Hellhound straightened from his crouch beside the doorway. "Everythin' okay?" he demanded, his gaze still locked on the door behind me.

I drew a deep breath and tried to hide the tremor of residual adrenaline in my voice. "Yeah. Sorry about that."

Just to be on the safe side, I extracted my bug detector and checked its reassuring green light before speaking again. "Long story. I need to get home. I'm getting an important email." When I tried to tuck the bug detector back in my waist pouch, my hands shook so hard I dropped it.

Hellhound scooped it up and passed it back to me, his warm hands closing around my icy fingers. "First we get ya somethin' to eat, darlin'."

I started to argue, but reconsidered. "Okay. It'll probably take him a while to send the email anyway."

As we turned for the door again, Hellhound stepped in front of me. "This time I go first."

"It's fine, he's gone," I reassured him. "And he won't hurt me anyway. He was just threatening you to scare me." I sighed as the truth of that hit home. "Shit. I really wish he hadn't seen you. I was hoping to keep you out of this."

We stepped out on the sidewalk and Hellhound's gaze flicked over the quiet street. "Outta what?"

"I promise I'll tell you as much as I can while we eat." I hesitated. "Shit, I don't want to fight the crowd at Eddy's tonight, but the only other thing that's open this time of night is the hotel bar. I hate that place."

"We could grab somethin' at your place."

A recollection of the chaos at home made me wince. "No. Meet you at the hotel."

"Okay. I'll walk ya to your car."

When we arrived, Hellhound eyed my tape-and-plastic window without expression. "I'm guessin' this's part a' the story?"

I sighed. "Yeah. See you in a few minutes."

At the hotel, I braced myself for the auditory assault of another hockey game as we stepped into the bar. Making our way to a table as far away from the big screen as possible, we sank into chairs with our backs to the wall.

I vented a long groan that must have been audible even over the blaring of the TV and Hellhound slid his arm around me. I let my head drop to his bulky shoulder, wishing I could just fall asleep and never wake up.

"Fresh meat tonight, eh?" The waitress's sarcastic voice roused me. She eyed Hellhound's bruised, bearded face and scuffed leather jacket before turning her curled lip toward me. "Scraping out the barrel with this one, aren't you?"

I had exactly one nerve left, and she had just gotten on it. I erupted to my feet, blind with the need to beat the ever-loving hell out of whatever my fists encountered.

She jumped back, her mouth dropping into an 'O' as Hellhound's powerful arms clamped around me and pinned my arms.

"Easy, darlin'," he growled in my ear before turning to the waitress. "Bring us a coupla burgers an' beers an' hold the attitude."

"Wh-what kind of b-"

"I don't give a shit," Hellhound rasped. "Just bring 'em."

She scuttled away faster than I'd ever seen her move, and Hellhound eased his grip. "Ya okay?"

I nodded and dropped back into the chair, the last of my energy draining away. He sat down and tucked his arm around me again before brushing a whiskery kiss over my forehead.

"Okay, darlin'," he murmured. "Talk to me."

I sighed and surreptitiously checked my bug detector. As

long as nobody was listening, I could probably tell him at least part of the story without endangering him or getting in trouble for blabbing classified information. I hesitated, sifting through facts and mentally editing.

Hellhound frowned. "Come on, Aydan. I can help, but I gotta know what's goin' on."

"I know, Arnie, but there's only so much I can tell you. Sorry, but some of it's classified."

Hellhound leaned down to meet my eyes squarely. "Ya gotta make your own decisions about that. But I'm just gonna say, remember who got sent to pick up that top-secret weapon from ya after the crash."

I leaned closer to whisper. "I asked Dermott about that during the debriefing. He only said you were a weapons specialist. He wouldn't tell me how high your security clearance is."

Hellhound's gaze sank to the tabletop. "I can't tell ya either, darlin'. Sorry."

I eased out a breath between my teeth. I trusted Hellhound with my life. And he obviously had a sky-high security clearance if Dermott had sent him despite his injuries instead of assigning someone else.

"Screw it," I said aloud. I hitched my chair closer and wrapped both arms around him, tucking my head into his shoulder to hide my lips in his beard. His arm tightened around me and I poured out the entire story, safe in his embrace.

When the beer arrived I pushed my bottle toward him, but he passed it back to me. "Drink up, darlin'. Sounds like ya need it."

When I began to demur, he shook his head. "Drink it. I'm drivin', an' you're stayin' here at the hotel with me tonight. If your place's trashed, an' bugged into the bargain, we'll go there long enough to get your email an' maybe straighten up a bit if ya feel like it, but ya don't need to deal with that shit tonight."

Relinquishing the burden of responsibility with relief, I tipped back a long swallow. The cold crisp bubbles tickled my palate, and I set the bottle down with a breath that felt like I'd been holding it for days.

"Thank you," I said with feeling, and leaned over to kiss him.

He grinned. "Hell, if ya kiss me just for a mouthful a' beer, I can hardly wait to see what I get for the burger."

I pulled a face. "I've had the burgers here. The most likely thing you'll get is food poisoning."

The food arrived more promptly than usual, but the waitress had obviously used the intervening time to repair her damaged snark. "I was just kidding, you know," she snipped as she plunked the plates down in front of us. "Everybody else knows how to take a joke."

We ignored her and dug into the burgers, which were either better than I remembered or else I was in such an advanced state of starvation that anything would have tasted good.

When the waitress slapped the bill on the table and marched away, Hellhound raised a conspiratorial eyebrow before carefully counting out exact change. Then he appropriated my pen and scrawled on the back of the bill, 'Here's your tip: Don't be a pissy bitch.'

I snickered, but shook my head at him. "You realize I'll never be able to come in here again."

He shrugged. "Why would ya wanna? Let's go."

As we pulled up in front of my house I cautioned, "Remember the bug."

"Yeah." Hellhound turned off the ignition and we headed for the door. When we stepped inside he shot a disgusted look around the mess. "Christ, darlin', what kinda fuckin' dickless asshat would do this?" He put extra emphasis on the epithet and I clapped a hand over my mouth to stifle a beer-induced giggle.

Grinning, he continued, "Whoever did this is a fuckin' clap-rotted dickcheese. Prob'ly got it ba-a-a-a-ad from fuckin' sheep. An' he prob'ly can't get it up anyway unless his mother's suckin' him off."

Caught between dismay and laughter, I smothered myself with both hands while he continued to spout the vilest insults imaginable. At last dismay won and I shushed him, trying not to giggle out loud.

I shot him a significant glance. "I'm just going to go and see if my computer still works."

"Okay, darlin'. Ya want some help?"

I considered that for a moment. "Yes, please."

It was worth a try. Maybe Hellhound would recognize Kane's friendly visitor.

We waded through the tumbled heaps of books and file folders in my office to get to my computer.

"It ain't busted." Hellhound sounded surprised.

"No, I think they were looking for something else," I replied for the benefit of the bug, and fired up the computer. Sure enough, I had new email. I selected the only message with an attachment, sent from a nondescript public address that had undoubtedly ceased to exist right after Sharkface sent the file.

Hellhound and I watched the video clip in silence.

Apparently Fuzzy Bunny was too cheap to install night-vision cameras. The murky streetlights revealed a slight figure in a hooded parka hurrying up Kane's front walk in the darkness. She pressed the doorbell, then waited.

When the door opened, I drew an involuntary breath. Either Kane had been caught changing clothes or... no, he was likely making it look as though we'd been in the middle of a passionate encounter.

Which we nearly had been, dammit.

Even in the poor-quality video, his shirtless torso showed the chiselled definition of his muscles. His half-zipped jeans and rumpled hair completed a delicious picture.

Apparently his visitor found him delicious, too. She hurled herself at him, wrapping her arms around his neck to draw him into a protracted kiss.

At last he extricated himself and leaned down as if to speak in her ear. The parka hood nodded, and the visitor turned back toward the street. The streetlight caught the curve of her cheek, the corner of her smiling lips, and the wing of a dark eyebrow. Then she tugged the hood down and hurried out of the camera view.

Was that the elusive Dawn White? And could Spider run any useful facial recognition on such a tiny flash of her features?

The clip ended and Hellhound and I exchanged a glance.

"Well, looks like the computer's workin' okay," he said casually. "Ya gonna be a while?"

I skimmed the list of emails and sighed. "Yeah, I need to deal with a few of these. I've been neglecting my bookkeeping clients lately."

"Okay. I'll just straighten up a bit," he said, and left.

Slumped in my chair, I stared at the screen, my mind churning through the implications of Sharkface's video. Maybe Kane was perfectly safe. Well, except for the imminent threat of a tonsillectomy from his visitor's tongue. But he hadn't seemed too concerned about that.

As long as nothing had gone wrong since then, he was probably fine.

I blew out a long breath. And if something had gone wrong, I had no way of knowing or helping him tonight, so I might as well try not to worry. Propping my eyelids open, I made short work of the most critical emails. I was just about to turn off the computer when a small flash caught my eye.

Every drop of blood squeezed from my heart as I stared open-mouthed at the tiny square blinking in the corner of my monitor.

It couldn't be.

The man who had controlled that signal was dead. I had killed him myself. I could still feel the kicks of the gun in my hand; see the devastation of splintered bone and tissue that used to be a face; feel the blood spattering my pant legs with each shot.

But the only other person who had used that signal was my dead husband.

CHAPTER 36

Transfixed, I stared at my computer screen. The tiny dot blinked back.

Drawing a deep breath, I raised trembling hands to the keyboard. Alt-Shift-click.

The text window popped onto my screen, its cursor zipping across to form the words, "Are you unobserved?"

It took two tries for my shaking fingers to fumble out, "Who is this?"

"Dickhead."

My mouth dropped open. Well, fuck you, whoever you are.

I typed, "Fuckface!" and slammed the Enter key.

The cursor zipped across the screen again. "No; this is Dickhead."

My heart gave a great thump as Stemp's dry voice spoke again in my memory. *'As much as I don't particularly appreciate being called a dickhead yet again...'*

Of course. I had noted this obscure communication system in one of my reports a couple of months ago. And Stemp was a computer expert.

"Where are you? What's happening?" The words spilled from my shaking fingers.

"Have item. Can't call home but all OK. Stall D 12 hrs."

I had only typed the first few letters of my many questions when the text screen vanished.

Heart pounding, I slumped in my chair, staring at the blank screen without seeing it.

The 'item' must be the weapon, and 'all OK' made sense. But what the hell did the last sentence mean? Was it a numbered parking stall somewhere? And what about Kane? Did the 'all OK' include him?

I was about to write the cryptic message on a scrap of paper, but laid the pen down unused. Probably better not to have any physical evidence.

Staring at the blank screen, I replayed the message in my mind. Was he telling me to be at Stall D in twelve hours? Where the hell was Stall D? Or was '12 HRS' an alphanumeric code that I'd know if I was a real agent?

I groaned and massaged my aching temples. No frickin' idea. Maybe Hellhound knew the secret code. I turned off the computer and trailed out the door.

When I emerged from the hallway, Hellhound was righting my upended sofa, the bulky muscles rippling across his back and shoulders as he set it on its feet. When he stooped to retrieve the cushions, the view was too good to resist. I padded over and ran an appreciative hand over his hard-muscled ass.

He whirled, his startled expression giving way to a smile. "Hey, darlin', didn't hear ya sneakin' up on me. But I ain't complainin'."

I was just leaning in for a kiss when my phone vibrated. Swallowing hard, I yanked the phone out of my waist pouch and squinted at the text message. My pulse quickened when I read Spider's message: "Want to come over for a beer?"

My shaking fingers fumbled out, 'See you in 20 minutes' and I turned to Hellhound, groping for some plausible excuse to leave immediately without alerting the listeners on the other end of the bug.

"Are you going to be ready for bed soon?" I blurted, and held my phone up so he could read Spider's text.

He frowned but replied with his usual teasing rasp. "Shit, darlin', I been ready for weeks. Let's go."

We hurried into our boots and jackets, and as soon as the SUV's doors closed behind us Hellhound nodded at my waist pouch. I showed him the bug detector's green light, and he demanded, "What the hell? Webb doesn't drink."

"I know. He must have found something and couldn't risk saying anything on an unsecured line." I clicked my seatbelt on and forced myself to sit back in the seat instead of perching on the edge. "Hurry up and drive."

Despite my nervousness, the hum of tires on pavement and the warmth of the SUV had nearly lulled me to sleep by the time we parked in front of Spider's small bungalow. A series of jaw-cracking yawns made my eyes water, and Hellhound glanced over.

"Guess ya ain't been sleepin' much lately."

"No." Another yawn threatened to dislocate my jaw as I hauled myself upright. "Let's go."

When I tapped on Spider's door, it popped open so quickly I guessed he'd been standing right beside it. His bright-eyed smile loosened the knots in my belly, and I peered over his shoulder into the house before leaning in to whisper, "Did you find something?"

"Yes, come on in." He beckoned us in and closed the door behind us. "I just scanned for bugs and Linda's working the night shift tonight, so we can talk..." He hesitated, his gaze flicking to Hellhound before eyeing me questioningly.

"I've told him everything about the weapon, and about Stemp and John," I reassured him.

"Oh, good. Kane's okay!" His words tumbled out before we even finished removing our boots. "The facial recognition program caught him at a gas station in Calgary about half an hour ago. He's with a woman." He shot me a quick glance before continuing, "I'm running a cross-check to see if her face pops up in any official databases."

The tension left my body on a whoosh of released breath. "Thank God. Can you show us the footage?"

"Sure, come on."

He turned and hurried down the hall, and we followed him into a basement that looked like a NASA command centre.

"Holy shit, Spider!" I turned in a slow circle, taking in the banks of computer screens and tables covered with various electronic oddments. "You've got a better setup here than the bunker under-"

I snapped my mouth shut as I remembered Hellhound's presence.

"It's okay, darlin', I know about the bunker under Webb's office," he reassured me. "An' the one under Sirius."

"Good." I let out a breath and slid my arm around him. "It's so nice to be able to relax around you."

He grinned and bounced his eyebrows. "Gimme a few minutes alone with ya, darlin', an' you'll be so relaxed-"

"Um, do you want to see the video?" Spider interrupted, colour rising in his face.

"Yes, please."

He slid into a chair and his fingers flew across one of the

several keyboards arranged on the desk. Then his fingers stilled and the tips of his ears turned pink. "Um, Aydan..." He gave me an awkward glance over his shoulder.

"Yeah?"

"Um..." He let out a breath and his colour deepened. "Never mind." He punched a key and a moment later a grainy black-and-white video flickered onto one of the screens.

Together we watched the silent footage as Kane emerged from the passenger side of a small, sleek sports car and paced around to its gas cap.

Hellhound whistled. "Nice ride. I ain't much of a car guy; what is that thing, darlin'?"

I squinted at the screen. "Looks like a Saturn Sky. They were great little cars. Wish I could have afforded one before Saturn went belly-up."

The driver's door opened and a slim dark-haired woman got out to wrap her arms around Kane for a lengthy kiss before heading for the convenience store.

Kane finished gassing up the car, and a few minutes later his companion returned and they drove away.

"Same chick," Hellhound said.

I turned to study him. "Are you sure?"

He shrugged. "I ain't sayin' I'm as good as a fancy facial recognition program, but she sure looks like the same chick to me."

I hugged him. "I'd bet your memory against a computer program any day."

"What video?" Spider demanded.

"Sharkf... um, Barnett sent me some footage from the surveillance video at John's house last night," I explained. "Remember how I said John kicked me out of the house in a big hurry? That woman came to his door shortly afterward. I'd say there's a pretty good chance she's Dawn White, and the message on his answering machine must have been a coded message from her, telling him she was coming."

I resolutely ignored my own double entendre. Judging by their body language, she probably *had* been coming last night. Repeatedly.

Spider's face was a study in consternation as he avoided my gaze. "Oh... um... sorry." He scuffed a toe at the carpet.

Comprehension dawned. "Don't worry, Spider, it's okay. I'm not upset. John and I don't have that kind of relationship."

"But you..." He pressed his lips together, his cheeks turning crimson.

I held in a sigh. Life would have been so much easier if he hadn't read my mind at the precise moment I was reliving the memory of red-hot sex with Kane.

"It's okay," I repeated. "Not a big deal." I changed the subject, hoping for a reprieve from the awkwardness. "I got a secret message from Stemp tonight."

"What? When?" Hellhound's eyes narrowed with comprehension. "Oh. That's what you meant by bookkeepin' clients. Ya couldn't tell me because a' the bug."

"No, actually I had no idea he was going to contact me." I conveniently omitted the classified details. "Anyway, he said he has the weapon and everything's okay, but the last sentence was 'Stall D 12 HRS. Is that some kind of code I should know?"

Spider's brow furrowed. "Um... not that I recognize."

Hellhound shook his head, too. "Doesn't fit anythin' I know."

"I thought it might be a parking stall somewhere," I said.

"Maybe he left something there for us to find."

"I dunno, darlin'." Hellhound objected. "Stemp's smart. If he can't call in to Dermott, he musta gone to a lotta trouble for this, so he'd make sure his message made sense to ya."

Weariness overcame me and I sagged against Hellhound's warm bulk. "Well, it doesn't. He has a lot more faith in my abilities than he should. I'm just an idiot civilian bookkeeper." I straightened as a thought struck me. "Wait a minute. What you just said... if he can't call in to Dermott... 'Dermott' starts with a 'd'."

Hellhound grinned. "'Stall Dermott twelve hours'. Good job, darlin'."

"That's it!" I planted a big smacking kiss on his lips. "You're brilliant!"

He shuffled his feet, smiling. "Hey, I didn't do anythin' 'cept hold ya up while ya were thinkin'. I'm just a dumb ugly biker, remember?"

"Biker, yeah, I'll give you that. Dumb and ugly, not a chance."

He laughed. "Thanks, darlin'. You're good for my ego even if my mirror tells me you're lyin'."

My tension ebbed away leaving leaden fatigue in its place, and I leaned against Hellhound again. "Thanks for calling tonight, Spider. I'm glad John's safe." I stifled a yawn. "Let's all get some sleep. Maybe by tomorrow morning your magic program will tell us who that woman is, and that'll give us a better idea what John and Stemp are planning. And maybe that'll help stall Dermott and Holt."

Spider nodded, his face clearing. "Okay. I've widened the geographic radius for the facial recognition's search, so it's crunching through all the available data collected since last night. Maybe we'll find Stemp, too."

"That'd be great," I agreed as I turned to stumble up the stairs, my eyes half-closed.

Thank God Kane and Stemp were all right. Now if I could just convince Sharkface not to kill me tomorrow, everything would be dandy.

CHAPTER 37

My eyes kept closing during the short drive to the hotel. When the motion of the SUV stopped, Hellhound's soft rasp roused me from a semi-doze.

"Come on, darlin', let's get ya to bed." He slid out of the vehicle and came around to collect me from the passenger side. Shepherded by his arm around my shoulders, I stumbled into the hotel and up the stairs to his room. When he opened the door, the bed beckoned like the Promised Land and I sleepwalked over to fall onto it.

He chuckled. "Here, lemme take your boots off an' ya can crawl right in." He began to unlace my boots, but I sat up and linked my arms around his neck to kiss him.

"I'm not planning on crawling in alone." I shucked off my boots and lay back, pulling him on top of me.

He propped himself on his elbows, his smile softened by the mellow lamplight. "You're wiped out, darlin'. Let's leave the mattress dancin' for mornin'."

"I'm not that tired." I pulled him down to me. "And I've permanently renounced deferred pleasure. You know what they say; 'life is short and nothing is certain, so eat dessert first'."

"Tell ya what, darlin'." He lowered his lips to mine and I

sighed in sheer bliss when he kissed me slowly. My knotted muscles softened in the rising heat while his mouth explored mine with his usual leisurely finesse. A brush of his tongue sent a sizzle down my spine, and a little moan escaped me when he deepened the kiss.

His lips traced whiskery pleasure over my jaw and neck while his hand migrated down to curve around my ass. "How 'bout if I eat dessert first," he rumbled in my ear. "An' if you're still conscious when I'm done, we'll see about the main course."

His kiss claimed me again and a hot shiver shook me when his hand slipped under my sweatshirt to unfasten my bra. His palm coasted lightly over my breast, the whisper of sensation making me arch to meet it. I tugged at his T-shirt as he paved a trail of tingling whisker-kisses over my throat.

"Take your clothes off," I whispered. "I want you naked."

"The feelin's mutual, darlin'." Hellhound rolled off me to stand beside the bed and peel off his T-shirt.

I skimmed out of my top, emerging from my sweatshirt just in time to see him drop his jeans. "Nice," I breathed. "Now that's what I call a main course."

He grinned. "I still want dessert first."

Holding his gaze, I slowly undid the button of my jeans. He licked his lips, his eyes igniting as I slid the zipper down.

"Mmmm." He knelt onto the bed astride me. "Lemme help ya with that."

I arched to rub against him as he shimmied my jeans over my hips and he let out a raspy half-groan-half-purr, his eyelids drooping in the lazy smile that promised mind-altering pleasure to come. He eased the denim down, his hands hot on my skin as he moved lower in the bed.

Suddenly the slow caress stopped. "Aw, shit, Aydan,

what happened?"

I propped myself up on my elbows to see him frowning at my blackened knee.

"Oh, I just banged it. No big deal."

His fingertips floated over the bruise. "It sure as hell looks like a big deal. Any other sore spots I should know about?"

"No. Well... actually my hip and my elbow are a little bruised, too." I sat up to kiss him. "But you can make them all better."

He gave me that lazy smile again. "Then I better get started on my mission a' mercy." He dropped my jeans and thong over the side of the bed and moved up to kiss me again, easing me unhurriedly onto the pillows.

I wrapped my arms around him, reveling in the feel of his hard bulky body against mine. "God, Arnie, you feel so good. It's been too long."

"Two months. 'Way too fuckin' long," he mumbled against my neck. "Lemme see if I can make it up to ya."

He nibbled his way over my collarbone, his beard and moustache igniting sparks of desire that flared into a conflagration when he cupped my breast, his magic fingertips teasing my nipple. I gasped when his mouth moved down to take over from his fingers, hot suction awakening the deep ache of need.

His hand traced the line of my ribcage before gliding over my hip and down my belly as if drawn by the liquid heat pooling below. His touch wrenched a moan from me, my body bowing upward under the combined pleasure from his mouth and fingers.

"Ah, darlin'," he rasped, his lips sending quivers through my body as they trailed down my stomach. He flicked the tip of his tongue into my belly button in a teasing promise and I whimpered anticipation, my body already tightening under the languid stroking of his hand.

He moved lower in the bed, drawing my knee up to nibble tingling kisses across the sensitive skin of my inner thigh. My breath stopped, every nerve hyperaware as he drew closer.

The first touch of his tongue exploded sensation through me, my hips bucking under his mouth and fingers. My world faded to nothing but his exquisite touch while he played my body like the masterful musician he was. Whimpers leaked from my throat, quickening into rising moans while the hot tension wound tighter, then tighter still.

Tremors vibrated my body, my breath catching as time slowed.

Stopped for a measureless moment...

Shattered into blinding ecstasy, my body rocking on wave after wave of glorious sensation, my cries soaring heedlessly to the ceiling.

As I lay panting in the ebbing ripples of bliss, Hellhound stretched out beside me. His arms gathered me in, cuddling me close to brush kisses on my cheeks and closed eyelids.

"Relax. Go to sleep, darlin'," he murmured.

I wrapped trembling arms around him, trying to pull him on top of me, and he stroked the hair back from my sweat-damp forehead. "It's okay, Aydan, just relax. Ya don't hafta..."

"Please..." Barely able to form the words, I clutched at him. "Now... want you... inside..." I wrapped my hand around the delicious hardness of his erection, fondling and urging.

He rumbled gratification and kissed me before rolling

over to delve into his jeans pocket. The crinkling sound of a condom wrapper made me whimper with desire.

A moment later his weight pressed me to the bed. When he slid into me the glorious sensation drew a strangled cry from my throat. *"God, Arnie! Yes!"*

I locked my legs behind his back while he rocked into a perfect rhythm. Long, steady strokes rewound my tension so fast the explosion of orgasm took me by surprise, my body spasming around him, my fingers digging into his powerful shoulders.

He slowed to almost nothing, pulsing gently while he propped himself on his hands to smile down at me with his sleepy-eyed grin.

"More," I gasped.

Still propped on his hands, he began to move again, gradually increasing his tempo and power. Each delicious stroke pumped more pleasure into my body, the sensation spiralling into dizzying need, my hips rising to meet him again and again while little cries escaped me.

"Love... watchin' ya..." His voice was hoarse and breathless, his arms steel-hard under my clutching fingers. "Come for me now, darlin'..."

"Harder..." The word wrenched from my throat. *"Arnie oh God!"*

I tumbled into blind ecstasy, swept higher with each powerful thrust. A few moments later his raw-throated groan underscored my cries, his body stiffening above me before he collapsed onto his elbows, pulling me tight against him. Locked together, we rode the storm of orgasm, our gasps and groans entwining like our bodies.

"Hey, darlin'." Hellhound's soft rasp roused me and I burrowed deeper into the pillow, clinging to the blissful oblivion of sleep.

"Hey, Aydan, time to wake up." A warm hand stroked slowly down my back. "I let ya sleep as long as I could, but ya gotta wake up now."

I groaned and mumbled into the pillow. "Not waking up unless I get an orgasm. No; three."

His chuckle vibrated the nape of my neck before his lips and whiskers traced tingling kisses down my backbone. "Hell, darlin', three's barely a good start. An' I'm happy to oblige, but you're gonna be late for work if I do."

"Fuck work."

A moment later my sleepy brain dragged itself into action and I jerked up to squint at the bedside clock. "Shit!" I scrubbed both hands over my face and blinked myself fully awake. "Yeah, today would be a bad day to skip work. Thanks, Arnie. And thanks for giving me a really, *really* good sleep." I kissed his smile and hauled myself out of bed to stumble in the direction of the bathroom. "But I want a rain check on those orgasms."

"Ya got it, darlin'."

In the shower, my mind darted from one thought to the next while I rapidly soaped and shampooed. Would Kane or Stemp make contact today? If they didn't, was Spider's video enough to convince Holt and Dermott that Kane was working undercover, or would they say it proved he'd gone rogue and redouble their efforts to apprehend him?

I pushed my face into the hot spray. And today was my deadline. How could I stall Sharkface? Would I even be alive this time tomorrow?

Grimacing, I turned off that thought along with the

water.

An unworthy idea crept into my mind while I was towelling off.

I could just say screw it all. Take Hellhound back to bed for a long hot round of morning sex, and then get in my car and drive away from all this. Vanish just like Stemp.

Kane didn't need me. I certainly wasn't going to contribute anything useful as an agent, and they didn't need me for decryptions anymore. Sooner or later they'd gather the evidence they needed to convict Parr, and I only had to evade Fuzzy Bunny's minions long enough for that to happen.

I could cut off my hair and dye it some nondescript colour; go vanish in some big city. I'd miss my friends, but it wouldn't be forever.

I sighed. But then the Department would think I'd gone rogue, so I'd have to evade them, too. And it would break my heart to leave my farm. My beautiful garage and my beloved cars. My garden...

Anger straightened my spine. Dammit, those bastards weren't going to take my dreams. And I owed Sharkface some major payback.

When I emerged from the bathroom, Hellhound jerked a thumb at my waist pouch. "Your phone's been ringin'."

I hurried over to extract it. When I accessed my messages, Sharkface's unwelcome voice greeted me. "Today's the day, sweet-ass. Call me. Or else."

I flopped onto the bed, yanking the pillow over my face with a groan.

The corner of the pillow lifted to reveal Hellhound's worried face hovering above me. "Aydan? What's wrong?"

"Nothing. Just my daily threat from Sharkface." I

groaned my way upright and made a face at my phone. "Might as well get this over with. Maybe I can stall him."

I punched in the number and waited.

After a couple of rings, he answered. "What have you got for me, sweet-ass?"

"I have a picture of George Harrison," I lied. "And I'm tracking down Kane and the bottle. I know where he was last night. I just need a little more time."

"You're out of time." His threatening tone shifted into fake warmth. "But you know what? I like you, sweet-ass. So if you deliver that picture to me by noon today, I'll put in a good word for you with Mr. Parr. See if he'll give you an extension to find the bottle."

I swallowed my instinctive scoff and adopted a scared, hopeful tone. "Would you really? Thank you! Where should I meet you?"

"Nose Hill Park, in the 14th Street parking lot."

"Um, that's in Calgary."

"Oh, you're a bright one, sweet-ass. Be there." He hung up.

"Asshole," I muttered.

Hellhound eyed me with concern. "What, darlin'?"

"He expects me to drive down to Calgary and meet him in a godforsaken parking lot. How stupid does he think I am?"

"I'm guessin' he thinks you're desperate," Hellhound growled. "An' I'm guessin' he ain't plannin' for ya to leave afterwards."

"Maybe." I flopped back on the bed again. "But likely Parr wants to keep me around a little longer and this is his way of throwing some fear into me without appearing to back down. I doubt if he'll burn any bridges until he has the weapon."

"Ya wanna take a chance on that?"

I sighed. "Not really. But I don't have a choice."

"Tell me where an' when you're meetin' him."

"Holt can back me up, so don't worry. I don't want you involved-"

"Too late, darlin'." He rose to loom over me, his jaw jutting with characteristic stubbornness. "I'm already involved. Ya can tell me where an' when or I can follow ya for the rest a' the mornin', but either way I'm gonna be there. An' it'll be a helluva lot safer for all of us if ya tell me now so I can get in position before ya get there."

I studied his widely-planted legs and crossed arms with a mixture of gratitude and frustration. Gratitude won, and I rose to hug him. "Thanks. Noon in the 14th Street parking lot at Nose Hill Park. Just stay out of sight and if anything goes wrong, call Dermott. And if anything changes I'll let you know."

His arms closed around me. "Thanks, darlin'." He stared into middle distance for a moment. "I been in that parkin' lot. Rollin' terrain an' some trees, so I'll set up on the west side where I got a clear sight line." He dropped a kiss on my forehead. "See how much easier it is when ya just plan me into your missions to start with?"

"Don't thank me," I muttered. "I'm sure there are all kinds of ways this can go wrong."

"Yeah, prob'ly," he agreed cheerfully as we headed for the door. "But we been through shit before, an' it worked out okay. I'm headin' out now so I got time to get in position. Call me when you're gettin' close."

"Okay." I extracted a burner phone from my waist pouch and handed it to him. "I'll call you on this."

CHAPTER 38

I had barely shed my coat at Sirius Dynamics when Spider tapped on my door, his eyes sparkling. "Guess what?"

"What?"

"Kane called in on the secured line last night." He raised a restraining hand as I opened my mouth to demand more information. "That's all I know so far. Dermott mentioned it when I told him about the footage I found last night. He's briefing us in ten minutes."

I slid into my chair to check my computer, where the meeting request glowed like a beacon of hope. "Thank God. That's one less thing to worry about."

"Oh. Um... speaking of worrying..." Spider's suddenly downcast face made my chest tighten.

"What? Spit it out, Spider."

"I, uh... my facial recognition software flagged Stemp last night, too. He showed up in the widened search area." He hesitated. "He flew out of Edmonton airport wearing his George Harrison disguise the night before last. Destination Frankfurt."

My heart sank. "Shit. He must have left the meeting in Drumheller and driven directly to the Edmonton airport."

Spider leaned in to whisper, "Should we tell Dermott

about Katya now?"

"I don't know." I frowned up at his troubled expression. "If she was sick or something, that would explain his personal emergency, and it would make sense that he'd fly overseas. And that would explain why he wanted me to stall Dermott, too, but why would he fly as George Harrison? And why would he take the weapon with him?" I stared into space, tugging a lock of hair.

How much did I really trust Stemp? I didn't know the man at all. My gut told me he wouldn't betray us, but what the hell did my gut know? This was the same gut that thought it was a good idea to pig out on beer and burgers right before bed.

"Well, let's see how the briefing goes." Spider's uncertain voice interrupted my thoughts. "It's time to go anyway."

I nodded and followed him down the hall, my prescient gut squirming with trepidation.

When we arrived at the meeting room, Dermott's grim face did nothing to ease my worry. And it didn't help that Holt looked as though he was trying to conceal satisfaction.

As soon as the door closed behind us, Dermott rose to pace. "Kane made contact last night." He gave me a nod. "You were right when you guessed there was another player involved in the original weapon deal. Yana was supposed to deliver the weapon to Fuzzy Bunny, but instead she planned to divert it to another arms dealer, Volslav. We don't know yet whether Volslav is a person or an organization, but Yana probably intended to set Kane up to take the fall with Fuzzy Bunny when the weapon vanished."

He cracked a knuckle and continued, "Thanks to Webb's facial recognition software, we have an identity for Dawn

White. On the surface, a quiet little secretary in a quiet little company, but Kane says she's connected with Volslav. And she's the one who gave him the information to convict those arms couriers seven years ago."

"What does that mean?" I asked. "Why would she show up now?"

Dermott shrugged. "I don't know, and Kane didn't have time to elaborate. White and Kane are meeting Volslav at six tonight so I assume Kane is maintaining his cover as an arms dealer. And more good news; the expert they met in Drumheller identified the developer of the weapon. I've set up teams to raid the developer's lab and Volslav's meeting at the same time."

"But what about Parr and Fuzzy Bunny?" I asked. "I thought the whole point of this operation was to nail them."

Dermott grimaced. "Yeah, that'd be nice, but we've stumbled onto an important power struggle here. It looks as though Volslav controls Europe, and Fuzzy Bunny is angling to expand there. If they control this weapon, they could do it. But if Volslav controls the weapon, that gives them a foothold in Fuzzy Bunny's territory here. If we nail Volslav now, it cripples their move into North America. We can't afford to miss this chance. And you're still building the case against Fuzzy Bunny anyway."

"But won't it blow Kane's cover if you hit the lab and his meeting with Volslav?"

Dermott shrugged. "It's a chance we have to take. And we have more important problems, because now we know Stemp's up to no good. Kane was expecting him to be at the meeting with Volslav tonight. He had no idea Stemp had escaped overseas with the weapon. And if Stemp has been an agent for Volslav all along, we're fucked. He could be delivering the weapon right into their hands, along with all our classified intel."

Holt turned a sardonic smile on me. "Still feeling warm and fuzzy about Stemp?"

"Actually... yeah, I think so." I turned to Dermott. "Stemp sent me a message last night. He said he had the weapon and everything was okay, but he couldn't call in. He expects to have everything resolved today. He'll probably be in touch soon with instructions for Kane."

At least I hoped that's why he wanted me to stall.

"What the hell, Kelly?" Dermott snapped. "How and when did he contact you and why didn't you call it in right away?"

"Um..."

I blinked stupidly. It hadn't even occurred to me to call in last night. Apparently my subconscious had already cast its vote of confidence in Stemp.

"Um, it was the middle of the night and all he said was 'have item, all okay but can't call in, need twelve hours'. He used the message system from, um..." I trailed off, glancing at Holt. "...another mission. Sorry, classified."

"And you believed him?" Holt demanded. "Fuck, what kind of chump are you? He's got the weapon and he's using you to help him cover his tracks-"

I interrupted, "Or he's doing his job and using the weapon to track down-"

"He fled the fucking country, Kelly! With a fucking top-secret weapon!" The vein was bulging in Dermott's forehead again. "How fucking naive are you? Stemp's been playing you from day one. Don't you know he's got a complete psych profile on you, documenting all the best ways to manipulate you?"

Suddenly I'd had enough of Dermott's shit. My voice came out hard and cold. "I'm sure he does. He told me right from the beginning that he'd manipulate me in any way necessary to protect national security. I'm equally sure he's got a file like that on everybody. It's what he does. It's why he's good at his job. And he's innocent until proven guilty, so cut him some slack."

"Not in our world, Kelly," Dermott spat. "In our world we stop assholes like him before innocent people die. I'd throw you in the brig for colluding with him if I didn't think you're too fucking dumb to even realize you were being played."

Red suffused my vision and I rocketed to my feet, fists clenching. "Listen, you fu-"

A hard shoe poked my shin and I barely suppressed the urge to lash out in return. Shooting me a warning look from across the table, Holt murmured, "Anger management, Kelly."

I sucked in a long breath through my nose. Then I faced Dermott, my teeth creaking under the strain of my clenched jaw.

"I'm going to work on Fuzzy Bunny's case," I grated. "I have a meeting with Barnett at noon in Calgary." I turned to Holt. "Can you back me up?"

"No." Dermott answered before Holt could open his mouth. "As of now, I'm promoting Holt to lead the mission to apprehend Stemp. And you better hope he doesn't find anything to compromise you in the process." He returned my glare. "You're lucky I still need you on the Fuzzy Bunny case, or you'd be in lockdown. Get out of my sight."

I forced my rigid muscles into motion and stalked out with all the limber grace of a rust-ridden robot. Practically snorting steam, I strode to my office and grabbed my coat. I was halfway down the stairs when Spider's tremulous voice halted me.

"Aydan, wait!" He hurried down behind me, his lanky limbs flailing awkwardly in his haste. "You can't go without any backup!"

I drew a long slow breath and held my voice level. "It's okay. Arnie's going to back me up. And I'm going to pick up some weapons and a vest at Stores. Barnett is going to be pissed that I lied about having the photo of George Harrison. I hope he won't be pissed enough to shoot me, but..." I shrugged, grimacing. "I hope those vests work. And I hope he doesn't go for a head shot."

"But, Aydan..." He stopped, his hazel eyes troubled. "Okay, I know it's your job. Just... be careful. And don't leave right away. I'll meet you at Stores with a screen capture of Stemp in his George Harrison disguise. At least you'll have something to give Barnett."

Gratitude warmed my heart. "Thanks, Spider, you're the best!"

He turned to hurry back upstairs and I headed for Stores, my anger dissolving as I switched to planning mode.

Who knew when I'd make it back, so I'd better make sure I was well supplied. My steps slowed. Damn. A bulletproof vest and trank guns seemed like a good idea at first blush, but what if Sharkface caught me with them? My cover would be blown sky-high. And if I somehow managed to survive that, Dermott would have my hide for letting Sharkface see a classified weapon.

I hissed out a breath between my teeth. Either way, the vest was still my best choice. If Parr still needed me, Sharkface wouldn't lay a hand on me so he'd never know about it. And if Sharkface had orders to kill me, I'd have to breach my cover and shoot him anyway. Assuming he didn't shoot me first.

I pushed that thought away and strode into Stores.

I was just emerging laden with gear when Spider hurried up. "Here's the photo," he said, his youthful face scrunched into worried lines. "I hope it's good enough. I thought about doing a quick sim and making a screen capture that would show his face, but..." He trailed off, looking miserable. "I didn't know what to do."

"It's okay, Spider, this is fine." I studied the photo he had handed me, frowning at the file folder blocking Stemp's features. "Maybe this is why Stemp got into his disguise for the benefit of our cameras," I said slowly. "Maybe he was trying to cover my ass by giving me something to pass on to Fuzzy Bunny without giving away the whole show."

"I hope so." Spider's lips trembled. "Be careful, Aydan." He threw his arms around me, and I patted his shoulder before withdrawing to put on my most reassuring expression.

"I'll be fine. Don't worry."

"Call me if you need anything."

I tossed off a salute and smile to hide my fear and headed for the stairs, leaving him gnawing his lip in the corridor behind me.

Sliding into my car, I drew a long breath and let it out slowly. A meeting in a public place in the middle of the day. How dangerous could it be? I'd be perfectly safe.

I swallowed hard. I'd just keep telling myself that. Never mind the flock of deranged butterflies doing kamikaze aerobatics in my stomach.

I pulled out my phone, and Hellhound answered on the

first ring. "Hey, darlin'. Ya headin' out already? I ain't even halfway to Calgary yet."

"Yeah." I blew out a breath and rubbed ineffectually at the knotted muscles at the back of my neck. "Dermott was being a prick and it was either leave now or shoot the fucker."

He grunted amusement. "Probl'y shoulda shot him."

"Yeah, well, I'm holding that in reserve for Plan B." I paused as a thought struck me. "Speaking of Plan B, I'm going to give you the number for Germain's burner phone. I don't know exactly where he is, but I think he's in Calgary somewhere. If anything goes wrong he'll be more help than Dermott. Have you got a pen handy?"

Hellhound chuckled. "Don't need one. Just read it off to me."

I complied, shaking my head. "Damn, I wish I had your memory."

"Well, it ain't always all it's cracked up to be, darlin', but it has its good points. Like on long drives when I get to replay all my mind-movies of havin' ya in my bed." His voice deepened. "An' other places. I just been thinkin' about that time in the passenger seat a' Dave's truck."

The memory brought a rush of warmth that left me slightly breathless. "Mmm. That's one of my favourites, too."

His voice dropped to a seductive rasp that vibrated my body like a big diesel engine. "We could talk dirty while we drive, darlin'. That'd make the trip a helluva lot more fun."

The vibrations spread to interesting places and I squirmed. "That would be a bad idea. When you use that voice on me I can't see straight. And I wouldn't want you to have an accident if you've got your hand on the wrong stickshift while you're driving."

"Which one's the wrong one?" His suggestive growl made me grin, imagining his bouncing eyebrows. "An' what kinda accident are ya talkin' about?"

"The kind that hurts you. I want you in one piece so I can play with your stickshift later," I teased. "So get your mind out of the gutter and focus on the mission."

"Hell, darlin', my mind'd hafta crawl up a helluva long way just to get into the gutter in the first place." His bantering tone levelled into seriousness. "Okay, I'm gonna set up behind a knoll above the west side a' the parkin' lot. I'll circle around on foot an' get there from the back so there ain't any tracks in the snow from the parkin' lot. The off-leash area is over the crest a' the hill, so nobody should spot me from above. Make sure ya park on the other side a' the lot from Barnett an' try an' keep him where I got a clear sight line."

"Okay." I drew a deep breath, easing the tension from my shoulders. "Thank you. You have no idea how much better it makes me feel to know you've got my back."

His rasp smoothed to a soft rumble. "I got a pretty good idea. Ya been coverin' my back for a while, an' it feels damn good." Before I could respond he added, "Call me if anythin' changes. Be safe, darlin'."

I whispered, "You, too," before he hung up. Smiling around the pleasant lump in my throat, I put the car in gear.

I arrived in Calgary early enough to stop at a drive-through, but the burger and fries sat in a cold greasy lump in the pit of my stomach while I drove toward Nose Hill Park.

What if Sharkface simply shot me as soon as I got out of

my car?   Or hell, as soon as I drove up?   What could
Hellhound do from his vantage point who-knew-how-far
away? Call the police and the coroner; that was about it.

But Nose Hill's big off-leash area was a favourite with
dog walkers and there were bound to be people there at
noon. Shooting me in front of witnesses would be stupid.
And anyway, Parr probably didn't want me killed outright.
More likely he'd want to extract as much information from
me as he could.   Sharkface probably had instructions to
abduct me so they could torture me at their leisure.

Gee, there was a cheery thought. I swallowed hard and
adjusted my sweaty grip on the steering wheel while the
greasy lump rotated in my stomach.

Nothing bad would happen.   Hellhound would be
watching over me. And I was armed.

Nothing bad would happen.

I repeated the mantra over and over as I turned into the
parking lot. Breathing a quiet 'thank you' at the sight of
Sharkface's dark SUV at the south end, I parked at the north
end. Hellhound would have his sight line.

But so much for 'lots of witnesses'. There were only two
other empty cars in the lot besides Hellhound's Forester.
Damn.

I was quivering in the driver's seat wondering what to do
when Sharkface got out of his SUV and strode toward my car.
That made up my mind. No way I'd let him walk up to my
car and trap me inside. I sprang out and hurried across the
lot to meet him halfway.

His flat eyes appraised me when I stopped several feet
away. "Where's my picture?" he growled.

"H-here." I extracted the folded sheet from my parka
pocket and held it out left-handed. The paper fluttered in

the dead-calm air as if shaken by a strong wind, and he gave me his shark-toothed grin.

"Whatsamatter, sweet-ass? Don't you trust me?"

"Hell, no." I turned away slightly as he approached, extending the photo as if to keep as far away from him as possible. With any luck its movement would distract him from my right hand, hovering over the concealed holster that contained my trank gun.

Instead of taking the photo, his hand flashed out to clamp around my wrist. I let out a yelp and made a not-too-vigorous effort to jerk away. Let him underestimate me.

His grip tightened like a vise. "Settle down. I just want to make sure you don't run off." With his free hand, he snatched the paper and snapped it open. Then his face darkened as he crumpled the photo and shoved it in his pocket. "What the hell is that supposed to be?"

"It's a p-picture of George Harriso-" I ducked as he swung at me. His open-handed slap glanced off the top of my head instead of my cheek, jolting pain down my neck.

He yanked me close to growl down into my face. "It's a picture of a file folder with a guy hiding behind it, you dumb bitch. It's fucking useless. And so are you."

"I'm not useless," I babbled, letting my voice go shrill in not-too-simulated terror. "You still need me. I can get that bottle from Kane."

He barked mirthless laughter. "We've got Kane. You're just a nuisance now." He twisted my arm behind my back and shoved me in the direction of the SUV. "And you know what I do with nuisances."

My heart stopped, my limbs freezing in place.

They had Kane.

No, no...

Sharkface jerked my arm, yanking me back to awareness. "Move, bitch, or I'll break it."

Up on tiptoe to ease the pain in my arm, I bared my teeth in a feral snarl. The dumb fuck thought I was left-handed and helpless in his grip.

Surprise, asshole.

Just as I grabbed for my trank gun, Sharkface's weight slammed into me.

The ground rushed up, fading into nothingness before I met it.

CHAPTER 39

I woke to the movement of a vehicle and a male voice. "...she's still out of it. Where can ya meet us?"

An inarticulate mumble of relief escaped me when I recognized Hellhound's distinctive rasp.

"Hang on, she's wakin' up," he said. "Aydan? Can ya hear me?"

"Yuh..." I dragged open my leaden eyelids just long enough to catch a blurred glimpse of the inside of Hellhound's SUV. My eyes fell shut again while my thick tongue slurred, "Whadda... fu..."

"Don't worry, darlin', ya just breathed in the trank gas. You'll be okay in a few minutes. I got Germain on the line an' he's gonna meet us." I tried to nod and achieved a spastic twitch while he spoke to Germain again. "Okay. See ya in ten."

My eyes opened more easily the next time, and I fumbled for the seat control with clumsy fingers. As I raised the seat from its reclined position, Hellhound shot me a quick smile from behind the wheel. "Hey, darlin'. How ya doin'?"

"Better." I blinked and shook my head, fighting the foggy feeling. "What happened? Please tell me I didn't shoot myself with my own trank gun."

He laughed, but sobered quickly. "Nah. I saw him grab ya an' waited to see what you'd do, but when he locked your arm an' started pushin' ya to the truck I took the shot. Hope I didn't fuck anythin' up."

"No, I was just about to shoot him anyway." My sluggish brain ground into gear, accompanied by a surge of adrenaline that made my stomach lurch into my throat. I clutched Hellhound's sleeve. "Arnie, they've got John!"

"Shit!" His hands clenched on the wheel. "What's your plan?"

"I don't know!" My voice rose in a frantic squeak and I clamped my lips together before the hysteria could spill out.

Panicking won't help. Think.

I had to find out where they were holding him.

"What did you do with Sharkface?" I snapped.

"He's takin' a little nap in the back." Hellhound jerked a thumb toward the rear of the SUV. "I nailed him twice so he's gonna be out at least another twenty minutes."

"Okay." I settled tensely into the seat. "We'll question him. Maybe he knows where they're holding John. Where are we meeting Germain?"

"Weasel's place."

"Is that a good idea?"

"Only one I got." He grimaced. "I'm hopin' Weasel ain't there. But if he is, he'll keep his mouth shut. He likes ya, an' he ain't gonna cross me."

I sighed. "Good thinking. At least this way you won't get caught with an unconscious guy in the back of your SUV."

I subsided, my hands worrying at the seatbelt while my mind ricocheted through useless plans. Kane could be anywhere, and I didn't have a clue how to find him.

But I could get help with that.

I yanked out a secured phone and punched the speed dial before activating the speaker so Hellhound could listen. This time it only rang twice before Dermott picked up.

"It's Kelly," I snapped. "Barnett said they have Kane. I'm meeting Germain in a few minutes and we'll question Barnett. Instructions?"

"Shit!" A series of muffled pops on the other end sounded like cracking knuckles. "We're up to our asses with Interpol and Stemp right now. Two tac teams are tied up with those busts tonight and I'm completely out of resources. Get Germain to back you up if he can, but otherwise you'll have to handle it on your own."

"I need Spider to trace Kane's burner phone."

"I'll transfer you now." The line went dead for a few moments before Spider's tremulous voice spoke in my ear.

"Aydan? Dermott said they have Kane." His voice cracked. "What can I do to help?"

"Anything you can think of that might help us locate him. Can you trace the burner phone he used last night?"

"Yes, but it'll take a while. I'll have to call you back. Hang on." The muffled clatter of computer keys sounded in the background. After a moment he spoke again. "Dermott can't spare any resources but I'm sending police officers to Dawn White's home and work addresses. If she's there, they'll ask her when she last saw Kane and hold her so you can question her." His gulp was audible, and his voice trembled when he spoke again. "I'll get the police to watch for Kane's or White's vehicles, and I'll call you right away if they spot anything. Hang onto that burner phone and I'll call you back on it as soon as I can." He swallowed again. "I know you'll find him."

My heart twisted. "I'll find him."

I had to. I'd never forgive myself if I didn't.

I hung up and eyed Hellhound's grim profile. "Can you think of anything else we can do?"

"Not 'til we hear back from Webb. But maybe Germain'll have some ideas."

I nodded, gnawing the inside of my cheek. Thank God Germain was meeting us and he could take over. If this was left up to my blundering attempts, I'd probably end up killing us all.

As if reading my mind, Hellhound glanced over. "Don't worry, darlin', we'll find him. You an' me an' Germain, we'll kick some serious ass. Just take it easy an' let the last a' that trank wear off. Ya can't do anythin' else right now."

I massaged my throbbing temples. "Why did I get knocked out by the aerosolized trank? I thought that only happened if I shot somebody point-blank indoors."

"Ya gotta be more'n three feet away on a calm day, just like bein' inside. An' I hit him twice, one right after the other, so there was extra knockout gas."

My brain got up to speed at last and I gave him a sharp appraisal, taking in his white fatigues patterned with random splotches of gray and beige.

Winter camo. And a couple hundred yards might not be a big deal for a marksman with a good rifle and bullets, but it was a hell of a shot for trank darts.

"Weapons specialist," I said slowly. "So that's it. You're a sniper."

He stiffened. "Ya didn't hear it from me."

"But..." I ground the heel of my hand into the frown lines between my eyebrows. "Then why did Stemp say you didn't have a restricted weapons license when we were debriefing a couple of months ago?"

Hellhound shrugged, watching the road with intense concentration. "Why does Stemp do anythin'?"

"Him and his goddamn 'need-to-know'." I shook my head. "God, he's twisty."

That thought made my guts clench even more. He *was* a twisty bastard. What if Dermott was right? What if Stemp had been playing me all along? And what if Stemp was the one who had sold Kane out?

Those thoughts marinated in my stomach acid while we drove in silence. When Hellhound gave me a sidelong glance for the third time before returning his gaze resolutely to the road, I turned to face him.

"What's wrong?"

He scowled at the windshield, the bunching of his shoulders visible even under his parka. "Hell, this ain't the time, but..." He hesitated, his face taut. "But it's buggin' the shit outta me, an' I gotta know."

My stress level ratcheted up to 'impending coronary'. I held my voice calm and level with all my will. "What is it?"

"I..." He thumped a fist on the steering wheel, still scowling. "Shit, Aydan, I was kinda hopin' you'd never find out what I really do, but I guess in some stupid fucked-up way I was tryin' to tell ya when I sent ya over to my place a coupla weeks ago knowin' you'd find my gear..." He trailed off, not looking at me.

After a few moments I prompted, "I don't know where you're going with this. What's bothering you?"

He shot me a defiant look. "I'm a professional killer. Been a sniper with Special Forces for damn near thirty years. I told ya I was a fuckin' sick bastard, but ya didn't really get it 'til now, did ya?" He turned back to stare at the road. "Go ahead an' dump me if ya want. I won't blame ya if ya do."

"What?" I gaped at his rigid profile. "Of course I'm not going to dump you! Why the hell would I do that? We're friends." I reached over to fondle his thigh, trying to lighten the mood. "And how dumb would I be to dump a guy who figures three orgasms is just a good start?"

He didn't smile. "Maybe we *were* friends, but that was before ya knew I'm a stone-cold killer. Aydan, I pick guys off in cold blood an' then go for a beer afterwards. It's just a day's work for me. I'm seriously fucked up."

"Arnie..." I groped for a rebuttal and found none. I blew out a breath. "Okay, you're right. You're a little fucked up." His hands clenched on the wheel and I stroked his bone-white knuckles and continued, "And that's okay. I can't fit into a normal life anymore, either. I've killed seven people in the past nine months. And you saw me shoot Doytchevsky's face off. I'm as fucked up as you."

Hellhound barked out a harsh laugh. "Ya don't wanna know my body count. An' ya never killed in cold blood. Those guys deserved it after what they did to ya."

"It doesn't matter, Arnie," I said gently. "I love you for who you are, not for what you do in the line of duty. I'm keeping you unless you kick my ass out the door."

He braked for a red light and sat staring through the windshield, utterly still. After a moment, he cleared his throat and his voice came out in a cracked whisper. "Did ya just use the L-word?"

Oh, shit.

I summoned up a grin and shoved gently on his shoulder. "Yeah. *Lo-o-ove*. What are you going to do about it, you big chickenshit?"

The corner of his mouth twitched into a cautious smile. "If ya say anythin' about commitment or livin' together, I'm gonna bail outta the truck right now an' run all the way to Tijuana."

"That's good. Because if you say anything about commitment or moving in, I'm going to bail out of the truck right now and run all the way to Tuktoyaktuk."

The light changed and he relaxed as we pulled away. "Bad choice, darlin'. It's fuckin' cold up there. Always head south if you're gonna run. Beaches an' palm trees beat the hell outta snow."

I let out the breath I'd been holding. "I'll keep that in mind." After a moment, I added, "So is that all that was bothering you?"

He tossed me a quick sheepish smile before returning his gaze to the road. "Yeah. But I hadta know, darlin'. It's been eatin' at me for a helluva long time, an' I just never had the guts to say it."

"Well, now you know." I leaned over to plant a kiss on his cheek. "If in doubt, trust me."

He laughed. "Says the chick with trust issues."

I grinned. "Do as I say, not as I do."

We both sobered and I went back to my futile worrying, but the silence between us was easy and I took small comfort from the warmth of his hand cupping my knee while he drove.

A few minutes later we pulled into a parking lot behind an industrial cinderblock building and Hellhound stopped in front of a large overhead door.

I sighed. "God, I hope he's not here." Hellhound nodded and began to get out of the SUV but I stopped him. "Hang on. I'll cover you."

He raised an eyebrow. "That little shit ain't gonna hurt me. An' ya know ya can't shoot him anyway, darlin'."

"But if he takes a swing at you with his tire iron, I'll trank him into oblivion."

"Ya know ya can't. Classified weapon. I'll be fine."

I growled frustration as we both got out, and Hellhound strode over to punch a code into the keypad beside the overhead door. It rolled up to reveal a darkened bay.

Hellhound's shoulders relaxed. "Good. He ain't here. An' he doesn't hafta know we were ever here, either." He pulled out his phone and sent a brief text before climbing back into the driver's seat to pull into the bay.

He had just gotten out of the SUV when a rust-dotted silver Sunfire rounded the corner and drove straight for the still-open door. I tensed, but Hellhound waved a welcoming hand. A moment later a gush of relief weakened my knees when I recognized Germain behind the wheel.

As soon as he pulled in, I punched the button to roll the door down and turned on the overhead lights.

Germain parked and got out, casting an appraising glance around the grimy space strewn with car parts and automotive tools. "Chop shop?" he inquired.

Hellhound shrugged. "Never asked."

Germain nodded. "Okay, neither did I. What have we got?"

"Fuzzy Bunny has John," I blurted. "Spider's tracking the coordinates of his burner phone and he'll call me back as soon as he has them. And we have Kevin Barnett, so we can question him."

Germain's jaw clenched. "Dammit! How soon can we question Barnett?"

"I figure five or ten minutes." Hellhound popped the rear hatch of his SUV, revealing Sharkface's considerable bulk folded awkwardly into the cargo bay. "Say hello to

Sleepin' Beauty."

Germain raised an eyebrow. "Okay. Bring me up to speed."

I briefed him rapidly, and when I finished he nodded. "All right. How do you want to proceed?"

"I was hoping you'd take over." I gave him an imploring look. "You know what you're doing, and I'm just a-"

Germain waved me into silence. "Bookkeeper, I know. Don't worry, you can drop your cover with me. I know you can handle this, and I'm at a critical point with my own op. I've got less than an hour before I have to show up there again. Just tell me what you want me to do."

Fear sank cold fangs into my heart. Now Kane's life depended on an idiot civilian bookkeeper. This was exactly why I'd tried to get Stemp to demote me.

My guts froze into a solid block of ice.

Oh my God.

Stemp, the chessmaster. He had known I wasn't a real agent all along. And he had manoeuvred everyone into position, tying up the best agents on other jobs and using me to hide his escape with the weapon. And he had known I'd botch Kane's rescue and probably get myself killed into the bargain, eliminating the risk to his daughter once and for all.

Oh God. God help us all.

"Aydan?" Germain's voice penetrated my icy horror.

No, dammit, if I was Kane's only hope, I'd bloody well find a way.

I straightened. "Okay. First we question Barnett. Carl, are you up for a little game of Good Cop, Bad Cop?"

Germain nodded. "Sure. Which one am I?"

"You're the good cop. No, wait; you're the only cop. I'm going to hang onto my Arlene Widdenback cover for now." I hesitated, digging my fingertips into my knotted neck muscles. "You can tell him you're arresting him for murdering Hibbert and for extortion, and offer him a break if he tells us where they're holding Kane. Or any other information that might help us."

"What d'ya want me to do?" Hellhound asked.

"You can play the hired muscle, but don't let him see you unless it's necessary. And you should probably change clothes."

Hellhound nodded and peeled off his camo. "He oughta be wakin' up any minute, but he ain't goin' anywhere. I put restraints on him."

A groan from Sharkface made us all snap to attention. Hellhound faded into the gloom at the front of the bay, and I mouthed, "Showtime".

CHAPTER 40

Striding over to Hellhound's SUV, I delivered a smart slap to the back of Sharkface's head. "Wake up!"

"Don't leave a mark on him," Germain cautioned. "I don't want to have to explain anything."

Sharkface groaned again and half-opened his eyes. "Wha... fuck?" A moment later he tried to move and his eyes flew open all the way as he jerked against his bonds. "Wha' *fuck?*"

I grinned down at him, letting my pent-up animosity sharpen my teeth. "Wakey-wakey, asshole. Rise and shine." Just for the hell of it I smacked him in the head again, putting some shoulder behind it.

"Cut it out, Arlene!" Germain stepped forward to grab my wrist. "I told you, I don't want any marks on him for the arrest report."

"Wha'? *'Rest?'*" Barnett's face turned burgundy and he fought the restraints in earnest, grunting and sweating.

"Yes. You're under arrest for the murder of Paul Hibbert," Germain said calmly. "Also for blackmail and extortion. And I'm sure we'll discover a lot of other charges as we continue to investigate. You have the right to legal representation..."

Germain raised his voice to finish the recitation of rights over Sharkface's bellowed insults and obscenities, which culminated in '*Fuck you!*' His words were crystal-clear, and I filed that information away for future reference. Even with a double dose of tranquilizer, he recovered fast.

"No, thanks, you're not my type," Germain snapped. "But I'm sure you can find a bum-buddy in jail. Unless you decide to help us. Then I might be able to swing a deal for you."

"What deal?"

Germain shrugged. "Depends on how cooperative you are."

"Whaddaya want?"

"Kane," I snarled. "I've got some unfinished business with him. Tell me where he is."

Sharkface sneered. "I don't answer to you, bitch."

"You will if you're smart," Germain said. "Now tell us where Kane is."

"I don't know. And you're full of shit. You're no cop, and if you are, you know damn well I don't have to tell you anything."

"I'm a cop all right." Germain flashed his badge. "And you're right, you don't have to tell me anything, but if you do I might be able to help you get off with a lighter sentence."

"Bite me. And if you're really a cop, let me call my lawyer."

"If you tell us where Kane is, you may not even need your lawyer."

"I told you I don't know."

Germain eyed him expressionlessly. "Then who would know?"

"I don't know." Sharkface smirked. "And I want my

lawyer."

Germain drew me aside and turned his back on Sharkface to speak softly. "Now what?"

"Lean on him."

He grimaced. "You know as well as I do that once he refuses to talk and asks for a lawyer we've reached the legal limit of what we can do here. Maybe if we took him in and showed him the footage of Hibbert's murder we could shake him."

"We don't have time for that!"

Germain frowned, lines of strain bracketing his mouth. "I know, but unless you've got any other ideas we're at a standstill. And I have to leave." He grimaced, the torment clear in his eyes. "I want to rescue Kane as much as you do, but I can't leave my other mission unless there's imminent-"

"But they have John, you know they'll be torturing him!"

Germain's fists clenched. "Yes, but where are they holding him? They'll likely keep him alive until after the meeting with Volslav, but that's only a few hours away. Even if we had teams available and we could barge into all Parr's properties without a warrant, we still wouldn't have time to hit even half of them."

"But what can we do?" I clutched at his sleeve. "Carl, help!"

He clasped my shoulders with both hands, his normally cheerful brown eyes solemn. "Aydan, quit the bookkeeper act. I don't have your in-depth knowledge of Fuzzy Bunny, and this is your show. Call me as soon as you have a plan and I'll drop everything to help, but you know I'm no use to you until then."

Despair closed like a granite coffin around my heart.

That was it. Kane's death sentence.

My voice came out flat and hopeless. "Spider is trying to locate John's phone, but I don't know how long that will take. If I get a location, I'll call you right away." I bit back the futile urge to beg him to stay. "You're right, I can't think of anything else you could do right now. Thanks for trying with Barnett, though."

He sighed. "Keep me posted."

I nodded, and Germain turned back to Sharkface. "Last chance. Helping us now is the best deal you're going to get."

Sharkface began to describe in anatomically impossible detail what Germain could do with his offer, and Germain shrugged and turned away to get in his car. Heart sinking, I punched the door opener and watched while he drove away.

The vibration of the burner phone made my pulse leap. I hurried out of Sharkface's earshot and fumbled the phone from my pocket. "Anything?"

"No." Spider's voice was thin and strained. "Dawn White isn't at home and didn't show up for work today. Kane's call originated from a downtown hotel last night around two AM, so I hacked into their CCTV security camera. At eight-thirty this morning the security footage showed Kane and White leaving the hotel looking..." He hesitated. "Um... happy. And when I traced the current location of the burner phone, the GPS coordinates matched the landfill. So Kane ditched the burner phone as per protocol, and whatever happened to him, it happened after they left the hotel. He could be anywhere. I'm sorry, Aydan, I feel so useless." His voice quavered into a silence that echoed in the gaping hollow inside my chest.

After a moment I forced a firm, confident tone. "Don't worry, Spider, you've been a huge help, and we'll figure this out. Keep your facial recognition programs running and let me know if anything else turns up."

"Do you have a plan?" The desperate hope in his tone twisted my heart.

"I'm working on one," I lied. "Don't worry."

"Thank God, Aydan, I knew you'd think of something!"

"I'll call you later," I choked through the tightening noose of my guilt, and hung up.

Oh, God.

Sickness wrenched my guts and I wrapped my arms around myself. I knew first-hand what Kane would be suffering. And my failure would doom him to a prolonged and excruciating death.

"Hey, sweet-ass!"

Sharkface's voice lashed my raw emotions and I turned to see he had struggled out of the back of the SUV to stand precariously, feet bound together and hands still restrained behind his back. He grinned, his flat eyes devoid of humour.

"So much for your cop friend. Now I've got a deal for you. If you let me go right now, I'll give you a couple hours head start before I report to Mr. Parr."

"Fuck you."

He bared his teeth. "Wrong answer, bitch. Try again. Now you get one hour head start. And if I catch you, I'll fuck you once for each time you've told me to fuck off. And when I get tired of fucking you, I'll cut you and burn you and then fuck you some more. And believe me, bitch, I can make it last for days-"

The terror of a flashback seized me for a bare instant before white rage exploded behind my eyes.

I charged.

Reaching him in a few hard strides, I sidestepped at the last moment to drive a kick into his gut with all my strength.

The air barked out of his lungs as he doubled over. I whirled, my foot on its way to his head even while my ears belatedly registered the small, flat report of a trank gun.

I was already spewing garbled obscenities by the time I dragged my eyelids open to see the inside of Hellhound's SUV again.

"Take it easy, darlin'." Hellhound's blurred features swam beside me. "Just give it a coupla minutes."

I let my eyes fall shut and mumbled ineffectually, but he must have guessed my question.

"I tranked him an' ya breathed the gas again. Just take it easy."

I subsided, letting my body recover while I fought the mental fog. The nuclear holocaust of my rage slowly reshaped itself into bright cold fury, and I measured its breadth and depth as if hefting a new and lethal weapon.

Yes. This would serve me.

If it didn't destroy me.

But maybe it already had.

I opened my eyes and jerked the seat upright. "Is Sharkface in the back?"

"Yeah. What d'ya wanna-"

"Take us back to my car." My voice came out hard and brittle.

"Okay..." Hellhound eyed me with concern, but he got out to open the bay door and turn off the lights without further comment. By the time we drove away, I was dialling my phone.

If I'd had any emotion left in my body, I would have held my breath while it rang. Instead, I waited with icy composure until Dave picked up.

"Dave, it's Aydan," I said, and kept talking over his cheerful greeting. "Where are you?"

"Calgary. Just prepping a reefer."

Shit.

"Are you fit to drive?" I snapped.

"'Course." He sounded puzzled. "Heading out in about an hour. Why?"

That was enough to shift my focus. "What? You're toking up before you get on the road?"

"No!" His affront came through loud and clear. "Jeez, thought you knew me better than... oh." Comprehension gentled his tone. "Reefer's a refrigerated trailer. Keeps fruit and stuff cool in summer, but in winter it keeps it from freezing. Just pre-warming it before we load."

"Oh. Sorry." I gripped the phone and drew a deep breath. "I'm going to ask you for a really big favour, and feel free to say no."

"Like I told you; anything, anytime."

"This is illegal. And dangerous."

"Hel... Heck, what else is new?" His joke might have sounded more humorous without the slight tremor in his voice.

"And you'll probably miss your delivery and end up in deep shit..."

"Time's wasting, Aydan," he said firmly. "Tell me where you need me. I'll get unhooked and bobtail over-"

"No," I interrupted. "If the trailer's empty I need it, too."

Hellhound shot me a perplexed look from the driver's seat, and Dave's voice mirrored his bewilderment. "Okay... Where do you want me?"

"Does your trailer have a ramp?"

"Uh... yeah. I'm delivering to a bunch of small-town grocery stores. Most of 'em don't have loading docks-"

"Is the ramp strong enough to hold a car?"

"Uh, probably. Have to check the load rating, though."

"Okay, good. We're close to Nose Hill Park and 14th Street right now. Where can we meet where it's easy for you to get the truck in and out but nobody will pay attention to somebody driving a car into a reefer trailer?"

"Uh..." Dave hesitated. "Anybody that knows anything about trucking is gonna notice something like that. You talking about your Legacy? It'll be a tight fit."

I held onto my patience with both fists. "Just tell me where, Dave."

"Okay, uh... Maybe close to a car dealership or a leasing company? As long as nobody looks too close at the trailer we might be okay. There's a place just south of the airport where I delivered some cars once."

"Perfect. Hang on, I'm going to put you on speaker so Arnie can memorize the address."

I pressed the speaker button, and Dave's voice crackled out of the phone with unfortunate clarity. "*He's* with you?"

His inflection was distinctly unflattering, and Hellhound's mouth quirked. "Dave. Buddy. I missed ya, too."

"Shi... crap. Didn't mean it that way..." Dave trailed off. "I just meant..." He stopped, apparently giving it up as a bad job. "Don't know the address off-hand, but I'll give you directions." He recited them and added, "I'll be there in twenty minutes."

When he hung up I turned to frown at Hellhound. "You guys aren't going to get into another pissing match, are you?"

Hellhound snorted. "Hell, I got nothin' to prove. Long

as Dave can handle it, I'm good."

"I know you're good." Despite my tension, I paused to smile at his smug expression. "What I'm asking is whether you can work with Dave."

All traces of humour vanished from his face. "We're talkin' about savin' John's ass here. If ya need me to stand on my head an' cluck like a chicken, I'll go put on the fuckin' feathers right now. Dave ain't gonna be a problem."

When we pulled into the Nose Hill parking lot, I drew a breath of relief at the sight of my car parked in solitary splendour. The rising wind whipped little eddies of snow across the packed surface, and I guessed the dog walkers had lost interest. Perfect.

"Pull in next to me," I commanded, and hit the remote trunk release.

"What the hell, darlin'?"

I ignored Hellhound's question and hopped out as soon as the SUV stopped moving. After hurriedly relocating all my gear from the trunk to the back seat I turned to face his bemused expression.

"Help me move Barnett into the trunk."

"Why?" Hellhound eyed me suspiciously. "He's fine in the back a' my truck. An' cars have those interior trunk releases now. Ya don't want him jumpin' out in the middle a' traffic."

"He's going to be unconscious, so it won't be a problem. Hurry up, before somebody comes."

"But..."

"My op, my orders." The words tasted of bitter irony, but I forced them out anyway and fixed Hellhound with my best

'I-mean-business' glare.

He shrugged and popped the hatch of the SUV. "Okay. So, 'illegal an' dangerous', eh? Sounds like my kinda party. What's the plan?"

I avoided answering while we hefted Sharkface's limp bulk into my trunk.

As I reached for the lid Hellhound said, "Better trank him again. I only hit him with one, an' that was fifteen minutes ago."

"Right, thanks."

I aimed my trank gun, but Hellhound stopped my hand. "Hang on. If it's close quarters an' he's already out, ya can just do this." He appropriated the gun and ejected the magazine to carefully extract two darts. Reaching over, he pushed the points into Sharkface's neck and held them there for a moment.

"There." He withdrew the empty darts, leaving two tiny punctures. "The injected trank still works the same, but the gas doesn't spray out unless the dart hits somethin' when it's goin' close to muzzle velocity. This way ya don't hafta hold your breath."

I closed the trunk lid and tucked the gun back in my holster before leaning against him for a quick hug. "What would I do without you?"

He grinned. "Prob'ly die from lack of orgasms." His smile faded. "Now, are ya gonna tell me what the plan is?"

I hesitated. "When we get there. I need to make a stop on the way, so I'll meet you there later."

"Did ya memorize the directions?" he challenged.

I blew out a breath of resignation. "No."

"Awright, then, tell me where your stop is. We'll go there first an' then ya can follow me to meet Dave."

"Or you could just tell me the directions and I could memorize them," I suggested without much hope.

He just snorted, and I gave up. "Fine. I'm going to stop at Canadian Tire. If you could stay in the parking lot and watch my car while I'm in the store, that would be great."

"Canadian Tire?" Hellhound frowned. "What-"

"Let's go, the trank's wearing off while we stand here," I interrupted, and made for the driver's seat.

CHAPTER 41

Pulling up to where Dave's big semi grumbled quietly in an empty corner of the parking lot, I shot a wary glance around the area. The wind had picked up and there was nobody moving among the rows of cars near the leasing office Dave had chosen as our meeting place.

Good.

I loosened my white-knuckled grip on my steering wheel and drew a long slow breath, willing my rigid muscles to ease.

I could do this.

I had to do this. Kane's life depended on it.

As Dave swung down from the cab, Hellhound emerged from his SUV and they both hurried toward my car. I powered the passenger window down and Dave leaned in, his worried gaze travelling over the makeshift plastic window on the driver's side and the shopping bags in my back seat.

"What happ…" He stopped. "What do you want me to do?" he asked instead.

I drew a deep breath and held my voice steady. "Listen carefully, and do exactly what I say." He nodded, his brow furrowing.

"Okay," I continued. "First of all, if anybody asks, I'm

Arlene Widdenback."

"Not Jane?"

"Not this time."

His jaw firmed and he squared his shoulders. "'Kay. Arlene Widdenback. Got it."

"I want you to show Arnie how to operate the doors and ramp on your trailer," I went on. "Then I want you to get in the driver's seat and not look back. Keep your phone on, and I'll phone you with instructions. Don't try to see what we're doing. If you hear anything, ignore it. Drive around wherever you want, but stay inside city limits. Got it?"

"But, Aydan-"

I silenced him with an upraised hand. "If the shit hits the fan and we get caught, you tell the truth in court. Tell them I called you and said I needed your truck but I didn't tell you anything and I wouldn't let you watch. And you did what I told you because you knew I worked for the Department."

"But-"

"Do you still have those removable decals for your doors?"

"Got something better." He gave me a slightly sheepish look. "After the last time we were on the run in my truck, I got bogus ones made up. And bogus decals to cover my license plates, too. Just in case."

My tension eased enough to let the corners of my mouth crack into a smile. "Dave, you're brilliant." His ears turned scarlet and he shuffled his feet, grinning. I added, "Put them on while Arnie and I are loading the car. Then get in the driver's seat and wait for instructions."

He sobered. "Aydan, tell me what you're doing. I can help-"

"You're already helping. And this is all I want you to do. You'll be safe this way." I waved off his incipient protest. "Dave, I couldn't live with myself if anything happened to you. And imagine how Nichele would feel. You have to think about her now. Please, just do as I say."

His lips thinned, but he blew out a breath and nodded. "'Kay. Good luck." He jerked his chin at Hellhound. "Come on."

I eyed the proceedings worriedly while they opened the big back doors of the trailer and hauled out twin ramps. Shit, Dave was right. The car was going to be a damn tight squeeze. I'd probably have to climb out the window instead of opening the door.

And the trailer was higher than I'd realized. The ramps were so steep I'd be lucky if I didn't high-centre the car at the top. And that was assuming I didn't drive off the narrow ramps in the first place.

And dammit, twenty minutes had passed. Sharkface was going to wake up soon.

Ramps in place, the men shot expectant glances in my direction. I turned the car around and backed toward the ramps, silently praying. A few feet away I stopped and got out to examine the trailer before turning to Dave.

"Can I open the doors from the inside if I have to?"

"Yeah, there's an emergency release handle here." He indicated a recessed lever on the door.

"Okay, good. Thanks. Dave, this is where you head for the cab."

His jaw worked as if he was chewing on an argument, but he muttered, "'Kay," instead and obeyed.

As soon as he was out of earshot, Hellhound demanded, "Okay, darlin', what's the plan?"

"Now you guide me up the ramps and then close the doors behind me. Follow Dave wherever he goes. I'll call you if I have any other instructions."

He frowned down at me in silence for a moment before his expression smoothed into ominous calm. "Whatcha got in the shoppin' bags, darlin'?"

Before I could stop him, he opened the car door and rummaged for a moment before going still. Straightening, he turned slowly, holding the bag containing duct tape, rope, and waterproof plastic tarps.

Still expressionless, he studied my face for a long moment before speaking. "Ya sure about this, Aydan?"

I avoided his gaze. "Yes. John's out of time. We're out of ideas. Unless you have a better plan."

Silence stretched between us.

"Let me do it," he said.

"No. This is my decision. My responsibility." I took the bag out of his hands and tossed it back into the car. "Guide me up the ramps."

He crossed his arms over his broad chest, legs planted like tree trunks. "I ain't leavin' ya alone with him. If somethin' goes wrong an' he gets free, me an' Dave'd be drivin' around clueless while he does whatever he wants to ya."

Cold fear weakened my backbone, but I jerked it straight again. "Nothing will go wrong. I have the trank gun-"

"No." Hellhound's face was set like stone. "Ain't happenin', an' that's final. Here's what we're gonna do. I'm gonna get in the trailer an' guide ya up the ramps from inside. You're gonna call Dave an' tell him to close us in. Anythin' that happens after that, we're in it together."

"Arnie, no. I don't want you involved. And..." Sudden

foolish tears burned the backs of my eyes. My voice came out so choked he had to bend down to hear me. "I... don't want you to see me do this. I didn't want you to know..."

I stared down at my hands twisting in front of me.

Too late. He already knew.

Already saw the monster I had become.

"Aydan." His hand was gentle on my hair. "Sometimes good people gotta do bad things. It ain't gonna change the way I feel about ya." His fingertips coaxed my chin up and he brushed a kiss across my lips. "Get ready to load."

He straightened and strode up the ramp into the trailer before I could swallow the giant lump in my throat.

A few minutes of white-knuckled manoeuvring later I engaged the parking brake, eyeballing the inches of space between my car mirrors and the sides of the trailer. Easing out a breath, I punched the speed dial for Dave's cell phone and held my voice steady. "Change in plans, Dave. Arnie's riding with me now. Come and close us in, and then go back and start driving."

"'Kay." The single word vibrated with tension, and a few moments later he appeared at the rear of the trailer, his bushy brows nearly meeting above his nose.

The clang of the door latches reverberated like the knell of Judgement Day.

I drew a couple of deep breaths that failed to calm me before squirming out the passenger window to sidle to the back of the car, my shopping bags held high. In the murky interior lighting of the trailer, Hellhound's bruised face was dark and forbidding.

"What now?" he asked.

I swallowed against the papery dryness in my throat. "First this." Tearing off a short strip of duct tape, I popped the trunk and plastered the tape over Sharkface's eyes, trying not to wince at the thought that he'd probably lose both eyebrows when it came off.

A bleak smile wrenched my lips. With what I was planning for him, ripped-out eyebrows would be the least of his worries.

Hellhound had already unfolded the tarp and spread it in the front corner of the trailer. He appropriated the duct tape to shape the tarp into a shallow pan at the bottom and attach the top edges partway up the walls of the trailer. "That oughta catch most of it," he grunted as he straightened.

My stomach lurched and I turned hurriedly back to Sharkface. Staring down at him, I summoned all my anger and hatred. All the pain and fear of the last nine months. All the terror I'd suffered at his hands.

"Let's get him stripped and onto the tarp," I snapped. "Before he wakes up."

Staggering against the movement of the trailer, we half-dragged, half-carried Sharkface to the tarp. The sight of his naked body turned my stomach, but I kept my face impassive. Hellhound and I avoided each other's eyes while we worked in silence to secure Sharkface's hands behind his back again.

As Hellhound bent to secure his feet, I stopped him. "Legs apart. We can attach the rope to the tie-downs on the wall."

His face twisted for a bare instant before smoothing into emotionless composure. He nodded and we bent to our work.

When we were finished we turned away together and I tottered as far away as possible to sink to the floor of the trailer. Hiding my face in my hands, I concentrated on breathing.

In. Out. Nice and slow. Just like ocean waves...

Hellhound sat down beside me and his palm traced slow circles on my back. "Ya don't hafta do this, Aydan," he whispered. "Let me do it. I'm already as fucked up as I'm gonna get."

I clenched my fists in my hair. "No. I have to do it."

"But, darlin'-"

His argument was cut short by a groan from Sharkface, and I gathered my trembling legs under me and leaned on Hellhound's shoulder to stand wavering against the motion of the trailer.

When he began to rise I pressed him back to the floor. "Please stay here," I whispered.

"We're in this together." He stood and clasped my hand in his.

Tension vibrated between our palms while we navigated back to where Sharkface was beginning to spew remarkably intelligible obscenities.

Standing in front of him, I drew a deep breath and reached for the hard cold weapon of my anger. Choosing between Sharkface and Kane wasn't even a contest.

Do it.

I kicked Sharkface's foot. "Shut up!"

His generalized swearing altered to a shower of violent abuse, his voice rising to a shout.

I stepped forward and planted my foot none too gently on his naked genitals. "I said shut up."

He yelped and jerked at the contact of my icy hiking boot, but he shut.

"That's better." I kept my voice as cold as the slush dripping onto his balls. "Now we're going to have a little talk."

Dave braked and I staggered, hurriedly shifting my weight to avoid crushing Sharkface's nuts to a pulp.

Oh, yeah, I was a real badass, all right. Could I even do this?

I stiffened my spine.

Yes. All I had to do was imagine what they were doing to Kane right now.

I sank down on the floor before my shaking legs could drop me.

"Tell me where Kane is," I snapped.

"I don't know. And I want my lawyer."

My laugh sent a quiver of uncertainty over his face. "Your lawyer," I mocked. "It's far too late for that. You should have talked to the cop while you had the chance. Then you'd be safe in a nice cozy jail cell right now."

"You're not going to do anything," he sneered. "Your cop friend already told you not to leave a mark on me." His blindfolded face searched the air. "Where is he?"

"Long gone. Along with my patience. If you tell me where Kane is right now, I'll call the cop back and let him arrest you. Otherwise, you're going to feel pain like you've never even imagined."

His mouth flattened. "Take off this blindfold. I already know who you are anyway. Let's do a deal. You tell me why you want Kane, and I'll see if I can help you."

The muscles in his big shoulders rippled as he worked at the restraints behind his back. I handed my trank gun to Hellhound with a nod in Sharkface's direction. The metallic sound of the magazine ejecting made Sharkface freeze, his face snapping in that direction.

Hellhound gave me a grim smile and extracted a dart,

holding it at the ready.

"Recognize that sound?" I asked. "Good. Then maybe you won't be quite so eager to piss me off. Here's the only deal you're going to get. I'm going to tell you a little story. Then you're going to tell me where Kane is."

His face hardened, but he said nothing.

"You underestimated me, you dumb fuck," I snapped. "You and Parr and all you other testosterone-drenched idiots. Do you know what that *bottle* really was?"

"Yeah."

"Good. And do you know why Parr doesn't have it right now?" I didn't wait for an answer. "Because George Harrison works for me and he took it out of the country while you idiots were busy chasing Kane. I'm the only arms game in town now. And I've been working with my own developer, too. I have a few new weapons that nobody else knows about. If you don't tell me where they're holding Kane, I'm going to introduce one of them to you."

He twitched as I ran my fingertips over his hairy ankle. I dropped my voice to an ominous growl. "I guarantee you won't like it."

Please let this work.

"You're bluffing." He didn't sound sure.

"You wish. Tell me where Kane is."

"If I help you, Parr will kill me."

"If you don't help me, you'll be begging for death long before Parr ever finds you." I delved into my shopping bag, the rustle of the plastic making Sharkface whip his blindfolded face in that direction.

Then he leaned back, his mouth firming. "You're full of shit, just like your so-called cop friend. Give it up, bitch. And let me go, or you'll regret it."

"I'm done talking," I snapped. "Say hello to a brand-new weapon. It causes excruciating pain without leaving a mark on your skin. So my cop friend will still be happy if I decide to turn you over to him afterward."

My anger bubbled up and I flicked the switch, generating a chattering hum from the device in my hand.

"And I can make it last for days, *bitch*," I hissed, and swiped the business end across his ankle.

CHAPTER 42

Sharkface's scream was so horrible I jerked backward, adrenaline slamming into my veins. Beside me, Hellhound made a strangled sound and clapped his hand over his mouth.

"Who's there?" Sharkface's voice was a couple of octaves higher than normal. "Cop, is that you? Make her stop! I know my rights-"

"I told you, the cop is long gone," I snarled. "It's just you and me and this big fucking wimp who's supposed to be my hired muscle."

I glared at Hellhound, who scrubbed his hands vigorously over his grin. When he spoke, his rasp was wobbly with suppressed laughter. "Jesus, that's fuckin' sick."

I brandished the electric depilator I'd purchased from Canadian Tire's health and beauty section. "You think that's sick? Wait 'til I get started a little higher up." I leaned over to touch the rotating head to Sharkface's knee, the depilator growling and flinging uprooted leg hairs in all directions.

He screamed again, jerking against his bonds so hard I was afraid they might snap. A wave of guilt drowned my fierce amusement and I swallowed hard.

Yeah, he was a vicious killer. Yeah, he'd do much worse

to me and enjoy it. But intentionally causing pain and fear sickened me.

I put on my snarl again. "Oh, and did I mention that this weapon kills whatever it touches? When the pain starts to fade, you'll know the nerves are dying. Then after a while the tissue just rots and falls off. Doctors think it's an infection, but antibiotics won't touch it. Do you remember when that flesh-eating disease was big news a few years ago? That was when we were testing this weapon. And nobody had a clue."

I moved the device in widening circles on his knee, generating a flurry of hysterical shrieks and thrashing.

"Make her stop, make her stop!" Sharkface babbled. "Please, I don't know where they're holding Kane, I swear! I don't know!"

"Jesus," Hellhound choked. "That's just *wrong!*"

"Shut up!" I snapped, afraid to even glance at him in case he burst out laughing. "Do you like having a dick, Barnett? I hope not, 'cause you're about to lose it. *Where's Kane?*" I raked the depilator high across his inner thigh.

His scream held the mindless terror of a dying animal and his bladder and bowels released. The sudden stench made me double over gagging as my oldest nightmare flashed before my eyes. The horrible screams, the smell of shit from ruptured intestines...

Hellhound's grin vanished and he pulled me into the shelter of his arms.

Sharkface's blubbering was still audible even muffled by Hellhound's embrace. "*I-don't-know-I-don't-know-I-swear-to-God-I-don't-know-oh-please!*"

I gulped hard, trembling violently while I clung to Hellhound. Gulped again and again, willing the hot bile down from my throat.

After a long moment I managed to draw a breath without my stomach heaving. I straightened, and Hellhound stroked my cheek with gentle fingertips.

"Go sit in the car," he whispered. "I'll do it."

I shook my head and turned back to Sharkface, holding my voice flat. "Tell me who would know."

"I d-don't know f-for sure b-but-"

I flicked the depilator on, letting it buzz like an enraged hornet. "Names. Phone numbers. Addresses. Now!"

The names poured out of him so fast his tongue tangled, the information interspersed with sobs and pleas for mercy.

When he ran down at last, I shot a glance at Hellhound and he nodded. All data stored.

"Who should I start with?" I ground out.

"W-Willis Arlington. H-He should know."

"Good. You're going to call him for me. Set up a meeting so I can snatch him. Then I'll give you a nice shot of anaesthetic and you'll go to sleep. If he comes to the meeting, you'll wake up safe in the hospital and you'll only lose a few little patches of skin where I touched you. But if he doesn't show up..."

I moved the buzzing depilator close to his face and he reared back, whimpering. "...you'll wake up right here. And I'll use this all over your body. And you will suffer for a long, long time. But you won't die. By the time they find you, they'll have to amputate your arms and legs and dick and balls and most of your chest and face. You'll be nothing but a helpless lump of flesh. For the rest. Of. Your. Life."

I leaned closer, putting as much menace as possible into my voice. "Is there anything else you want to tell me?"

"P-Please, th-that's all I know, I s-swear!"

"Okay. I'm going to give you a minute to get yourself

together. And then you're going to call Arlington."

I dragged myself to my feet to stagger to the far end of the trailer and punch the speed dial for Dave's cell.

He answered on the first ring. "Everything okay?"

"Yes." I braced myself against my car as my stomach heaved again. "Where are we?"

"Westbound Stoney Trail at 14th Street."

"Okay, we'll stop soon. I'll call you back with a location."

"'Kay."

I wobbled back to the other end of the trailer, the smell of Sharkface's excrement twisting my guts into nauseated knots.

"It's time," I snapped. "You're going to tell Arlington that I'm bringing you the weapon but some idiot ran into your car in traffic and you can't meet me because you can't leave the scene while the police are there. Describe me. Tell him I'll be waiting in front of the liquor store in Crowfoot Crossing at..." I consulted my watch. "Two-thirty. Got it?"

"Accident. C-Crowfoot liquor store. Two-thirty."

I flipped the switch and he flinched at the buzz of the depilator. "Keep still," I crooned. "Very, very still. Because I'm going to hold this right next to your nuts while you make the call." He went rigid and a keening sound leaked from his throat as I knelt beside him.

"You're not going to do anything stupid, are you?" I asked softly.

"N-No! P-please don't..."

"And you're not going to sound scared at all when you talk to Arlington, are you?"

"N-No..."

"You sound scared. Try again."

He drew a short breath and cleared his throat, the

muscles of his thighs vibrating against the strain of the ropes. "No."

"That's better. Are you ready to make the call now? The sooner you do it, the sooner you get to a hospital."

He cleared his throat again. "I'm ready."

Hellhound punched the number into his phone and held it next to Sharkface's ear. I held my breath while the phone rang.

Please, God, let this work.

A 'hello' crackled from the speaker and Sharkface spoke, his voice faint but steady. "Arlene Widdenback has Mr. Parr's item but some fucking idiot ran into my car and I can't leave the scene while the cops are here. Can you get it from her? She'll be in front of the Crowfoot liquor store in Crowfoot Crossing at two-thirty. Tall redhead. Long hair, brown eyes."

A torrent of protest came from the phone and muscles rippled in Sharkface's jaw. "I don't trust anybody else. It's got to be you or we're both fucked..." The word trailed off with a tremor and I growled softly beside his ear.

"Do it, Arlington," he snapped. "Gotta go. Cops."

Hellhound punched the disconnect button and I turned off the depilator at the same time.

"Good job," I said. "Here's your anaesthetic. You'd better hope you don't wake up here."

Hellhound pressed the dart into Sharkface's neck and his rigid body went limp.

My legs gave out as though the trank had been injected into me instead. Slumped on the floor of the trailer, I wrapped my arms around my churning gut and concentrated on taking slow, even breaths.

Hellhound knelt beside me and gathered me into his

arms. "Ya okay, darlin'?" he murmured.

"No." The word wavered out and I jerked my chin up. "But I will be. As soon as we get John back safe and sound." I hauled out my phone again and punched the speed dial. "Dave, head for Crowfoot Crossing. Park in a loading bay where we can pull the car out without attracting attention, and then let us out."

"'Kay. Gonna be about ten minutes."

I hung up and burrowed into Hellhound's arms, but Sharkface's reek made my stomach do backflips. Pulling away, I hauled myself to my feet and wavered over to the shopping bag.

When I pulled out a second tarp, Hellhound nodded comprehension and rose to help me unfold it. As I reached for the duct tape, his hand closed over mine. "Ya look pretty green around the gills, darlin'. Why don't ya go sit in the car an' let me do this?"

I leaned my head against his chest. "Thank you."

He dropped a kiss on the top of my head, and I tottered back to squeeze through the window into my car again.

By the time the motion of the trailer ceased, Sharkface was concealed behind a curtain fashioned from the second tarp, taped securely to the walls and floor. Hellhound waited behind my car while the clanks of the door latches heralded Dave's arrival.

As soon as the ramps were extended I drove down and got out, sucking in breaths of clean, cold air. Hellhound and Dave rapidly stowed the ramps and Hellhound swung the doors shut against Dave's curious stare.

Dave's nose twitched. "What's that stink?"

"Must be a sewer backup somewhere," Hellhound said. "What's the plan, Aydan?"

"Dave, get back in the truck and promise me you won't get out until I text you that we're coming. When you get my text, open the doors and pull out the ramps, and then get back in the cab. Don't do anything else, and don't look in the trailer. Got it?"

He nodded reluctantly. "'Kay. But-"

"No buts. You're the most important part of this plan and I have to know I can count on you."

His ears went pink and he straightened, squaring his shoulders. "You can count on me."

"Thanks, Dave." I gave him a hug. "Now get in the cab and wait for my text."

"'Kay." He strode to the front of the truck and swung up into the cab without looking back.

Hellhound winked. "Good job, darlin'. Lucky he's still half in love with ya."

A flush warmed my cheeks. "He's in love with Nichele. And with the idea of playing James Bond."

"Whatever works. Ya got a plan?"

"Kind of." I glanced at my watch. "It's almost time. Let's talk in the car." We strapped in, and I put the car in gear and continued, "I need to go to the liquor store and buy a bottle of something so I've got a bottle-shaped paper bag to leave on the front seat. I'll tell him the weapon is in the car, and I'll park fairly far away from the liquor store. You can hide between a couple of cars in case anything goes wrong, but I plan to bring him to the car and hit him with a trank when he leans in. Then even if somebody's watching, it'll just look as though he got into the car."

"Good plan, darlin', but I'll go buy the bottle. If he's early, ya don't wanna get caught comin' outta the store with the bag."

"Okay, thanks."

I pulled into a parking spot and Hellhound got out to stride toward the liquor store as if he hadn't a care in the world. I watched tensely until he disappeared inside, then scanned the parking lot.

Shit, I should have made Sharkface give me a description of Arlington.

Too many damn details to think about.

But at least worrying about details kept me from dwelling on gut-wrenching thoughts of what was happening to Kane. They wouldn't be playing around with depilators.

Pushing away nightmare memories that bled terror into the edges of my mind, I stared at the liquor store until my eyes burned.

What was taking Hellhound? How fucking long did it take to grab a bottle and pay for it?

At last he strode out, paper-wrapped bottle in hand, and I let out a breath I hadn't realized I was holding. Getting out of the car, I left it unlocked and walked toward the store. Hellhound and I passed each other with no sign of recognition, and I heard the muffled thump of the car door behind me.

Everything in place.

Shivering in front of the liquor store a few minutes later, I checked my watch. Dammit, Arlington was late. What if he wasn't coming? What if Sharkface woke up and started yelling? Shit, shit, I should have taped his mouth.

"Arlene?" A rawboned man with pockmarked skin approached, his beady gaze flicking over me and skittering around the parking lot.

"Who are you?" I demanded.

"Kevin Barnett was in a car accident and he asked me to

meet you and pick up the item you were going to give him."

I gave him a suspicious glare. "Why should I believe you?"

He twitched his scarf aside to show the muzzle of the gun trained on me. "I don't give a shit whether you believe me or not. Give me the bottle."

CHAPTER 43

I didn't try to hide my surge of fear. "Okay, okay, you can have it. It's in my car. You can have the car, too, I'll give you the keys, just don't hurt me!"

Arlington jerked his chin toward the parking lot. "Move. I'll be right behind you. If you try anything, I'll shoot you."

"Okay, don't shoot." I walked as slowly as possible, my gaze scouring the parking lot. Where was Hellhound? Could he see what was happening?

We were halfway to the car when his burly figure emerged from between two pickup trucks ahead of us, frowning at one of the trucks as if surveying some invisible damage. As we approached, he turned his back and bent to poke at the sidewall of the rear tire.

I didn't dare glance his way as we passed, but I knew he'd be ready for the slightest opportunity. Thank God nobody else was nearby in the windswept parking lot.

I walked almost past my car before halting abruptly to stop Arlington near the centre of the back bumper.

"It's in the trunk," I said and pressed the trunk release, holding my breath.

I had just raised the lid when I heard a familiar flat report and Arlington began to topple. I shoved him toward the trunk and he collapsed into it with a thud that made me wince. An instant later Hellhound was beside me, and we bundled Arlington's legs in and slammed the lid.

Despite my thundering heart, a laugh bubbled up. "What a team!" I reached up to press a kiss against Hellhound's grin, and we hurried for the front of the car.

Dropping into the driver's seat, I massaged my chest in an attempt to soothe my heart back into a normal rhythm.

"Ya okay, darlin'?" Hellhound asked.

"Yeah." I drew a long breath, willing calm.

"We better head back to the truck now," he said. "Barnett's trank's gonna be wearin' off."

"I know." I hesitated. "I need one more thing, though. Do you know where I can get theatrical supplies? Like fake blood?"

Hellhound eyed me with interest. "There's a place close to here where I got that wig an' the dye for my beard. What're ya thinkin'?"

"I'm thinking we're running out of time and I'll probably puke if I have to t-torture..." The word choked out and I swallowed hard. "Anybody else. I don't know what I would have done if the depilator hadn't worked..." I trailed off, my stomach twisting.

I was pretty sure I did know.

I drew a deep breath. "I want to scare Arlington badly enough that I can avoid the whole thing," I finished shakily.

His face softened. "Darlin', ya didn't torture Barnett. Ya scared the shit outta him, that's all."

"Arnie, I tied him down and subjected him to pain and fear so intense he shit himself." I gulped down nausea. "That's torture."

"Ya only pulled out a few leg hairs," he insisted. "If that's torture, those fuckin' Brazilian wax places oughta be outlawed."

I shuddered. "I'm not arguing that." I put the car in gear. "I'll drop you at the truck. You can trank Barnett again and make sure Dave stays put while I go and get the fake blood. Tell me where the place is."

Fifteen minutes later I slammed on the brakes and took a hard right into the nearest alley, my heart thumping with sudden fear.

God, I was an idiot. I'd almost made a fatally stupid mistake.

Hell, it might still turn out to be fatal unless I was really, really lucky.

Pulling in behind a garbage dumpster, I drew my trank gun and got out of the car to hurry around to the trunk. My keys jingled in my trembling fingers and I silenced them in my fist.

Dammit.

Swallowing hard, I crept around beside the rear fender instead. Sucking in a deep breath, I hit the trunk release and took a rapid step forward to fling the trunk open and fire another dart into Arlington. He didn't move, and the wind swirled reassuringly around me. After waiting as long as I could hold my breath, I inhaled cautiously. When nothing untoward happened I blew out a long breath, the tension releasing from my shoulders.

Which saint watched over fools? Whoever it was, I owed him or her big-time.

I leaned in and confiscated Arlington's gun. God, that could have been bad if he had woken up.

After a moment of deep breathing, I rummaged through his pockets and took his cell phone as well before checking my watch. Okay, at least twenty minutes before he'd need another trank. With any luck I could make it back to the truck by then.

Apparently I'd used up all my luck in the alley. The voluble store owner subjected me to a relentless recitation of all the famous actors he had met, and pestered me with jovial questions about my need for fake blood and Halloween makeup in the middle of winter. Exercising the utmost restraint, I kept a smile on my face and refrained from tranking him.

Fifteen minutes had passed by the time I escaped, my shoulders knotted with tension. Leaning into the back of my car, I opened the folding rear seat and reached into the trunk to press another dart into Arlington's neck before getting behind the wheel.

At long last I backed cautiously up the ramps into the trailer, trying to ignore Dave's rubbernecking. The tarp curtain was still in place, and the smell seemed worse than ever after my respite in the fresh air.

Dave's nose was twitching again when he closed the doors, but I stayed behind the wheel of the car so I wouldn't have to face his questions.

As soon as the latches clanged shut, I squirmed out of the car with my bags.

Hellhound's strained face relaxed into a smile. "Shit, darlin', glad you're back. I used my last two darts on Barnett fifteen minutes ago."

"Oh, shit! Sorry, I should have thought of that!" I sidled

back to reach into the car. "Here's another magazine."

As he pocketed it, I popped the trunk and let out a breath of relief at the sight of Arlington's repose.

Hellhound leaned in to examine him. "How long d'ya figure before he wakes up?"

"I don't know. I dosed him fifteen minutes ago. Barnett recovered really fast, but Arlington's a lot smaller." My heart rate ratcheted up a notch. Kane's time was ticking away. "The sooner the better."

I snugged nylon restraints around Arlington's wrists and ankles and pulled the tuque from my winter survival gear down over his eyes before we lugged his limp body behind the curtain and tethered him to the wall. Then I hurried back to the trunk to retrieve my theatrical supplies.

Several minutes later, I glanced over as Hellhound's clever fingers put the finishing touches on a gruesome-looking wound on Barnett's leg.

"Nice work. You're really good at this." I reached over to peel up the bottom of Sharkface's duct-tape blindfold and dribble some fake blood down his cheeks before replacing the tape.

Hellhound nodded. "School drama club, thanks to Mom and Dad Kane."

We both went silent.

Doug Kane. Oh, God, how could I face him?

That thought was interrupted by a groan from behind us, and I turned to Hellhound and jerked a thumb at the tarp curtain.

He nodded, rapidly gathering up the makeup supplies before disappearing behind the tarp.

Arlington's drooping head rose slowly. "Wha' th'...?" His body went rigid against the restraints.

I let him struggle for a few moments before speaking. "Relax. You're not going anywhere."

He froze. "Wha... Arlene? Is that you?"

"Yeah." I knelt beside him, not too close. "I need you to answer a quick question for me."

"Why would I do that?"

I whisked the tuque off his head and watched his eyes widen at the grisly sight of Barnett's makeup. "Because that's what happens when I don't get the answers I want. Hold still."

I tore off a strip of duct tape and plastered it over his eyes. "Barnett said you had John Kane. And he said you'd know where he's being held."

"I don't know any John Kane, but..." His head twitched sideways as if expecting a blow and he spoke rapidly. "Don't hurt me. I can still help. Who do you figure this Kane guy crossed?"

"Parr. So if somebody pissed Parr off and he wanted information from them, where would they be?"

"Probably the butcher shop."

"What the hell is that supposed to mean?" I snapped.

He flinched. "An actual butcher shop. Good for interrogation. Lots of sharp tools, easy to hose down afterwards, and nobody questions some ground-up meat and bone being thrown away."

My stomach tried to climb my throat and my voice grated out as if edged with shards of broken glass. "Are you sure about that? Because this is your only chance. If you're lying to me now, the next thing coming out of your throat will be screams."

He shrank away as far as his bonds would allow. "N-no, I'm not sure. Like I said, I don't know this Kane guy. But if

Parr wants information, that's probably where he'll be."

My heart battered my ribs so hard I could barely hold my voice steady. "Give me the address and tell me how it's set up inside."

As he began to speak, Hellhound stepped silently around the tarp. When Arlington finished his recitation, I glanced up to see Hellhound's affirmative nod.

"You'd better be right," I snarled, and pressed a dart into Arlington's neck.

Lurching to my feet, I staggered to my car to extract a couple of secured phones. I handed one to Hellhound and croaked, "Call Germain. I'll call Dermott."

First I called Dave and told him to find the nearest possible place we could unload the car. Then I pressed Dermott's speed dial.

Heaping curses on his head with every ring, I clenched the phone hard enough to make its plastic creak. When he finally answered I rapped out a status update in a few sentences, finishing with, "I need backup!"

"I don't have it to give." Dermott's voice crackled with stress. "But I'll get Webb to coordinate with the police to back you up. They'll respond to a hostage situation, just don't tell them any classified details. Hang on, I'll transfer you to Webb and he'll set it up."

A moment later, Spider came on the line. "You found him? Thank God!"

"I don't know," I cautioned. "I just have an address and a possibility."

"That's better than what we had." His voice wavered and I heard him swallow. "Give me the address and I'll get a police team there. Do you have your police radio with you?"

"What police radio?"

"You don't have...?" He bit off the pointless question. "Maybe Germain has one."

"Hang on. Arnie? Does Carl have a police radio with him?"

Hellhound relayed the question and a moment later his nod made me suck in a breath of relief.

"Carl has one," I told Spider.

"Good. Tell him to give me five minutes and then call in to coordinate with the police." He drew a tremulous breath. "Good luck, Aydan."

"Thanks." I hung up and tapped Hellhound on the shoulder, staggering as Dave braked.

Hellhound said, "Hang on" into the phone and raised his eyebrows at me questioningly.

The trailer's door latches clanged and I jerked my chin at my car. "Finish talking while we drive."

CHAPTER 44

By the time we neared our rendezvous point, Hellhound and Germain had completed their phone conversation and developed a plan. If I hadn't been so terrified, my pride would have been smarting from the short but stinging rebuke Germain had delivered on the speakerphone when I lobbied to let the police handle it instead.

Hellhound glanced over from the passenger seat and his grim expression eased as he reached over to squeeze my knee. "Don't let Germain bother ya, darlin'. It's just battle nerves talkin'."

I hunched my shoulders. "No, he's right. He's such a good agent and he's sacrificing his mission for this. I'm just an idiot chickenshit-"

"Stop runnin' yourself down!" Hellhound's sudden bark made me jump, and his voice softened as his palm made a gentle circle on my thigh. "Listen, darlin', I know ya gotta hang onto your cover story, but now ain't the time. I know ya can kick your way through hell an' back, an' we need ya now. John needs ya."

My belly hollowed at the thought.

Around the corner from the butcher shop, I parked beside Germain's Sunfire. I couldn't see any police units, but

I knew they'd be somewhere nearby.

Too late for self-doubt now. A memory-flash of Doug Kane's steady grey eyes straightened my spine. No worries; no regrets.

"Let's do it." My voice came out ridiculously level.

Hellhound's soft rasp stopped me as I reached for the door handle. "Hey, Aydan. Ya know I love ya, don't ya?"

My stiff lips surprised me with a smile. "Yeah. Don't make me run for Tijuana."

He grinned and we got out.

Smiling was the last thing on my mind a few minutes later while we made our way down the sidewalk toward the butcher shop. I checked my watch and drew a shaky breath. Germain would already be in place at the back door. If Arlington hadn't lied to us about the layout, this should work.

A few pedestrians hurried along the windswept sidewalks in the late-afternoon twilight, and I could hardly believe they didn't seem suspicious of my jerky facsimile of a casual stroll.

Hellhound leaned down and made one more attempt to change our plan. "Let me go first."

"No. That's final." I made my voice as firm as my quivering belly would allow. "I'm wearing a vest; you're not. I go first. End of story."

My pulse thundered in my ears as we approached the shop, its glowing 'Closed' sign staining the drawn blinds blood-red. Too soon we arrived at the front door, and I stood close to block the view while Hellhound bent over the lock. An instant later it released and I shoved my way into the shop, my trank gun already swinging up to fire across the store at the startled-looking man with his pistol half-raised.

He collapsed without a sound as Hellhound crowded in behind me. Dodging around the meat counter, we had almost reached the door behind it when two gunshots slammed terror into my veins.

Momentum carried me to the door. Behind me, Hellhound roared our prearranged signal, "Incoming!"

Propelled through the door by Hellhound's battle cry, I snapped into a sidestep to clear the way even as my mind froze in horror.

Blood.

So much blood.

My nightmares came alive before my eyes. Kane's body dangling by its arms from a meathook, the obscenely sharp point protruding from his wrists. Slow runnels of blood shockingly scarlet on the white tile floor...

Kane's grey gaze met mine and reality rushed in to supplant the horrible memory.

He still had his eyes. They hadn't blinded him. The meathook wasn't impaling his wrists; they were bound and hooked over it. He was battered but I couldn't see any life-threatening injuries.

I jerked my gaze away to register the rest of the scene in a snapshot of adrenaline.

Germain holstered his weapon as he hurried in from the open back door. Two men lay unmoving on the floor, their guns spilled from lax fingers, their blood bright against the drying smears and spatters.

Beside me, Dawn White's naked body leaked crimson from so many wounds my mind shuddered away from cataloguing them. I instinctively moved toward her as she writhed, her clawed fingers scraping across the blood-covered floor to drag her closer...

Closer to the fallen man's gun.

Sheer reflex jerked my body into motion as she grabbed the gun and swung it up.

"Die, bastard," she gurgled, the words bubbling out on a gout of blood.

Shots deafened me. Impact slammed me to the floor.

More blasts. Her body jerked as Germain's bullets found their mark.

Silence bulged into my eardrums, an expanding hush that echoed the white explosion of pain in my shoulder. Muffled shouting pushed the silence aside and Hellhound's face appeared above me, his bruises dark against his bone-white pallor.

I dragged my good hand over to explore the hole high on the left side of my parka. "Vest," I croaked. "I'm okay."

He nodded and sprang up, vanishing from my field of view.

I gradually made sense of the shouting through the distortion of my damaged hearing.

Germain's voice. "Officers down! Medic!"

I tried to roll over but my body wouldn't cooperate.

More yelling. "Keep pressure on it! Help me get him down!"

I managed to haul myself up onto my good elbow just as a uniformed police officer and a paramedic dashed through the door. I glimpsed Germain and Hellhound crouched over Kane's body, now lying on the floor. Their crimson hands pressed to his chest, oh God...

A stretcher rattled through the door, more paramedics closing the circle around Kane. One crouched briefly beside Dawn White's body, checking for a pulse before turning away.

He knelt beside me instead, easing me back to the floor despite my protests. A few moments later Germain and Hellhound joined him, their faces grim while they wiped blood off their hands.

"Is he..." My words choked into silence.

"Hit in the chest." Germain's voice vibrated with tension. "But he's conscious. It might not be as bad as it looks."

Both men hunkered beside me as the paramedic unzipped my parka. His face cleared when he spotted the bulletproof vest, and he gently unfastened it to pull the neck of my sweatshirt aside and examine my left shoulder.

"Your collarbone doesn't look broken," he reassured me. "The impact mark is just below it. Can you move your arm?"

I managed a short and painful arc and he nodded. "You're probably just bruised, but we can take you in." He was interrupted by the stretcher's departure, Kane's motionless body drenched in blood, his face obscured by an oxygen mask.

I sat up, sucking in a breath through my teeth when my shoulder shifted. "I'll ride in the ambulance with him."

"No." The paramedic eyed me with sympathy. "I'm sorry, no passengers. They're taking him to the Foothills Hospital if you want to go there later. Don't hurry, though. He'll go straight into surgery and you won't be able to see him until he's out of recovery. Minimum three or four hours, a lot more if the damage is extensive."

"But he'll be okay, right?" I clutched his sleeve. "He's really tough, and he was still conscious..."

"I don't know; I didn't attend him." The paramedic must have seen the desperation in my eyes. "If he was still conscious and breathing on his own, I'd say that's a good sign. Do you want to go in for an x-ray just to make sure you don't have any cracked ribs?"

I stared blankly at Dawn White's ravaged remains, her blood slowly congealing in rivulets toward the floor drain.

Go in and wait for hours, praying for Kane's life while Parr wallowed in luxury bought with blood.

Not fucking happening.

I heaved myself to my feet, hugging my arm to keep it from moving too much. "No, I'm fine." I turned to Germain. "Carl, thank you. I hope you can still salvage your..." I pressed my lips shut, remembering the paramedic's presence in the nick of time. "Arnie, I have to go. Can you wait at the hospital and call me as soon as you have news?"

"Where ya goin'?"

I took one last glance around the carnage, the cold rage expanding to replace my heart. "Back to work." I turned on my heel and strode out into the store.

"Aydan, wait." Germain's voice stopped me at the door. He hurried over, his eyes dark and worried in his strained face. "I..." He made an awkward gesture as if he didn't know what to do with his hands. "When I said 'don't be a cowardly bookkeeper' on the phone earlier, I didn't mean you were a coward; you're the bravest woman I know and an excellent agent and-"

"It's okay." I patted him absently on the shoulder. "I have to go."

"Wait. Please. I thought you needed a pep-talk, but it came out wrong and I'm sorry. I just wanted you to drop your cover so we could plan..."

"I know, Carl, and it's fine. You're right, I needed to hear it just then. I'll talk to you later, okay? Good luck with your mission."

My words came as if from someone else's mouth, my mind already fully engaged in my planning. Slipping past the milling uniforms and flashing lights, I punched Dave's speed dial.

"Where are you?" I demanded as soon as he picked up.

"Northbound Deerfoot at McKnight. Everything okay?"

My throat closed and I forced my voice to stay level. "I hope so. Meet me where you dropped us off, as soon as you can get there. If there's anybody around, move on and phone me with a new location."

"'Kay."

Blessing his unquestioning trust, I hung up and nearly jumped out of my skin when Hellhound loomed out of the dusk beside me.

"Where d'ya think you're goin'?" he growled.

"Back to the truck. I've got work to do."

"An' ya thought you'd just go do it by yourself?"

I smiled up into his scowl. "Not if you're coming along."

"I'm comin'."

"Really? I thought you were just breathing hard." The reflexive joke fell from my lips without humour. He didn't exactly smile, but the harsh lines in his face relaxed. I squeezed his hand and added, "I'm glad you're here."

We slid into the car and I grabbed another secured phone.

Dermott took forever to answer. When he did, he sounded so distracted I wasn't sure if he'd gotten more than the most basic points in the hurried update I barked out.

"... and call me as soon as you hear anything from the hospital," I finished, but he hung up so fast I wasn't sure he'd heard me.

I swore and pointed the car toward our meeting place.

I could hear thumping from the trailer as soon as we pulled up.

"Shit, lucky we taped their mouths or they'd be yellin' their fuckin' heads off," Hellhound muttered. He jumped out almost before I stopped the car and Dave hurried toward us, wide-eyed. Hellhound scowled and flung up a silencing hand. "Don't ask."

Dave looked to me for confirmation, and I nodded. "What he said." I turned to Hellhound. "Is that coming from the front or the back?"

He cocked his head, listening for a moment before replying, "Front."

So they hadn't escaped their bonds. Thank God.

I let out a breath. "Dave, you don't see anything; you don't hear anything. Just let us back into the trailer and close the doors. I'll tell you where we're stopping next."

"But, uh... Aydan..." He leaned down to peer through my plastic window imploringly. "I *smelled* something."

"No, you didn't." I locked eyes with him and held his gaze until he nodded.

"'Kay." He turned away and busied himself with the door latches and ramps.

Hellhound leaned down to my window to speak softly. "I'll go in an' trank 'em both again while you're loadin' the car."

"No. I need Arlington awake."

"Okay. I'll shoot Barnett, an' the gas oughta knock Arlington out long enough to keep him quiet while we load."

"Perfect."

As soon as Dave put one of the ramps in place,

Hellhound hurried inside the trailer. A moment later the thumping ceased and he jogged out again, flashing an innocent look at Dave's perplexed expression.

"Thought you were gonna guide Aydan up the ramps from inside," Dave protested.

"Yeah, but I farted in there an' damn near burned my nose hairs off." Hellhound fanned a hand under his nose. "Christ, ya can smell it from here! Somethin' musta crawled up my ass an' died."

Dave recoiled, his nose twitching again. "That's *you*? You're sick! Aydan, come and ride up front with me. You don't have to put up with..." He shot a dark look at Hellhound before finishing, "...*that*." Hellhound smirked and Dave's fists clenched, his jaw jutting. "At least excuse yourself in front of a lady. Show some respect."

Hellhound's smile vanished and he took a threatening step forward. "I'm really fuckin' sick a' ya sayin' I don't respect Aydan," he ground out. "Shut your fuckin' pie-hole or I'll give ya a lesson in respect, ya fuckin' little-"

"Guys!" I sprang out of the car and planted myself between them. Glowering, they sidestepped to keep each other in view.

My ravelled nerves snapped.

Fists clenched, I flung my head back and let out a roar of sheer frustration. Both men jumped, their mouths falling open. Taking advantage of their instant of immobility, I jabbed a finger at Dave.

"You! In the cab! Now!" I whirled on Hellhound. "You! In the back! Move it!"

They didn't exactly leap to obey, but they did shuffle grudgingly in the directions I indicated.

"Guide me up the ramps," I snapped at Hellhound, and

got back in the car.

A few minutes later I sighed when I realized we still needed Dave to close the doors. I squeezed my eyes shut and pressed the speed dial.

"Sorry, Aydan," he said instead of hello. "I didn't mean to make you mad."

"It's okay, Dave. I know you were just looking out for me, but I really need you guys to work together. Lives are at stake. Can you come and close the doors now, please?"

"'Kay. Be right there. Sorry."

"It's okay."

A few moments later he appeared at the back doors, his expression contrite. I gave him what I hoped was a reassuring smile and drew a breath of relief when the latches clanked into place.

When I slithered out of the car and sidled to the back, I met another contrite expression.

"Sorry, Aydan." Hellhound hung his head. "I shouldn'ta let him get to me. I was just worryin' about..." He stopped. "Sorry. No excuse."

I slipped my arms around him and laid my head against his chest. "It's okay. I'm worrying about him, too." I straightened. "That's why I have to do this. You stay here."

I ducked behind the tarp curtain and my stomach heaved.

CHAPTER 45

Still tethered to the wall of the trailer, Arlington jerked at the rustle of the plastic tarp. I registered his movement with half my attention, my gaze still frozen on Barnett's unconscious form.

His struggles had churned up the fetid contents of his tarp. The theatrical makeup was mixed with liberal splatters of his own excrement, leaving him looking like a half-rotted corpse. We hadn't over-tightened the ropes when we tied him, but his frantic efforts to escape had ground them into his ankles and broken skin swelled around the bright yellow nylon. My stomach tried again to empty its contents at the thought of the bacteria crawling into that vulnerable flesh.

Drawing a deep breath, I turned away. Only rope burns, and he was tranked. He wasn't suffering at the moment, and soon I'd get him to a hospital.

Make it count.

Kneeling beside Arlington, I pulled the duct tape off his eyes and mouth. He yelped, blinking away the involuntary tears caused by the loss of one eyebrow and a goodly portion of his weedy moustache.

A moment later he focused on the scene across from him.

"*God!*" He recoiled so violently the back of his head thudded against the wall of the trailer. "*Jesus!*" His eyes widened and he thrashed against his bonds, fighting to get farther away from me. "I told you I didn't know! It's not my fault, I told you I was just guessing-"

I cut off his shrill protests. "Shut up. We found him at the butcher shop. And I'm not going to hurt you if you cooperate."

He sagged, panting, and his gaze skittered back to Barnett's gruesome presence. "Christ. What..."

"Shut up and listen."

Arlington clamped his lips together and stared up at me, trembling.

The memory of the butcher shop made my voice hard and cold. "Parr is finished. I'm the new game in town and if you're smart, you'll switch sides. I have Parr's weapon prototype, and I have some new weapons, too. One of them does that." I nodded at Barnett. "It causes excruciating pain without leaving a mark on the skin initially. Then everything it touched dies slowly, rots and falls off. You can see the start of it there." I pointed at a particularly unattractive combination of makeup and shit on Barnett's leg.

Arlington darted a fearful glance at it before returning his undivided attention to me.

"I'll give you the same deal as I offered Barnett," I continued. "You can stay loyal to Parr and suffer the consequences, or you can help me collect Parr's people and ultimately take down Parr. I've got a friend who's a cop. If you help me, I'll turn you over to him and you'll get to go through the justice system into a nice comfortable jail cell. Maybe even get a break on your sentence. If you don't, well..." I shrugged and cast a pointed look at Barnett. "He'll survive, but they'll probably have to amputate."

"H-how do I know you won't just k-kill me?"

"You don't." I flashed him a pointy-toothed grin. "But disposing of bodies is a pain in the ass, and I'd rather foster good relations with my law enforcement friends. I'm in this game for the long term. Anyway, death is better than that." I jerked a thumb at Barnett. "And if you don't help me, that's what you're going to get."

"I'll help." The words were out of his mouth almost before I finished speaking. "What do you want?"

"Names, positions in the organization, addresses, and evidence. And I want you to lure each of them to a meeting. As soon as I have them all, you'll be safe. If you steer me wrong, you'll be screaming." I glared at him. "Start now."

It was a lengthy recitation, and I was glad of Hellhound's listening ears and infallible memory on the other side of the curtain.

When Arlington ran down at last, I eyed him in silence for a moment before speaking. "Okay. You're going to call the first guy and set up a meeting. You're going to say you need to meet right away and you're going to be very convincing, because if he doesn't show up you're going to end up like Barnett. Then I'm going to go and collect your guy, and you're going to keep nice and quiet while you wait."

I gestured at the inside of the trailer. "You've probably already figured out you're on the highway. Nobody can hear you banging or yelling, so don't bother. And even if you do manage to get loose, you won't survive jumping out at highway speed. So if you're not sitting here tied up nice and quiet when I get back with the next body, I'm going to be Very Pissed Off. And Very Pissed Off is not a nice look for me. Got it?"

He nodded, wide-eyed.

"Good. Start thinking about what you're going to say. Hold still." I tore off another strip of duct tape and plastered it over his eyes, managing to avoid most of his remaining eyebrow.

Slipping around the tarp curtain, I wobbled over to where Hellhound leaned against my car. He tucked an arm around me and bent to whisper. "Coupla those names matched the ones Barnett gave us, so that's prob'ly a good sign."

"Good." I leaned closer, drawing strength from his warm bulk. "Are you ready to do this?"

"Hell, yeah."

I eased out a breath and called Dave.

Hours later, we were tethering our latest catch to the inside of the trailer when my waist pouch vibrated. Punch-drunk with pain and fatigue, I didn't register the meaning of the two-word text message at first.

'Call home'.

Then my heart kicked my aching chest and a wave of adrenaline made me light-headed. Hellhound finished taping our captive's eyes and mouth and glanced up, colour draining from his face at the sight of my expression.

"What..." he began.

"I don't know." I showed him the text and we hurried around our tarp curtain to get as far away from our human cargo as possible.

Clutching Hellhound's hand, I drew a deep breath and punched the speed dial on my last secured phone.

This time it only rang once.

"Dermott."

"It's Arlene. Is he..." My voice choked off.

Oh, please...

"He's out of surgery and stable. The bullet broke a rib, but that deflected it enough that it missed everything vital. We're airlifting him back here to debrief. Get back as soon as you can."

My mind refused to process anything beyond the first sentence. "He's going to be okay?"

Beside me, Hellhound drew in a sharp breath.

"Yeah, that's what I just said. When can you get back?"

I nodded at Hellhound and he slumped against my car, the white lines of strain easing from his face. I squeezed his hand and dragged my attention back to Dermott.

"I have one more loose end to tie up. Probably about an hour, and then two hours to drive back."

I hung up and wrapped my arms around Hellhound to hide my face in his chest. He held me tightly, rocking me in his embrace, and we stood that way for long moments until at last I regained my composure and straightened.

"One more."

Hellhound grinned. "Let's do it, darlin'."

I wriggled out my car window for the last time, suppressing a whimper when I had to raise my aching arm. Guilt gnawed at me as I walked down the ramp and out of the trailer, leaving ten captives plus Barnett and his stench behind. Poor Barnett. In about twenty minutes his trank was going to wear off, and he'd probably struggle all the way to Silverside.

I stiffened my spine. Dammit, I'd seen what he did to

Hibbert. If there was such a thing as karma, this was it. All I did was tie him up and pull out a few leg hairs, and he'd done the rest to himself.

My rationalizations didn't help much, and I swallowed nausea as Dave locked the trailer doors for the last time.

He turned from his work and gave Hellhound a dark look. "Only letting you ride up front on one condition. If you need to..." He hesitated, shooting a quick glance at me as his ears reddened. "...*do anything*, you tell me and I'll stop so you can get out. Got it?"

To my relief, Hellhound laughed. "Yeah. But I think the burritos have worn off. We're safe."

"Didn't smell like it to me," Dave muttered, and headed for the driver's door.

Hellhound looked up at the passenger door before turning to me. "Can ya make it up there? Looks like your shoulder's pretty sore."

I eyed the high door and suppressed a whimper. "I can make it. It's only bruised."

"D'ya want shotgun or d'ya wanna lie down in the sleeper?"

I drew a breath of relief at the memory of Dave's tidy custom sleeper and the pristine sheets in his bunk. "Sleeper. Thanks." I reached for the handle beside the door and groaned. "Maybe I could use a boost after all."

I only registered the first few minutes of the trip. The steady thrum of the big diesel and the quiet rumble of male conversation lulled me into fitful sleep broken by violent nightmares. Hellhound's gentle touch and voice soothed me back to sleep time and again, and it seemed only moments before he was smoothing the hair back from my forehead and calling my name.

"Time to wake up, darlin'. We're gettin' close to Silverside, an' Dave needs to know where to go."

"Uh." I dragged myself upright, wincing. "Right." I rubbed bleary eyes and tried to shake some coherent thought into my sleep-fogged brain. "Um, the hospital. Secure entrance. Barnett's ankles will need to be cleaned up. And I can call Dermott from there and get instructions about where he wants our..." I bit off my words when I realized Dave was listening avidly. "...um, cargo," I finished.

"Where's the secure entrance?" Dave asked.

"Around back. It just looks like a blank door, so I'll give you directions."

Dave had just pulled to a stop outside the door when it opened and a scrubs-clad man hurried out to stand frowning up at the huge truck. He gesticulated, and Dave rolled down his window.

"You can't park here," the orderly snapped. "Loading dock is around the side."

I leaned across Dave to speak out the window. "No, we have a delivery for this entrance."

Maybe he recognized me from my previous misadventures, or maybe I'd simply hit on the correct code words. In any case, his frown vanished, to be replaced with furrows of concern.

"Where?" he demanded.

"In the back. Hang on." I retreated into the cab. "Dave, stay here. I'll let you know when we're done unloading. Arnie, I'll need your help with the doors and ramps. We'll have to unload my car first."

Hellhound nodded and swung down from the cab, reaching up to help me as I winced my way down after him.

Thumping came from Barnett's corner of the trailer, and I sighed. "Can you go in and trank him again while I talk to the orderly?"

"Yeah. Let's get your car out, an' then I'll go take care of him."

I hurried around the truck, and the orderly rapped out, "Status of the injuries?"

"Just some rope burns that need to be disinfected and dressed. We'll bring him out. Can I borrow a couple of masks and some gloves and maybe a couple of those disposable paper suits?"

The orderly's eyes widened. "Biohazard? Wait here!"

He darted back through the door before I could stop him, and I sighed and turned toward the back of the trailer.

The stench hit me as soon as the trailer doors opened, and I spared a moment of sympathy for the captives with their mouths taped shut, forced to breathe that reek through their noses for the last couple of hours.

Then again, considering the crimes they'd committed, they probably deserved it.

I drove down the ramps for what I sincerely hoped was the last time and parked a few car-lengths away. Hellhound hurried into the trailer and vanished behind the tarp curtain.

I was just getting out of the driver's seat when a crew of aliens in space suits rushed out of the hospital. Two guided a stretcher while three more began to set up what looked like an inflatable tent.

"Shit! No, no!" I scurried over to tug on the nearest alien's sleeve. "It's not a biohazard, he's just got shit all over him. He stinks, that's all. He just needs to be hosed off."

"Oh." The alien muttered into his headset before reaching up to turn off his respirator and remove the bubble head of his suit. Around him the others did the same, casting baleful looks at me.

"Sorry," I mumbled. "Um, could you please bring out the tarp he's sitting in, too? I don't want to get shit all over the inside of the trailer."

The orderly let out a 'hmmph' and stalked up the ramps, followed by his brethren pushing the stretcher. Hellhound beckoned them in, and a few minutes later they all emerged with Sharkface cocooned unconscious inside his malodorous tarp.

They whisked him through the door and Hellhound leaned down to inspect his jeans with distaste. "Fuck, now I stink like shit, too. Didn't dare use the gun on him with the docs comin' in right afterwards. He was thrashin' around so much he got some on me when I stuck the dart in his neck."

"Let's close up the trailer and then you can go in and get washed off," I suggested. "I'm going to tell Dave to just idle in the parking lot for now, and I have to go in and call Dermott. Meet you at the nurses' desk."

When I rounded the corner a few minutes later, Spider's fiancée Linda hurried out from the nurses' station. "Aydan! Thank God you're all right!" She gave me a quick hug. "Spider was so worried! I'll tell him you're here; he's just sitting with John."

"Wait, Linda." I caught her arm as she turned to rush away. "I do want to see Spider and John, but first I have to talk to Dermott. Can I use your secured line to call him?"

She dimpled. "No need. He's with John, too. Go on in, it's the second room on the left."

"Thanks. If you see Arnie, could you tell him where I am?"

She nodded and I turned toward the room, drawing a deep breath. God, I didn't want to face Dermott. But I had to see Kane and prove to myself that he was really alive.

I hesitated outside the door, heart thumping. This was it.

Would Dermott throw me in jail for aiding Stemp? Or for torturing Barnett? Or hell, for some other crime I hadn't even realized I'd committed?

Would he free my captives because I'd skipped some legal technicality that I would have known about if I was a real agent? Or worse, would he charge me with kidnapping and coercing confessions from them?

I groaned and leaned my forehead against the cool metal door frame. Maybe I should just run out to my car and drive far, far away.

I recoiled as Dermott himself strode through the door. He jerked to a halt, his ruddy features only inches away.

"Fuck!" he exclaimed. "What took you? Get in here."

CHAPTER 46

Pulse pounding, I followed Dermott into the large hospital room, my gaze searching out Kane's battered face on the pillow. Deep lines of pain carved his features sharp against his greyish pallor, but his eyes blazed above his smile.

"Oh, Aydan, you did it! I knew you would! You're amazing!" Spider lunged out of his chair to fling lanky arms around me, nearly hugging the breath out of me. "Oh, thank God!" He wiped his eyes unabashed, and I hugged him in return.

Glancing over his shoulder, I froze. The hospital noises receded, leaving only the sound of my blood draining into my socks while I stared at the silent figure I'd just noticed in the corner of the room. My mouth fell open, but nothing came out.

Then my heart restarted with a tremendous thud and I gasped a breath that tasted of glorious vindication.

"You... it's you," I stammered. My smile widened until my ears ached. "You're here! You're..." I glanced at Dermott's dour expression before returning my grin to Stemp. "Welcome back!"

Stemp rose, smiling the smile that warmed his amber

eyes and made him look like a human being instead of a reptilian robot. "Thank you. I'm pleased to be back."

I returned my attention to Kane, drinking in the glorious sight of his living, breathing form.

"Thank God you're all right," he murmured. He cast a rueful glance at his semi-reclined state against the pillows. "Excuse me for not getting up to greet you."

Mindful of Stemp's and Dermott's presence, I managed not to smother him with kisses but my smile was wide enough to hurt my face. "Thank God *you're* all right!" I hurried forward to squeeze his hand. "You scared the shit out of me." My voice wobbled at the end and I concealed it in a cough.

A tap at the door made me swing around to see Hellhound sidle into the room, his gaze anxiously searching out the figure in the bed. Then a grin split his face and he strode forward to grip Kane's forearm in a warrior's armclasp. "Fuck, ya goddamn asshole, ya scared the shit outta me! Don't fuckin' do that!"

Kane grinned and inclined his chin toward Hellhound's bruised features. "I owed you a scare. Payback's a bitch."

Hellhound barked laughter. "No shit."

"Since we're all here..." Stemp's composed voice cut through the conversation. "...and since Kane will need to rest soon, let's debrief. This room is secure. Dermott, if you please?" He nodded toward the door and Dermott swung it shut.

I sank into one of the chairs, my knees suddenly weak. What if this was my last moment of freedom? My guts clenched and I beat back claustrophobic terror. I could probably still make a run for it. Only Dermott was between me and the door.

"Kane, please begin while you have the strength," Stemp said. "If it becomes too much for you, please say so and we'll resume at another time."

"I'm fine." Kane hitched himself higher on the pillow, his face taut with pain.

Hellhound leaned over to support him with one powerful arm while he expertly plumped the pillow with the other, then eased Kane back into position.

The hard lines around Kane's mouth softened into a smile. "You haven't lost your touch."

Hellhound returned a twisted smile. "Wasn't that fuckin' long ago. Told ya then I didn't wanna hafta do it for ya again."

"If not for Aydan, you wouldn't have to." Kane met my eyes. "Thank you for taking that bullet for me."

Heat flooded my face. "Um, you're welcome... I mean, um... not that you're welcome to shoot me, but... shit, you know what I mean. I'm glad you're okay. Well, kind of okay." I pressed my lips together to silence my babbling, and studied my toes.

"Kane? If you please." Stemp's dry tone did nothing to ease the fire in my cheeks.

"You're all up to date as of my last report?" Kane asked.

Thankful for the shift in attention, I looked up in time to see nods all around.

Stemp raised an eyebrow. "Helmand, too?"

"I briefed him," I said. "He's been involved from the start."

"Very well. Kane, continue."

Kane eased in a breath, wincing. "As I mentioned in my last report, I didn't trust Dawn White. I was posing as an arms dealer when I had dealings with her seven years ago and I knew she had contacts in the arms game, but it turned out she was working for Volslav all along. When Volslav didn't receive the weapon from Yana a couple of weeks ago, they traced our flight and obtained a passenger manifest. Dawn recognized my name and assumed I had acquired the weapon, so she contacted me using our old code. I resumed my cover..."

He paused, his gaze fixed on the corner of the ceiling. "...along with the relationship we'd had seven years ago," he went on without looking at me. "As promised, her expert identified the origin of the weapon. After the meeting, Dawn told me about Volslav and indicated there was an opportunity to sell the prototype to them. In my cover as an arms dealer, I couldn't refuse, and in any case, I hoped to gain valuable intel from meeting with Volslav."

Kane shifted, his lips tightening with pain. "What I didn't know was that Dawn had been playing both ends against the middle. She worked openly for Volslav but she had been leaking information to Fuzzy Bunny on the side. She contacted Parr, hoping to gain a reward while still securing her position with Volslav." He closed his eyes for a moment. "She got her reward from Parr."

Sickness twisted my belly.

Kane continued, his features an impassive mask, his tone remote. "Dawn told me she had arranged another meeting before our scheduled one with Volslav, but she didn't say with whom. When Parr's men pulled their guns, I realized Dawn had sold me out to Fuzzy Bunny. I assumed she was safe with them since she was their informant, and I knew she still needed me for the meeting with Volslav later, so I didn't expect things to escalate the way they did. I held onto my cover and didn't fight back when they captured us. When they demanded the weapon, I told them my associate currently had it but I could offer them a deal if they let us go. They didn't go for it."

He glanced at Stemp. "By then I knew you had taken the weapon out of the country, so stalling was my only option. And in any case I didn't want to draw attention to George Harrison, since you were supposed to be dead and Parr had already been asking questions."

He fell silent and my muscles clenched with morbid suspense even though I knew how the story ended.

After a moment Kane spoke again, his voice raw with pain. "I had played my relationship with Dawn too convincingly. In an attempt to coerce the location of the weapon from me, they tortured her and forced me to watch. I tried to protect her by insisting she meant nothing to me. It didn't work."

Nausea wrenched my guts. Kane closed his eyes, his voice fading. "They finished with her and started with me. That's when you found us."

After a moment of silence, Stemp spoke. "I suspected that not everyone had believed George Harrison's faked death originally, so I seeded our personnel list with that name when Kelly supplied it to Parr a couple of weeks ago. When Parr started asking questions, I knew the cover wouldn't hold up much longer anyway, so I went to the meeting wearing my George Harrison disguise to see if it drew any interest."

He glanced over at Kane. "I'm sorry I didn't get a chance to inform you of that before the meeting."

Kane nodded understanding and Stemp went on, "I recognized Volslav's arms expert, and I knew he had identified me in my George Harrison cover. I couldn't risk contact with the Department, so I flew directly to Europe to mitigate the damage to my old informants before contacting Interpol. Some of my informants had new information, and by showing the weapon to a couple of key players I was able to successfully reactivate our original case. As a result, Interpol made a clean sweep of arrests, dealing a crippling blow to Volslav overseas."

Stemp inclined his head in my direction. "Unfortunately, our concentration on Volslav may have compromised your investigation of Fuzzy Bunny, but we had little choice."

"Um... about that..." My voice came out hoarse, and I cleared my throat. "Actually, I've got a truckload of guys waiting out in the parking lot to testify against Parr. What do you want me to do with them?"

Dermott erupted from his chair. "What?"

"Well, not a truckload, exactly," I amended. "Ten."

A tap on the door interrupted me, and Stemp barked, "Come!"

Dr. Roth cracked the door open and poked her head in. "Aydan, that man you brought in... Kevin Barnett?"

Dermott shot me a suspicious look, and I focused on Dr. Roth's serious expression, my toes curling. "Um, yeah?"

She glanced at the assembled men, and I sighed. "It's okay, you can say whatever you need to."

She slipped into the room and closed the door behind her. "Mr. Barnett was quite distraught when he recovered from your tranquilizer. He kept screaming about being tortured..."

Everyone stiffened and the air temperature in the room dropped several degrees.

"...and insisting that his leg was going to rot and fall off as a result of what you did to him," Dr. Roth continued, apparently oblivious to the tension. "After I cleaned the urine and feces and theatrical makeup off him, I did a thorough examination but I couldn't find anything wrong with him other than ligature marks on his wrists and ankles and a bruise near his solar plexus. When I told him that, it only seemed to agitate him more. He became hysterical, insisting that the effects of your secret weapon were invisible but his tissue was dying and he would soon lose, in his words, 'chunks of his leg'."

She frowned. "Then he said he was losing sensation in the affected areas because your weapon had killed his nerves and his tissue would soon begin to deteriorate. I did a standard sensory test and he reacted normally, but he wouldn't believe me when I told him. He was so agitated I had to sedate him."

"He's on drugs or somethin'." Hellhound linked his hands behind his head and stretched out his legs as though the hard chair under him was the height of comfort. "He was fuckin' loony-tunes when we picked him up."

Dr. Roth's frown deepened. "I did a full tox screen. It was negative for all common recreational drugs, and also any prescription drugs that could potentially induce psychosis. Aydan, what exactly happened to him?"

"Um..." I gulped down the dryness in my throat.

"We tranked him an' had him tied up when he came to," Hellhound interjected smoothly. "He freaked the fuck out an' shit himself, so we tranked him again an' stripped him 'cause the stink was fuckin' disgustin'. Put a tarp under him, an' then the fuckin' coward woke up an' shit an' pissed himself again. That's when we figured maybe he was scared enough to tell us where Kane was, so we pulled out a coupla his leg hairs an' Aydan made up this bullshit story about a secret weapon."

He laughed and shook his head. "Fuckin' idiot fell for it hook, line, an' sinker. He gave us a name an' we picked up the next guy, Willis Arlington. In the mean time, we got some stage makeup an' did up Barnett with a buncha fake blood. Arlington took one look an' gave us the location of the butcher shop, an' then started spillin' names. We picked 'em all up, an' they're all out in Dave's truck ready to testify."

"Dave?" Stemp's eyes sharpened. "The redoubtable Mr. Shore?"

Hellhound grinned. "Yeah."

Dr. Roth's shoulders relaxed. "I did note that the areas Mr. Barnett seemed concerned about were lacking hair, but plucking a few leg hairs certainly wouldn't account for the level of agony he described. He said the areas were hairless because the hairs had already died and fallen out and the tissue of his leg would be next." Her solemn expression didn't waver. "So you're saying Mr. Barnett is simply... misinformed and overly anxious?"

"Yep." Hellhound raised an eyebrow. "Good luck convincin' him of that, though. He's gonna spend the next coupla months waitin' for his leg to rot an' fall off no matter what ya tell him." His lips twisted in a sardonic smile. "Couldn't happen to a nicer guy."

Dr. Roth's lips quirked, but she held onto her expression of professional gravity. "Perhaps some anti-anxiety medication," she murmured, and left.

Dermott turned to me, frowning. "I have Germain's report. He said he formally arrested Barnett and offered him a deal if he cooperated, and Barnett turned it down and lawyered up. That doesn't sound like a panicky guy to me.

What really happened?"

"Yeah, that's right." Hellhound dove in again. "An' then Germain hadta leave an' we were gonna bring Barnett in, so we tranked him. When he woke up an' realized Germain was gone an' we weren't cops, he totally lost his shit." He snorted. "Literally."

"Kelly." Stemp's dispassionate voice sent a chill down my spine. "*Your* report, please." He sent a quelling glance in Hellhound's direction.

I swallowed hard. If I revealed Hellhound's lies and half-truths, he'd be in deep trouble.

"That's pretty close," I equivocated. "When I met Barnett originally he told me they had John and he was going to kill me, and he tried to abduct me. Arnie tranked him and that's when we brought Carl in to try to get Barnett to tell us what he knew."

I forced my spine straight and raised my chin. "It's my fault Barnett was so scared. I pulled out his leg hairs and told him the story about the so-called secret weapon."

I glanced at Kane and froze in the anguished grey of his eyes. After what he had just experienced, the thought of me intentionally inflicting pain and fear must utterly repulse him.

"I t-tortured Barnett," I choked. "It was my idea and I take full responsibility. Dave doesn't know anything, and Arnie never touched him. He was just following my orders."

"Ya didn't torture him," Hellhound growled. "Doc Roth just finished sayin' there ain't a mark on him 'cept from the restraints, an' he did that to himself by freakin' out."

"Good enough for me," Dermott seconded. "Tell me about this truckload of witnesses."

"Not good enough for me," Stemp snapped. "We can't

ignore allegations of torture. Particularly not when an agent admits to it."

Everyone stared at him as though he had just reared up and hissed like the snake he was.

Icy fear trickled down my backbone.

I was going to jail after all...

CHAPTER 47

"Bullshit!" Dermott barked. "This case is still under my jurisdiction, Stemp. There's no evidence of torture according to a medical professional. We're done here." He turned to me. "Kelly, tell me about the witnesses."

"And tell us how their testimony was coerced," Stemp added quietly.

"They weren't!" Hellhound jerked upright in his chair, glowering. "That's fuckin' bullshit! It was a sting, plain an' simple. Aydan told 'em she was the new arms dealer in town an' she had the weapon prototype, an' they decided to switch sides an' rat Parr out." He glowered at Stemp. "It ain't against the law to lie when you're doin' a sting. An' there's lotsa legal precedent for convictions based on evidence gathered through Mr. Big operations."

My jaw dropped and we all stared at him in silence.

"What?" He crossed his arms, flushing. "I was just readin' a piece on it a while ago. So yeah, sometimes I use big words. I ain't as much of a dumbass as I let on."

"And you can recite that article word for word, can't you?" I eyed him fondly. "And you probably looked up the cases just for fun as well. And I bet you know them verbatim, too."

His flush deepened. "Yeah."

Dermott shot a triumphant look at Stemp. "Case closed." He returned his attention to me. "Tell me about the witnesses."

"They're all tied up in the back of Dave's truck. He's waiting out in the parking lot." I gave Stemp a wary glance. "Nobody has legally arrested them or read them their rights or anything."

"Fine, we'll process them out," Dermott said. "Get..." He frowned at me. "...Shore, is it?" I nodded and he went on, "Get him to take them over to Sirius. We'll keep them separated in the secured area until we can sort them out. I'll have a team meet him there."

He paused. "Oh, that reminds me. The tac teams picked up everybody at the Volslav meeting and cleaned out the weapons lab, too." A grin spread over his face. "Full house in the brig tonight. Good job, everybody. Kelly, do you have the records for each of your prisoners?"

I pointed to Hellhound's head. "Up there. Safe and sound and one hundred percent accurate."

"Good. Helmand, come by Sirius as soon as you have time." Dermott rose. "See you, Stemp. I've got some cases to wrap up."

My heart sank at the sight of his victorious grin as he strode out. Shit, would he be promoted now? As much as Stemp unfailingly pissed me off, he was still a far better director.

"We better go," Hellhound said, casting a significant glance at Kane's pallor.

Spider nodded and slipped out, but I searched out Kane's grey gaze. "You go ahead, Arnie. I'll be there in a minute."

Kane closed his eyes. "I'm really tired, Aydan. I need to

rest for a while. I'll talk to you later."

"Oh." I swallowed. "Um, okay. I hope you feel better." I turned to feel my way out, a chill settling around my heart.

Kane spoke again behind me. "Director, please stay."

"Very well." Stemp's dispassionate tone didn't alter. "Kelly, please wait for me. I have a matter to discuss with you."

I nodded without turning back.

In the hallway, Hellhound's arm closed around my shoulders. "He didn't mean it that way, darlin'. He's gotta use his strength to take care of official business first."

"I don't know, Arnie." I leaned against him, seeking comfort. "I think I've disappointed him one too many times. You know how by-the-book he is. I went too far."

"That's bullshit, darlin'," he began, but I pulled away to fumble in my waist pouch, hiding the foolish tears that stung my eyes.

"I have to phone Dave," I mumbled, and pressed the speed dial. He answered on the first ring, and I summoned up a cheerful tone. "Everything's fine, Dave. Can you drive over to Sirius Dynamics? A team will meet you there to unload your cargo. Give me a call when you're done, and I'll buy you as much beer as you can drink over at Blue Eddy's."

It would be better than dwelling on what I'd lost.

When I hung up, Hellhound appraised me for a moment before speaking. "Ya kicked ass today, darlin'. Hard to believe ya did it all with that hair-pullin' thing. Does it really hurt that much?"

I pulled the depilator out of my pocket and handed it to him. "See for yourself."

He flicked its switch and eyed the spinning head dubiously before pulling down his sock to touch it to his ankle. "Aagh, *fuck!*" He jerked upright, hopping on one foot. "Christ, that hurts like a motherfucker!"

I gave him a smile, letting his clowning cheer me as I knew he'd intended. He turned the device off and pushed it at me. "Jesus, darlin', why would ya do that to yourself on purpose?"

"It doesn't hurt that much when you do it regularly," I explained. "And it hurts worst on your ankle and knee and inner thigh. That's why I used it in those places on Barnett. If you'd tried it on your calf it wouldn't hurt as much."

"Fuck that. I ain't tryin' it again." He frowned. "Why the hell d'ya rip out your leg hair anyway? That's fuckin' sick. Leg hair just ain't that bad."

I planted my hands on my hips. "You're saying if you could choose between getting it on with a woman with hairy legs and armpits and one who'd shaved, you'd choose the hairy one?"

A devilish twinkle lit his eye. "Jeez, darlin', I dunno. Hafta do more research. Line up a buncha chicks for me an' I'll start testin'."

"Yeah, right." I leaned against him, grinning. "Nice try."

"Hey, a guy can dream."

"Helmand." Stemp's expressionless voice pulled us apart. "I need to speak with Kelly privately. And you're needed at Sirius to help document the prisoner intake."

"I'll meet you at Blue Eddy's afterward," I said, and Hellhound nodded, shooting me a look of concern before striding away.

"Walk with me," Stemp commanded, and set off at a brisk pace.

I followed him down the hall and outside, where a gust of wind-driven snow made me zip up my parka and huddle into my hood. Stemp strode on into the snowy darkness and I hurried to catch up.

A block away from the hospital, he withdrew his hand from his pocket to show me the green light of a bug detector. Slowing his pace, he said, "I want to thank you. And apologize."

"Uh?" Shock made me stumble over my own feet, and he waited patiently while I recovered.

"I'll begin with the apology," he said. "I apologize for seeming antagonistic in the debriefing. I wanted to be very certain there would be no repercussions for you as a result of your... unorthodox methods. An allegation of torture is potentially disastrous. By playing devil's advocate I made sure that Dermott would back you. Having taken a public stand against me in your support, he's extremely unlikely to reverse his position on the issue."

"Oh."

My tired brain churned through his logic. Always the chessmaster, two moves ahead of everybody else. But he was covering my ass.

"There's no need to apologize," I said. "Thank you."

"You're welcome. And thank you, too, for several things." A smile warmed his face. "Firstly, thank you for your care and concern over my home and plants. Bud Weems told me what you did. Secondly, thank you for believing in me when I contacted you secretly."

He sobered. "Your trust both honours and concerns me. If I had been in your place, I doubt if I would have reacted that way. But a good agent relies on gut instinct, and in this case it served us both well. I hope it continues to do so."

"And lastly." He stopped walking and turned to face me. "Thank you for guarding the secret of Katya and Anna. As you probably guessed, I wasn't entirely forthcoming in tonight's debriefing. When I realized I had been recognized as George Harrison, I knew Katya and Anna could be endangered and I left immediately, putting their safety ahead of national security. That is..."

He hesitated, his mouth flattening. "...clearly contrary to the letter of my job description, but to be perfectly frank, I don't care. My family comes first. I've relocated them and given them different identities. The mission with Interpol was secondary to my true motivation, but it worked out well nonetheless. So thank you for your discretion."

I nodded. "I thought it might be something like that. I'm glad they're okay. And I'm glad I don't know where they are anymore. They'll be safe now even if I get captured and... coerced."

"Yes. And that brings me to ask you a tremendous favour."

Aw, shit.

I braced myself. "What is it?"

He eyed me gravely. "May I entrust you with their new names and location?"

I stared at him in silence for a moment. Then I closed my dangling jaw. "Why the hell would you do that? You just got them safely hidden."

"Life is uncertain." His dispassionate tone never altered. "If something should happen to me, they would never know whether I had been killed or captured, or if I had simply abandoned them. I would like to spare them that uncertainty. You could contact them in the event of an emergency or accident."

"But..."

He fixed me with his intense amber gaze. "I understand

the significance of what I'm asking. But it would mean a lot to me. And to them."

I stood for a moment, grappling with the urge to refuse. I didn't want to be responsible for more lives. I didn't want to acknowledge the lengths I was willing to go to protect them. Trying to save Kane's life had been bad enough. To have a child's life on my conscience?

No.

No, no, no.

But to let a child believe her father had heartlessly abandoned her?

I sighed. "Okay."

"Thank you. I'll send the information via the secret communication system on your computer. Be prepared for a transmission tonight."

I nodded and turned back toward the hospital, the weight of responsibility bowing my aching shoulders.

"One more thing." Stemp's voice halted me.

God, now what?

I turned to face him. "What?"

"I should advise you that Kane has requested reassignment."

I stared at him, the winter wind slipping like a dagger through my parka and into my heart.

"Kelly?" Stemp frowned. "Did you hear me? Kane-"

"Doesn't want to work with me anymore." The wind howled through the black empty space enclosed by my ribs. My numb lips spoke of their own volition. "Yeah, I got it. Is that all?"

"Actually, no." He gave me a narrow-eyed appraisal. "You need to maintain a low profile until we've completed all the arrests and finished tying up the loose ends pertaining to

Parr, Fuzzy Bunny, and Volslav. I would suggest witness protection or a safe house..."

He raised a hand at my incipient protest. "...but I know you would oppose it. However, I have another assignment which I believe is an excellent fit, and it is also in the nature of a personal favour to me."

"What is it?" My words came out completely flat.

"Reactivating my George Harrison cover came with the risk of drawing attention to myself in my current persona. I'll deal directly with any personal threats, but I fear repercussions to my loved ones."

"You just relocated Katya and Anna," I pointed out. "If you don't tell me where they are, they'll be perfectly safe."

"I don't mean Katya and Anna. I mean my parents." He sighed. "Despite our fundamental differences in ideology, they are... dear to me. I would like you to stay with them for a few months to ensure their safety."

"Stay...?"

"Yes. It solves several problems. Firstly, they live in an extremely isolated area with little connection to the outside world, so it would be a relatively safe haven for you until the situation with Fuzzy Bunny settles. Secondly, they are..." He grimaced. "...unfortunately knowledgeable in dealing with someone suffering from post-traumatic stress. If you don't accept this assignment, I'll be forced to place you on administrative leave and mandate treatment for you, and I know how much you wish to avoid that. If you accept this assignment, you can call in to Dr. Rawling for phone consultations, and my parents will support you through the nightmares, anger, anxiety, or other symptoms you may be dealing with. And lastly, you can protect them should the need arise. I doubt it will, but..." He shrugged. "As you know, I prefer to be prepared."

My mind steadfastly refused to comprehend his words. I stared at him for a moment before inquiring faintly, "You want me to move to a hippie commune?"

He laughed, startling me back to reality. "Precisely."

My brain slowly rebooted. "But only for a couple of months."

"Yes. You can leave this behind..." He indicated the snowy world around us with a sweep of his arm. "...and move to a secluded raincoast paradise until spring arrives here. I'll arrange for someone to take care of your home during that time." He smiled. "You'll be taking what amounts to a lengthy paid vacation."

I stared at him, my mind sluggishly turning the idea over and over.

Well, shit. Why not? It would let me avoid awkwardness with Kane while he was recovering, and he'd likely be gone by the time I got back. Tammy Mellor could handle the decryptions. And Hellhound had a high enough security clearance to be told where I was. He might even come and visit me in B.C., lured by the promise of ice-free roads for his Harley.

And I desperately needed a break. God, I just wanted to curl up in a ball and disappear.

"Okay." The word fell flatly from my lips.

"Excellent. Be ready to leave tomorrow morning. A car will pick you up at your house at ten hundred."

I nodded and turned away to slog back to the hospital.

His voice stopped me again. "Also..."

A dull throbbing began at the base of my skull. "What?"

"Kane asked me to send you in to see him."

CHAPTER 48

I hesitated for a long moment outside the door to Kane's hospital room, bone-deep fatigue dragging at me. My bruised shoulder throbbed in time with my tension headache, and I squeezed my eyes shut.

I should just walk away.

I had already seen the cool distance in Kane's eyes. He had requested reassignment. What was left for us to talk about? This conversation could only end in ashes and bitterness.

I turned away.

Fuck it. I'd go and meet Dave and Hellhound at Blue Eddy's and drink myself senseless. Hellhound would haul my stinking carcass home and put me to bed, soothe my hangover in the morning, and get me out the door by ten...

"Aydan!" Linda hurried out of one of the other rooms, her perky smile making me feel like seven kinds of shit. "John has been asking for you. Have you talked to him yet?"

"Um, no. I don't want to disturb him tonight," I mumbled. "Maybe I'll drop by tomorrow after he's had a chance to rest."

Or maybe not.

"No, you need to see him. He said he wanted to see you

no matter how late it was." She latched onto my arm and ushered my dragging feet back to his door. "Go on in."

"Aydan? Is that you?" Kane's voice emanated from the room, sounding exhausted but wide awake.

Shit.

"See, I told you." Linda's smile sparkled up at me. "Go on in."

There was nothing else for it. I trudged into the room.

"You came." Kane's smile looked strained. "Thank you. Would you please close the door?"

I did as he asked before turning reluctantly to face him.

He held out his hand. "Please... come closer?"

I sighed and crossed the room to stand beside the bed. In the dim light his features looked carved from white stone, hard pain lines etched around his mouth and eyes.

My heart clenched and my hand flew to his despite my attempt to hold myself aloof.

His eyes closed for a moment, his hand gripping mine. "Aydan..."

"It's all right," I interrupted softly. "Stemp already told me you want to be reassigned, and I understand. I stepped over the line today, and I don't blame you for being disgusted by me. Just rest. Get better. I'll go now."

"No!" His hand clenched around mine so hard I let out a yelp of surprise. "Aydan, no, dammit!" He struggled up on the pillow and a groan wrenched from between his teeth. He took a couple of shallow breaths before growling, "Damn Stemp. I wanted to tell you."

"It's okay," I soothed. "Don't worry about it. Just take it easy and get better-"

"No, dammit!" His grip tightened and I winced.

"John, you're hurting me."

"I'm sorry!" He eased his grip without letting go of my hand. "Dammit, Aydan, I'm sorry, this isn't what I wanted..." He waved me to silence when I began to speak again. "Stop. Please let me explain. Will you do that?" He gazed up at me imploringly. "Will you please just stand there and listen until I'm finished talking?"

"Of course." I stroked his hand, afraid he'd overtax himself. "Just relax. Say whatever you need to say." I swallowed the hard lump in my throat. "I'm listening."

"Thank you." He closed his eyes and breathed for a moment, sweat glistening on his forehead.

My heart twisted again. "John, can't this wait? You should be resting."

"No." His eyes flew open. "Aydan, I did request reassignment, but it's not for the reason you think. I..." He swallowed convulsively and his hand trembled in mine. "I... Today shook me. More than any mission I've ever had. Dawn..."

I touched his face, his pain slashing my heart. "I'm sorry. I'm sorry I didn't get there in time to save her."

"No, that's not it. Aydan, she didn't mean anything to me." His face twisted. "That's the hell of it. Nobody deserves to suffer like that, but I never liked her. Never trusted her. And she betrayed me in the end. But..."

He gave me an imploring look. "I couldn't help thinking, Aydan, what if it had been you? What if they had captured us and I had to pretend, had to say you meant nothing to me? Had to watch them..." His voice choked off.

He swallowed and continued evenly, "I couldn't. Can't. And that weakness could mean the failure of a mission. So I requested reassignment. If we're not working together, that can't happen. And..." He gazed up at me, his eyes dark and vulnerable. "If we're not working together, we could…"

He drew a shallow breath, his hand tightening on mine. "I'm going to be on med leave for at least six weeks, probably more. I was hoping maybe we could… take some time and get to know each other like normal people. When we're not hopped up on adrenaline or facing death. Just… talking… or going for walks. Or maybe working on your car. I don't know. What do normal people do?"

I stared down at him, open-mouthed. "I… uh…" Sudden comprehension exploded into fury. "*Bastard!*" I spat.

He flinched, pain twisting his face.

"I'm sorry, not you!" I amended hurriedly. "Stemp! That lousy fucking twisty bastard! He dumped your reassignment request on me to manipulate me into doing what he wanted. Again, for fucksakes! As usual!"

"What…?"

"I'm going to be guarding his parents on a hippie commune in B.C. for the next two months. I leave tomorrow morning."

Kane stared at me for a few moments before the corners of his mouth quirked up. "You're kidding me."

"No!" I knotted my fists in my hair and tugged savagely. "I'm not kidding! I couldn't make up shit like this!"

He began to laugh feebly, clutching his chest. "That bastard. That rotten bastard." He sobered, panting shallowly. "Well, then."

"Well, then," I echoed.

A mischievous spark kindled in his eyes. "Maybe my convalescence will require a stay in a place with more temperate weather."

"I've heard that can be very beneficial," I agreed, giving in to the smile tugging at my mouth.

"And since we're not working together anymore..." He pulled gently on my hand, grinning. "Come closer. I seem to recall I owe you the last half of a kiss. And then some."

I leaned down to his lips. "I'll take a kiss as a down-payment for now..."

Book 9 is available!

Visit my Books page at dianehenders.com/books for progress updates and announcements.

A Request

Thanks for reading!

If you enjoyed this book, I'd really appreciate it if you'd take a moment to review it online.

Here are some suggestions for the "star" ratings:
Five stars: Loved the book and can hardly wait for the next one.
Four stars: Liked the book and plan to read the next one.
Three stars: The book was okay. Might read the next one.
Two stars: Didn't like the book. Probably won't read the next one.
One star: Hated the book. Would never read another in the series.

You can help prospective readers by writing a few sentences about what you liked or disliked about the book.

Thanks for taking the time to do a review!

About Me

Before I started writing fiction, I had a checkered career: technical writer, computer geek, and interior designer. I'm good at two out of three of those. Fortunately, I had the sense to quit the one I sucked at (interior design).

When my mid-life crisis hit, I took up muay thai and started writing thrillers featuring a middle-aged female protagonist. ('Walter Mitty', you say? Nope, never heard of him.)

Writing and kicking the hell out of stuff seemed more productive than more typical mid-life-crisis activities like getting a divorce, buying a Harley Crossbones, and cruising across the country picking up men in sleazy bars; especially since it's winter most months of the year here in Canada.

It's much more comfortable to sit at my computer. And Harleys are expensive. Come to think of it, so are beer and gasoline.

Oh, and I still love my husband. There's that. So I stuck with the writing.

Diane Henders

And here's my "professional" bio, in case you need something more suitable for mixed company:

Diane Henders is the Kindle best-selling author of the NEVER SAY SPY series: Sexy thrillers packed with tension, laughs, profanity, and sometimes warm fuzzies.

The first book in the series, NEVER SAY SPY, has had over 450,000 downloads to date, and stayed on Kindle's 'Women Sleuths' Top 100 list for 60 consecutive months.

Diane enjoys target shooting, gardening, auto mechanics, painting (art, not walls), music, and martial arts; and loves food and drink almost as much as she loves her husband. They live in the wilds of British Columbia, Canada, where they get all the adrenaline rush they could ever want by growing fruit trees in bear country.

Want to know what else is roiling around in the cesspit of my mind? Drop by my blog and website at dianehenders.com, check out the extras, and don't forget to leave a comment in the guest book to say hi – I love hearing from you! Or you can connect with me on Facebook at:
https://www.facebook.com/authordianehenders.
See you there!